KU-216-053

Integrated
SCIENCE 2

Integrated SCIENCE 2

George Bethell
David Coppock
Lynne Pebworth

OXFORD

Oxford University Press, Walton Street, Oxford OX2 6DP

Oxford New York Toronto
Delhi Bombay Calcutta Madras Karachi
Petaling Jaya Singapore Hong Kong Tokyo
Nairobi Dar es Salaam Cape Town
Melbourne Auckland

and associated companies in
Berlin Ibadan

Oxford is a trade mark of Oxford University Press

First published 1991

A CIP catalogue record for this book is available from the
British Library.

ISBN 0 19 914269 6

Typeset in Plantin Light by
Tradespools Ltd, Frome, Somerset
Printed in Hong Kong

Acknowledgements

The publishers wish to thank the following for permission to
reproduce photographs:

AEA Technology: p47; **Allsport UK:** p84 (bottom/**Bob Martin**,
p88 (top left and right)/**Pascal Rondeau; Argos:** p63 (centre right),
p100, p115, p120 (bottom right), p141; **Barnaby's Picture Library:**
p50 (centre); **British Airways:** p69 (bottom right), p206; **British
Gas:** p73 (bottom); **British Steel:** p64; **Bruce Coleman:** p31
(bottom), p134/**Kim Taylor**, p155 (top)/**L.C. Marigo**, p155
(bottom)/**Norman Myers**, p173 (right)/**Kim Taylor**, p176 (top)/
Eric Crichton, p176 (bottom)/**Andy Purcell; Electrolux Domestic
Appliances:** p156; **Sally & Richard Greenhill:** p123 (top), p129
(left and far right), p130; **Robert Harding Picture Library:** p137;
Michael Holford: p60 (top); **Holt Studios:** p9 (left and right), p18,
p21 (bottom), p173 (left), p176 (bottom), p241/**Nigel Catlin; The
Hulton-Deutsch Collection:** p40; **The Hutchison Library:** p34/
Pierrette Collomb, p69 (top right), p129 (centre)/**Robert Francis;
IBM UK:** p115; **Dr Terry Jennings:** p25, p63 (bottom left), p185,
p192 (top), p217; **Labatt Brewing UK:** p88 (bottom); **Mary Evans
Picture Library:** p35, p45 (top); **Mercedes-Benz:** p87 (top); **Tony
and Marion Morrison, South American Pictures:** p240; **The
National Grid Company:** 192 (bottom); **National Power PLC:**
p184 (bottom), p188; **NASA** front cover background, p222 (left and
right), p223, p225 (top), p226 top and bottom), p227 (top and
bottom), p228; **Oxford Scientific Films:** p10 (top)/**M. Wilding** p10
(bottom)/**Paul Franklin**, p17/ (top)/**Terry Heathcote**, p17 (centre)/
Stan Osolinski, p21 (top)/**Avril Ramage**, p24/**Ronald Toms**, p31
(top)/**Doug Allan** p33/**W. Johnson**, p36 (top)/**Waina Cheng**, p 36
(centre)/**Peter Parks**, p36 (bottom)/**Alastair Shay**, p56 (bottom
right)/**G.I. Bernard**, p61 (bottom) **Kathie Atkinson**, p85 (bottom
left)/**Mike Birkhead**, p85 (bottom right)/**Chris Catton**, p86 (top)/
David Cayless, p91 (top left)/**B.P. Kent**, p153 (bottom/**John
McCammon**, p212 **Press-tige Pictures**, p214/**G.A. Maclean**, p221
(left and right)/**David Thompson; Pilkington Glass:** p83;
Potterton International: p115; **Rex Features:** p60 (bottom), p90
(left), p114; **The Rover Group:** p87 (bottom); **The Royal Society
for the Protection of Birds/M.W. Richards:** p85 (top), p90 (right);
Science Photo Library: p20/**Dr Jeremy Burgess**, p51 (right)/
James Stevenson, p83 (top)/**Andrew McClenaghan** p140/**David
Parker**, p146/**Dr T.E. Thompson**, p148 (bottom right)/**Martin
Bond**, p152/**CNRI**, p157 (top)/**Malcolm Fielding**, p158 (right)/
Simon Fraser, p169 (bottom)/**Will McIntyre**, p179 (centre/**Dr
Jeremy Burgess**, p180/**Martin Dohrn**, p205/**NASA**, p216 (centre)/
Ronald Rover, p225 (bottom)/**NASA**, pp232 (left)/**Hank Morgan**,
p232 (top)/**Tektoff**, p232 (centre)/**Dr A. Lesk**, p232 (bottom)/
Alexander Tsiarras, p237/**Chris Priest and Mark Clarke; A Shell
Photograph:** p148 (bottom left), p201; **Sky Television:** p115;
Topham Picture Source: p45 (bottom); **TRH/Vickers:** p153 (top);
Vauxhall Motors: p157 (bottom); **VELA/Educational Electronics:**
p117; **ZEFA:** front cover, three inset photographs, p49, p50 (left
and far right), p57 (top), p63 (centre left), p69 (below), p72
(bottom), p73 (top and centre), p81, p84 (top), p86 (centre and
bottom), p89, p91 (bottom left), p105 (top right), p111, p120 (top
left, top right, bottom left), p123 (centre & bottom), p127, p128,
p143 (top), p148 (top), p165, p179 (top), p184 (top right), p196,
p198 (left, top centre right, bottom), p207, p208 (top and centre),
p220, p222 (right) p244..

Additional Photography by: Chris Honeywell
Picture research: Suzanne Williams

Introduction

This book has been written for students like you, studying science at (senior) secondary level. It contains 12 chapters covering many important topics, particularly those that affect us in our everyday lives. The topics are usually presented over two or four pages and there are lots of diagrams and photographs to help you. There are also questions to check that you have understood the main ideas. Where the topics overlap cross-references are given to guide you.

Of course, science is more than just reading books, however good they are, and your school's programme of practical work will help you develop experimental skills. To support this you will find 'activity items' throughout the book. These are things that you can do at school under the guidance of a teacher or at home on your own. Some of the activities suggest experimental work, others ask you to carry out surveys or collect data from sources such as newspapers and magazines. They are all there to help you develop a scientific attitude.

We obviously hope that this book will help you to pass your examinations but we also hope that it will increase your interest in science and its applications. It does contain many examples of how modern technology has improved our lives but it also considers the harmful effects of the way in which we use science. It tries to give information and a balanced view on some of the most important issues of the day; environmental pollution, the human population explosion, recycling of materials, and others. Using this information you will be able to make up your own mind and take part in discussions on these matters as a well-informed person.

Above all, we hope that you will enjoy using this book and that you will finish it feeling more confident that you can use scientific ideas and methods to understand the way our world works.

George Bethell
David Coppock
Lynne Pebworth

1991

Contents

1 Food chains and webs

Where does our food come from?
What happens when plants and animals die?
How easily can the balance of nature be upset?
Where does the energy in our food go to?

A food web

A **food chain** is a way of showing how food passes from a plant to an animal and from one animal to another. Sometimes food chains are short, sometimes they are long. It all depends on how many links there are in the chain.

Plants are called **producers** because they make, or produce, their own food by photosynthesis using energy from the Sun. Animals that eat plants are called **herbivores**. Animals that eat other animals are called **carnivores**. **Omnivores** are animals that feed on both plants and animals.

Food chains are linked together in **food webs**. Each plant or animal in one chain is likely to be a link in another chain. Food webs show more information about what animals eat.

Questions

1 What is **a**) a producer **b**) a herbivore **c**) a carnivore **d**) an omnivore?

2 Write down one food chain in the food web shown above.

3 Make a list of **a**) the herbivores **b**) the carnivores in the food web shown above.

4 Suggest what might happen if all the bluetits in the food web shown above were killed.

Producers and consumers

The first link in a food chain is always a producer. As you have seen, producers are plants which photosynthesize.

The producers in aquatic (water) ecosystems are mainly algae.

The producers in land ecosystems are much more varied.

Herbivores that feed on producers are called **primary** or **first-order consumers**. Mice, rabbits, horses and sheep are primary consumers.

Carnivores that feed on primary consumers are called **secondary** or **second-order consumers**. **Tertiary** or **third-order consumers** feed on secondary consumers, and so on up the food chain. Herring, owls, foxes, cats and dogs are carnivores that could be secondary or tertiary consumers. It all depends on what they are eating at the time!

Look at this food web for the North Sea.

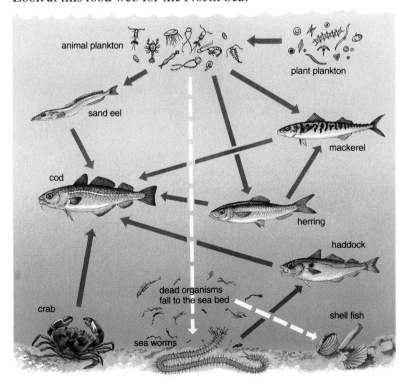

The producers in this food web are plant **plankton**. Plankton live near to the surface of the sea. Animal plankton are the primary consumers. There are many examples of secondary and tertiary consumers, such as herring and mackerel.

Questions

1 What is the difference between a primary and a secondary consumer?

2 Use the North Sea food web to answer the following questions.

a) Name   i) the producer   ii) the primary consumer   iii) a secondary consumer.

b) Give one occasion when a mackerel is   i) a secondary consumer   ii) a tertiary consumer.

c) Explain why the cod can be called a quaternary (fourth-order) consumer.

3 A student was telling her friend about some things she saw happening in and around a local pond. She said that she had seen tiny water fleas eating algae; a heron with a perch in its beak; minnows eating water fleas; and a perch chasing minnows around the pond.

a) Write down   i) the shortest   ii) the longest food chain.

b) Name   i) the producer   ii) the primary consumer   iii) the secondary consumer   iv) the tertiary consumer in the longest food chain.

Scavengers and decomposers

So far we have looked only at carnivores that feed on other living animals. Many animals avoid being eaten. They live on and reproduce in order to keep their species going. However, all animals die sometime, so what happens to their dead bodies?

In every ecosystem there are consumers that feed only on the dead remains of others. These animals prevent the environment from getting cluttered up with dead bodies and waste. They also ensure that materials are recycled in ecosystems. These consumers are of two types, **scavengers** and **decomposers**.

A scavenger is an animal that feeds on dead animal or plant remains. Snails in a pond eat dead fish. Crows feed on dead insects, birds, rabbits, and anything that might be killed on the roads by passing cars and lorries. Seagulls are often seen scavenging on rubbish tips for scraps of our discarded food. Of course these animals can fill other 'slots' in food chains as well – they're not scavengers all the time. Pond snails eat algae, crows eat corn, and seagulls eat fish; it all depends upon what is available at the time.

Decomposers don't eat dead animals and plants. They digest them by releasing enzymes on to the remains to break them down into simpler substances. Some of this digested material is then absorbed into the decomposers' own cells. Fungi and bacteria are decomposers. These organisms are important in the cycling of materials in the soil environment. Producers then take up the materials which decomposers have made, use them to grow and so make them available for living animals in food chains.

Bracket fungus on a tree

Questions

1 a) What is the difference between a scavenger and a decomposer?
b) What do scavengers and decomposers have in common?

2 In many large towns and cities foxes can be seen at night rummaging through litter bins. In the countryside foxes can be seen hunting, catching, and eating small animals such as rabbits.
Explain why a fox can be called both a scavenger and a secondary consumer.

3 People often put out bread for birds to eat. In winter this bread usually disappears quickly.
However, in summer the bread may lie around for several days, eventually becoming covered in mould (a fungus).
Suggest reasons for these observations.

Activities

1 Look carefully in your garden or around your school grounds for either a dead animal or a pile of faeces left by an animal. Make a note of its position, its size, and the date you found it. **Do not touch the animal or faeces**.

Over a period of several days or weeks note any changes that take place to your sample. You may like to consider the following:

- Has it changed its position?
- Has it changed in appearance?
- Has it changed in size?
- How long did it take to disappear completely?
- Was its disappearance due to the activity of a scavenger or decomposers?

Investigating food webs

A group of school students were studying a corner of their school field. They identified dead leaves, woodlice, millipedes, and centipedes. Their teacher asked them to investigate the feeding relationships between these organisms.

The students set up five dishes as shown below. Each dish was covered with a lid with several holes in it. The dishes were put in a cool, dark place and left for a few days.

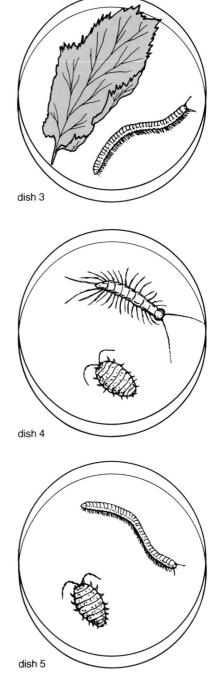

dish 3

dish 4

dish 5

dish 1

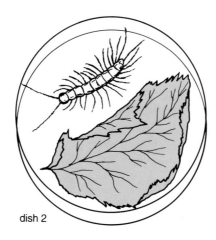

dish 2

The students presented the results of their investigation in the form of a table. This is what they wrote.

dish	organisms inside	what had happened
1	dead leaf and woodlouse	part-eaten leaf and live woodlouse
2	dead leaf and centipede	dead leaf and dead centipede
3	dead leaf and millipede	part-eaten leaf and live millipede
4	woodlouse and centipede	part-eaten woodlouse and live centipede
5	woodlouse and millipede	dead woodlouse and dead millipede

Questions

1 Which of the organisms in the dishes is **a**) a producer **b**) a primary consumer **c**) a secondary consumer **d**) a predator **e**) a herbivore **f**) a carnivore?

2 Write down one food chain. Explain how you used the evidence from the investigation to do this.

3 Write down a food web linking all the organisms.

4 Suggest reasons why the students **a**) covered the dishes **b**) put holes in the lids **c**) put the dishes in a cool dark place.

Ecological pyramids (1): a pyramid of numbers

When you study an ecosystem you will probably realize that there are usually more producers than consumers. For example, if you studied this food chain:

grass → rabbit → fox

you may well find that there were 1 000 000 individual grass plants, 15 rabbits and 1 fox.

It is sometimes useful to have this extra information about a food chain. If the single fox was killed or moved away from the area we may want to know how the rabbit population was affected and, in turn, how this change affected the number of grass plants, especially if the grass was a food crop!

This extra information can be shown as a sort of bar chart. The length of each bar represents the number of organisms forming that link of the chain.

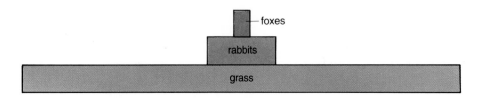

Another way of presenting the same information would be:

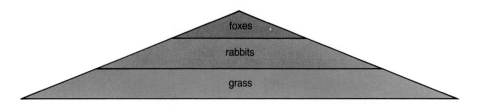

Notice the shape of each diagram. They are both called **pyramids of numbers**.

Not all pyramids are as neat and tidy as the ones shown above. Sometimes the producer may be a single, large plant such as an oak tree. Living and feeding on this oak tree could be thousands of caterpillars. Small birds feed on the caterpillars. In turn, hundreds of fleas could be feeding on the blood that they suck in small amounts from the birds.

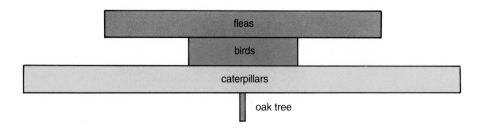

Questions

1 How does a pyramid of numbers get its name?

2 What does the length of each bar in a pyramid of numbers represent?

3 Explain briefly why pyramids of numbers can be many different shapes.

4 Draw a pyramid of numbers for this information taken from a survey of a woodland ecosystem

> 1 elm tree
> 400 caterpillars
> 9 sparrows

Ecological pyramids (2): a pyramid of biomass

Biomass is a word used to describe the mass of living material in an ecosystem.

If we measured the mass of organisms in each level of this food chain:

grass → **rabbit** → **fox**

we may well find that the mass of grass was 500 kg, the mass of rabbits was 50 kg, and the mass of foxes was 10 kg.

These figures can also be shown as a bar chart.

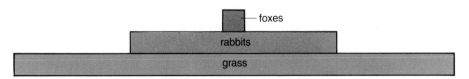

Notice that we get another pyramid – a pyramid of **biomass**. Ideally we should measure dry biomass but this is often not practicable because the organisms have to be killed and dried out. Good estimates can be made from wet (living) biomasses.

If we use this method of showing the feeding relationships in an oak tree you will notice that we get a different picture to that shown on the opposite page.

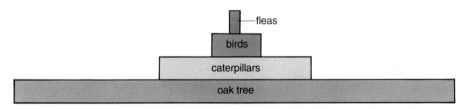

This looks much more like a true pyramid now!

Questions

1 What is biomass?

2 What is your **wet** biomass?

3 Give one similarity and one difference between a pyramid of numbers and a pyramid of biomass.

4 A group of students were studying this food chain that they had observed in a corner of their school field:

leaves → **woodlice** → **centipedes**

They collected all the leaves, woodlice and centipedes they could find and weighed them. The results are shown in the table.

a) Use this information to draw a pyramid of biomass for this food chain.

b) Why is it important that the students **weigh** all the organisms in this food chain?

c) Suggest what might happen if another 10 grams of woodlice were added to the food chain.

organism	biomass
leaves	4.5 kg
woodlice	5 g
centipedes	1 g

Energy flow through ecosystems (1)

Carbon, oxygen, nitrogen, and water circulate in the environment. Even though they continuously change from one form to another, these materials stay in roughly the same proportions within ecosystems. Energy, however, does not cycle. Instead it flows through ecosystems in a straight line.

Producers convert the light energy from the Sun into chemical energy in sugar molecules. Some of this energy is used by plants in respiration, while the rest is stored as starch or used to build other chemicals like protein and fat. When consumers feed on plants they release this stored energy by digestion and respiration. They can use it for activities such as movement. Some energy, however, will be 'locked up' in the animal's body in fat and protein. This whole process is repeated at each link in a food chain. In the end all the energy is 'lost', usually as heat, to the environment. The trapping of energy from the Sun by producers maintains a continuous flow of energy through ecosystems.

Let's follow the flow of energy through a food chain which is important to humans:

grass → bullock → human

What happens in one year to the energy from the Sun when it falls on to just one square metre of grass?

Questions

1 a) How much energy is i) 'locked up' by the square metre of grass each year ii) taken up by the bullock each year from a square metre of grass?
b) Calculate the percentage of energy from the grass taken up by the bullock.
c) Explain why this figure is so small.

2 a) How much energy is i) used by the bullock in growing ii) lost in faeces and urine iii) 'locked up' in the bullock?
b) Calculate the percentage of energy from the Sun that eventually gets 'locked up' in the bullock.

3 a) Make a list of the parts of the bullock that humans usually feed on.
b) Explain why humans take up only a small proportion of the energy 'locked up' in the bullock. Suggest where the rest might go.
c) Suggest where the energy might go after a human has taken it from the bullock.

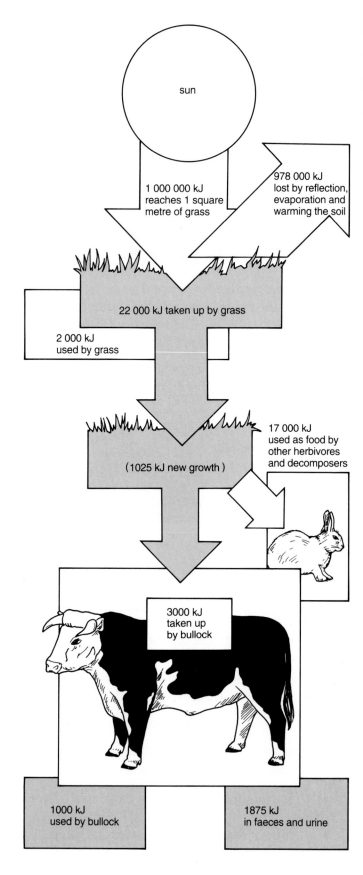

Energy flow along a food chain in one year

By now you should understand that the transfer of energy along a food chain is very inefficient. In most food chains there is usually a high loss of energy between each link:

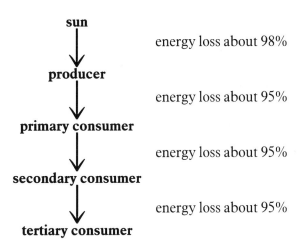

sun

↓   energy loss about 98%

producer

↓   energy loss about 95%

primary consumer

↓   energy loss about 95%

secondary consumer

↓   energy loss about 95%

tertiary consumer

This energy loss could be cut down if people were to eat food from further down the food chain. Eating plants instead of the animals that feed on them makes better use of the available energy. This is why cereals are grown in such large quantities all over the world, particularly in North America, Russia, and China.

The main cereals grown are wheat, barley, oats, rye, maize, and rice. All these plants started out millions of years ago as wild grasses. Early humans selected the seeds that they gathered from these grasses and used them to grow 'new' varieties. Gradually this artificial selection led to the evolution of the modern cereals that we see today.

Wheat is one of the most common cereals produced in the world today. More than 300 million tonnes are produced each year. It can be used for making:

flour . . .   . . . pasta . . . 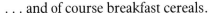   . . . and of course breakfast cereals.

Wheat for food

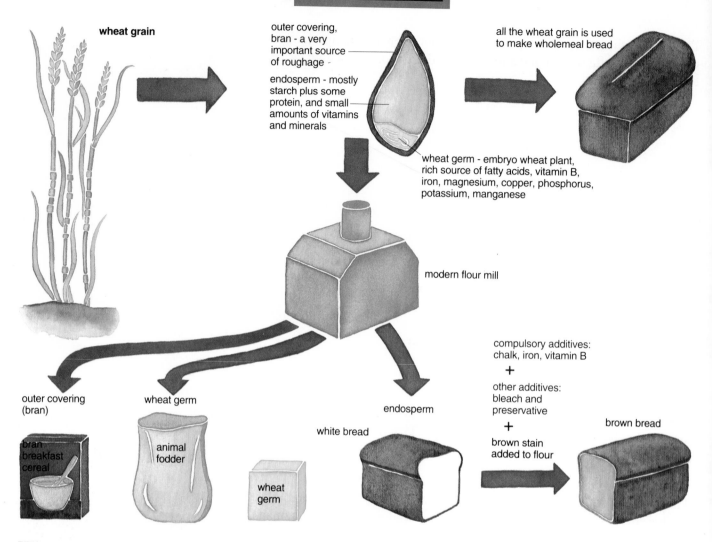

wheat grain

outer covering, bran - a very important source of roughage

endosperm - mostly starch plus some protein, and small amounts of vitamins and minerals

all the wheat grain is used to make wholemeal bread

wheat germ - embryo wheat plant, rich source of fatty acids, vitamin B, iron, magnesium, copper, phosphorus, potassium, manganese

modern flour mill

outer covering (bran)

bran breakfast cereal

wheat germ

animal fodder

wheat germ

endosperm

white bread

compulsory additives: chalk, iron, vitamin B

+

other additives: bleach and preservative

+

brown stain added to flour

brown bread

Wheat or meat?

An average person can get enough energy for one day by eating:

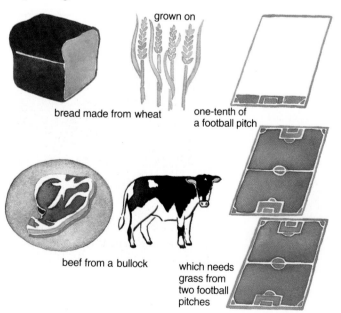

bread made from wheat

grown on

one-tenth of a football pitch

beef from a bullock

which needs grass from two football pitches

Questions

1 Which part of a wheat plant is used for **a)** animal bedding **b)** making flour?

2 During harvesting, farmers cut the wheat plants near to the ground. This leaves stubble behind. Many farmers burn this stubble before ploughing it into the ground.

    a) What is the point of ploughing the plant material back into the ground?

    b) Suggest **i)** one advantage **ii)** one disadvantage of burning stubble. (*Hint*: plant cells are broken down by burning.)

3 What is the difference between wholemeal bread and brown bread?

4 In some countries there is not enough food to go round.

    a) What should the people in these countries eat, bread or meat?

    b) Briefly explain your answer.

Competition

In any ecosystem there are always more organisms produced than can ever survive. Only those best adapted to their environment will survive. This was one of Charles Darwin's important observations which helped him to develop his theory of evolution. Competition takes place between organisms of the same species and between organisms of different species.

What do plants compete for?

Plants make energy available to other organisms by 'trapping' it from sunlight. Plants must therefore try to get as much light as they can in order to make as much food as possible. This competition for light can be seen in a wood. The faster growing trees usually win the race!

Water and mineral salts are essential for plant survival. Food cannot be made without them. Plants with root systems that spread deeper and wider in the soil will be more likely to survive at the expense of those with smaller roots.

Bright, sweet-smelling flowers attract insects. The more insects that visit a flower, the more chance the plant has of pollinating other flowers and therefore reproducing itself.

Trees competing for food and light in a woodland environment.

What do animals compete for?

Food and water are vital to animals for survival. The more food and water an animal can get, the better its chances of survival. Animals, unlike plants, can move from one place to another. So animals can hide from predators or shelter from bad weather.

Like plants, animal species can only survive if individuals can find a suitable mate. The bigger, fitter males usually win the battle to mate with the females.

In many species males fight for a mate.

Activities

1   Make up some thick gravy and pour it on to an old saucer and let it cool down. Put the saucer outside where it is open to the air.

After a day or so cover the saucer with clingfilm and put it in a warm place. Look closely at the surface of the gravy after a few days. Note the positions and sizes of the bacteria and/or fungi colonies.

Keep a check on the growth of colonies until the surface of the gravy is completely covered with microbes. Is there any evidence that competition between organisms has taken place?

Look at an area of gravy where two or more colonies have grown close together. What has happened there? Suggest what the microbes may have been competing for.

The fungi are furry and the bacteria are smooth, round blobs.

Safety warning: Do not attempt to remove the cover from the dish at any time during this activity. When you have finished, throw the whole lot away or, better still, burn it!

Knocking out the competition

The more people there are in the world, the more food is required to feed them. As the world population increases so too does the demand for efficient farming methods. Farmers must get the highest crop yields that they can.

In order to produce more food crops, farmers add **fertilizers** to the soil. Unfortunately, fertilizers don't just help the crops to grow, other plants grow better as well. These other plants compete with the food crop for light, water, and minerals. So to improve the chances of success for the food crops, chemicals are used to kill the unwanted plants (weeds). These chemicals are called **selective weedkillers** or **herbicides** because they kill the weeds without harming the crops.

Fungicides are used to kill any fungal competitors that may also affect the successful growth of food crops. A fungus called wheat rust feeds on living wheat plants as they grow. This reduces the amount of wheat produced.

There are animal competitors, too. Small mammals such as mice eat the crop before and after it is harvested. Insects present a much greater problem. In some parts of the world one-third of all food crops are eaten by insect pests. Chemicals have also been developed that kill insects. These chemicals are called **insecticides**.

Questions

1 **a)** Why do farmers need to grow more and more food crops?
b) Suggest one way in which farmers can grow more crops.
c) Why is it important for farmers to 'knock out the competition'?

2 What are   i) herbicides   ii) fungicides
iii) insecticides?

3 Name   i) a plant pest   ii) a fungal pest
iii) an insect pest.

4 Herbicides, fungicides, and insecticides are sometimes put together under one name, pesticides. Suggest why this is.

5 A gardener discovers spots of mould on the leaves of his tomato plants. After a few days these spots spread into patches. The leaves eventually die. No tomatoes are produced from these plants.

a) Suggest why no tomatoes are produced from the infected plants.
(*Hint*: remember what job leaves do.)
b) How might the gardener have saved his crop of tomatoes?

Activities

1 Go into a garden centre and look around for the shelves where pesticides are kept. Make a list of as many pesticides as you can under the following headings:

weedkillers (herbicides)
fungicides
insecticides

Make a note of any warnings given on the packets or bottles. What do these warnings indicate?

Messing about with food chains (1): DDT

One insecticide has done more than any other to enable farmers to grow more food crops. The name of this insecticide is dichlorodiphenyltrichloethane, known as **DDT**.

DDT was developed by scientists in the early 1940s. For many years DDT seemed to be the 'perfect insecticide'. It was used to kill off not only many of the insects that attacked food crops, but also those that live off humans such as lice and mosquitoes. However, scientists gradually became aware that DDT is not biodegradable. Levels of DDT build up in the soil. From the soil DDT can pass into streams and rivers and the oceans. It can therefore enter food chains. As it is passed from consumer to consumer it it stored in their fat layers, becoming more and more concentrated. The animals at the ends of food chains are eventually killed.

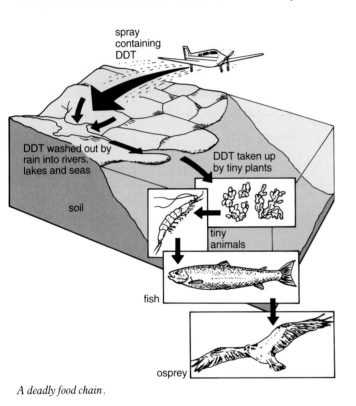

A deadly food chain.

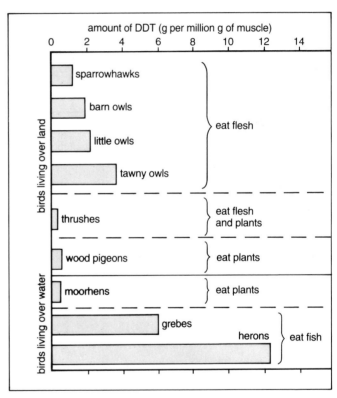

Questions

1 In the 1960s scientists noticed that there was a fall in the numbers of certain types of birds of prey. They also noticed that this fall took place at about the same time as DDT was being widely used as an insecticide. As a result of these observations a large-scale survey was carried out. The survey showed the levels of DDT in predatory birds living in a number of different places. The results of the survey are shown in the chart.

   a) How much DDT was there in every million grams of grebe muscle?

   b) Which of the birds had about 2 grams of DDT in every million grams of its muscle?

   c) Suggest why carnivores that live near water have higher levels of DDT in their bodies than carnivores that live and feed over land.

The development of new high-yield cereals has helped to meet the world's increasing demand for food. However, these new cereals need much more fertilizer than the older varieties. This has caused another serious problem for food chains.

Modern artificial fertilizers are soluble. Therefore much of the fertilizer used on the land gets washed away into nearby streams, rivers, and lakes. Most of the cereal produced in England comes from East Anglia. So it is not surprising that there are high concentrations of nitrogen and phosphorus in rivers in East Anglia, which come from land drainage.

The large amounts of nitrogen and phosphorus in the water encourage the growth of algae. The animals that feed on water plants cannot keep up with this rapid growth and soon the water becomes full of algae. As the algae die, poisonous substances are produced. This makes the water unfit for drinking and kills the animals living in it. Decomposers use up all the oxygen in the water, making it impossible for animals such as fish to breathe. Eventually the food web of the stream, river or lake is broken down.

Checking the effects of land drainage

It is possible to see what effect fertilizers have on water ecosystems by studying the kinds of animals living there. The chart shows the kinds of animals you might expect to find in water with different oxygen levels.

Questions

1 How do fertilizers get into waterways?

2 Explain briefly how fertilizers upset the balance of life in streams, rivers and lakes.

3 List three fish you would expect to see in a river with a high level of oxygen.

4 Roughly how much oxygen would you expect to find in a river that had no fish in it at all?

5 What effect does temperature have on the oxygen content of a river?

6 Suggest how the pollution of waterways by fertilizers could be reduced.

amount of pollution	animals present	volume of oxygen (cm³/litre of water)	
		at 5 °C	at 20 °C
clean unpolluted water	stonefly nymph, mayfly nymph, salmon, trout, grayling, good coarse fishing	6.5-9.0	4.5-6
little pollution	caddis fly larvae, freshwater shrimp, good coarse fishing - trout rarely seen	6.0-6.5	4.0-4.5
some pollution	water louse, blood worm (ridge larvae), leech, roach, gudgeon, moderate to poor fishing	3.5-6.0	2.5-4.0
heavy pollution	sludge worm, cat-tailed maggot, no fish life	0-3.5	0-2.5

Another way of knocking out the competition

Greenfly are eaten by ladybirds – greenfly are the prey of ladybirds, ladybirds are predators.

Greenfly feed on roses. A rose grower therefore needs to protect his or her plants against greenfly attack. Insecticide sprays are often the only answer. They kill the insects and the plants go on to produce lovely flowers that the grower can sell. However, insecticides are harmful to the environment, especially when used incorrectly. So what can a rose grower do to protect the plants and yet not harm the environment?

The answer lies with the ladybird. If ladybirds are released on to rose plants, they eat all the greenfly and the roses are saved. Ladybirds are used to control the number of greenfly. This is an example of **biological control**.

There are other examples of biological control. Whitefly damage food crops such as tomatoes. They are a particular menace in greenhouses where conditions are ideal for their rapid growth – warm, moist, and with plenty of food. The parasitic wasp (*Encarsia*) is an insect which lays its eggs inside the larvae (grubs) of the whitefly. When the eggs hatch they slowly feed on the larvae, eventually killing them. No whitefly larvae means no adult whitefly.

Ladybird feeding on greenfly

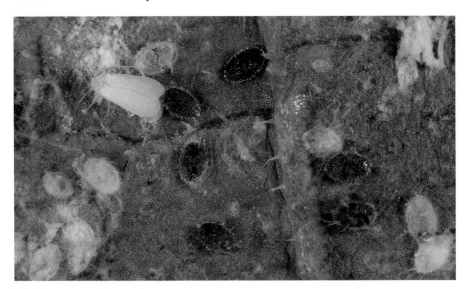

Whitefly parasitised by wasp larvae

People are becoming more concerned about the use of insecticides on their food, especially foods which are eaten raw like tomatoes. Biological control agents such as the parasitic wasp can provide an acceptable alternative to insecticide spraying.

To be really effective, the predator used for biological control must be able to find its prey easily. Also, it should only feed on one kind of prey. Just imagine what might happen if ladybirds also fed on roses, or whitefly parasites took a liking to tomatoes!

Scientists have to carry out many tests in the laboratory before releasing any new biological control agents into the environment.

Questions

1 What is the difference between a prey and a predator?

2 Give two reasons why biological control agents have an advantage over insecticides.

3 Give two important features which make a predator a suitable agent for biological control.

4 What do you suppose happens to the ladybirds when they have removed all the greenfly from a rose grower's crop?

21

Other relationships between organisms

Earlier in this chapter you read about the part played by scavengers and decomposers in food chains. **Parasites** form another group of consumers.

Parasites are organisms that get their food from the body of another living organism. This second organism is called the **host**. Parasites live on or in the body of the host, but do not usually kill it. If they did they would kill their food supply and themselves as well!

There are many kinds of parasites. They are usually small. Some, like the tapeworm, live inside the host. Others, such as the flea, live on the outside.

louse: live on head and body; They suck blood and spread typhus

flea: body flattened from side to side, which enables it to move easily between victims' hairs; has long claws to cling to host; sucks blood and spreads typhus germs and some tapeworm eggs

tapeworm: uses suckers on head to attach itself to host's intestine wall; absorbs host's digested food

mouth sucker

leech: uses teeth inside mouth to cut open skin and suck blood; lives in fresh water

rear sucker

segment full of eggs

Commensalism is a relationship between two organisms where only one of them benefits. This organism is called the **commensal**. However, unlike a parasite, the commensal does not harm its host.

The relationship between the sucker fish and the shark is an example of commensalism. The dorsal fin of the sucker fish is modified into a sucker which enables it to attach itself to the underside of the shark. The shark doesn't attempt to eat the sucker fish. When the shark feeds, the sucker fish picks up any food scraps that escape from the shark's mouth.

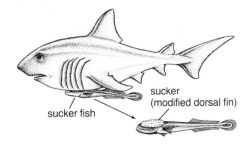

sucker fish

sucker (modified dorsal fin)

Shark with sucker fish

Sometimes two completely different organisms live together and form a relationship in which neither is harmed. This relationship is called **mutualism** because both organisms help each other, they mutually benefit. Mutualism is sometimes called **symbiosis**.

Lichens look as though they are single organisms. In fact they are made up of two quite different partners. One of these is a green alga and the other is a fungus. The alga produces enough food and oxygen for both organisms by photosynthesis. The sponge-like fungus encloses and protects the alga. It also absorbs water and minerals for the complete lichen.

Questions

1 Explain parasitism, commensalism, and mutualism.

2 How are commensals and parasites **a)** similar **b)** different.

3 Rabbits have bacteria living in their digestive system. These bacteria feed on the cellulose that makes up the walls of plant cells. Rabbits have a constant body temperature. How do **a)** rabbits **b)** bacteria benefit from this relationship?

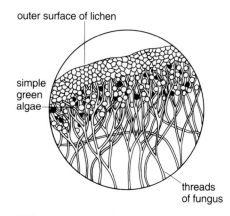

outer surface of lichen

simple green algae

threads of fungus

Lichen, as seen through a microscope

Questions

1 The diagram shows a food web for a pond ecosystem.

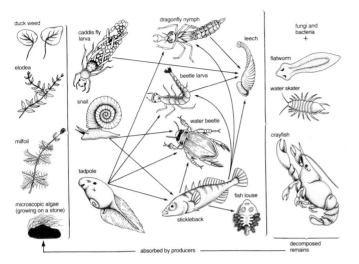

a) Write down two food chains ending at the water beetle.

b) Name i) a primary consumer   ii) a secondary consumer   iii) a tertiary consumer   iv) a scavenger   v) a decomposer.

c) Suggest what might happen if all of the water beetles were removed from the pond.

d) Give i) one difference   ii) one similarity between the parts played by scavengers and decomposers in keeping the pond ecosystem in balance.

2 The diagrams show four different pyramids of numbers.

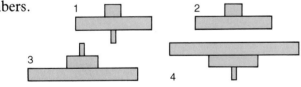

a) What does each pyramid represent?

b) Match each pyramid to the following:

 i) grass → antelope → lion
 ii) oak tree → caterpillar → sparrow
 iii) animals living in a balanced pond ecosystem
 iv) rose bush → greenfly → parasites of greenfly.

c) Briefly explain why pyramids of numbers can have different shapes while pyramids of biomass have one basic shape.

3 Carol has some apple trees in her garden. Unfortunately she got very few good apples from these trees. Most of them were damaged by insects and had to be thrown away.

However, a few years ago Carol made some bird boxes to encourage more birds into the garden. Since the installation of the bird boxes, the quality of apples collected from the trees improved considerably.

a) Suggest a reason for the improvement in the quality of apples after the installation of the bird boxes.

b) What is this an example of?

c) What other remedy could Carol have used to improve the apple crop?

d) Give i) one advantage   ii) one disadvantage of this action.

4 Write down the words 'parasitism', 'mutualism', 'commensalism', 'competition', and 'predation' in a column. Alongside each word write a suitable example taken from the list below.

a) moss growing near the top of a tree trunk

b) head lice or 'nits' sucking blood from the head of a schoolboy

c) two stags fighting for control over a herd of deer

d) farm cats killing mice and stopping the mice eating cereal crops

e) bacteria in the appendix of a rabbit feeding on the cellulose cell walls of plants.

5 Some people living in a small village in a poor country survive by planting vegetable and cereal crops each year. They keep a few cows to provide milk. One year there is not enough rain and their crops fail. The villagers face starvation. All they have is a store of vegetables and seed corn and their cattle. However, they do have a well that provides just enough water for them to drink. Help from other countries will probably take many months to reach them.
A village meeting is called to decide what should be done. There are a number of suggestions. These are:

- eat the vegetables and feed the seed corn to the cows to maintain a milk supply

- eat the cows and vegetables and plant the seed corn in the hope that it will grow before they all die

- eat the cows, then the vegetables, followed by the seed corn.

a) Which suggestion do you think best?

b) Explain why you think this is the best solution to this serious problem.

c) What is the best way that other countries can help in situations like this? Explain why.

What is a community?

What is a population?

How fast do populations grow?

How can we measure a population?

How do populations affect each other?

What effect do humans have on other populations?

If left on their own with plenty of food and space, the number of individuals in a group of plants or animals like these rabbits will get bigger and bigger. Eventually, however, a point will be reached when the group will get no larger. The environment will no longer support extra individuals. There will be competition for food and shelter, many individuals will be eaten by other animals, and some will die of disease. The numbers of individuals in natural groups of plants and animals are therefore kept under control – there is a natural limit.

The number of individuals in a breeding group never stays the same. It changes over a period of time. The seasons affect the supply of food and create harsh conditions in which to live. Many animals and birds die in winter in Britain, for example. Sometimes it is the actions of humans that change the living conditions for plants and animals. Many of these actions are due to lack of thought, while some are actually deliberate.

It is not always easy to see how the number of individuals in a group changes. Sometimes it is necessary to carry out surveys to find out exactly what is happening. In this chapter you will read about techniques that will enable you to make some surveys of your own.

Questions

1 Why does a group of animals or plants increase in number when it has plenty of food and space?

2 When will the growth of the group come to a stop?

3 Suggest reasons for the change in numbers in a group of plants and animals over a period of time.

4 Why is it useful to carry out surveys of groups of plants and animals?

5 List some examples of ways in which humans might affect the numbers of plants and animals living in the wild.

Some terms to know

All living things live in places that are best suited to their needs. The place where an animal or plant lives is called a **habitat**. Bluebells are usually found in woodland, so the habitat of bluebells is woodland. Sometimes the word **microhabitat** is used to describe a small part of a habitat. A rotting log in a woodland habitat provides a microhabitat for many plants and animals. Microhabitats usually provide different conditions from the main habitat.

If an organism is to live successfully, its habitat must contain food, shelter, and a place to breed.

A **species** is group of organisms of the same type that live and breed successfully together to produce fertile offspring. Individuals of different species will not usually interbreed. If breeding does take place the offspring will probably be sterile. The horse and the donkey are different species. However, they can interbreed because they are similar to each other. The offspring of this cross is called a mule. Mules are sterile and so cannot produce baby mules.

Organisms do not live their lives on their own. They usually form breeding groups. These groups are called **populations**. Populations of animals and plants are made up of individuals of different ages, which live in habitats which are most suitable for them. For example, a population of wood mice is made up of young and old mice living in a woodland habitat.

A habitat is usually occupied by a number of different plant and animal populations. This collection of organisms living together in one habitat is called a **community**. A wood is a good example of a community. It is made up of populations of trees, shrubs, grasses, ferns, birds, wood mice, squirrels, insects, and many more kinds of plants and animals. There are close links between members of a community. These links are usually to do with food. Many organisms are the food of others living in the same community. There are many complex food webs in a woodland habitat.

Sometimes a community may contain more of one particular species than any other. These are called **dominant species**. A wood dominated by oak trees is called an oak wood. Oak woods are very different habitats from beech woods or birch woods.

A woodland habitat

Questions

1   What is your habitat?

2   Make a list of the people that make up your school community.

3   **a)**   What is a species?
    b)   If the horse and the donkey are different species, why can they breed?
    c)   How do you know that the horse and the donkey belong to different species?

4   What is a community?

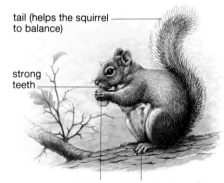

tail (helps the squirrel to balance)

strong teeth

feet have 'fingers' and 'toes' for gripping

The squirrel is well adapted to life in a woodland habitat.

Colonization and succession

If you are a keen gardener you've probably noticed that plants soon grow on a piece of bare earth. An uncultivated field soon turns to scrubland as tall grasses, shrubs and small trees **colonize** the land.

When bare rock is exposed above the surface of the ground it soon becomes colonized by lichens. These are called a **pioneer species** or **pioneer community** because they are the first organisms to occupy the new area. In Chapter 1 you read that a lichen is a symbiotic relationship between a fungus and an alga. One of the advantages of this relationship is that the fungus prevents the alga from drying out and dying. This is important because bare rock does not hold water like soil does.

Weathering of the rock will gradually produce sand and soil. However, to be of use to other organisms the soil must have nutrients in it. These nutrients come from the lichens when they eventually die and decompose. Mosses and ferns are the next organisms to move into the new area. As more rock is weathered and more plants die, a rich layer of fertile soil is built up. Grasses, shrubs, and trees slowly colonize the ground until it is completely covered. Animals move in to feed on and make homes in the vegetation.

The colonization of bare earth followed by the build-up of communities is called **succession**. The final stage of succession is known as a **climax community**. In Britain, the climax community is usually deciduous woodland with oak as the most common tree. In Scotland it is coniferous pine forest. There are many kinds of climax communities. Oak and pine are called the dominant species of these two climax communities.

Succession from completely bare and infertile ground such as rock is called **primary succession**. Organisms that grow in these places are the first sign of life ever to appear. However, there is a difference between completely infertile rock and ground that has simply been cleared of vegetation. Gardeners dig and farmers plough their land to aerate the soil before growing crops. Forest fires clear the land in a similar way. Seeds and roots of plants still remain in the ground. Other seeds may be blown by the wind or carried by animals from surrounding areas. This time colonization will not be by pioneer species. Succession will begin with more advanced plants. This kind of succession is called **secondary succession**.

Questions

1 What does colonization mean?

2 What is a pioneer species?

3 What is succession?

4 What is the difference between primary and secondary succession?

5 **a)** What is a climax community? **b)** Name a climax community.

6 A minor earthquake causes the soil to slip from a hillside. The dominant species was oak. A large area of rock is exposed.
   a) What kind of plants are likely to colonize the area i) in the first year   ii) in the first 5 years?
   b) What will the area look like after about 50 years?
   c) In what way will the vegetation be different from that which was growing in the area before the earthquake?

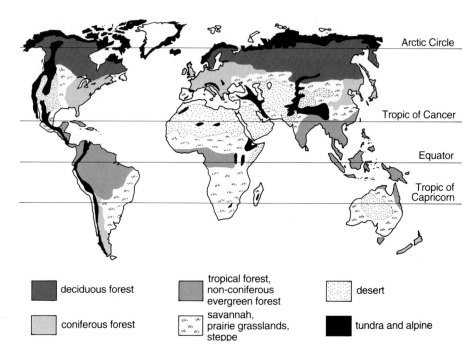

deciduous forest

coniferous forest

tropical forest, non-coniferous evergreen forest

savannah, prairie grasslands, steppe

desert

tundra and alpine

Arctic Circle

Tropic of Cancer

Equator

Tropic of Capricorn

The kind of climax community depends upon climate. Climate depends on where the community is located on the Earth. The map shows the positions of main climax communities of the world.

A closer look at a woodland community

A wood is usually a stable community, the result of the final stage of plant succession. Such communities are full of many different species of both plants and animals.

In a wood the plants are arranged in four layers.

- The tree layer consists of large trees with big trunks. Their leaves form a canopy covering the rest of the wood.
- The shrub layer contains shrubs such as hawthorn and bramble.
- The field layer is made up of herbaceous or non-woody plants like grasses, ferns, and woodland flowers such as primrose and bluebell.
- The ground layer covers the surface of the soil. Mosses and lichens are found here.

The layering of plants in a wood is called **stratification**.

Animals move freely between layers. For example, squirrels search for food in the ground layer but move to the tree layer to sleep and breed. Birds nest in the tree layer and feed on berries in the shrub layer.

tree layer (5-20 m and above)

dominant species eg oak; some codominants, eg sycamore; birds, eg barn owl, sparrowhawk, wood pigeon, magpie, jackdaw, crow, songthrush, chaffinch, great tit, blue tit, jay, woodpecker, nuthatch, tree creeper; grey squirrel; many insects, larvae (caterpillars) of winter moth

shrub layer (2-5 m)

several species eg hawthorn, blackthorn, dogweed, elder, dog rose, buckthorn; birds, eg robin, blackbird, pied flycatcher, redstart, woodpecker, nuthatch, tree creeper; many insects as in field layer; grey squirrel

field layer (0-2 m)

herbs, low woody plants, tree saplings, woodland flowers, ferns; birds, eg coal tit, warbler, wren, hedge sparrow; fallow deer, roe deer; small mammals, eg dormouse; butterflies, moths, bees, wasps, hoverflies, gnats, flies, mosquitoes, beetles, spiders

ground layer (up to 3 cm)

flies, beetles, spiders, grasshoppers, voles, shrews, wood mice, harvestmen, ants; lichens, mosses, liverworts, low herbs

Questions

1 Sometimes the tree layer is called the canopy layer. Why do you think this is?

2 a) What is an herbaceous plant? **b)** Name two herbaceous plants.

3 List **a)** two animals **b)** two plants of the ground layer.

4 Why do you suppose grasshoppers are not found above the field layer?

5 Explain why:
  a) Woodland plants like the primrose always flower in spring.
  b) Bluebells have a store of food in their bulbs. They can burst into growth early in the year.
  c) Ivy is a plant that climbs up the trunks of large trees.
  d) Mosses are delicate plants that quickly dry out. However, they grow well in the ground layer of a wood.

Counting populations

It is impossible to count all the plants and animals that live in a particular habitat. Think how difficult it would be to count the plants in just a small section of field.

To make things easier we can use a method called **sampling**. A sample is a small part of a habitat that is studied very closely. If the sample is typical of the area, the distribution of plants and animals in the whole habitat will be similar to that in the sample. **Random sampling** makes sure that every part of a habitat has an equal chance of being chosen.

Counting plant populations in a sample

This is best done using a wooden or metal frame called a **quadrat**. Quadrats are usually made so that they cover a known area of ground such as $0.25\,m^2$ or $1\,m^2$. Gridded quadrats are divided up into smaller quadrats by wires running from top to bottom and from side to side. This forms a sort of grid. Every square in the grid has the same area.

Quadrats can be used to see how often particular plant species occur across a habitat. This is called the **species frequency**. When the quadrat is lying on the ground you simply add up the number of squares that contain plants of the same species. It doesn't matter how many plants there are in each square. The final number is then calculated as a percentage of the total number of squares in the quadrat.

You can also use a quadrat to measure how much ground is covered by a plant species. This is called the **species cover**. You estimate how many squares would be filled up if you were able to move the plants together.

Activities

1   Calculate the percentage frequency and percentage cover of plantain using the information in the quadrat above.
Which species is most frequent?
Which species covers most ground?
What is the relationship between the frequency and cover of a plant species and its size?

Sampling along a transect line

This method is best to measure population distribution in an area that is not the same all over. You may want to see how populations change as you move from a shaded part of a wood to an area which is in full sunlight.

A **transect line** is a piece of string or measuring tape stretched tightly between two poles across the survey area. The quadrat is then placed carefully in position along the line at regular intervals. These positions are called **stations**. The spaces between stations are usually 1 metre. This kind of transect is sometimes called a **belt transect** because a strip or belt of land is being surveyed.

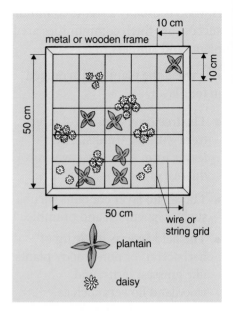

metal or wooden frame
10 cm
10 cm
50 cm
50 cm
wire or string grid
plantain
daisy

Worked example

The diagram shows a quadrat lying on the ground. In the quadrat are two different plants, daisy and plantain.

Frequency of daisy

Number of squares containing daisies = $^{13}/_{25}$
Frequency of daisies = **52%**

Cover of daisy

Total number of daisies in quadrat = 26
Number of daisies that would fit in one square = 16
Number of squares filled (approx.) = $^{26}/_{16}$
Cover of daisies = **6.5%**

Measuring plant distribution using the line transect method

Counting animals

Animals, unlike plants, are not always easy to see. If you are lucky you may be able to count some larger animals and birds, but usually you will only see footprints or droppings. However, we can use a number of methods to count animal populations.

Collection

A sweep net can be used to collect insects and spiders from the ground, field, and shrub layers. Animals can be collected from ponds and streams in a similar way. Once collected, the animals can be identified and kept in suitable containers until the count is finished. When all the animals have been counted they should be released safely back into their natural habitats.

Capture-recapture

This method is very useful if you want to count the number of individuals in one species. It involves capturing a group of animals, marking them in a way that does not harm them, and releasing them back into their habitat. After a day or so more animals are trapped at random. If the animals come from a large population the chance of collecting a marked animal the second time will be small. On the other hand, if you recapture all of your marked animals then you have probably seen the whole population!

You can estimate the size of the population by using the formula:

$$\text{estimated population} = \frac{\text{number of animals in first sample} \times \text{number of animals in second sample}}{\text{number of marked animals recaptured}}$$

There are some things that you need to be aware of when using this method.

- The habitat should have fixed boundaries.
- You must leave sufficient time before recapturing the animals: don't wait too long otherwise your marked animals may be dead.
- Marking methods must not affect the life of the animal. For example, it's no use marking snails in a way that makes them easily seen by birds.

Recording your results

It is very important to write down the results of your population counts as soon as you make them. Your notebook needs to be carefully organized so that no information is left out. With so much information to collect, it is very easy to forget something vital to your investigation.

Below is a page from a student's notebook. It shows information about the distribution of plant species in a wood. A line transect ran from a clearing into an area of deep shade. Quadrats were used at stations which were 1 metre apart.

species \ station	1	2	3	4	5	6	7	8	9	10	11	12	13	14	15	16	17
grass	100/80	100/70	60/40	60/40	50/20	40/20	20/20	20/20	10/10	10/10	10/10	10/10	10/10	10/10	10/10	10/10	10/10
primrose	0/0	0/0	20/20	50/40	50/40	80/40	80/40	40/20	20/10	0/0	0/0	0/0	0/0	0/0	0/0	0/0	0/0
fern	0/0	0/0	0/0	0/0	0/0	0/0	0/0	0/0	30/50	30/50	30/50	30/50	30/50	40/50	40/50	30/70	30/70
moss	20/10	20/10	10/10	10/10	10/10	20/30	20/30	30/20	40/20	40/20	40/20	40/20	40/20	40/20	40/20	40/20	40/20

frequency / cover

Page from a field notebook

Population growth

A population will grow if more individual plants or animals are born than die. However, populations do not grow at the same rate all the time. The size of the population at any one time affects its growth rate.

Suppose a single yeast cell is put into a flask containing a glucose solution. The flask is put in a warm place. Conditions are ideal for the yeast to start reproducing and increasing the population. By counting the number of yeast cells at regular intervals we can gather enough information to plot a graph. The graph is called a **growth curve**. A typical growth curve for a population is shown here.

Growth cannot continue forever at the same rapid rate. Sooner or later there will be a shortage of necessities like food or space. When this happens the population growth slows down and becomes stable. The birth rate and death rate balance each other. This is called the **stationary phase**.

A large population may eventually begin to have an effect on its environment. For example, the population may begin to produce more waste than the environment can take. This will cause more individuals to die than are born. The growth curve now enters its **death phase**. The population begins to fall.

Population size

If a species is going to survive it must reproduce. Most plants and animals reproduce sexually so their lives begin as a fertilized egg.

The number of fertilized eggs produced per individual varies enormously from species to species. It may be as many as a hundred million in the oyster, or as few as one or two in a lifetime in a human. The average number of fertilized eggs produced in the lifetime of an organism is called its **fecundity**.

In most animals the **birth rate** is a measure of fecundity. **Death rate** or **mortality** is the number of individuals that die over a fixed period of time such as a year.

The balance between fecundity and mortality usually controls the size of a population. However, don't forget that individuals may leave or join a population at any time. They can **emigrate** or **immigrate**.

Emigration is often the result of overcrowding. For example, bees swarm when their colony becomes too large. A group of bees, the swarm, leaves the main group and forms a new population somewhere else.

Sometimes emigrants leave their own population to join another one. They then become immigrants to the new population, making it larger.

Questions

1 Why does the growth of a population start slowly?

2 Explain why the number of individuals in a population increases so rapidly in the exponential phase.

3 Suggest two things that might cause a fall in a population of rabbits living in a wood.

4 Bacteria reproduce by one cell dividing into two new cells. This division happens once every 20 minutes. Starting with one bacterium living in ideal conditions,
   a) draw a chart showing the population increase over a 5-hour period
   b) use this information to draw a growth curve. Plot time on the horizontal axis.

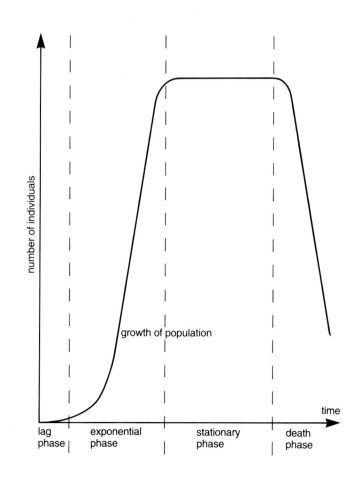

Environmental pressures

Anything which prevents growth in a population is called **environmental pressure**. There are a number of things which affect population growth. They can be divided up into two main groups.

Population-dependent pressures

These are due to the size of the population itself.

- A shortage of food, water, or oxygen affects all organisms. No living thing can survive without these necessities for life.
- Low levels of light severely limit the growth of plant populations. Without sufficient light, plants cannot photosynthesize. Without photosynthesis they die.
- A lack of space leads to overcrowding. This can affect the breeding habits of some animals, especially those like birds that have their own territories.
- The more individuals there are in a population, the closer they are to each other. If one becomes ill then the chances of others getting the disease are increased. If the disease is fatal, the population will decrease.
- Predators find it easier to catch prey if they are available in large numbers.

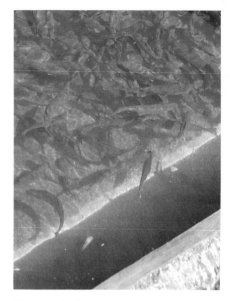

Overcrowding?

Population-independent pressures

These are things the population has no control over. They have the same effect whether the population is large or small.

- A sudden change in temperature may kill large numbers of organisms. For example, many birds die during a severe winter in Britain.
- Forest fires destroy not only large numbers of plants but also the animals that live in the forest habitat.
- Severe storms and floods wash away the homes of burrowing animals like rabbits. Plants covered with water for long periods also die.

Questions

1 List three things other than shortage of food, water, and oxygen that can cause the number of individuals in a population to fall.

2 What is the difference between population-dependent and population-independent pressures?

3 Suggest one other environmental pressure that a population has no control over.

4 In the 1950s the rabbit population in Britain was dramatically reduced by the disease myxomatosis. Suggest how the rapid spread of the disease could have taken place.

A cold winter can check population growth

The human population – the rule breaker

Most populations of plants and animals are controlled by predators, disease, seasonal changes in climate, and the availability of food. Populations frequently grow very fast or 'explode', and then suddenly crash when environmental pressures come into play.

Humans are at the top of food chains. They have little to fear from predators. Humans have the skill and knowledge to overcome many diseases. They build homes which protect them from the worst effects of changes in climate. Agricultural techniques have improved to the point where many countries produce more food than they need.

All these factors have resulted in the human population growing bigger and bigger, especially in recent times.

The graph shows the growth of the human population over a period of 500 000 years.

At the moment the human population is growing by about 1.5 million every week – that's 150 a minute!

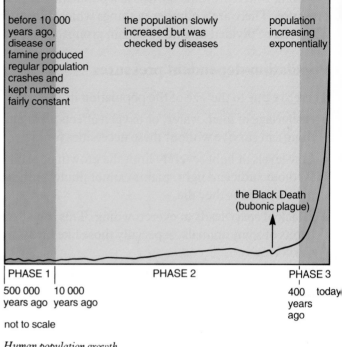

Human population growth

Patterns in human populations

In the developed countries of the world the growth of the human population is beginning to decline. In fact, in some Western European countries the population is no longer rising at all. The birth rate is being matched by the death rate.

As well as the total number of people in a population, it is useful to know the age and sex of the individuals in it. One way of showing this information is by a **population pyramid**.

A population pyramid is similar to the pyramid of numbers that you read about in Chapter 1. However, it usually involves much larger numbers. Each bar represents the number and sex of individuals in a particular age group. The youngest are at the bottom and the oldest at the top. Females are on the left and males are on the right. Two population pyramids are shown here.

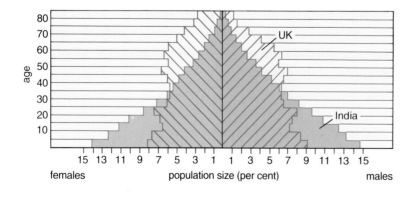

Questions

1 **a)** What is the difference between a population explosion and a population crash?
b) List three things which could cause a population crash.

2 Explain briefly why the human population is not affected by environmental pressures as much as other populations.

3 Use the graph showing human population growth to answer the following questions.
a) When was there no real increase in the human population?
b) Why do you suppose the human population only rose slowly up to about 400 years ago?
c) What has happened to the balance between fecundity and mortality in the exponential part of the graph?

Interactions between populations

A habitat is very rarely occupied by a single species of plant or animal. Communities contain many species, all of which interact with each other. There is competition for things like food, space, and shelter both within a species and between species.

One obvious relationship between two species is that between a **predator** and its **prey**. Predator–prey relationships play an important part in controlling populations. When a predator eats its prey it removes particular individuals from the population. These individuals are usually the sick or the old. Neither of these are of use to the species as a whole. Sick animals spread disease to others and the old use up valuable food supplies without breeding. This all sounds very heartless, but the future of a species depends on those healthy individuals that are able to breed successfully.

What happens when the young and healthy are eaten? Obviously the prey population begins to fall. If it falls too far the population of predators falls with it. Fewer predators means that fewer prey will be eaten. This allows the prey population to increase again. An example of this cycle is shown in the graph below.

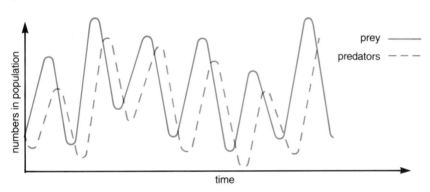

Notice that the number of predators is always lower than the number of prey and that the predator cycle closely follows that of the prey.

Questions

1 a) What is a predator–prey relationship?

b) Explain why such a relationship is important in controlling populations.

2 The graph opposite shows the effect of adding some *Paramecium* (single-celled animals) to a population of yeast.

a) What happens to the yeast population as soon as the *Paramecium* are added?

b) Why is there a time lag between the two population cycles?

c) If the *Paramecium* were removed, suggest what might happen to the yeast population.

3 In what way are predator–prey relationships good for the evolution of species?

4 In what way are predator–prey relationships an example of negative feedback?

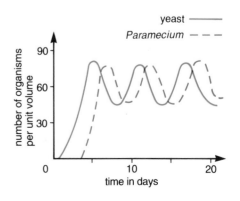

Two thousand years ago the climax community in Britain and much of Northern Europe was woodland. Oak and beech woods were a familiar sight all over Britain. Very few areas were not populated by trees. Only high mountain areas and those covered with bogs and swamps remained clear. As the human population began to grow, so grew the need for more land. Forests were cleared in order to provide space for the cultivation of crops and grazing of domesticated animals. This affected not only tree populations but also populations of other plants and the animals that depended on them for food and shelter. Animals such as the brown bear, the wolf, and the wild boar were once common in Britain. As their habitats were destroyed, so were they. People thought bears were dangerous, so didn't try to save them. The last British brown bear was killed in the tenth century. The removal of natural food supplies forced wolves to eat domestic flocks and herds. By AD 1500 the wolf was extinct in Britain. The seventeenth century saw the end of the wild boar. They were hunted mainly for food; the piglets were especially good to eat.

A growing population means more and more waste is produced. Pollution of the land, the water, and the air are the direct result of a population growing beyond its natural limits. Waste chemicals are dumped into rivers and seas killing fish and other aquatic life. Oil from spills at sea has reached even the most distant parts of the largest oceans, spoiling natural habitats. The burning of fossil fuels is the main cause of acid rain. Scandinavian countries are particularly affected – Norway has almost 2000 lakes without fish.

The size of the human population across the world is the direct cause of these ecological disasters.

Just as humans affected the natural populations of ancient Britain, today we can see the same kind of thing happening in the tropical rainforests of Southeast Asia and South America. Exploding populations in these countries are demanding more and more land on which to grow food. The only land that is available is that which is taken from the forests. Rainforests are a huge source of natural resources such as drugs, hardwoods, rubber, and chocolate. They also play a major part in maintaining the balance of carbon dioxide, water, and oxygen in the air. Removal of the forests (**deforestation**) will mean these resources are gone forever. The greenhouse effect will probably get worse and it is likely that there will be wholesale changes to the climate patterns of the Earth.

Activities

1 Imagine you are writing to the Brazilian government or a large multi-national company. In your letter try to explain the probable results of the destruction of the tropical rainforests.

When you have finished your letter, suggest some reasons why the Brazilians or multi-national companies might ignore your opinion (and those of other people who share your views) and continue to cut down rainforests.

Even as long as 600 years ago there was a high demand for fuel. Peat was extracted from boggy areas on an enormous scale. The Norfolk Broads in the east of England were the result of this peat removal. The area then flooded. A totally different type of habitat was created.

Questions

1 What was the climax community of Britain 2000 years ago?

2 Why were the forests cleared?

3 Briefly explain how the Norfolk Broads were formed.

4 **a)** Name three species that have been affected by the human population in Britain.
b) Sketch a graph showing the interaction of the human population with one of these species.

5 Where in the world can you find tropical rainforests?

6 Suggest how removal of the tropical rainforests could influence the greenhouse effect.

Classifying organisms

Imagine how difficult it would be to find a particular book in a library if the thousands of books were scattered all over the place in no logical order. If libraries didn't have systems of classification none of us would ever find the book we were looking for.

In the same way, no one can ever hope to know the names of all the living organisms found on Earth. Scientists have therefore devised a classification system for all known living things. Organisms are sorted into groups on the basis of features that they have in common.

Grouping together

The **species** is the smallest classification group. Members of a species can breed together to produce fertile offspring.

Similar species are grouped into **genera** (singular: **genus**). All members of a genus have common features. For example, the domestic cat, *Felis domestica*, the lynx, *Felis lynx*, and the mountain lion, *Felis concolor*, belong to the same genus, *Felis*.

The classification system continues by grouping related genera into **families**. The cat family, Felidae, includes the domestic cat, the lion (*Panthera leo*), and the cheetah (*Acinonyx jubatus*).

A group of similar families is called an **order**. Cats, dogs (Canidae), bears (Ursidae), and weasels (Mustelidae) are all from the order Carnivora.

Orders with common features are grouped into **classes**. The order Carnivora belongs to a most important class, the Mammalia, which includes bats, monkeys, horses, whales, kangaroos, apes, and humans.

Classes are grouped into **phyla** (singular: **phylum**). Mammals are members of the phylum Chordata which contains all the animals with a spinal cord. Fish, amphibians, reptiles, and birds are also chordates.

The biggest groups of all are the **kingdoms**. The Chordates, along with the Arthropoda and Mollusca, belong to the **Animal Kingdom**. Other kingdoms include the **Plant Kingdom** and the **Kingdom Fungi**.

Scientific names

Organisms have a scientific name in addition to a common name. An organism must have a name which refers to it and it alone, and is understood all over the world. For example, in North America the names puma, cougar, and mountain lion all refer to the same animal. By using the single scientific name, *Felis concolor*, any possible confusion is avoided.

The modern system of classification is based on the work of the Swedish naturalist, Carl von Linné (1707–78). He gave every known plant and animal a Latin name and grouped together organisms according to their similar features. Latin was chosen because it was the international language of science. Linné even Latinized his own name to Carolus Linnaeus!

group	example (animal)	example (plant)
kingdom	Animal	Plant
phylum	Chordata	Angiospermae
class	Mammalia	Dicotyledons
order	Carnivora	Ranales
family	Canidae	Ranunculaceae
genus	*Canis*	*Ranunculus*
species	*familiaris*	*bulbosus*
scientific name	*Canis familiaris* (domestic dog)	*Ranunculus bulbosus* (bulbous buttercup)

Levels of classification

Questions

1 Why is classification necessary?

2 Which is **a)** the largest **b)** the smallest classification group?

3 How many classes in the Animal Kingdom can you name?

    a) Why was Latin chosen for naming organisms?
    b) Explain why Latin names are useful.

5 Write a classification table like the above for **a)** the brown bear (*Ursus arctos*) **b)** the stoat (*Mustela erminea*).

For many years only two kingdoms were recognized, the plant and animal kingdoms. However, there are thousands of organisms, mostly very small, that are neither plant nor animal, or have both plant and animal features. These organisms are grouped separately from plants and animals. Today, many scientists recognize five kingdoms.

Kingdom Monera

Monera are living organisms which closely resemble the earliest forms of life on Earth. They live as single cells, or in colonies of identical cells. Their cells don't have a true nucleus. Instead, their genetic material (DNA) lies free in the cytoplasm, not enclosed by a nuclear membrane. Their cell walls are rigid, like plant cells, but they are made of materials not found in any other kingdom. Bacteria and blue–green algae are typical monerans. Over 3000 species are known.

Kingdom Protista

Protists are single-celled organisms living individually or in colonies. The kingdom is very varied having over 28 000 known species. The cells of protists have true nuclei. Genetic material is enclosed by a nuclear membrane. All protists live in water or moist places. Examples of protists are simple forms of algae and protozoa. Protozoa are sometimes called 'the first animals' because they feed by digesting complex food materials, just like us!

Kingdom Fungi

The **Fungi** form a large group of organisms made up of about 75 000 named species. For many years fungi were classified with plants, but are now recognized as a separate kingdom. Some fungi, like yeasts, live as single cells. Most, however, have a more complex structure – pin mould and the mushroom are good examples. The body of a fungus is made up of a **mycelium** (network) of thread-like **hyphae**. A hypha contains true nuclei and other typical cell structures but doesn't have cross walls to divide it up into individual cells. Fungi do not have chlorophyll and therefore cannot make food by photosynthesis. They feed by digesting their food outside themselves and then absorbing it.

Purple bacteria growing on seaweed

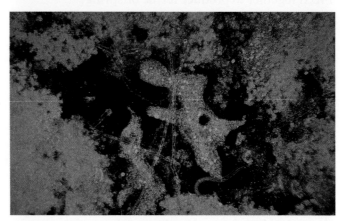

Amoeba (a protozoan) in pond debris

Fungi

Questions

1 What single feature would help you to identify a member of the Kingdom Monera?

2 Why are the protists sometimes called 'the first animals'?

3 Suggest two ways in which fungi differ from plants.

4 Explain why scientists today divide all known organisms into five kingdoms instead of two.

Who's related to whom? (2)

The Plant Kingdom

Most plants consist of more than one cell. In fact, they usually have many thousands of cells specialized into different tissues and systems. Plants have chlorophyll and make their own food by photosynthesis. Over 300 000 plant species have been listed.

The diagram below shows how plants are classified.

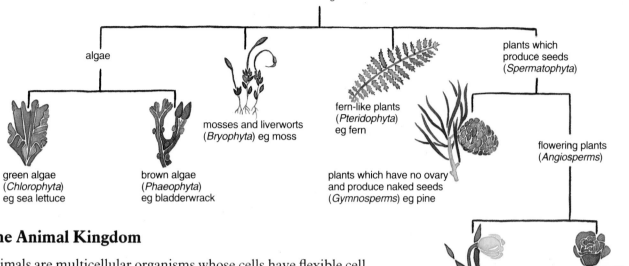

The Animal Kingdom

Animals are multicellular organisms whose cells have flexible cell membranes and no cell wall. Their cells are specialized into tissues, organs, and systems. Animals usually move to get their food, which is swallowed and digested inside the body. Of the 1.5 million listed animal species over 1 million are insects.

Animals are classified like this:

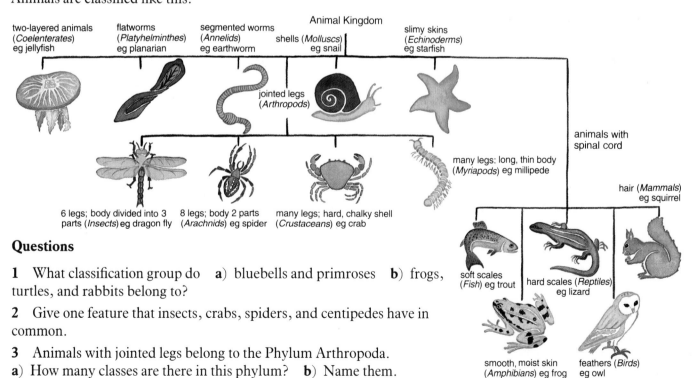

Questions

1 What classification group do **a)** bluebells and primroses **b)** frogs, turtles, and rabbits belong to?

2 Give one feature that insects, crabs, spiders, and centipedes have in common.

3 Animals with jointed legs belong to the Phylum Arthropoda.
a) How many classes are there in this phylum? **b)** Name them.

4 What is **a)** the largest **b)** the smallest classification group shown in the above diagrams?

37

Using keys

What do we do when we want to know the name of an organism that we cannot recognize? The answer is to use a **key**. A key is a series of questions which we ask ourselves. Each answer leads on to another question. This goes on until eventually the name of the organism is found.

Here is a simple key which will help you to name the four 'unknown' animals shown opposite.

Question 1   Does the animal have flippers?
          Answer: Yes   **dolphin**
                     No   Go to question 2

Question 2   Does the animal have wings?
          Answer: Yes   **bat**
                     No   Go to question 3

Question 3   Does the animal have a bushy tail?
          Answer: Yes   **squirrel**
                     No   **otter**

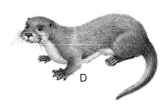

Here is a different kind of key. It works in just the same way as the one above, but it is presented in the form of a flow chart. Use it to identify the wild flowers shown opposite.

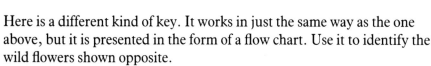

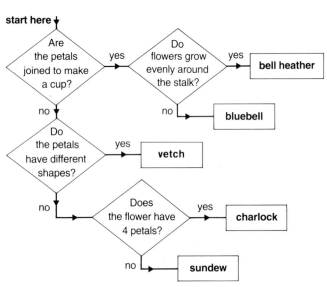

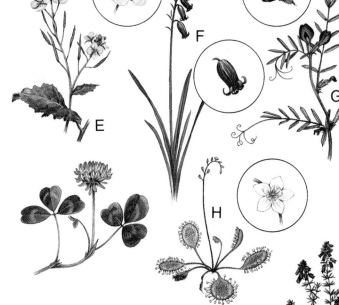

Questions

1   What are the names of organisms A–I on this page?

2   Why are keys useful?

3   Explain briefly how to use a key.

4   Make up a key to help someone identify the following items of laboratory glassware: beaker, test tube, filter funnel, measuring cylinder, conical flask.

5   Why do you think the classification of living organisms is more difficult than the classification of books in a library or food in a supermarket?

Questions

1 The diagram shows a simple graph of population growth curve.

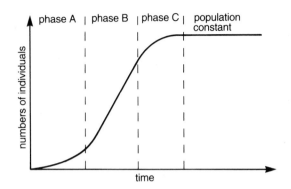

a) Why does the population i) increase slowly in phase A   ii) increase quickly in phase B   iii) start to slow down in phase C?

b) Give at least five reasons why the growth of a population eventually stops.

c) In most populations the number of individuals does not remain constant, it rises and falls. Explain why this happens.

d) How is the growth curve for the human population i) similar to   ii) different from the curve shown in the graph?

e) Suggest reasons for this difference.

2 Some students carried out a survey to find out the distribution of four plant species on some sand dunes. Their results are shown below.

a) Describe the distribution of the plants across the survey area.

b) What is the percentage frequency of
i) *Ammophila arenaria* at station 5   ii) *Hydrocotyle vulgaris* at station 13?

c) Briefly explain how this information could have been collected. Mention the methods used and any precautions that might have been taken.

d) Suggest reasons for the plants only appearing in particular places in this habitat.

3 The diagram shows a population pyramid for China.

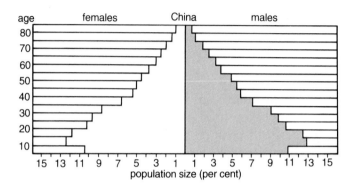

a) What does a population pyramid show?

b) Does the pyramid in the diagram show the population of China to be stable or unstable? Explain your answer.

c) Suggest how the birth rate of a country might be reduced.

d) The birth rate in China is falling.
 i) Draw a population pyramid for China as it might appear in 50 years' time if this trend continues.
ii) What effects might this have on the Chinese people and their way of life?

e) Draw a population pyramid for a developed country in Western Europe. List three differences between this and the pyramid for China today.

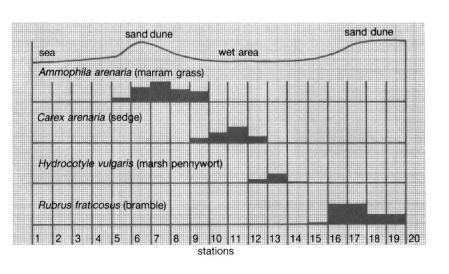

How many elements are there?

How do they behave?

Can we group them according to their properties?

How does this help scientists and technologists?

An element is a substance which contains only one type of atom. For example, the element copper only contains copper atoms. There are over 100 elements, each with its own set of properties that identifies it from the others. It would be very difficult to remember how all these individual elements behave, so we put elements which behave in a similar way into **groups**.

The **periodic table** is one way of arranging elements into groups that share similar properties. It was developed gradually over many years. In the early nineteenth century, a scientist called Wolfgang Döbereiner noticed that elements could be grouped in threes, each member of the group having similar properties to the other two. One of Döbereiner's groups (called a **triad**) contains the three metals lithium, sodium, and potassium. They have similar melting points, densities, and strengths, and undergo similar chemical reactions. Each of these elements is very reactive, as you will see later (page 46).

This idea was developed further in 1864 by a British scientist, John Newlands. He arranged all the known elements in order of increasing atomic mass and noticed that each element had similar properties to the element seven places after it. This was called the 'law of octaves'. However, it could only be used with the first 21 elements.

element	symbol
aluminium	Al
argon	Ar
barium	Ba
beryllium	Be
boron	B
bromine	Br
caesium	Cs
calcium	Ca
carbon	C
copper	Cu
fluorine	F
helium	He
hydrogen	H
iodine	I
iron	Fe
lead	Pb
lithium	Li
magnesium	Mg
neon	Ne
nitrogen	N
oxygen	O
phosphorus	P
potassium	K
silicon	Si
sodium	Na
sulphur	S
zinc	Zn

This list of elements is in alphabetical order. It is easy to find an element but it does not help us to understand how the element behaves chemically.

H	Li	Be	B	C	N	O
F	Na	Mg	Al	Si	P	S
Cl	K	Ca	Cr	Ti	Mn	Fe

Newlands' octaves

In 1869 the Russian chemist Dmitri Mendeleev arranged the elements in order of relative atomic mass. However, he left gaps for elements that had not yet been discovered, and predicted the properties of those elements. These predictions proved correct when the elements were eventually discovered. He also recognized that groups of elements with similar properties did not all have to contain the same number of elements.

Dmitri Mendeleev

Li	Cl
lithium	chlorine
Na	Br
sodium	bromine
K	I
potassium	iodine

Two examples of Döbereiner's triads

Modern periodic tables

Periodic tables used today have horizontal rows called **periods** and vertical columns called **groups**.

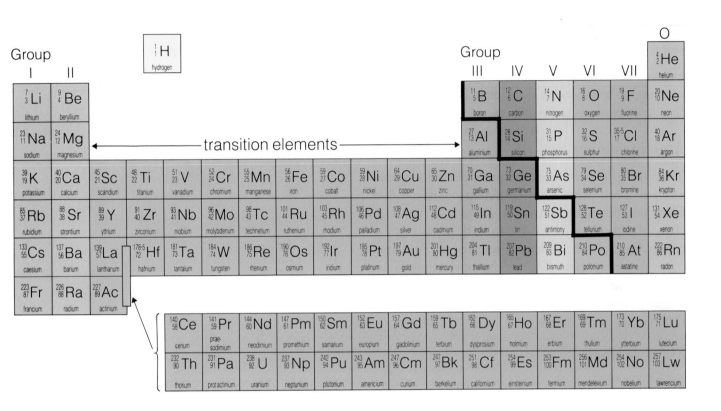

The periodic table of the elements

Elements within a group share similar properties. The groups are numbered, starting at group I on the left-hand side. The elements in group I are called the **alkali metals** and they include lithium, Li, sodium, Na, and potassium, K. The elements in group II are sometimes called the **alkaline earth metals**. Calcium, Ca, and magnesium, Mg, are in this group. Between groups II and III, in the fourth period, there is a large group called the **transition elements**. The last group is called 0, the **noble gases**, including helium, He, neon, Ne, argon, Ar, and krypton, Kr.

Each of the elements in the periodic table is shown by a symbol, a number above it, and a number below it. The smaller number, the lower one, is the **atomic number**. This gives information about the number of positive and negative particles in an atom. The larger number, the upper one, is the **relative atomic mass** –

it shows how that element's mass compares with the mass of other elements. This is explained on the next page.

mass number ———— 19

F

atomic number ———— 9

fluorine

Questions

1   Explain what is meant by the words **periodic table**, **group**, and **period**.

2   Draw a labelled diagram to show how the element calcium, Ca, is shown on the period table.

3   Explain the importance of early attempts to classify the elements. What were the limitations of Döbereiner's and Newlands' work?

The structure of the atom

An atom is far too small to be seen by the naked eye. Only by using very powerful microscopes is it possible to obtain a 'picture' of an atom. If you put 100 million atoms side by side, they would only measure 1 cm across. It is very difficult to imagine anything this small. Despite these difficulties, scientists have been able to find out a great deal about atoms.

Every atom is thought to be made up of a **nucleus** surrounded by a cloud of **electrons**. The nucleus consists of **protons** and **neutrons**.

Atomic number

The number of protons in an atom is called its **atomic number**. Each element has a different atomic number. Elements contain neutral atoms. Protons are positively charged particles, so there must also be negatively charged particles in an atom. These negatively charged particles are electrons. The number of electrons is equal to the number of protons in an element, so the atomic number also tells us how many electrons the atom has.

Mass number

Protons and neutrons have approximately the same mass. Electrons have a mass close to zero. The mass of an atom depends on how many protons and neutrons it has:

$$\text{mass number (or nucleon number)} = \text{number of protons + neutrons in an atom}$$

From this it follows that:

$$\text{mass number} - \text{atomic number} = \text{number of neutrons}$$

Relative atomic mass

Elements may contain atoms that have the same numbers of protons, but different numbers of neutrons. These are called **isotopes**. Some elements have only one isotope, but most elements have more than one.

Atomic masses are measured by comparing the mass of the atom with the carbon-12 isotope. For example, chlorine, Cl, has two isotopes, one with a mass number of 35 and the other with 37. Seventy five percent of all naturally occurring chlorine has a mass number of 35.

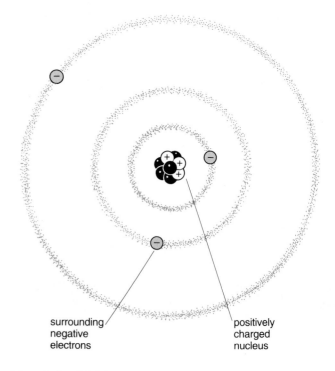

surrounding negative electrons

positively charged nucleus

Theoretical model of the atom

The other 25% has a mass number of 37. The **relative atomic mass** of an element is defined as the average mass of its isotopes compared with the mass of one atom of carbon-12. This explains why the relative atomic mass of chlorine is not a whole number – it is 35.5.

percentage of chlorine with mass number 35 = 75

percentage of chlorine with mass number 37 = 25

$$\textbf{relative atomic mass} = \frac{(35 \times 75) + (37 \times 25)}{100} = \textbf{35.5}$$

Questions

1 Calculate the relative atomic mass of the following elements. You are given the percentages of each isotope. Give your answer to one decimal place.

    a) copper: 69% of isotope of mass 63
                     31% of isotope of mass 65

    b) zinc: 49% of isotope of mass 64
                     28% of isotope of mass 66
                     4% of isotope of mass 67
                     18% of isotope of mass 68
                     1% of isotope of mass 69

The arrangement of electrons

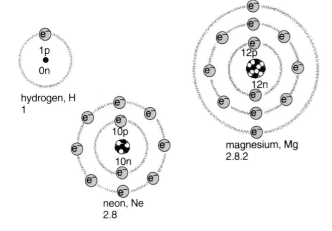

hydrogen, H
1

neon, Ne
2.8

magnesium, Mg
2.8.2

The arrangement of electrons in three different atoms

Scientists have worked out a theoretical model of the atom in which the electrons are arranged in definite layers or levels of energy around the nucleus. Each layer or **shell** can hold a certain number of electrons. The first **energy shell**, which is at the lowest energy level, can hold a maximum of two electrons. The second and third shells can hold a maximum of eight electrons each. The electrons build up from the first shell, filling each one until all the electrons are in place. This means that the atom has the minimum amount of energy and all the electrons are as close to the nucleus as they can be. The table below shows how the electrons are arranged for the first 20 elements.

element	symbol	atomic number	number of electrons	first shell	second shell	third shell	fourth shell
hydrogen	H	1	1	1			
helium	He	2	2	2			
lithium	Li	3	3	2	1		
beryllium	Be	4	4	2	2		
boron	B	5	5	2	3		
carbon	C	6	6	2	4		
nitrogen	N	7	7	2	5		
oxyygen	O	8	8	2	6		
fluorine	F	9	9	2	7		
neon	Ne	10	10	2	8		
sodium	Na	11	11	2	8	1	
magnesium	Mg	12	12	2	8	2	
aluminium	Al	13	13	2	8	3	
silicon	Si	14	14	2	8	4	
phosphorus	P	15	15	2	8	5	
sulphur	S	16	16	2	8	6	
chlorine	Cl	17	17	2	8	7	
argon	Ar	18	18	2	8	8	
potassium	K	19	19	2	8	8	1
calcium	Ca	20	20	2	8	8	2

What are ions?

In some chemical reactions, the electrons that surround the nucleus move from one atom to another. An atom with one or more additional electrons is called a **negative ion**; an atom which has lost one or more electrons is called a **positive ion**. Metal atoms lose electrons in chemical reactions so their atoms become ions with a positive charge. Non-metal atoms accept these extra electrons to become negatively charged ions.

	atom	configuration	ion	configuration
metals	Na sodium atom	2.8.1 electron configuration	Na^+ sodium ion	2.8 electron configuration
	Ca calcium atom	2.8.8.2 electron configuration	Ca^{2+} calcium ion	2.8.8 electron configuration
non-metals	F fluorine atom	2.7 electron configuration	F^- fluoride ion	2.8 electron configuration
	S sulphur atom	2.8.6 electron configuration	S^{2-} sulphide ion	2.8.8 electron configuration

During chemical reactions, electrons move from one atom to another. The number of neutrons and protons stays the same

Questions

1 Explain the following terms: **atomic number**, **mass number**, **relative atomic mass**, **ion**.

2 Draw diagrams to show the structures of the following atoms:
a) sodium, Na
b) fluorine, F
c) calcium, Ca
d) sulphur, S
e) carbon, C

3 What are the charges on the following ions?
a) potassium
b) chloride
c) oxide
d) magnesium

Metals and non-metals

There are two types of elements, **metals** and **non-metals**. There are many more **metal** elements than **non-metal** elements. The metals are on the left-hand side of the periodic table, the non-metals on the right. They are separated on the periodic table by a stepped line. The metals close to this line have some of the properties of the non-metals. Similarly, the non-metals close to the line have some metallic properties. The properties of metals and non-metals are shown in the table below.

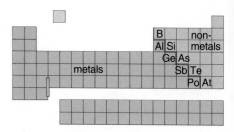

Metals are on the left-hand side of the periodic table and non-metals on the right.

metals	non-metals
usually solids at room temperature	usually solids or gases at room temperature
good conductors of electricity and heat	do not usually conduct heat or electricity
lustrous (shiny)	not usually shiny
malleable (can be hammered into a different shape)	brittle when solid and shatter when hammered
ductile (can be stretched)	too brittle to be stretched
usually sonorous (ring like a bell when hit)	not sonorous
usually very dense	generally have a low density
nearly all have high melting points	have low melting points, with a few exceptions
When they react with dilute acids, hydrogen gas is given off	do not react with dilute acids

Properties of metal and non-metal elements

There are far more metals than non-metals.

Questions

1   Choose two metals which you are familiar with, e.g. copper and iron, and look at them closely. What kind of properties would you use to describe them?

2   Oxygen and sulphur are two non-metals. How do their properties differ from those of metals?

3   Using the headings below, make a list of uses for some metals and non-metals. One is done for you.

element	symbol	used for	reason for using it
copper	Cu	water pipes	does not rust, easily bent into shape, can be joined by soldering

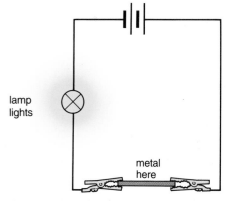

When a metal is placed in an electric circuit containing a bulb, the bulb lights. Metals conduct electricity. If a piece of sulphur was placed in the same circuit, what would happen?

Mercury – a liquid metal

The general properties of metals and non-metals apply to nearly all the elements. However, there are exceptions. For example, silicon, Si, is a shiny non-metal; the metal lead, Pb, is not sonorous; group I metals have low densities and melting points, and iodine, I, has a higher density than many metals. Metals and non-metals are all either solids or gases. The two exceptions to this are the metal **mercury**, Hg, and the non-metal **bromine**, Br. They are both liquids at room temperature. The properties of bromine are shown on page 48. The properties of mercury are shown in the table below.

Mercury

atomic number	80
atomic mass	201
melting point	$-39\,°C$
boiling point	$357\,°C$
density	$13.55\,\mathrm{g\,cm^{-3}}$

Mercury is a very dense silvery liquid with many uses. The electrolysis of brine in the manufacture of chlorine and sodium hydroxide uses mercury as the negative electrode in the cell (this is described on page 61). However, efforts are being made to develop a new method for this process without using mercury, since leakages from cells have caused pollution problems. Mercury is used in thermometers covering a range of $0\,°C$ to $100\,°C$. Mercury expands evenly as the temperature rises and it is a good conductor of heat. It is also used in barometers to measure changes in air pressure. As the weather changes, so does the air pressure.

Other metals such as aluminium mix easily with mercury to form **alloys** which are called **amalgams**. Some tooth fillings are made with an amalgam of mercury with tin and silver. If mercury is absorbed through the skin or by inhalation, it can cause severe brain damage. Hatters used to use mercury to make top hats and were exposed a great deal to the metal. This may explain the expression 'mad as a hatter'!

The 'Mad Hatter' from Alice in Wonderland

Mercury pollution

It is now known that exposure to mercury can cause serious health problems. It is no longer used in school laboratories. If you break a mercury thermometer, it must be cleared up by someone who knows how to do this safely.

About 30 years ago, mercury was discharged into the Minimata Bay in Japan by a local factory. It was noticed that the local fishermen became very tired and suffered from headaches. This soon spread to the rest of the community, including the population of cats. The fish in the bay had become poisoned by the mercury, which was passed on to the people who ate the fish. Many people died or suffered severe nervous disabilities.

Mercury poisoning can have devastating effects.

The alkali metals

The members of group I, the alkali metals, are:

lithium   **Li**
sodium   **Na**
potassium   **K**
rubidium   **Rb**
caesium   **Cs**

This group is found on the far left of the periodic table. They are all metals. Group I elements are sometimes called the alkali metals because they react with water to form an alkali, as you will see on the opposite page. The metals are all very reactive, and because of this, they must be stored under oil to protect them from coming into contact with either air or water. It is because of this high reactivity that the alkali metals are only found naturally combined with other elements. They show similar physical properties (see table below). For example, they are shiny, conduct electricity, and have other metallic properties. However, they also have some properties that are not usually associated with the majority of metals. Lithium, sodium, and potassium each have a density which is less than that of water ($1\,g/cm^3$). This means that they float on water. Both their melting and boiling points are lower than expected for metals. One other unexpected property is that the alkali metals are soft – they can be easily cut with a knife. When they are first cut, you can see how shiny they are. After a few minutes they become very dull due to reaction with the air.

Sodium, potassium, and lithium are stored under oil.

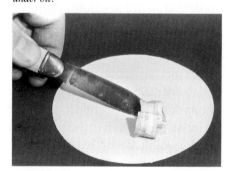

When the alkali metals are first cut, the surface is shiny. It rapidly tarnishes as the metal reacts with the air.

element	relative atomic mass	melting point in °C	boiling point in °C	density in g/cm³
Li	6.9	180	1331	0.53
Na	23.0	98	890	0.97
K	39.1	63	766	0.86
Rb	85.5	39	701	1.5

Questions

1 Plot a graph of melting point against relative atomic mass for the alkali metals. On the same graph, plot the boiling points. Write a sentence to describe the information the graph gives you.

2 Look at the table of electronic configurations on page 43. Write down the arrangement of electrons in lithium, sodium, and potassium. Do you notice any trend? Write a sentence to explain what you have found.

3 'The alkali metals are all typical metals.' Explain why this statement is not completely correct.

Chemical properties of group I

On exposure to moist air, the alkali metals rapidly react with oxygen (they tarnish). They all react violently with cold water to give off hydrogen gas and form alkaline solutions:

potassium + water → potassium hydroxide + hydrogen
$$2K \ + \ 2H_2O \ \rightarrow \ 2KOH \ + \ H_2$$

The chemical reactions of the alkali metals are similar, but not exactly the same. When they are placed in contact with cold water, they all react immediately. They move about rapidly on the surface of the water and give off a colourless gas, hydrogen. The heat given off during the reaction is enough to make the metals melt. The metals become more reactive as you go down the group. Potassium is more reactive than sodium, which is more reactive than lithium. Potassium bursts into lilac coloured flame. Sodium may burst into yellow flames, but only if it is prevented from moving about on the water. Lithium does not burst into flames.

When the alkali metals burn in air or oxygen they burn with characteristic coloured flames. Potassium reacts the most vigorously. If the burning metals are placed in a gas jar of chlorine, they continue to burn, giving off a lot of white smoke. The smoke is made up of small metal chloride particles. Once again, potassium is more reactive than sodium, which is more reactive than lithium.

Properties of compounds of group I elements

The compounds of group I metals are soluble in water. Even their carbonates are soluble, which is unusual. All group I compounds are ionic (this is explained on page 54). When the group I compounds are heated, they melt but do not decompose. They are said to be very stable to heat. The more reactive the metal, the more stable its compounds.

Activities

1 Design and carry out an experiment to compare **a**) the solubility in water and **b**) the stability when heated of group I compounds with other metal compounds. Use sodium carbonate, calcium carbonate, and copper carbonate in your experiments. Put your results in a table.

Uses of the alkali metals

The pure elements do not have many uses, since they corrode very easily. The high thermal capacity of sodium makes it a useful coolant in nuclear power stations. The orange glow from street lamps is provided by sodium vapour. Sodium is in plentiful supply in the form of sodium chloride (common salt). The UK also has considerable underground reserves of rock salt in Cheshire. Impure salt is used on roads during the winter to prevent ice. Salt is also used in cooking. Concentrated salt solution is called brine and is used to make sodium and its compounds. It is also used to preserve foods in tins such as sausages, sardines, and tuna fish.

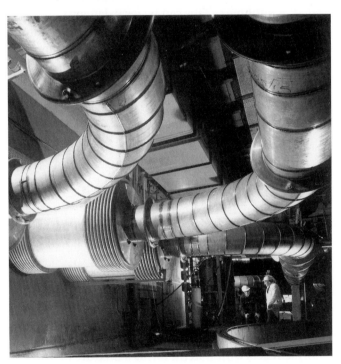

These pipes carry liquid sodium which is used as a coolant at the Dounreay fast-breeder nuclear reactor.

Questions

1 Write a word equation for the reaction of caesium with water. Is the reaction likely to be more or less vigorous than the reaction of sodium with water? Explain the reason for your answer.

2 Look at the table on page 46. By following the pattern, make predictions about the melting and boiling points of caesium, then look up the actual values in a reference book.

The halogens

Halogens form a group of elements on the right of the periodic table. The first four halogens are fairly common:

fluorine	**F**	**bromine**	**Br**
chlorine	**Cl**	**iodine**	**I**

The first three elements are very reactive at room temperature. Halogens are all non-metals. As a group of elements they show trends in their physical properties – going down the group, their melting points, boiling points, and densities increase. Bromine is a liquid at room temperature and iodine is a solid. Iodine turns (almost) directly into a vapour when it is heated; it **sublimes**. This can be very dangerous in a school laboratory, especially if the vapour comes into contact with broken skin or your eyes. When using iodine, always wear safety spectacles. The other halogens are very dangerous to use in the laboratory and should only be used in a fume cupboard by a teacher.

element	relative atomic mass	appearance at room temperature	melting point in °C	boiling point in °C	density in g/dm³
fluorine	19.0	pale yellow gas	−220	−188	1.69
chlorine	35.5	pale green gas	−101	− 35	3.21
bromine	79.9	red-brown liquid	−7	58	2930
iodine	126.9	dark grey solid	114	183	4930

Chemical properties of group VII

The halogen elements are very reactive. When chlorine reacts with water it forms a mixture of acids which have strong bleaching properties. Household **bleaches** contain chlorine compounds.

chlorine	+	water	→	hydrochloric acid	+	hypochlorous acid
Cl_2	+	H_2O	→	HCl	+	HClO

Bromine does not react as easily as chlorine, and iodine only dissolves slightly in water.

Chlorine is a very reactive non-metal. It will react with all metals (even unreactive gold), to form metal chlorides. For example, if dry chlorine gas is passed over heated iron wool, as in the apparatus shown above, iron(III) chloride is produced. Bromine and iodine react in a similar way, but need a great deal more heat for a reaction to take place.

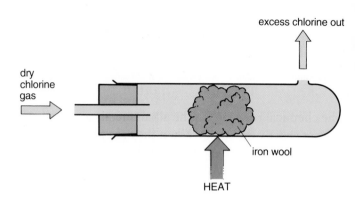

The iron wool is heated and the Bunsen removed before passing the chlorine gas through the combustion tube. This experiment needs to be carried out in a fume cupboard. Why?

Activities

1 Household bleaches usually contain a compound of chlorine called sodium hypochlorite. **They must be handled with extreme care and safety spectacles must be worn when using them. Do not let bleach come into contact with your skin or clothing**.

Carry out a survey of as many different bleaches as you can find. List the chemical contents of the bleach.

2 Collect $10\,cm^3$ samples of two different household bleaches.
Add water to the samples to make $50\,cm^3$ solutions of each sample.
See how effective each sample is by testing it on different fabrics.

Displacement reactions

You can compare the reactivities of the halogens by carrying out **displacement reactions**. If a solution of chlorine dissolved in water is added to a solution of potassium iodide, iodine is formed and the solution turns dark brown. This happens because chlorine is more reactive than iodine and displaces it:

chlorine	+	potassium iodide	→	potassium chloride	+	iodine
Cl_2	+	2KI	→	2KCl	+	I_2

If iodine is added to a solution of potassium chloride, nothing happens. This is because iodine is not reactive enough to take the chlorine from the potassium.

iodine	+	potassium chloride	→	no reaction
I_2	+	2KCl		

Uses of the halogens

Fluorine and chlorine are both very poisonous gases. Chlorine was used in the First World War as a chemical weapon. It has a pungent, irritating smell and must be treated with extreme care.

Because of their high reactivity the halogens as elements do not have many uses. Chlorine is an exception, as both it and its compounds have a great many uses. Its bleaching and disinfecting properties are used when chlorine is added in small quantities to drinking water. It kills the bacteria in the water without harming people or animals. Larger quantities are added to swimming pools.

A great deal of the chlorine produced is used to make **hydrochloric acid**. Chlorine is burnt in hydrogen to produce hydrogen chloride, which then dissolves very easily in water to produce the acid. This acid is used in the manufacture of many other chemicals. Other uses of halogen compounds are shown in the diagram below.

Why does this swimmer wear goggles?

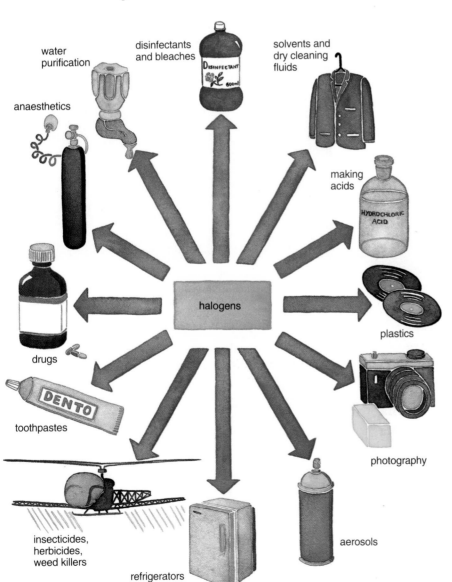

Halogens have many uses.

Activities

1 Plot a graph of melting point against relative atomic mass for the halogens. Put the relative atomic mass on the horizontal axis and the melting point on the vertical axis. Use a relative atomic mass scale from 1 to 130 and melting point scale from −220°C to 200°C. Plot the boiling points on the same axes. What do you notice?

Questions

1 Does the reactivity of the halogens increase or decrease going down the group? Support your answer with suitable examples.

2 Explain what you would expect to see if bromine water was added to a solution of potassium iodide. Write an equation to illustrate your answer.

3 Look at the table on page 43. What is the pattern in the arrangement of electrons in group VII elements?

49

Other families of elements

There are other groups of elements in the periodic table which have similar properties to each other. Here are some examples.

Group 0, the noble gases

helium	He	krypton	Kr
neon	Ne	xenon	Xe
argon	Ar	radon	Rn

The gases in this group do not react easily. The gases do not form molecules. They used to be called the **inert gases** because people thought that they could not form any compounds. However, a small number of compounds have now been made so the name has been changed to the noble gases. By looking at the arrangement of electrons in their atoms (see page 43) it is possible to suggest why this is so. This is explained in more detail on page 52.

These elements are of limited use. Argon is used to fill light bulbs since it does not react with the hot filament. Similarly, neon is used in fluorescent tubes. Helium can be used in airships because it is non-flammable and has a low density. It is safer to use than hydrogen which forms an explosive mixture with air.

The noble gases help to create colourful light displays.

Helium is safe and much lighter than air – it is used for balloons.

Group II, the alkaline earth metals

beryllium	Be	strontium	Sr
magnesium	Mg	barium	Ba
calcium	Ca	radium	Ra

All the members of this group are metals. They are less reactive than the group I elements. The reactivity of the group II metals increases as you go down the group – compare the reactivities of magnesium and calcium in cold water. Calcium reacts fairly quickly in cold water giving off hydrogen gas and forming an alkali, calcium hydroxide.

$$\text{calcium} + \text{water} \rightarrow \text{calcium hydroxide} + \text{hydrogen}$$
$$\text{Ca} + 2H_2O \rightarrow Ca(OH)_2 + 2H_2$$

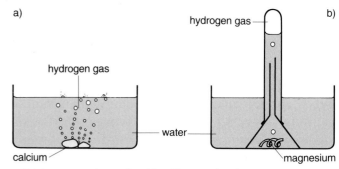

a Calcium reacts vigorously with cold water, in minutes.

b Magnesium reacts very slowly with cold water. This experiment needs to be set up and left for a few days before there is enough hydrogen to test.

Clean magnesium reacts slowly with cold water, but reacts more quickly with steam to form magnesium hydroxide and hydrogen. Magnesium is a very useful metal. It is very light, and is used extensively in making alloys (see page 69). Since magnesium burns with a very bright light it is used in fireworks and flares.

When burning magnesium in the laboratory, it is important not to look directly at the brilliant white light. Some fireworks contain magnesium.

Calcium compounds have important uses:

calcium compound	common name	use
calcium sulphate	gypsum	making 'plaster of Paris', wall and ceiling plaster, plasterboard, etc.
calcium hydroxide	lime	neutralizing acid soils
calcium phosphate		fertilizer
calcium carbonate	limestone	making cement

Transition elements

These elements are between groups II and III of the periodic table. They are all metals. Some examples of transition elements are:

titanium	Ti	iron	Fe
vanadium	V	cobalt	Co
chromium	Cr	nickel	Ni
manganese	Mn	copper	Cu

They all have metallic properties. As well as having similar properties going down the group, this family of elements also has similar properties going across a period. They generally have high melting points, which are similar across the period. Compounds of the transition metals are usually coloured, for example, copper sulphate is blue, copper carbonate is green. The metals and their compounds are often used as catalysts in industrial processes, for example iron is used in the manufacture of ammonia and vanadium(V) oxide in the production of sulphuric acid. Iron is an important mineral for healthy living. Many alloys contain transition elements.

Titanium is strong and inert (unreactive) – it is used for replacement hip joints.

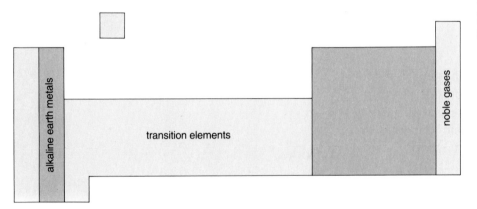

The positions of the alkaline earth metals, transition elements, and noble gases in the periodic table

Activities

1 Limestone (calcium carbonate) is a very common material and has many uses and interesting properties. Make a poster showing where it is found and how it is used.

2 Look at all the different compounds of transition metals you can and note down what they look like. **Be careful, many are poisonous.** Comment on any similarities you notice.

Questions

1 Suggest why the elements in group 0 of the periodic table are called the noble gases.

2 With suitable examples, show how the reactivity of group II elements compares with that of group I elements.

3 List as many uses of transition metals and their compounds as you can.

Information from the periodic table

The arrangement of electrons in an atom gives a great deal of information about an element. For example, it allows you to predict how the element will react.

Reactivity

The elements in group I of the periodic table all have one electron in their outside shell, and are very reactive.

lithium	**Li**	**2.1**
sodium	**Na**	**2.8.1**
potassium	**K**	**2.8.8.1**

The noble gases, on the other hand, are very unreactive. They are also very stable at room temperature. This is because they all have a full outer shell of electrons, so they cannot take any more.

helium	**He**	**2**
neon	**Ne**	**2.8**
argon	**Ar**	**2.8.8**

Stability

In order for a group I element to have the same kind of stability as a noble gas, it must lose its outside electron. When it does this its ions have a positive charge. To lose electrons, an element must give them to another element. This can happen in a chemical reaction.

lithium $= $ **Li**   **2.1** $-$ **electron** $=$ **Li$^+$ ion 2**
sodium $= $ **Na**   **2.8.1** $-$ **electron** $=$ **Na$^+$ ion 2.8**
potassium $=$ **K**   **2.8.8.1** $-$ **electron** $=$ **K$^+$ ion 2.8.8**

The group VII elements, the halogens, are very reactive non-metals. They all have seven electrons in their outside shells.

fluorine	**F**	**2.7**
chlorine	**Cl**	**2.8.7**

For these elements to become stable, they must take an extra electron to fill their outer shell. When they do this, they become negative ions.

fluoride $=$ **F**   **2.7** $+$ **electron** $=$ **F$^-$ ion 2.8**
chloride $=$ **Cl**   **2.8.7** $+$ **electron** $=$ **Cl$^-$ ion 2.8.8**

Summary

Metals can lose electrons and become positive ions during reactions:

metals	number of electrons lost	ion charge
group I	1	1+
group II	2	2+

Non-metals can gain electrons and become negative ions during reactions:

non-metals	number of electrons gained	ion charge
group VII	1	1−
group VI	2	2−

The gases in group 0 do not lose or gain electrons. They are very unreactive.

Activities

1 Carefully study the information in the periodic table and write down the arrangement of electrons in an atom of magnesium, Mg, and calcium, Ca.

- How many electrons are there in the outside shells of these atoms?
- Do you think that these elements will lose or gain electrons in chemical reactions? Give a reason for your answer.
- What will be the charges on their ions, positive or negative?
- What will be the size of the charges, one, two, or three?

Repeat this activity for oxygen, O, and aluminium, Al.

Describe any pattern you have discovered.

Using the periodic table

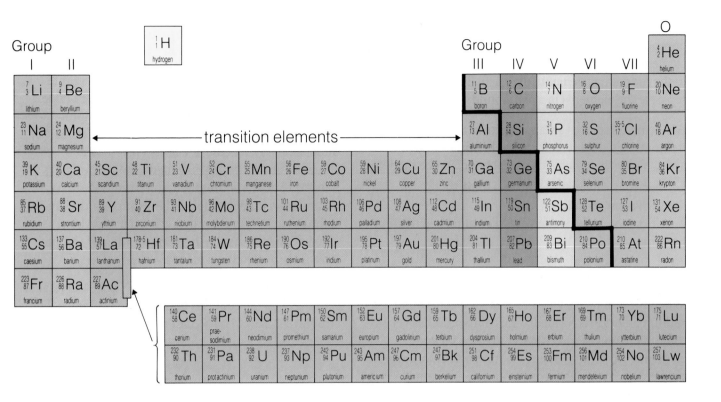

If you know what group of the periodic table an element is in, you can predict how it will react. For example, if you are told that an element is in group I of the periodic table, you will know that it is a metal which reacts violently with cold water. You should also be able to predict its physical properties, since all group I elements can be easily cut with a knife and have low densities.

If the properties and reactions of an element are known it is also possible to predict which group of the periodic table it is in. For example, if you are told that an element is a gas at room temperature, doesn't seem to react with any other elements, and exists as a molecule with only one atom in, then you could suggest that it is likely to be in group 0.

By knowing how many electrons there are in the outside shell of an atom, it is possible to say which group of the periodic table it is in. From this information you can predict its likely reactions and properties.

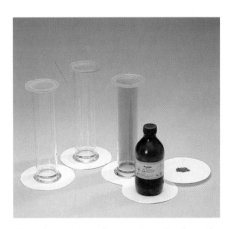

The halogens become less reactive going down the group. Fluorine is the most reactive and iodine the least reactive.

Questions

1 Predict the reactions and properties of the following elements:

a) element X in group II

b) element Y, a metal which reacts quite vigorously with dilute acids but not with cold water. Its compounds are all white solids and are insoluble in water.

c) element Z which has seven electrons in its outside shell.

53

Bonding (1): ionic

When two or more elements react together to form a **compound**, a chemical bond is formed between the elements. The compound has very different properties to the individual elements. It is usually very difficult to separate the elements in a compound.

An element requires a stable electron arrangement in its atoms. To do this, it forms a chemical **bond**. There are two ways in which a chemical bond can be made:

1 electrons can be transferred – **ionic** (or **electrovalent**) **bonding**
2 electrons can be shared between atoms – **covalent bonding**.

Ionic bonding

When sodium reacts with chlorine, the compound sodium chloride is formed. The compound has very different properties to either of the two separate elements. Both the elements sodium and chlorine are very reactive and dangerous to handle. Sodium chloride is eaten as table salt!

The outer electron in the sodium atom is readily given to any other atom that needs it. When sodium loses its outer electron it forms sodium ions, Na^+. Chlorine has seven electrons in its outer shell and during the reaction uses the electron from sodium to give it a full outer shell of electrons. It then becomes a chloride ion, Cl^-.

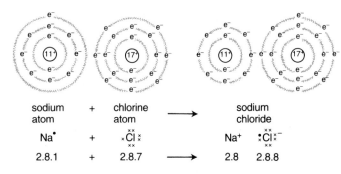

sodium atom	+	chlorine atom		sodium chloride	
Na•	+	×Cl×		Na⁺	:Cl×⁻
2.8.1	+	2.8.7		2.8	2.8.8

The transfer of electrons during the reaction between sodium and chlorine

Ionic bonding usually takes place between a metal and a non-metal. Ionic compounds cannot be separated very easily into their elements. It takes a large amount of electricity to separate the sodium from sodium chloride by electrolysis.

Structure of ionic compounds

From studies of ionic compounds using X-rays, it has been found that the ions are arranged in a definite pattern. This means that they have a regular shape. Look at the diagram of the structure of sodium chloride. The sodium ion is surrounded in three dimensions by six chloride ions. Now look at a chloride ion and count how many sodium ions it is bonded to. Each sodium ion is surrounded by six chloride ions. Each chloride ion is surrounded by six sodium ions. Therefore in any crystal of sodium chloride there must be the same number of sodium ions as there are chloride ions.

The formula for sodium chloride is NaCl. A crystal of sodium chloride contains many millions of ions. The structure is said to be a **giant ionic lattice**.

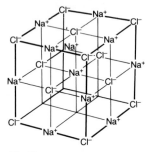

Crystal lattice of sodium chloride

Properties of ionic compounds

Ionic compounds:

- are hard
- have high melting points
- have high boiling points
- dissolve in water
- do not conduct electricity when solid
- do conduct electricity when liquid or dissolved in water.

Questions

1 What is ionic bonding?

2 Solid sodium chloride does not conduct electricity, though when molten or dissolved in water it does. Why do you think this is?

3 Make a list of ten ionic compounds and find out their melting points. What do you notice?

Bonding (2): covalent

A **covalent bond** is found in compounds that contain only non-metals. Electrons are shared between the atoms in a covalent compound. A covalent compound does not contain any ions, since non-metals are generally unable to donate electrons from their outer shells to other atoms. The electrons are shared by the atoms which overlap each other. The covalent bond is a very strong bond. However, the bonds holding the molecules together may be either weak or strong (as explained on page 57). Here are some examples of covalent bonding.

The chlorine molecule, Cl_2

A chlorine atom has seven electrons in its outside shell. If it had one more electron in its outer shell, it would have a full outer shell, and be more stable. If there are no metal atoms available to give electrons to the chlorine atom, then it can share an electron with another chlorine atom. When it does so, both the chlorine atoms share an electron and both have a full outer shell. This means that each molecule of chlorine contains two atoms. It is said to be a **diatomic molecule**, Cl_2.

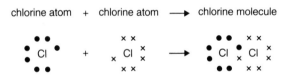

The sharing of electrons in the chlorine molecule

The hydrogen chloride molecule, HCl

Hydrogen only has one electron in its outside shell, and needs another to make a stable electron arrangement. Chloride needs one more electron, and shares one of its outer electrons with hydrogen. This means that hydrogen now has two electrons in its outside shell and chlorine has eight.

The hydrogen chloride covalent bond

The methane molecule, CH_4

Carbon has four electrons in its outside shell and needs to share four other electrons before it has a stable electron arrangement. Four atoms of hydrogen will share their electrons with carbon to form a methane molecule.

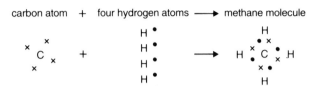

Covalent bonds in methane

The carbon dioxide molecule, CO_2

When two pairs of electrons are shared, a double covalent bond is made.

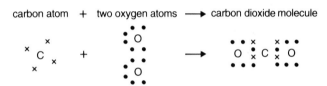

Covalent bonds in carbon dioxide

Properties of covalent compounds

Covalent compounds:
- are not usually very hard
- have low melting points
- have low boiling points
- do not usually dissolve in water
- do not conduct electricity.

Questions

1 What is covalent bonding?

2 Draw up a table to show the differences in properties between ionic and covalent compounds.

3 Draw diagrams to show how the electrons are shared in the following covalent compounds: tetrachloromethane, CCl_4, and water, H_2O.

4 Put the following compounds into groups of ionic and covalent compounds. (You may find the periodic table useful.)

calcium oxide, CaO, potassium bromide, KBr, sulphur dioxide, SO_2, lithium oxide, Li_2O, hydrogen bromide, HBr, ethane, C_2H_6, carbon monoxide, CO, zinc chloride, $ZnCl_2$.

Simple molecules

Covalent bonds between atoms in molecules are very strong bonds. However, the bonds holding covalent molecules to each other can be quite weak. Covalent compounds do not conduct electricity, and do not contain any ions. The atoms in a 'simple molecule' are held together by covalent bonds. The compounds contain non-metals. There are some very weak forces holding these covalent compounds together, called **intermolecular forces**. These very weak forces between covalent molecules can be easily broken. When a solid melts, the bonds between the molecules have to be loosened or broken. If the forces holding the molecules together are weak, then it does not take much heat to break these bonds. It is because of this that simple molecular substances, such as methane, CH_4, have such low melting and boiling points.

compound	formula	molecular structure
oxygen	O_2	
hydrogen chloride	HCl	
bromine	Br_2	
sulphur	S_8	

Simple covalent molecules

The element iodine, I_2, is an example of a simple covalent molecule. The two atoms in an iodine molecule are bonded together covalently. The forces between the molecules are very weak compared with the covalent bond holding the two atoms together. Iodine is a solid at room temperature. It is soft and flakes easily. It has low melting and boiling points and smells like disinfectant. Iodine has these properties because the weak forces holding the molecules together can easily be broken.

*Iodine is a purple solid at room temperature. It **sublimes** – it turns straight into a gas on heating.*

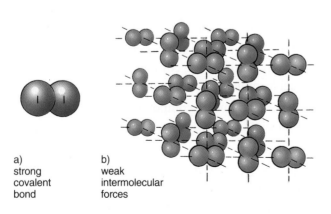

a)
strong
covalent
bond

b)
weak
intermolecular
forces

a) One iodine molecule b) Iodine molecules are held together by weak bonds.

The seaweed Laminaria contains iodine.

Giant molecules

Diamond and **graphite** both contain only carbon atoms. The atoms are bonded together covalently, and each forms a different giant structure. There are considerable differences between the properties of diamond and graphite. These differences are due to the different structures of diamond and graphite.

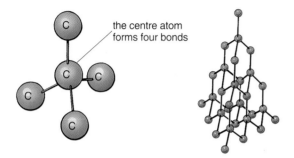

Each carbon atom in diamond is bonded to four others.

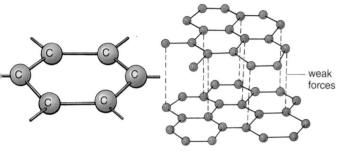

Graphite consists of hexagonal layers of carbon atoms. The layers have weak bonds holding them together.

Each carbon atom in diamond is bonded covalently to four other carbon atoms. They are arranged in the shape of a tetrahedron. In graphite, each carbon atom is bonded covalently to three other carbon atoms in layers. Each layer is a giant structure of carbon atoms which is arranged in hexagons. The layers are only held together by weak forces. This means that the layers slide over each other easily. Graphite is often used as a lubricant and is part of the 'lead' in pencils. Graphite has a high melting point, 3730 °C, because the covalent bonds (in the hexagons) are difficult to break. Graphite fibres are used to make objects that require strength, for example golf clubs and tennis rackets. The structure of diamond gives it different properties – it is the hardest natural substance known. This makes it useful for cutting other hard substances such as rocks. Dentists' drills contain diamonds. Diamond does not conduct electricity, though graphite does. Diamond and graphite are **allotropes** of carbon. Allotropes are different structural arrangements of the same element in the solid state.

Graphite's lubricant properties make it useful in pencils.

Diamonds are used to cut delicate patterns on glass.

Questions

1 How do the properties of a simple covalent structure such as iodine compare with those of a giant covalent structure such as diamond?

2 What is an allotrope?

3 List as many uses as you can for diamond. How do the structure and properties of diamond relate to these properties?

4 Carbon is a non-metal. Graphite is one form of carbon. Graphite is a non-metal that conducts electricity. Diamond is another form of carbon, but it does not conduct electricity. Can you think of a reason why this is?

Patterns in the periodic table

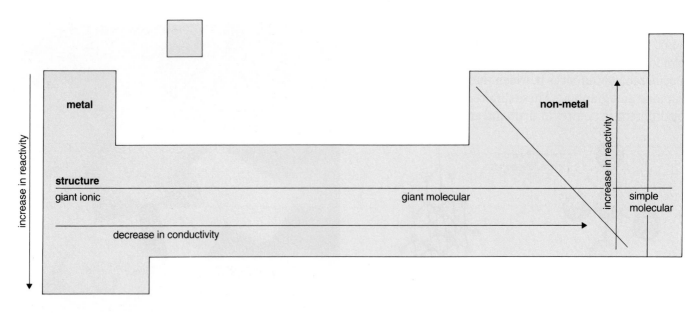

Summary of trends in the periodic table

Each group in the periodic table shows patterns in its elements' properties and reactions. These properties and reactions follow a trend. For example, the melting points of group I metals, the alkali metals, decrease going down the group. The reactivity increases going down the group.

The melting points of the group VII elements, the halogens, increase going down the group, and the reactivity decreases.

In addition to the trends within groups of the periodic table, there are also trends across a period. Some of these trends in period 3 are shown in the table below.

Questions

1   List the trends in the properties of the elements and compounds of period 3 of the periodic table.

2   How do you think the properties of periods 2 and 4 will compare with those of period 3? Illustrate your answer with specific examples.

element	Na	Mg	Al	Si	P	S	Cl	Ar
melting point in °C	98	650	659	1410	44	119	−101	−189
boiling point in °C	890	1117	2447	2677	281	445	−34	−186
metal or non-metal	⊢——— metal ———⊣			⊢——————— non-metal ———————⊣				
electrical conductivity	⊢——— good ———⊣			⊢— moderate —⊣		⊢——— poor ———⊣		
formula of oxide	Na_2O	MgO	Al_2O_3	SiO_2	P_2O_3	SO_2	Cl_2O	—
type of oxide	⊢— basic —⊣		basic and acidic	⊢——————— acidic ———————⊣				
type of structure	⊢——— giant ionic ———⊣			giant molecular	⊢——— simple molecular ———⊣			
atomic number	11	12	13	14	15	16	17	18

Questions

1 This question refers to the outline of the periodic table below. The letters on the table are **not** the symbols of the elements.

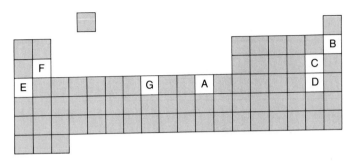

a) Which element is a noble gas?

b) Which element would you expect to have a violent reaction with cold water?

c) Which two elements would you expect to have similar chemical properties?

d) Which element is likely to have compounds which are coloured?

e) Will element D be more or less reactive than element C?

f) Which element will have two electrons in its outer shell?

2 An element X has atomic number 13 and mass number 27.

a) How many protons does an atom of this element have?

b) How many neutrons does it have?

c) Write down the electron arrangement of this element.

d) What group in the periodic table is this element in?

e) Is this element likely to be a metal or a non-metal?

3 Copy and complete the table below, then use the information to answer the following questions.

element	atomic number	mass number	electron arrangement
A	12	24	
B		40	2.8.8
C		19	2.7
D	19	39	

a) Is element D a metal or a non-metal? Give a reason for your answer.

b) If elements D and C reacted together, would they form a covalent or ionic bond?

c) What group in the periodic table does element B belong to?

d) Draw a diagram to show the arrangement of particles in an atom of A.

e) Element D has an isotope with mass number 41. What information does this give you about element D?

4 Look up the properties and reactions of the halogens. Astatine, At, is a halogen. It is below iodine in the periodic table. Predict the properties and chemical reactivity of astatine.

5 Choose elements from the second period of the periodic table to answer the following questions.

Li   Be   B   C   N   O   F   Ne

a) Which of these elements are non-metals?

b) Which element is a noble gas?

c) How do the structures of the compounds of these elements vary going from left to right?

Where do we find metals?

How can we extract them?

What other materials are used in place of metals?

How can we change the properties of materials to make them more useful?

How do new materials such as plastics compare with metals?

What are the differences between solids, liquids, and gases?

How does heating change the state of a material?

What is temperature?

How do gases behave when conditions change?

Early artefacts were made of bronze and copper.

The history of materials

We use a large variety of materials every day. Many of them are relatively new materials, such as plastics (see page 76) and composite materials (see page 84). Some of the most important 'old' materials in use today are **metals**. During the **Bronze Age**, people found that if they heated rock containing copper with carbon, they produced copper. This was then mixed with tin to make an alloy called **bronze**. Bronze is very hard and was used to make tools.

A more reactive metal, **iron**, was obtained in a similar way. The properties of iron made it a much more useful metal than copper. However, it wasn't until the early nineteenth century that today's most important metals were discovered. In general, the more difficult it is to extract a metal, the later it was discovered.

Other materials that were used a long time ago, and that are still used today, include **glass** (see page 83) and **concrete** (see page 82).

Today's cars are made mostly of steel.

Metal ores

An **ore** is a rock or mineral that contains a metal (usually in the form of an oxide). Most of the metals in use today are found combined with other chemicals as ores in the Earth's crust. The names of some ores are given in the table opposite. People mine ores to extract the metals, and some ores are running out. We need to think of ways to make more economical use of our natural resources, for example through recycling (see pages 85–6). More metal has been used by our society since 1950 than in the previous history of the world.

name of ore	metal it contains
haematite	iron
chalcopyrite (copper pyrites)	copper and iron
malachite	copper
litharge	lead
galena	lead
bauxite	aluminium
alumina	aluminium

Extracting metals from their ores

There are three main stages in obtaining metals from their ores:

- mining
- extraction
- purification.

A few unreactive metals are found uncombined with other elements, for example gold is mined straight from the ground. The decision as to whether it is worth mining an ore is based on many factors such as:

- How much ore is there?
- How much will it cost to mine?
- How much will the extraction cost?
- Does someone want to buy the metal?
- How much profit is there?
- What environmental problems are there?

Extraction methods

There are three main methods of extracting pure metals from their ores: electrolysis, reduction, or roasting in air. The method used depends on the metal.

Very reactive metals such as sodium and aluminium require a great deal of energy to separate them from their compounds. **Electrolysis** is used for these (see page 62). It is a very costly process because it uses a lot of energy. Less reactive metals can be extracted by cheaper methods such as reduction.

Reduction is a chemical reaction which involves taking away the oxygen (or other similar element) from a compound. Metals such as iron and lead are extracted using reduction.

Copper and mercury are extracted from their ores by **roasting them in air**. Some copper is found uncombined, but most copper is found in chalcopyrite (copper(I) sulphide, also called copper pyrites).

copper(I) sulphide + oxygen → copper + sulphur dioxide
$$Cu_2S \quad + \quad O_2 \quad \rightarrow \quad Cu \quad + \quad SO_2$$

Questions

1 What is an ore?

2 What factors have to be considered when deciding whether or not to mine an ore?

3 Explain what is meant by reduction.

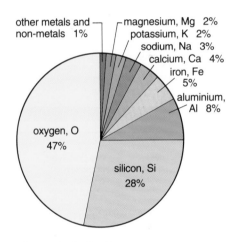

Elements in the Earth's crust

Copper pyrites ore

Extracting aluminium

Aluminium is the most abundant metal in the Earth's crust, but one of the most expensive to extract. The main ore of aluminium is **bauxite**, which contains aluminium oxide (Al_2O_3), sand, and some iron oxide. The first stage in the extraction is the removal of the impurities, sand and iron oxide. The pure aluminium oxide left is called **alumina**, which melts at 2045 °C. It will not conduct electricity when solid, so to save heating it to this temperature it is dissolved in molten **cryolite** (Na_3AlF_6) at about 950 °C. This solution is a better conductor of electricity than molten alumina.

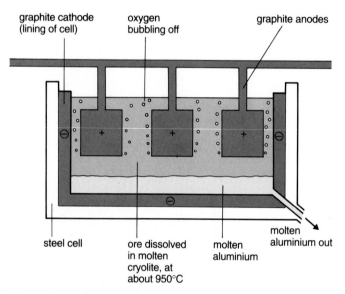

The extraction of aluminium using electrolysis

Electricity is passed through the alumina solution via electrodes. The electrode that is connected to the positive terminal is called the **anode**. The negative electrode is called the **cathode**. Both these electrodes are made of graphite. During electrolysis, the alumina is split up into its elements, aluminium and oxygen. Liquid aluminium collects at the negative electrode. Oxygen is released at the positive electrode. The liquid aluminium is siphoned off from time to time. Some of the oxygen reacts with the carbon electrodes to form carbon dioxide. This corrodes the electrode, which has to be replaced frequently.

What happens during electrolysis?

Solid aluminium oxide does not conduct electricity. However, when it is dissolved in liquid cryolite, it does. Chemicals which conduct electricity are called **electrolytes**. To conduct electricity, a substance has to have charged particles which can move. These particles are called **ions**. Aluminium oxide contains positive aluminium ions and negative oxide ions. When aluminium oxide conducts electricity, the positive aluminium ions move towards the negative electrode. The negative oxide ions move towards the positive electrode. Each aluminium ion has three positive charges. At the negative electrode, the aluminium ions can take some negative charges (**electrons**) to cancel out this charge. The ions then become aluminium atoms.

$$\text{aluminium ions} \quad + \quad \text{electrons} \quad \rightarrow \quad \text{aluminium atoms}$$
$$2Al^{3+} \quad + \quad 6e^- \quad \rightarrow \quad 2Al$$

At the cathode, oxide ions give their electrons away.

$$\text{oxide ions} \quad - \quad \text{electrons} \quad \rightarrow \quad \text{oxygen molecules}$$
$$3O^{2-} \quad - \quad 6e^- \quad \rightarrow \quad 1\tfrac{1}{2}O_2$$

The whole process requires a great deal of electricity, which makes it very expensive.

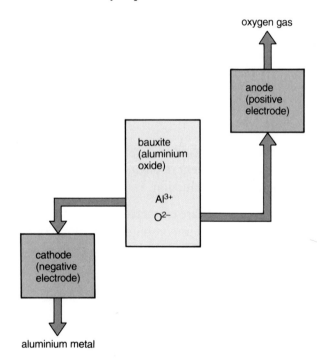

Aluminium ions move to the cathode; Oxide ions move to the anode.

Questions

1 What is the main ore of aluminium?

2 Describe how aluminium is extracted from its ore.

3 Why is the aluminium ore dissolved in cryolite?

4 What happens at the cathode and anode during the electrolysis of aluminium ore?

Uses of aluminium

Pure aluminium is a very reactive metal, much more reactive than iron, for example. However, if you try to react a piece of aluminium with dilute acid in the laboratory, it appears to be unreactive. This is because when pure aluminium is exposed to air it becomes coated with a very thin layer of aluminium oxide. This layer is almost transparent, and protects the aluminium underneath from further corrosion.

Aluminium is also a very strong metal, especially when alloyed with other metals (see page 69). Aluminium is a light metal with a relatively low density (steel is three times as dense). It is used to make light objects that need to last for a long time, for example aeroplanes. Its good conductivity of electricity makes aluminium useful for cables and wires in the electrical industry. The main restriction on the use of aluminium is its cost of production. It is possible to produce six times as much iron for the same cost. About 272 000 tonnes of aluminium are produced in the UK each year.

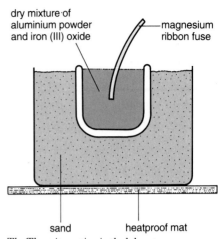

The Thermit reaction in the laboratory (see Activity 3 below)

construction	wall facings roofing windows and doors
transport	engines superstructures of ships aeroplanes
packaging	drinks cans milk bottle tops food containers cooking foil

How aluminium is used

Aluminium has many uses. What properties of aluminium make it such a useful material?

Activities

1 Gather together as many different objects as you can that are made from aluminium. Discuss their uses and decide what property of aluminium makes it suitable for each object.
Display your findings on a poster.

2 Find out the prices of aluminium, iron, gold, and zinc from a newspaper. Suggest reasons for their differences.

3 Find out how aluminium is used to weld steels together in the Thermit process.

Extracting iron

Iron is the second most abundant metal in the Earth's crust, and is the most used. The main ore of iron is called **haematite** and contains iron oxide, Fe_2O_3, and sand. The iron oxide is reduced (the oxygen is taken away) in a **blast furnace**. Over 700 million tonnes of iron are produced in this way each year.

The reactions that take place in the blast furnace are as follows:

- Coke (carbon) reacts with the oxygen in the air to make carbon dioxide.

  $$C + O_2 \rightarrow CO_2$$

- Limestone decomposes when heated to make calcium oxide and carbon dioxide.

  $$CaCO_3 \xrightarrow{heat} CaO + CO_2$$

- The carbon dioxide from these reactions reacts with more coke, making carbon monoxide.

  $$CO_2 + C \rightarrow 2CO$$

- The carbon monoxide reacts with the iron oxide. Liquid iron is made. This reaction is a reduction: the iron oxide is reduced to iron.

  $$\underset{\text{oxidized}}{\underbrace{3CO + \overset{\text{reduced}}{\overbrace{Fe_2O_3 \rightarrow 2Fe}} + 3CO_2}}$$

- The impurities, mainly sand, react with the calcium oxide to form calcium silicate or **slag**.

  $$CaO + SiO_2 \rightarrow CaSiO_3$$

The iron that is made in the blast furnace contains about 93% iron. This impure form of iron is called **pig iron**. Pig iron has very few uses because it is weak and brittle. Most of it is converted into **steel**. The slag is used for building roads. The blast furnace runs continuously. To save energy, the hot waste gases are used to heat the air going into the bottom of the furnace.

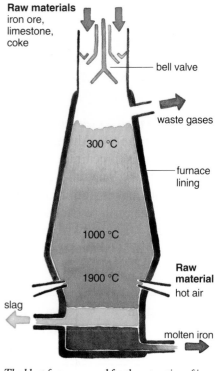

The blast furnace – used for the extraction of iron

7000–8000 tonnes of iron a day are produced in the blast furnace.

Making steel

Most of the steel made today is manufactured in the **basic oxygen steel-making** (BOS) **furnace**. Steel is an alloy of iron. Different steels contain different amounts of iron. All steels contain some carbon which forms crystals of iron carbide. This strengthens the steel. The more carbon steel contains, the harder it is. However, adding carbon makes steel more brittle – to overcome this, the steel is heated and then allowed to cool. Sometimes other metals are added to the steel to change its properties.

type of steel	contents (other than iron)	uses
soft	up to 0.15% carbon	sheets, wires
mild	0.5% carbon	building (e.g. bridges), car bodies
hard	1.0% carbon	hammers, cutting tools
stainless	18% chromium, 8% nickel	cutlery, sinks

The properties of steels can be altered by heating them in different ways. The table below shows the effects of heating and cooling steel in three different ways.

treatment	properties
heat until red-hot, leave to cool very slowly	soft and easy to bend
heat until red-hot, cool by plunging into cold water	harder to bend, becomes brittle
heat until red-hot, cool in water, reheat, cool slowly	like original steel

Cooling rapidly by plunging into water is called **quenching**. This freezes the structure of the steel in the high temperature form, which is hard and brittle. Reheating steel and cooling it slowly is called **tempering**. This returns the steel to its original form. The structure of iron crystals is different above and below 900 °C.

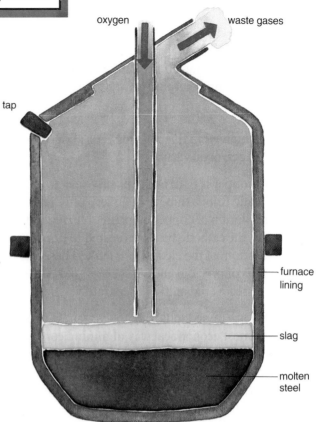

*The basic oxygen furnace. Oxygen is blown on to molten pig iron. The carbon and sulphur present are converted to their oxides and leave the furnace as waste gases. The other impurities form **slag** which is skimmed off, leaving steel.*

Questions

1 What are the raw materials used in the blast furnace?

2 Write down the five chemical reactions that take place in the blast furnace.

3 Why is limestone added to the furnace?

4 What is the difference between pig iron and steel?

5 Give five uses of steel.

6 Where would the most economical site for a blast furnace be? Explain your answer.

Activities

1 Bend a piece of thick copper wire backwards and forwards. Does this change the properties of the copper? How do you think that this might be applied usefully in steel production?

2 Pull a piece of copper wire using two pairs of pliers. (Wear safety spectacles.) Describe what happens.

3 Look at a broken end of a piece of copper wire under a microscope and describe it.

Extracting copper

Copper is less reactive than iron. Some copper is found uncombined in the Earth, but most is extracted from its ore, **chalcopyrite** or **copper pyrites** which contains copper sulphide, Cu_2S.

$$Cu_2S + O_2 \rightarrow Cu + SO_2$$

The copper obtained in this way contains about 3% impurities. To purify the copper, **electrolysis** is used.

The impure copper is used as the positive electrode, the anode. The cathode is made from a thin piece of very pure copper. The electrodes are dipped in a solution of copper sulphate. During the electrolysis, the anode dissolves and the cathode becomes coated in pure copper. The impurities sink to the bottom of the electrolysis tank. These impurities may contain small amounts of precious metals such as gold, silver, and platinum. These can be recovered and sold separately.

The ores that are mined today do not contain very large amounts of copper. The most economical way of mining copper ore is by **opencast mining** (mining from the Earth's surface). This destroys large amounts of the countryside, since it is not considered financially feasible to fill in the mine once it has been used. It is thought that our reserves of copper may run out within the next century.

Electroplating

Electroplating is a process which coats an object with a metal layer using electrolysis. If a metal sheet is coated with a less reactive metal, this protects the sheet from rusting (see page 73). The object to be electroplated is used as the cathode in the electrolysis tank. The electrolyte that the electrodes are dipped in contains ions of the metal which will form the plating. The anode is also made of the plating metal. Some metals need to be plated with an intermediate metal before being plated with their final metal coating. For example, steel objects that need to be plated with chromium, such as car bumpers, have to be coated with nickel and copper, before being plated with chromium. The object to be electroplated has to be clean and free of grease.

Jewellery is often plated with gold or silver. Cutlery is sometimes coated with nickel and silver.

Activities

1   Carry out a survey on the use of metal objects in the home, and what coatings (if any) they may have. Find as many metal objects as you can and try to find out what metal they are made of. Record your results in a table like the one below.

object	use	metal	reason for choice	coating
knives and forks	eating	stainless steel	looks good, does not corrode	none

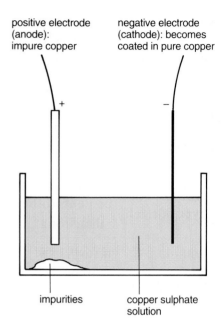

positive electrode (anode): impure copper

negative electrode (cathode): becomes coated in pure copper

impurities

copper sulphate solution

Purifying copper using electrolysis

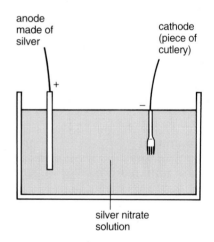

anode made of silver

cathode (piece of cutlery)

silver nitrate solution

Silver plating cutlery. The current must not be too large or the coating will not 'stick'.

Questions

1   What is the main ore of copper?

2   Give one reason why it is not necessary to extract copper from its ore using electrolysis.

3   Describe how copper is purified.

4   What is electroplating?

Metals are crystalline materials. If you look at something made of **galvanized** iron (iron coated with zinc), such as a dustbin or a new lamppost, you may be able to see zinc crystals. These crystals are irregular in shape. You can grow lead crystals easily in the laboratory by putting a strip of zinc metal into a solution of lead nitrate. After a short time crystals of lead form. This is because zinc is more reactive than lead. Zinc displaces lead from solution.

By looking at metals with X-rays (**X-ray diffraction**), it can be seen that the atoms in a metal are held closely together in a regular pattern. There are three different types of arrangement of atoms in metals: **hexagonal close packed** (HCP), **face centred cubic** (FCC), and **body centred cubic** (BCC). The BCC structure is a more open structure than the other two. Metals such as sodium and potassium have this structure.

If you look closely at galvanized iron you can see zinc crystals.

Zinc is more reactive than lead. Zinc displaces lead from solution.

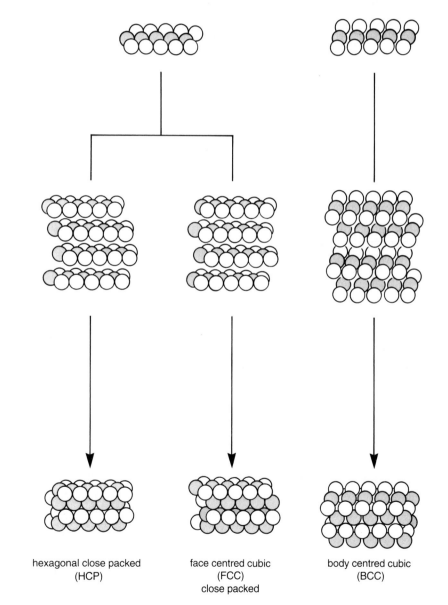

hexagonal close packed
(HCP)

face centred cubic
(FCC)
close packed

body centred cubic
(BCC)

Three structures of metals

Activities

1 Using polystyrene spheres or marbles, try to construct models of the three different structures of metals.

2 Find out all you can about X-ray diffraction.

Understanding the properties of metals

The general physical properties of metals are:

- high densities
- high melting and boiling points
- good conductors of heat and electricity
- malleability (can be shaped by hammering)
- ductility (can be drawn into a wire).

The properties of a particular metal depend on the way the atoms are arranged in the crystal, and on the crystal size.

The average density of metals is about $8\,g/cm^3$. This is much higher than that of non-metals. One factor which affects the density of an element is the atomic structure – the way in which the atoms are packed together. A FCC structure usually has a higher density than a BCC structure. Sodium and potassium both have BCC structures and are both less dense than copper, which has an FCC structure.

Atoms in metals are packed closely together.

metal	symbol	density in $g\,cm^{-3}$	structure
copper	Cu	8.9	FCC
gold	Au	19.3	FCC
iron	Fe	7.9	FCC
magnesium	Mg	1.74	HCP
nickel	Ni	8.9	FCC
potassium	K	0.86	BCC
sodium	Na	0.97	BCC

Densities and crystal structures of some metals

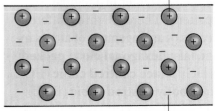

large ions in crystal structure

electrons free to move

Electrons move around the metal ions.

The outer electrons in a metal atom are able to move freely through the metal as a whole. We can think of the electrons as forming a 'sea' around the much larger positive ions. The bonds between the metal ions are strong so it takes a lot of energy to melt or boil a metal.
The 'sea' of moving electrons in a metal enables the metal to conduct electricity.

Metals can be hammered into different shapes (they are **malleable**) and can be pulled into wires (they are **ductile**). When a force is applied to a metal by pulling or hammering, the layers of atoms slip over each other. Groups of crystalline areas are called **grains**. By making the grain size smaller, through heating and cooling the metal for different lengths of time, it is possible to make the metal stronger, harder, and more brittle. In this way properties of metals can be adapted for particular jobs.

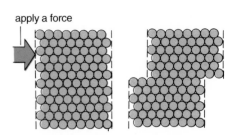

apply a force

When a force is applied to a metal, the layers of atoms slip over each other.

Questions

1 Write down the general properties of metals.

2 Why do metals **a)** have high melting points **b)** have high densities **c)** conduct electricity?

3 What properties of metals are useful for making **a)** hammers **b)** fuse wire **c)** bridges **d)** cars?

Alloys

The properties of a pure metal can be changed by mixing it with a small amount of another element. The different size of the 'new' element's atoms disrupts the regular pattern of the metal crystal. This can make metals harder and stronger. The new metal is called an **alloy**. The atoms which are added make it more difficult for the metal atoms to slip past one another, so alloys are usually less malleable and less ductile than pure metals. Alloys also tend to have lower melting and boiling points and are not such good conductors of electricity.

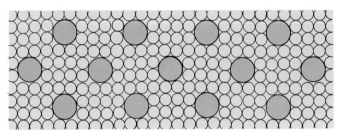

Atoms in an alloy

Brass and bronze

Brass is an alloy made from a mixture of 60% copper and 40% zinc. It is much stronger than either of the metals on their own. Brass is very resistant to corrosion and conducts electricity well. It has many everyday uses including plumbing and electrical equipment, ships' propellers, and ornaments. **Bronze** contains 90% copper and 10% tin. It is used for statues.

50p coins are made of 75% copper and 25% nickel. 2p coins are made of 97% copper, 2.5% zinc, and 0.5% nickel.

To make statues, molten bronze is poured into a mould and allowed to harden.

Solder

Solder is made by melting lead, which has a low melting point (328°C), and mixing it with molten tin. (Solder sometimes contains other metals.) Solder melts at an even lower temperature than pure lead. When it is solid, it is strong. These properties make solder useful for joining two pieces of metal together. Electrical wires can be joined together using solder.

Solder melts at a low temperature. It can hold two metals together quite firmly.

Duralumin

Aluminium alloys are becoming increasingly important. The cost of aluminium alloys is high, but their properties make them very useful for making, for example, aircraft and window frames. The alloys contain about 4% copper plus very small amounts of other metals such as magnesium, silicon, and zinc. They are extremely resistant to corrosion, and are strong and light.

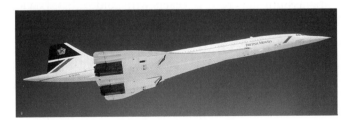

Aluminium alloys are used to make aeroplanes.

Questions

1 What is an alloy?

2 Make a table with the following headings. Write in it all the alloys you can find out about.

name of alloy	main elements	properties	uses

69

Knowing about the chemical reactions of metals is vital when working out how to use them. For example, knowing how a metal reacts with dilute acids can help us decide what metal to make a can out of. (The can may be used to store fruit, which contains natural, weak acids.) How easily a metal is attacked by the oxygen in the air tells us how quickly a metal will corrode.

Reactions of metals with acids

When a metal reacts with a dilute acid, hydrogen gas is given off and a salt is formed.

$$\text{magnesium} + \text{sulphuric acid} \rightarrow \text{magnesium sulphate} + \text{hydrogen}$$
$$Mg + H_2SO_4 \rightarrow MgSO_4 + H_2$$

Magnesium reacts very quickly with the acids found in the school laboratory. Not all metals react with acids. Sometimes metals react very slowly with weak acids, over many years. **Acid rain** attacks some metals quite severely.

Reactions of metals with water and steam

The more reactive metals such as sodium react violently with cold water, giving off hydrogen gas and forming an alkali, sodium hydroxide.

$$\text{metal} + \text{water/steam} \rightarrow \text{metal oxide} + \text{hydrogen}$$
$$\text{(or hydroxide)}$$

Metals which are less reactive such as zinc and iron react very slowly with cold water, but react vigorously with steam. Other even less reactive metals such as silver do not react with water or steam.

Reactions of metals with oxygen

Many metals react slowly with the oxygen in the air. Moist air causes some metals to corrode (see page 72). However, if metals burn in oxygen the reaction is much faster. **Oxidation** takes place when metals burn in air.

$$\text{metal} + \text{oxygen} \rightarrow \text{metal oxide}$$

Metal oxides are **basic oxides**. Most metal oxides do not dissolve in water. Those that do, for example oxides of sodium or potassium, form alkalis (see page 174), which turn universal indicator blue/purple.

Activities

1 Look at the packaging of acidic foods such as tinned fruit, chutneys, etc., and list the types of packaging used.
What do you notice about the insides of cans used to store fruit?

metal	symbol	reactivity with water	reactivity with dilute acids
potassium	K	reacts with cold water	violent reaction
sodium	Na		
calcium	Ca	reactivity decreases going down table	reacts
magnesium	Mg		reactivity decreases going down table
aluminium	Al	protected by oxide	
zinc	Zn	reacts with steam	
iron	Fe		
lead	Pb	no reaction with water or steam (lead reacts very slowly with steam)	no reaction
copper	Cu		
silver	Ag		
platinum	Pt		
gold	Au		

Summary of reactions of metals with water and dilute acids

Corrosion of metals is a problem.

Displacement reactions

When a metal reacts with an acid, it replaces the hydrogen atoms in the acid to form a salt. For example, when magnesium reacts with dilute hydrochloric acid, magnesium chloride solution and hydrogen gas are formed. It is possible to compare the reactivity of the metals by their reaction with dilute acids. Not all metals react with acids, so **displacement reactions** can be used instead to work out the order of reactivity. If a more reactive metal is placed in a solution containing metal ions which are less reactive, then the more reactive metal will displace the less reactive one. For example, if magnesium is placed in a solution of copper sulphate, the magnesium will displace the copper from solution. Red-brown copper is seen which settles on the bottom of the container. However, if a piece of copper was placed in a solution containing magnesium ions, there would be no reaction. The displacement reactions of some metals are given in the table above.

metal	solution to which metal is added				
	$MgCl_2$	$FeSO_4$	$Pb(NO_3)_2$	$CuSO_4$	$AgNO_3$
magnesium, Mg	no reaction	D	D	D	D
iron, Fe	no reaction	no reaction	D	D	D
lead, Pb	no reaction	no reaction	no reaction	D	D
copper, Cu	no reaction	no reaction	no reaction	no reaction	D
silver, Ag	no reaction	no reaction	no reaction	no reaction	no reaction

D = displacement reaction observed

Magnesium displaces copper from copper (II) sulphate solution after only a few minutes.

Questions

1   Write down the order of reactivity of the metals shown in the table above, putting the most reactive first.

2   Use the table opposite to answer the following questions.

  a)   Which metal is the most reactive? Give reasons for your answer.
  b)   What do you think the reaction of metal B is likely to be with dilute hydrochloric acid?
  c)   What would you expect to see when metal D is placed in a solution of copper(II) sulphate?

metal	solution to which metal is added		
	iron(II) sulphate	copper(II) sulphate	silver nitrate
A		no reaction	displacement
B	no reaction	displacement	
C	no reaction	no reaction	no reaction
D	displacement		

Rusting of iron

Iron and steel are among the most widely used materials in our society. This is because iron is one of the easiest and cheapest metals to extract from its ore. However, when iron and steel are exposed to the damp weather over a long period of time, they **rust**. During rusting, iron combines with oxygen to form a red powder called iron oxide, $Fe_2O_3.H_2O$. The rusting of iron and steel causes a great deal of damage, so it is very important to try to prevent rusting.

Activities

1   The conditions which cause rusting can be investigated by carrying out the following experiment and leaving it for a week or two.

- Place four clean iron nails into each of five test tubes. Label the test tubes **A)** to **E)**.
- Leave test tube **A)** without a bung in.
- Half fill test tube **B)** with distilled water.
- Place boiled distilled water in test tube **C)** and pour on a thin layer of oil. This will float on the water and prevent any air from entering it. Put a bung in the top of the tube for extra protection from air.
- Dissolve some salt in water and add this to test tube **D)**.
- Put some solid calcium chloride into test tube **E)** to take away any moisture from the air, and place a bung in the top.
- Record you results in a table with the following headings.

test tube	appearance after two days	appearance after one week	appearance after two weeks

- In which test tube did the nails rust the most?
- In which test tube did the nails rust the least?
- Under what conditions do iron and steel rust most?

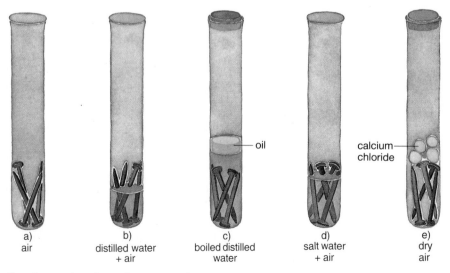

a)
air

b)
distilled water
+ air

c)
boiled distilled
water

d)
salt water
+ air

e)
dry
air

oil

calcium
chloride

Experiment to investigate what causes rusting

Car manufacturers go to a lot of trouble to prevent this from happening too quickly.

Corrosion of other metals

Metals such as the reactive alkali metals (see page 47) corrode so easily in air that they are kept under oil for safety. Other metals are very resistant to corrosion – gold and silver are good examples. Not all corrosion of metals causes problems. Copper reacts with oxygen and carbon dioxide in the atmosphere and becomes coated in green **verdigris**. This protects the copper underneath from further attack. Aluminium reacts with oxygen to form a thin layer of aluminium oxide. This layer protects the aluminium from further corrosion in the same way. The aluminium oxide layer is made thicker if the aluminium is to be used for window frames. This is carried out using electrolysis and is called **anodizing**.

*Copper roofing with a coating of **verdigris**. What compound of copper do you think this is?*

72

Preventing rusting

Many common objects in the modern world, such as motor cars, engineering tools, bridges, etc., are made from iron and steel. There are a number of relatively simple ways to protect these metals from corrosion. The method used depends on how much metal there is, and what the metal is used for. Some methods of protection are much cheaper than others.

Coating with grease or paint prevents air from reaching the metal. Large objects such as bridges and ships can be protected with paint. The paints that are used often contain lead or zinc, because these metals are good at preventing rust. Oiling bicycle chains at regular intervals helps to stop them rusting, and also ensures that they move freely. If a metal object needs to be protected from rust and look attractive, it can be coated in coloured plastic. Old gas and water pipes which are rusting can be coated inside with a new high density plastic.

A protective coat of paint

What advantages does the plastic coating give to this furniture?

The gas board uses high-density plastics to line old gas pipes. This provides a relatively cheap method of replacing old pipes.

Electroplating (see page 66) is used to coat cans that are used for storing food. The steel cans are coated with a thin layer of tin by electrolysis. Tin is used because it is non-toxic. If a can becomes dented, the protective layer of tin may become damaged and allow the acid from the fruit to react with the steel. Car bumpers, bicycle handlebars, taps, and kettles are all electroplated with chromium.

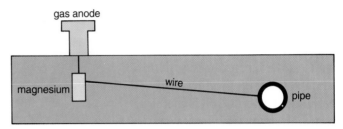

Gas and water pipes can be protected from corroding using sacrificial protection.

Iron sheds and dustbins are usually galvanized with zinc by immersing them in molten metal. They are coated with zinc because it is less likely to corrode the iron. Thirty per cent of all the zinc extracted from the Earth is used for galvanizing.

A more reactive metal can protect a less reactive metal in a method called **sacrificial protection**. Pieces of fairly reactive metals such as magnesium or zinc are 'sacrificed' to save such metals as iron or steel from rusting. Ships are protected by this method. A bar of magnesium is attached to the side of the ship under the water line. The magnesium corrodes before the less reactive iron. When the magnesium is used up, it is replaced. Underground gas and water pipes can be protected in a similar way.

Questions

1   What conditions encourage rusting?

2   Rusting is oxidation. Explain this statement.

3   Name five different ways in which a metal can be prevented from corroding.

4   Why doesn't aluminium corrode easily?

5   How does sacrificial protection work?

Activities

1   Find out how car manufacturers try to stop cars from rusting. Gather information by looking at various cars and from advertisements in newspapers and magazines.

Refining oil

Where is crude oil found?

Oil is made over millions of years by dead sea creatures being compressed. It is trapped by non-porous rock under the sea bed. Many reserves of oil have been found on the bed of the North Sea and **crude oil** is obtained from them by drilling. Crude oil is a thick, black, pungent liquid which is not very useful in its natural state. However, it can be split up into many useful products by **refining**. The crude oil is therefore transported to oil refineries on land.

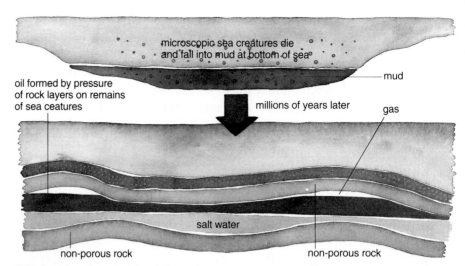

*Oil is formed on the sea bed from billions of sea creatures called **plankton**. They fall to the bottom of the sea and become trapped in mud. Millions of years later, other layers of rock have trapped the oil underneath non-porous rock.*

What is crude oil?

It is a mixture of compounds called **hydrocarbons**. These are compounds containing only carbon and hydrogen. They belong to the **carbon** (carbon-based) group of compounds. The various hydrocarbons present in crude oil have different numbers of carbon atoms in their molecules. The carbon atoms are arranged in chains. Groups of hydrocarbons with similar length carbon chains are separated out from crude oil at an oil refinery.

Questions

1   How was crude oil formed?

2   What is a hydrocarbon?

3   Crude oil is said to be a mixture of hydrocarbons. How is this mixture separated?

4   List the groups of hydrocarbons obtained from crude oil.

Separating crude oil

Crude oil can be separated by **fractional distillation**. Each group of hydrocarbons has a different range of boiling points. As the oil is heated to about 500 °C, gases are collected at different temperature ranges. This takes place continuously in a tall tower called a **fractionating column**. The groups of hydrocarbons are called **fractions**. The fractions with larger molecules (longer carbon chains) and higher boiling points are collected at the bottom of the fractionating column, and the fractions with smaller molecules at the top. The fractions are then refined further to produce chemicals that can be used.

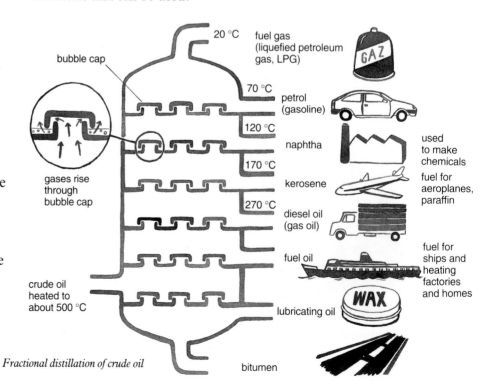

Fractional distillation of crude oil

Chemicals from crude oil

To produce more petrol and other important chemicals, the heavier fractions go through the process of **cracking**. This causes the long carbon chains to vibrate, and eventually split up. A **catalyst** is used. One of the new molecules is a **saturated** hydrocarbon and the other is an **unsaturated** hydrocarbon. Saturated hydrocarbons are called **alkanes**. Each carbon atom in an alkane is bonded to four other atoms. All the bonds in the molecule are **single**. **Alkenes** are unsaturated hydrocarbons. Some carbon atoms in alkenes are only bonded to three other atoms. The molecules contain **double** bonds.

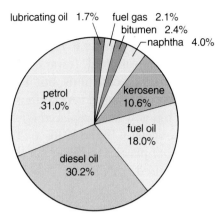

The distillation of crude oil makes a variety of products.

During the catalytic craking of long-chain hydrocarbons, smaller chained alkanes and alkenes are made.

Properties and uses of alkanes

Alkanes, when they are burnt in air, generate a lot of heat. They are therefore used as fuels. Methane is natural gas. Propane is sold under a variety of manufacturers' names such as Propagas, and butane as Calor gas. When alkanes burn they form carbon dioxide and water.

methane + oxygen (from air) → carbon dioxide + water + HEAT
$$CH_4 + 2O_2 \rightarrow CO_2 + 2H_2O + HEAT$$

Petrol (which contains octanes) does not burn completely and some poisonous carbon monoxide is produced. The high temperature of the engine converts some of the nitrogen from the air into nitrogen oxides. These gases are also poisonous, and are acidic.

Alkanes are also used as lubricating oils and waxes, and to make more alkenes.

Properties and uses of alkenes

Alkenes take part in many reactions. Because they are unsaturated they burn, but not as easily or cleanly as alkanes.

Ethene is used mainly in the production of plastics such as polyethene and in the manufacture of alcohol and antifreeze.

Questions

1 What is meant by **catalytic cracking**?

2 Give an example of a saturated hydrocarbon.

3 Why do alkanes make good fuels?

4 How could you test a hydrocarbon liquid to see whether it was an alkane or an alkene?

alkanes			alkenes		
name	formula		name	formula	
methane	CH_4		ethene	C_2H_4	
ethane	C_2H_6		propene	C_3H_6	

Plastics

Many objects that used to be made of metal are now made of **plastic**. One of the first plastics to be invented was celluloid. It was once used for making cine films, but it is flammable and caused very serious fires. It has now been replaced by cellulose acetate. In the 1940s many other plastics were manufactured.

The list of uses of plastics is endless.

A plastic is a synthetic material which can easily be shaped. Plastics are usually tough and versatile. They are very good electrical insulators. They can be spun into fibres to make clothes and carpets, or moulded to make objects such as cups or chairs. Plastics are **polymers**. Polymers contain very large molecules that are made by adding together many small molecules called **monomers**. (Poly means many, mono means single.) Some familiar polymers are polyethene (polythene), polystyrene, and poly(vinyl chloride) (PVC). The names of the corresponding monomers are ethene, styrene, and vinyl chloride. Nylon, Perspex, and Terylene are the common names of some other important plastics.

monomer

polymer

Each monomer unit can be linked to the next to form one large polymer unit. This is similar to linking together a string of paperclips.

Addition polymerization

Addition polymers are made from alkenes. Alkenes are unsaturated organic compounds – they contain a double bond between two carbon atoms. When polymers are made from alkenes, the monomers 'add' to each other forming long chains of polymer. This is called an **addition reaction**. Alkenes are not found naturally – they are obtained by catalytic cracking of crude oil products.

In polyethene each monomer unit is the same. It is like a string of beads all the same type connected together.

Condensation polymerization

Condensation polymers are made by reacting different monomers together. Usually a small molecule such as water or hydrogen chloride is also made during the process, which is called **condensation polymerization**. Nylon is made using this method.

In nylon, the monomers are not all the same type. It is like a string of alternately coloured beads.

Activities

1 Make a list of all the plastic objects you come across in one day.

2 Collect information about different uses and types of plastics, relating the properties of each plastic to its use.

Questions

1 Explain the words **plastic**, **monomer**, and **polymer**.

2 What is meant by **addition polymerization**?

3 How does condensation polymerization differ from addition polymerization?

Polyethene and nylon

Polyethene and nylon

Polyethene (**polythene**) is one of the most common plastics. It was first made in 1933 by heating molecules of ethene to a temperature of 200 °C at 2000 times atmospheric pressure. The product was an unstable white waxy solid which sometimes exploded! After some research, polyethene was made safer and was found to be a good electrical insulator. One type of polyethene can be made into thin transparent sheets that float on water. This is called **low-density polyethene**. However, it softens and loses its shape when heated, for example in boiling water. It is used for making food bags, washing-up bowls, and 'squeezy' bottles.

In 1953 a German chemist, Professor Ziegler, produced a variety of polyethene using a new method. Ethene was polymerized at atmospheric pressure using a catalyst. The resulting polyethene had slightly different properties. It did not soften when put into boiling water, was more rigid, and had a higher density. It is called **high-density polyethene**. Milk crates are made of high-density polyethene.

Polyethene is made by addition polymerization. The monomer is ethene. If high pressures and temperatures are used, low-density polyethene is made. At lower pressures and using a catalyst, high-density polyethene is produced. In both cases, long chains of about 50 000 ethene molecules added together are formed.

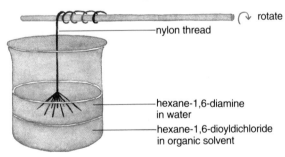

Addition polymerization. Polyethene is made from the monomer ethene. n = *a very large number.*

Nylon

Nylon is a plastic that can be made into thin fibres, which can be woven into cloth. Nylon is made by condensation polymerization. The two chemicals used have reactive 'ends'. When they join together, a small molecule – hydrogen chloride – is split off.

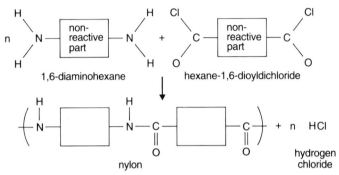

Condensation polymerization. Two different monomers are joined together. Nylon is made by this reaction.

Nylon can be made in the laboratory in the following way: hexane-1,6-dioyl dichloride is dissolved in an organic solvent, and 1,6-diaminohexane is dissolved in water. Both are poured carefully into a small beaker, and the two layers do not mix. Where the layers meet, the chemicals react to form nylon. If this nylon is slowly pulled out of the beaker, more nylon is formed. This is sometimes called the 'nylon rope trick'.

In the 'nylon rope trick', the reaction only takes place where the two chemicals meet.

Questions

1 Write a word equation to represent making polyethene.

2 What is the difference between low-density polyethene and high-density polyethene?

3 What two chemicals are used to make nylon in the laboratory?

4 Why is the laboratory manufacture of nylon sometimes called the 'nylon rope trick'?

Advantages and disadvantages of plastics

Plastics are synthetic (made, not natural). They have many advantages over natural materials such as wood, and other materials such as glass and metals. In recent years more and more use has been made of them.

Advantages of plastics

- They do not rot.
- They do not corrode.
- They can insulate.
- They can be moulded into convenient shapes.
- They are generally light materials.
- Some plastics are very strong without being heavy.
- They can be coloured during manufacture.
- They can be very cheap to produce.

Disadvantages of plastics

- They do not rot and so are difficult to dispose of.
- They give off poisonous fumes when burnt. (This is especially dangerous when foam furniture burns.)
- They are very cheap to produce compared with the cost of recycling them, so are usually thrown away.
- They often don't look as good as 'natural' materials.

Some of the advantages of plastics are also disadvantages. If plastics were more expensive to make, then we would think twice about using them so extensively. Since plastics don't rot, they can be used to make heart valves and other body parts. However, 5% of household waste is plastic. Most of the plastics we use are not biodegradable. It takes many thousands of years for a plastic yoghurt pot to disintegrate. Can you imagine how many yoghurt pots we get through in one year?

Plastics cannot easily be burnt because of the poisonous fumes which they give off. Plastics can be recycled, but at a large cost. If they were recycled, people would have to sort their rubbish into different types of plastic. This would take time and effort.

Scientists are trying to make goods out of **biodegradable plastics** which can be broken down by bacteria in the soil or by sunlight. There are some plastics today which do break down, but unfortunately they are not being used extensively. When oil runs out, plastics will become more expensive to make, so perhaps we will think more carefully about recycling them.

Some of the more dangerous foam furniture is now banned.

NEAL'S YARD WHOLEFOOD WAREHOUSE

Golden Cross
off Cornmarket Street
· Oxford
Telephone
0865 792102

*Open seven days
a week*

◼▶ OXFORD ◀◼

Made from PHOTODEGRADABLE film.... decomposes in Sun & Soil

Recycling plastics can be a problem. Making objects from degradable plastics is one way to reduce plastic pollution.

Activities

1 Do you think the advantages of plastics outweigh the disadvantages? Give reasons for your answer.

Uses of plastics

How many uses for plastics can you add to the lists below?

plastics	uses
polyethene	plastic bags beakers buckets bowls washing-up bottles milk crates dustbins
polystyrene	cups packaging materials ceiling tiles ball-point pens model construction kits thermal insulation
polypropylene	washing-up bowls carpets string
poly (vinyl chloride), PVC	car seat covers raincoats records hose pipes curtain rails electrical insulation

plastics	uses
poly (tetra-fluoroethene), PTFE	non-stick saucepans soles of irons bridge bearings oven floors plumbing tape
nylon	rope brush bristles tights clothing
Terylene (polyester)	seat belts yacht sails clothing
melamine	unbreakable plates and mugs work surfaces
phenolic resins	electric plugs saucepan handles
Perspex	rulers car windscreens advertising signs substitute for glass
Bakelite	electrical fittings

The contents of the dustbin provide an interesting insight to the use of materials in today's society.

Activities

1 Carry out a survey of all the rubbish thrown away at home for a week. List the rubbish in different groups, such as plastics, paper, glass, metals and wood. What proportion of the rubbish is plastics?

Polyethene, nylon, and PVC are all **thermoplastics**. They become soft when they are heated. When they are cooled, they become hard again. They are also called thermosoftening plastics. They can be shaped when heated. It is possible to heat and cool thermoplastics again and again. Thermoplastics can be shaped in a number of ways.

Extrusion

The plastic is heated to make it soft, and squeezed through a small hole. It is then cooled with cold air, which hardens it. Plastics to be made into long, thin strips are made in this way, for example garden hose pipes.

Vacuum forming

Toys and baths are made by placing a sheet of plastic over a mould. The plastic is then heated and air sucked from between it and the cold mould.

Injection moulding

Soft plastic is forced into a mould. After it has cooled, it is taken out of the mould. Dustbins and combs are made in this way.

Blow moulding

This is similar to injection moulding, but the soft plastic is blown into a cold mould which is usually made of two halves. Plastic bottles and objects with complicated shapes are made like this.

Elastomeric polymers

All rubbers are elastic. They can be pulled into different shapes, and return to their original shape afterwards. Natural rubber comes from the sap of the rubber tree. However, there is not enough natural rubber available for all needs. Synthetic rubber is a polymer made from an alkene called butadiene. Sulphur is added to the rubber to improve its elastic properties and strength. This is called **vulcanizing**. Vulcanized rubber is used to make tyres.

Nylon fibres are made by extrusion.

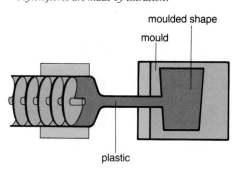

Injection moulding

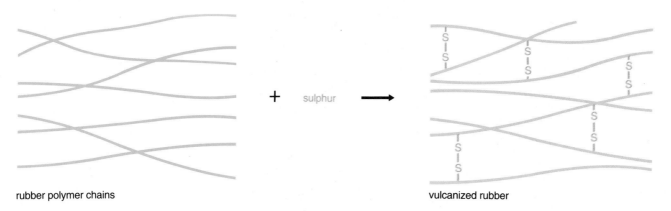

rubber polymer chains

vulcanized rubber

When rubber is heated with sulphur, the polymer chains are linked together by sulphur atoms. The cross-links stop the polymer chains stretching.

Thermosetting plastics

Plastics that remain hard after heating are called **thermosetting plastics** or **thermosets**. If they are heated again, they do not soften so they cannot be remoulded. Examples include Bakelite, melamine, and glass reinforced plastic (GRP). Thermosetting plastics are usually very tough, rigid, and resistant to high temperatures. Melamine is often used for unbreakable plates and mugs. Bakelite was the first plastic to be manufactured and is very resistant to heat. It is used as an electrical insulator. GRP is glass mixed with polymers to make a light, strong material. It is used to make boats and canoes, roofing, piping, etc., since it also resists corrosion. There are two ways of shaping thermosetting plastics.

Compression moulding

The plastic is heated and moulded at the same time, and compressed into shape.

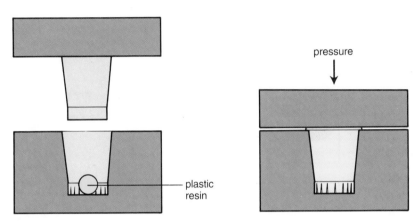

Thermosetting plastics can be moulded using compression.

Lamination

Laminated plastics such as Formica are made by sandwiching layers of plastic with another material, such as paper or wood, and pressing them into thin sheets. This form of plastic is very heat resistant.

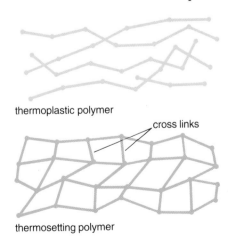

The structures of a thermoplastic and a thermosetting polymer

Canoes made of GRP are light and strong.

Questions

1 What is a thermoplastic?

2 How do thermosetting plastics differ from thermoplastics?

3 Explain, with the aid of a diagram, what extrusion is.

4 Why can't Bakelite be extruded?

5 Draw a diagram to show the difference in structure between a thermoplastic and a thermosetting plastic.

6 Why is sulphur added to rubber? What is this process called?

81

Calcium carbonate, CaCO₃, is one of the most abundant minerals in the Earth's crust, second only to the group of silicates. There are different forms of calcium carbonate, namely **chalk**, **limestone**, and **marble**. Chalk was formed from the shells of dead sea animals and is a fairly soft material. Where it has been subjected to a great deal of pressure, it has turned to the harder form, limestone. Marble was formed by the effects of both pressure and heat on chalk. The most common of the three forms of calcium carbonate is limestone. It is used in the blast furnace for the extraction of iron (see page 64), and for neutralizing acid soil. Limestone is also used to make two very important materials – concrete and glass.

Concrete

Many buildings and bridges are made of **concrete**. Concrete is a mixture of cement, sand, water, and gravel or small stones. Cement is made from limestone or chalk, depending which part of the country it is made in. Limestone is mixed with shale, while chalk is mixed with clay.

When added to water, the cement grows crystals which interlock with the sand and gravel, causing them to bind together. Using different sized pieces of stones, you can make different types of concrete. Mortar for bricklaying is made in a similar way, using a mixture of sand and cement.

Concrete is used in the building industry in many ways. It is often strengthened by pouring it over a framework of steel rods. This is called **reinforced concrete**.

History of cement

The Egyptians used lime as a cementing material to build their pyramids. The Romans developed cement and made it stronger. In 1842 Joseph Aspidin patented Portland cement, which is still manufactured today. He called it Portland because he thought it looked like Portland stone. The cement was made in kilns shaped like beehives, which can still be seen in parts of the UK today. The chalk used to make (early) cement was mined by men with pickaxes, and then loaded into the kilns which were often kept burning for months. Cement made like this was used by Brunel to build a tunnel under the River Thames in 1838.

Many buildings are made of limestone. Limestones are fairly easy to cut and look very pleasant when they are slightly weathered in appearance. Normal weathering does not do much harm to the stones. However, since carbonates react with acid, buildings that are subjected to acid rain and a great deal of exhaust pollution from traffic can crumble and disintegrate over a number of years.

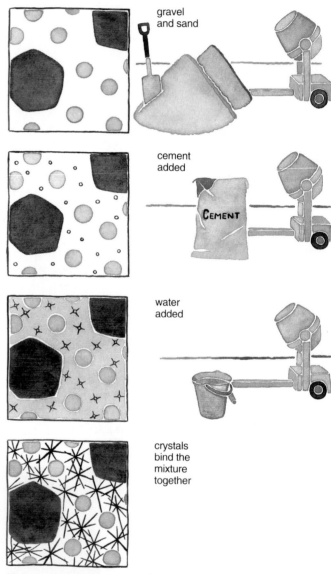

gravel and sand

cement added

water added

crystals bind the mixture together

How concrete and mortar are made

Questions

1 What are the main uses of limestone?
2 How were chalk, limestone, and marble made?
3 What are the starting materials for cement?
4 How is concrete made?
5 List as many different uses of concrete as you can.

Glass

Glass is a very versatile material, also made from limestone. The raw materials for the manufacture of glass are sand (silicon dioxide, SiO_2), sodium carbonate, Na_2CO_3, and limestone. These three compounds are mixed together and heated to a temperature of 1500 °C. The sand and sodium carbonate react together making sodium silicate, Na_2SiO_3. (This is called **water glass** since it dissolves in water.) The limestone helps to form a structure of calcium silicate and sodium silicate, which is not soluble in water.

$$SiO_2 \ + \ Na_2CO_3 \ \rightarrow \ Na_2SiO_3 \ + \ CO_2$$

Clean scrap glass called **cullet** is added to help the mixture melt. The cullet comes from glass containers that have been returned, such as medicine bottles, beer bottles, and chipped milk bottles. The glass can be coloured by adding small amounts of compounds such as iron compounds for brown glass, cobalt oxide for blue glass, and copper compounds for green glass. The most expensive red glasses contain gold!

Making glass bottles

When the glass is at 1500 °C it looks like treacle. It is drained from the furnace or tank and cut into large lumps called **gobs**. Each gob falls into a mould and compressed air is blown in to force the glass into a bottle shape. Throughout the process, the glass is kept hot – problems with stresses might develop if the glass were allowed to cool too rapidly. Milk bottles are coated with titanium oxide to prevent them from becoming too scratched.

A ribbon of float glass being washed before it is automatically cut and stacked

Where is your nearest bottle bank?

Making float glass

The raw materials for **float glass** are sand (silica), soda ash, limestone, dolomite, saltcake, and cullet. These are fed into a furnace and melted at 1500 °C. The molten glass formed is floated out as a continuous ribbon on a bath of tin. The surface of the tin is very smooth and, along with the high temperature, this makes the surface of the glass flat. Any irregularities are smoothed out. The glass is then cooled slowly and cut automatically, according to the customers' requirements. This type of glass is used for shop windows, cars, mirrors, and anywhere a distortion-free glass surface is required.

History of glass

The Egyptians are thought to have been the first people to make glass objects. They coiled molten glass into jars and used them for oils and perfumes. Much later, glass bottles were made by blowing through a pipe with a lump of molten glass on its end. This is still carried out to make special objects, but the majority of today's glass products are made by machine.

Glass is really a liquid! However, it looks like a solid. If you look at some very old glass window panes, they are thicker at the bottom than at the top, because the glass has 'flowed' like a liquid.

Questions

1   What are the raw materials for the manufacture of glass?

2   How is float glass made? What special property does it have?

Composite materials

A **composite material** contains two or more types of material combined together to provide a 'new' material with different properties. One of the materials is usually a fibre. A composite material can be modified to give an object the properties desired. For example, reinforced concrete is much stronger than concrete on its own. Concrete alone is too brittle for bridges to support a large volume of traffic. By pouring the concrete over rods of steel, which act like fibres, the problem is overcome.

Glass composites

Glass reinforced polyester (GRP) is made by mixing glass fibres with a polyester resin and adding a chemical hardener. The resulting plastic is very tough but very light. It is often used to make boats, since it is also very resistant to corrosion. Its other uses include piping, car body repairs, and roofing materials.

A layer of steel wire mesh can be sandwiched between two plates of glass, making the glass very tough. This is done as part of the rolling process during the manufacture of float glass. If a transparent mesh is used instead of the wire mesh, the reinforced glass can be used on the outside walls of a building.

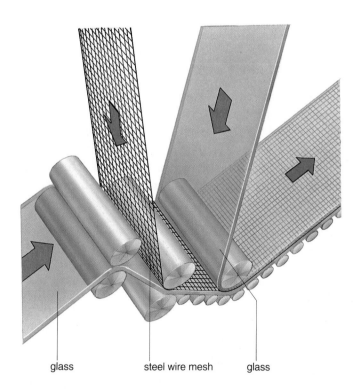

glass   steel wire mesh   glass

Steel wire mesh can be welded in between sheets of glass to provide toughened glass.

Toughened glass is used in buildings to provide security and strength.

Graphite composites

Sports equipment is increasingly being made of graphite fibres. The fibres are very strong and are also very thin. Squash and tennis rackets are first made of an alloy with a low melting point. This is then dipped into a mixture of graphite in a plastic which sets very hard when heated. When the plastic has set, the alloy melts away leaving a very strong racket.

Plastics reinforced with carbon fibres are also used in the manufacture of Formula One racing car bodies.

Graphite composites are used for sports equipment.

Activities

1   Carry out a survey of either glass or graphite composites. Find out about their uses, their particular properties, and their manufacture. Write to different organizations and manufacturers for help. Present your findings in the form of a written report to the rest of the class.

About one tonne of rubbish is thrown away by the average UK home every year. The cost of disposing of all this waste is very high. It is possible to cover much of this cost by collecting and recycling as much waste as possible.

Recycling would reduce the volume of rubbish to be disposed of.

What is the point of recycling?

Not all our natural resources are going to last forever. Minerals such as bauxite (aluminium ore) may run out in our lifetimes. Oil, which is used as a raw material for the manufacture of many plastics, is running out now. Scientists might discover new ways of producing aluminium and plastics without using these raw materials, or they may develop new, different materials to use in their place. However, we have the technology and the resources to reclaim many materials such as plastic and aluminium from our household rubbish now. Do you think we should recycle materials before it's too late?

Glass

Glass is not biodegradable. The raw materials for the manufacture of glass are plentiful and relatively cheap to extract. However, the mining of both limestone and sand cause scarring of the landscape. Recycling glass would reduce this problem. Bottle banks are used increasingly in the UK to collect glass to make cullet. Producing new glass using cullet can save up to 25% of the energy costs during manufacture. By recycling glass we can also save on space in landfill sites.

Glass needs to be disposed of safely.

Plastics

Since a great deal of our household rubbish is plastic, it may seem to be the best material to start recycling. However, there are many problems. There are about 30 different plastics in our rubbish, mainly in packaging materials. In order to recycle plastic, it has to be sorted out into these different types first. Who will do this sorting out? To make the recycling of large drinks bottles cost effective, 10 000 bottles would have to be collected to make just one tonne of plastic. Since the disposal of plastics is very difficult to carry out without damaging the environment (for example, burning them can give off toxic fumes), alternatives must be found. The search is on for a truly biodegradable plastic. A new polymer is being developed using sugar as a raw material. However, it is still cheaper to produce plastics from oil than from sugar! Other countries have made efforts to solve the problem. In some states of the USA companies can be charged a fine if they do not meet a recycling target each year. In Germany laws have been introduced so that a deposit is charged on all plastic bottles which are then returned to the shop. In Dublin a company uses unsorted plastics to make road signs for local authorities.

Plastic waste can kill.

85

Oil

Waste oil can be re-refined to provide more fuel. Waste lubricating oil, used in car engines, contains up to 20% harmful additives. Used oil also contains more lead than new oil. Oil can be recovered from most waste oil, but at present only about 30% of waste oil is recycled. The rest is usually dumped down drains or burned. The pollution costs of this action are severe. Waste oil needs to be taken to certified recycling collection points. Do you know where your nearest one is?

A small amount of crude oil can cause a great deal of pollution.

Costs of recycling

Whether to recycle or not depends on many factors.

- Is the material or mineral running out?
- Can it be recycled?
- If so, how can the material be collected?
- Does it cost more to recycle than to throw away?
- Should the cost only be considered in terms of money?
- What effects are there on the environment?

Activities

1 Choose one material and find out about how easy it is to recycle.

Find out about any local schemes in operation near where you live. Try and organize a collection of recyclable waste in your school.

Metals

If a metal is expensive, then people think twice about throwing it away. The scrap industry recycles large amounts of metal every year. Fifty per cent of copper is recycled from pipes and old wiring, and 80% of the lead from car batteries is reclaimed. Producing pure copper from scrap copper only costs 3% as much as mining it.

Scrapyards are full of a variety of metals. A large proportion of these metals can be separated and recycled.

It is relatively easy to recycle large pieces of metal, but less easy to recycle metals which we throw away on a daily basis, such as drinks cans. Drinks cans are made from either pure aluminium or tin plate. Both aluminium and tin are expensive to produce and are running out, so recycling them is worthwhile. Over half of drinks cans are 100% aluminium. They can be separated out from tin plate cans using a magnet – tin is magnetic, aluminium is not. Recycling aluminium not only saves bauxite, but also saves energy. Recycling needs only 5% of the energy used to produce aluminium from its ore. Different countries have different attitudes towards recycling cans. The problems are not usually concerned with the process of recycling, but rather with collecting the cans. In Denmark legislation was introduced which banned the sale of drinks in non-returnable containers. Charities can make money by organizing collections of cans for recycling.

The mining of some raw materials, such as limestone or metal ores, can cause scarring of the landscape.

Case study (1): today's cars

A variety of materials are used in the manufacture of a motor car. The properties of these different materials are used in different ways. There are parts of the car that need to be protected from corrosion; parts that need to be very strong and inflexible such as the car body shell; parts that need to be very strong yet flexible such as safety belts. The development of new materials has revolutionized the motor car since Benz built the first in 1885. Plastics have played a major part in preventing rust and in producing objects that need to be hard-wearing yet soft. Metals are now designed to be as free from rust as possible over a long period of time. Cars have become much safer through the use of more advanced materials, and the search is still on for even better materials.

Benz's first petrol powered car, 1885

Glass in cars

Car headlamps are traditionally made of glass, but can now be made of strong plastics. However, car windscreens are still made of glass. The glass can be cut exactly to the manufacturer's requirements. It is also made stronger by lamination (i.e. made in layers) to prevent glass fragments injuring people inside during an accident. In modern car manufacturing plants, windows are coated with plastic so that they can be put into cars safely using full automation. Problems with visibility during sudden changes in temperature have held back the development of completely plastic windows.

Metals in cars

A large amount of the steel manufactured in the UK goes into making car bodies. It is a tough, relatively cheap material that can easily be shaped. The steel is protected from rusting by using several layers of paint. Car engines made from aluminium are lighter than those made from other metals such as cast iron. Aluminium is also a better conductor of heat, which makes for more effective cooling of the engine. All moving parts in the engine are coated with oil to help reduce friction and prevent rust. Many parts of the car are electroplated with chrome. Chrome is shiny so looks attractive, and is also less likely to corrode than iron.

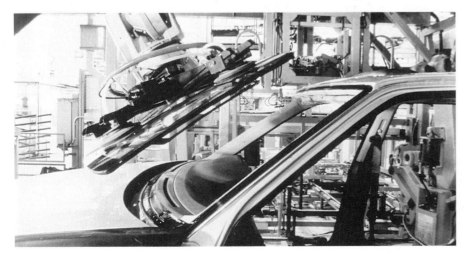

A large part of modern car production is mechanized.

Synthetic materials

Nylon is often used to make seat belts since it is flexible but very strong. Seats are often covered in a synthetic fibre. They can be almost any colour and texture and are hard-wearing. PVC (poly vinyl chloride) is used to cover (insulate) electrical wires where needed. Many items inside a car such as door handles and steering wheels are also either formed from or coated with plastic.

Activities

1   Look carefully at a modern car and list all the different materials that are used in its manufacture. Give reasons why each material has been chosen for its purpose.

Case study (2): safer cars for the future?

Formula One racing cars are safer than ever before. This is mainly due to the use of composite materials in the manufacture of the car bodies. Drivers are now able to literally walk away from crashes at speeds of up to 240 kilometres per hour (150 miles per hour). It is important for a racing car to be as light as possible so that it can be as fast as possible. Racing cars were originally made of steel, as motor cars are today. Aluminium replaced steel, being lighter, until about ten years ago. Although the metals were very strong, the nuts and bolts that held the pieces together formed weak spots. They also did little to help the aerodynamics. A plastic was introduced which was reinforced with carbon fibres which not only solved these problems and made the car lighter, but also reduced the time taken to produce a car body.

Composites in motor cars?

If this composite material can give all these safety features, in addition to reducing rusting, why are motor cars on the road today not made of plastic reinforced with carbon fibre? One of the main reasons concerns the problems involved in mass producing cars in a short space of time. At the moment, producing the carbon-fibre reinforced plastic bodies is very labour intensive and would not be cost effective. Steel is still the cheapest material to make car bodies. However, there have been developments in the manufacturing of car components made of composite

Formula One cars are now built to such high safety standards that many drivers are able to walk away from crashes such as this one without serious injury.

materials. For example, suspension systems have been tested in cars and have been proved to be successful. These components have been mass produced. Car companies use composites to make roofs and body panels on a large scale by compression moulding. The suppliers of the plastics are working on a method of producing sheets of composite material that are stiff enough to be handled and flexible enough to be moulded. The day of the corrosion-free car may soon be with us!

A Formula One racing car has a car body made of composites.

A twentieth-century problem (1)

Siting a production plant

The development of any new material is carried out only after very thorough research. Unless there is a market for the particular material, then its large-scale production will not be economically viable. The production of any material on a large scale has to be carefully thought out before the production plant is sited. For example, there are different numbers of people seeking employment in different parts of the country. If one of the raw materials has to be shipped in from another country, for example, bauxite for the production of aluminium from countries such as Jamaica, then it may be worth building the production plant near a sea port to reduce transport costs. However, there may be problems recruiting a large enough workforce there.

The manufacture of plastics uses large quantities of ethene and other products from the distillation of crude oil. Most oil refineries are situated near ports with special terminals for the delivery of oil. It may help to have a plastics factory situated nearby to reduce transport costs. This may also help reduce the costs of storing hazardous chemicals, since they can be bought direct and at relatively short notice.

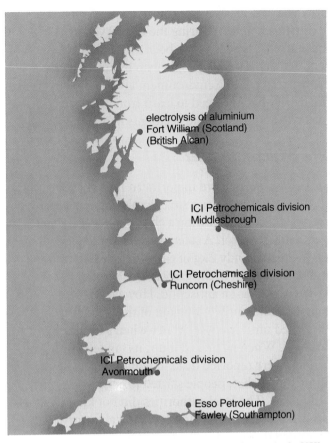

Can you think why these industries are situated where they are in the UK?

Another major consideration is the effect on the environment. Recently, more effort has been made to make factories blend in with their environments. Many processes involve problems such as waste gases and the safe disposal of by-products. These have to conform to legislation from the Health and Safety bodies. No one really wants a smelly factory in their back garden! Sometimes things can go tragically wrong, but usually the laws are obeyed and the risk of pollution is reduced. This was not the case during the Industrial Revolution of the 18th century. Little care was taken over the health of the workforce and workers suffered dreadful side effects and even death from their work. Iron works and factories appeared rapidly from 1750 with minimal care for the effects of the environment. In this century the air has often been polluted. It wasn't until after the 'killer fogs' of 1952 and 1956 that a Clean Air Act was passed in Parliament to control the emission of waste gases from factories.

Activities

1 Make a plan of the local industries in your area. Think why they are sited where they are and comment on their effect on the environment.

2 Find out about the effects of the Industrial Revolution on the environment and on the people who worked in factories during that time.

3 Find out about the 'killer fog' of 1952.

The industrial pollution that was so prominent during the Industrial Revolution is now a thing of the past. Or is it?

There have been a number of tragic accidents involving chemicals during the last 20 years. Many of these accidents could have been avoided. The effects of such accidents on the people who live close to the factories and on the environment are too disastrous to put a price on. We need to learn from previous mistakes and try to avoid accidents happening again.

The Seveso disaster

Seveso is a small town in northern Italy. On Saturday 10 July 1976 there was a small explosion in a nearby chemical factory following a chemical reaction that went out of control. A safety valve allowed a cloud of gas to escape. Only 2 kg of gas were released into the atmosphere. Part of the gas was the harmless TCP which is used as an antiseptic. However, it also contained dioxin. Nothing out of the ordinary happened until two weeks later when a farmer found a dead cat. When he picked it up, its tail fell off. More animals were reported dead in neighbouring fields. Shortly after that, people started to experience burns and rashes. The local authorities did not know that the gas that had escaped from the chemical factory contained dioxin until this time. Over 2000 people were evacuated from the town and many were seriously affected by burns. Children were more seriously affected than adults. Many children born after the disaster were seriously deformed.

This accident need not have happened. The people who lived very close to the factory in Seveso were not told of the dangers of dioxin and the people who worked at the factory were oblivious to the problems. The last barrels of chemicals were destroyed there in 1983 and efforts are now being taken to clean the affected area so that people can move back into the town.

Seveso is still deserted.

Oil pollution

Crude oil is a valuable commodity. It is a thick, sticky, dark liquid which is used to make a variety of chemicals. It is transported in enormous tankers, or through long pipes from oil fields. There have been accidents involving the transport of crude oil which could have been avoided. For example, in 1989 the tanker Exxon Valdez lost 11 million gallons of oil which polluted the sea and coast of Alaska causing tremendous environmental problems. It is very difficult to disperse crude oil, but detergents can be used. These detergents also cause damage to the environment. The easiest way to solve these problems is to avoid accidents happening.

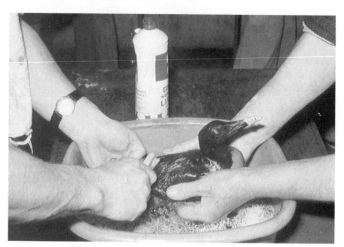

Birds and animals coated with oil die if they are not cleaned up. The oil also ruins the feeding grounds for many birds.

Disposal of toxic chemicals

It is very difficult to dispose of dangerous chemicals safely. Some countries have tighter controls than others on the treatment of toxic waste. Transporting toxic chemicals such as PCBs (polychlorinated biphenyls) can cause more problems than their disposal. The containers chemicals are transported in must be correctly labelled so that they are handled in the safest way possible. People are becoming increasingly more aware of the problems of disposing of this waste, and the amount of toxic waste is increasing.

Activities

1 Collect newspaper articles about problems associated with   **a)** pollution due to chemical factories   **b)** pollution of the sea and coasts by oil and   **c)** the disposal of toxic waste.

The kinetic theory of matter (1)

The substances around us can exist in three forms: solid, liquid, and gas. We call these the three **physical states**. The photographs on this page show typical solids and liquids, and containers full of gas.

Solids have well-defined, rigid shapes. The crystalline solids shown have flat faces and sharp edges. Like all solids they keep their shape and do not flow over surfaces. Substances like sand and sugar may not appear to obey these rules but close observation shows that each 'grain' is a hard solid which behaves just like a larger crystal.

Solids have well-defined shapes.

Liquids do not have well-defined shapes and they flow. When a liquid is poured into a jar or bottle it takes up the shape of the container, but only up to a certain level. The liquid has a well-defined volume which can be measured using a measuring cylinder.

Liquids take the shape of the container they are in but have a fixed volume.

Gases do not have a well-defined shape. When a gas is placed in a container it quickly takes up any available space. Gases can also flow and it is possible to pour heavy gases from one container to another.

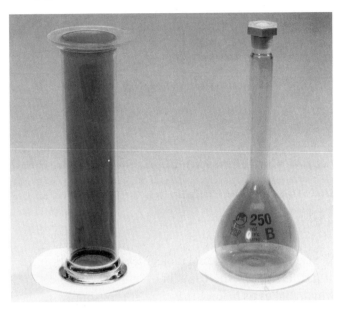

Gases take up all the available space.

Most materials can exist in all three physical states. Perhaps the best example is water. It comes out of the freezer as a solid (ice), out of the tap as a liquid, and out of a boiling kettle as a gas (steam). Heating or cooling water may change its state.

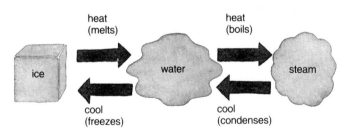

The kinetic theory of matter attempts to explain how solids, liquids, and gases behave. The theory is based on three assumptions:

- all matter is made up of tiny molecules or atoms which are continually in motion
- when the particles are close together there are attractive forces between them, and
- heating a material affects the movement of the particles.

The kinetic theory explains the behaviour of solids, liquids, and gases in terms of moving particles. When these particles are close together they attract each other. This gives us the following models:

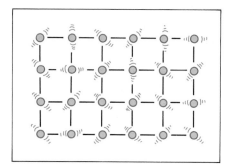

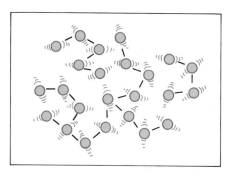

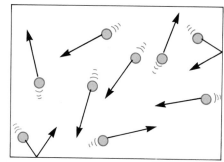

*In a **solid**, strong forces of attraction hold the atoms or molecules together in a regular grid or lattice. The particles vibrate but cannot break free. The solid has a fixed shape and volume.*

*In a **liquid**, the molecules are close together but they have enough energy to move about. As a result liquids can flow. At the surface the molecules attract one another forming a kind of skin above the liquid.*

*In a **gas**, the molecules are far apart and are moving so quickly that they do not really attract each other. They move in straight lines but have many collisions with other molecules and with the walls of the container they are in.*

We cannot see individual molecules in a solid, liquid, or gas. However, there is a lot of indirect evidence which makes us believe that they are constantly in motion.

Diffusion

When the cap is taken off a bottle of strong perfume the smell gradually spreads out. After a few minutes it can be detected several metres away. We say that the perfume's vapour (gas) has **diffused**. This means that some of the molecules which were in the bottle have escaped and moved across the room. On the way, they have collided with the moving molecules in the air, so their progress has been rather slow.

Diffusion can also take place in liquids, as demonstrated by Activity 1 opposite.

Brownian motion

We can get a better idea of molecular motion by looking at small particles of smoke suspended in air. A small glass cell is filled with smoke from a burning waxed straw. Through a microscope hundreds of bright specks can be seen. These are due to light reflecting from relatively large pieces of carbon and oil in the smoke.

If you look carefully you will see that these specks are moving in a jerky, zig-zagging motion. This is because the smoke particles are being bombarded by fast-moving molecules in the air. This random motion is

called **Brownian motion**. It is named after a Scottish scientist, Robert Brown. In 1827 Brown noticed that pollen grains moved jerkily when placed in water. In this case, the tiny pollen grains are being bombarded by fast-moving water molecules.

Surface tension

Evidence that molecules attract each other can be found from looking at the surfaces of liquids. These behave as if they were covered with a thin elastic skin. This is because the molecules in the surface layer are attracted to the molecules in the liquid below them.

Activities

1 Take a glass Petri dish or a white saucer and fill it with water. Then carefully place one drop of ink from a pipette in the centre of the water. Do not stir the water. Watch as the ink particles gradually diffuse outwards.
Design an experiment to calculate the average speed of diffusion for ink into water.

2 Fill a glass with water. Carefully add more water until the surface is above the rim. Sketch the top of the glass and the surface of the water. How does your diagram show that water molecules attract each other?

3 Put a very thin layer of lard or butter on a small plate. Put two or three drops of water on the plate. Sketch the shape of each drop as seen from the top and the side. How does this show that water molecules attract each other?

The kinetic theory gives us models for solids, liquids, and gases. These models can be used to explain some things which you may have noticed happening.

Expanding solids

Solids **expand** when they are heated. They don't usually expand much, but expanding solids can cause problems for engineers. For example, a 1 m length of steel expands 0.01 mm when its temperature rises by 1 °C. So a 100 m bridge would be 4 cm longer in summer (+30 °C) than in winter (−10 °C)! Engineers leave gaps at the ends of bridges to allow for this expansion. Without these gaps, the forces generated by the expanding metal could damage the bridge.

In steel the atoms are held in a regular structure called a **lattice**. Within the lattice the atoms vibrate. When the steel is heated the particles gain more energy and so vibrate more vigorously. This means that, on average, the atoms are further apart. The solid expands in all directions but keeps the same shape.

On cooling the atoms vibrate less as they lose energy and so the metal **contracts**.

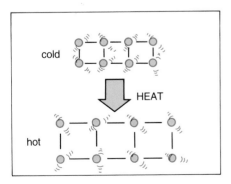

When a metal is heated the molecules vibrate more. On average they are further apart – the metal has expanded.

Conducting solids

The atoms in a metal are held in place by the forces between them. These bonds link the atoms together. When one end of a metal rod is heated the atoms near that end start to vibrate more vigorously. This makes nearby atoms vibrate more, and so gradually energy is passed along the rod. This is called **conduction**.

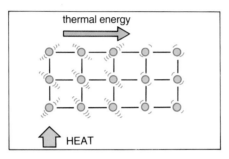

The molecules vibrate more vigorously when heated. Some of this energy is passed to neighbouring molecules, which pass it to their neighbours, and so on.

Evaporating liquids

In a liquid the molecules vibrate and move around, but they are still close enough to attract each other. The molecules stay under the surface layer. However, not all the molecules move at the same speed. Some move more quickly than average and some move more slowly. Sometimes a molecule gains enough energy to break free of the surface and escape. This is **evaporation**.

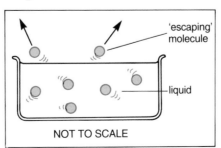

Only high-energy molecules can escape from the liquid.

Notice that only the faster molecules can break free. As a result the average speed of the molecules left is lower. This means that the liquid has a slightly lower temperature. Evaporation of a liquid causes cooling.

Questions

1 Explain, using the kinetic theory, why the handle of a metal spoon gets hot when the other end is dipped into hot tea.

2 A motorist travelling on a motorway notices that it is made up of concrete slabs 25 m long separated by a thin strip of bitumen (tar). An engineer says that these are **expansion joints**. Suggest why the road is made in this way.

3 A nurse preparing a patient for an injection cleans the skin by rubbing it with alcohol. The patient notices that this makes the skin feel cold. Suggest why.

4 The air in a room with central heating can get very dry and this can cause furniture to crack. To prevent this an open container filled with water can be placed near a radiator. Use the kinetic theory to explain why this increases the amount of water vapour in the air. Also explain why the container has to be topped up every so often.

Changing state

When a solid is heated it may reach a temperature at which it melts and turns into a liquid. According to the kinetic theory, the molecules in the solid get more energy as they are heated. Eventually they get enough energy to break free of the forces that hold them in place in the solid. If you keep heating, the liquid will boil and turn into a gas. This is because the molecules now have enough energy to break free completely.

Activities

1 Fill a beaker almost to the top with crushed ice taken from a deep freeze. Quickly place a thermometer in the ice and record its temperature. Heat the beaker over a Bunsen burner and record the temperature of the ice/water every 30 seconds. Continue to do this until the water has been boiling for about 3 minutes. Plot the results on a graph.

The diagram below shows the general shape of the results graph. The four stages can be explained using the kinetic theory.

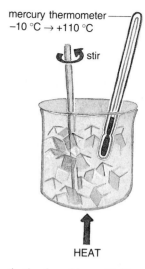

Investigating the melting and boiling of water

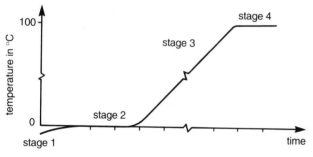

When a solid melts or a liquid boils the temperature remains constant.

Stage 1. Here the energy is raising the temperature of the ice up to 0 °C (melting point).

Stage 2. Here there is very little temperature rise. The energy is allowing molecules to break away from their fixed positions in the ice. The solid ice is turning to a liquid.

Stage 3. Here the energy is raising the temperature of the water up to 100 °C (boiling point).

Stage 4. Here there is no temperature rise. The energy is allowing molecules to break free completely. The liquid is changing to a gas.

Specific heat and specific latent heat

The energy needed to raise the temperature of 1 kg of a solid, liquid, or gas by 1 °C is called the material's **specific heat**. The energy needed to melt 1 kg of solid without changing its temperature is called the material's **specific latent heat of fusion**. The energy needed to change that 1 kg of liquid into a gas at its boiling point is called the material's **specific latent heat of vaporization**.

The diagram opposite gives the values for water. Notice that we have to supply energy to melt a solid or to boil a liquid. However, when a gas condenses or a liquid freezes energy is given out.

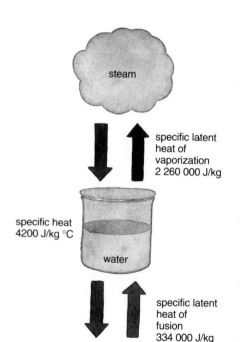

specific latent heat of vaporization 2 260 000 J/kg

specific heat 4200 J/kg °C

specific latent heat of fusion 334 000 J/kg

Molecular motion and temperature

A temperature scale gives us a simple way of comparing how hot objects are. The most commonly used temperature scale is the Celsius scale. The table below gives some common examples of temperatures on this scale. Notice that 0°C is the temperature of melting ice and 100°C is the temperature of boiling water.

object	temperature
surface of Sun	6000°C
light bulb filament	2500°C
Bunsen flame	1000°C
boiling water	100°C
human body	37°C
summer day (UK)	25°C
melting ice	0°C
cold winter day (UK)	−10°C
domestic deep freeze	−15°C

What is temperature?

We have already seen that, according to the kinetic theory, molecules move more quickly when a substance is heated. The energy from the heat source is transferred to the molecules as increased kinetic energy. At the same time the substance's temperature goes up.

We can think of temperature as a measure of the (average) kinetic energy of the molecules.

We can now use kinetic energy to explain what happens when a hot object is placed in contact with a cold object.

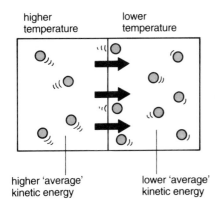

Thermal energy always flows from hot objects to cooler ones.

The hot object has many high-speed molecules. When these collide with the slower moving molecules in the cold object, they transfer some of their energy. The hot block gets slightly colder and the cold block gets slightly warmer. This goes on until eventually the two objects are at the same temperature. We say that they are then in **thermal equilibrium**.

When an object cools down its molecules slow down and have less kinetic energy. If we keep taking energy away the molecules will, in theory, stop moving! The temperature could never be lower because we could not take away any more energy. The lowest possible temperature is called **absolute zero**. Scientists have calculated this to be about −273°C!

For scientific work it is convenient to use a temperature scale starting at absolute zero. The Kelvin scale starts at absolute zero and has degrees which are the same size as degrees on the Celsius scale. This makes conversions easy.

Kelvin scale	Celsius scale
1273 K	1000°C
373 K	100°C
273 K	0°C
0 K	−273°C

Questions

1 Explain the following using the kinetic theory:
   a) A spoon placed in a cup of hot tea gets hot.
   b) Adding cold milk to hot black coffee cools it down.
   c) A teapot should be heated with boiling water before tea is made in it.
   d) A kettle placed over a gas flame gets hot.

2 Convert the following temperatures to the Kelvin scale:
   a) 0°C **b)** 100°C **c)** 180°C **d)** −173°C **e)** −100°C.

3 Convert the following temperatures to the Celsius scale:
   a) 0 K **b)** 73 K **c)** 150 K **d)** 473 K **e)** 561 K.

Investigating gases (1): volume and temperature

The expansion of a gas is more difficult to study than the expansion of a solid or a liquid because there is another factor to be taken into account: the **pressure** of the gas. The apparatus shown has a fixed mass of gas trapped in a thin tube under a bead of liquid. When the gas is heated it can expand and push the liquid upwards without its pressure changing. (The length of the air column can be taken to be a measure of volume because the cross-sectional area of the tube remains constant.)

Under these conditions the gas expands steadily as its temperature rises from 0 °C to 100 °C. In fact **the volume of the gas is proportional to its absolute (Kelvin) temperature**. If we double the temperature of the gas (in kelvin) its volume doubles.

We can write this in symbols as:

$V/T =$ **constant** (provided P is constant)

The graph shows typical results when this investigation is carried out using air. If we extended the line backwards it would meet the temperature axis at about −273 °C. At this temperature the gas would have no volume! This is because, according to the kinetic theory, all the molecules would be stationary at the bottom of the tube and taking up very little room. (In practice, all real gases would have turned to liquids long before absolute zero was reached.)

One of the most important points about this investigation is that when we repeat it with gases other than air we get exactly the same result. All gases behave in the same way and give the same value for absolute zero.

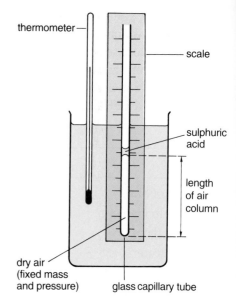

Experiment to investigate how the volume of a fixed mass of gas at constant pressure varies with temperature

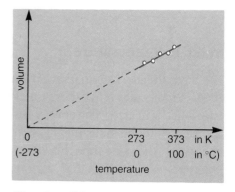

*The volume of the gas is **directly proportional** to its absolute temperature – provided that the pressure remains constant.*

Questions

1 Explain how the apparatus in the diagram could be turned into a gas thermometer.

2 The line on the graph has to be extended backwards to find absolute zero.

   a) Explain why 0 °C to 100 °C is a good range to use for this experiment in schools.

   b) Explain why the experiment would not work if you used liquid helium to cool the air to 4 K (−269 °C).

3 Copy the results graph shown on this page. Mark the line as 'air, volume V'.

   a) On the same axes draw the line you would expect if the same volume of carbon dioxide gas had been used.

   b) On the same axes draw the line you would expect if twice the volume of air ($2V$) had been used.

4 Suggest two reasons why mercury thermometers are of more use than gas thermometers.

Investigating gases (2): pressure and temperature

In the previous investigation the gas was trapped under a light, movable 'lid' so that the pressure would always stay the same. However, if the gas is heated in a rigid container with a fixed lid, it cannot expand. In this case the **pressure** of the gas increases. The diagram shows a suitable apparatus for this investigation. Notice that in this case it is the volume which is kept constant.

The gas (air) is enclosed in a sealed flask with a mercury thermometer to record its temperature. The pressure of the gas is measured using a **Bourdon pressure gauge** attached to the flask by a short length of tubing. The pressure readings are taken as the gas is heated and a graph is plotted. Typical results are shown opposite. Notice that **the pressure is proportional to the absolute (Kelvin) temperature of the gas**. This means that if we double the temperature of the gas (in Kelvin) the gas pressure doubles.

In symbols we can write this as:

P/T = **constant** (provided V is constant)

By extending the graph line we can see that the gas would exert no pressure at 0 K. We can explain these results using the kinetic theory. In a gas the molecules are continuously moving so at any time many of them are colliding with the sides of the container. They bounce off without losing any energy, and in doing so each one exerts a small outward force on the wall. Because many billions of molecules are doing this in each second, this force appears as a constant pressure.

As the gas is heated the molecules get more kinetic energy, so they strike the walls with a greater force. They also have more collisions with the walls in each second. These two factors make the pressure of the gas increase. Of course, at absolute zero the molecules would not be moving and colliding with the walls. The pressure would be zero!

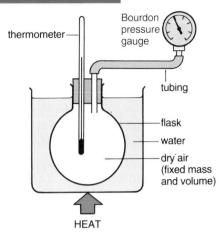

Experiment to investigate how the pressure of a fixed mass of gas at constant volume varies with temperature

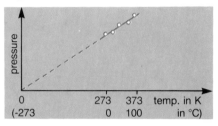

*The pressure of the gas is **directly proportional** to its absolute temperature – provided that the volume remains constant.*

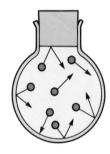

According to the kinetic theory, the pressure of the gas on the container is due to molecules colliding with the walls.

Questions

1 A tin can with a tight-fitting push-on lid contains a small quantity of water. When the can is heated over a ·Bunsen burner it fills up with steam. If the can is heated further the lid is forced off with a bang.
   a) Explain why the lid flies off. Use the words pressure, force, and temperature in your answer.
   b) Explain using the kinetic theory what is happening to the water molecules throughout this activity.
   c) Explain why it would be very dangerous to do this experiment with water contained in a metal can with a screw top.

2 A motorist checks the pressure in the tyres of his car before a long journey. After travelling for 200 km on a motorway he checks them again and finds that the pressure has gone up! Suggest why.

3 A pressure cooker contains steam at a temperature of 100 °C and at a pressure of 100 000 Pa. It is then heated until the pressure is 200 000 Pa. Calculate the new temperature of the steam.

Assume that the volume of the steam remains constant and don't forget to use the absolute (kelvin) temperature. (1 Pa = 1 N/m²)

If you trap some gas in a container and then try to reduce its volume, the pressure increases. If you try to make the trapped gas fill a bigger volume, then the pressure decreases. You can prove this quite easily by filling a bicycle pump with air and then placing your finger over the hole at the bottom of the pump. If you now press the handle down slowly you will notice that at first the gas (air) is very easy to compress. As you push the handle down still further you will notice that the air is pushing against your finger with a large force. If you release the handle at this stage the air pressure will force it to spring back out again. If you keep compressing the air you will get to a stage where the pressure becomes so great that your finger is pushed away and some of the air escapes.

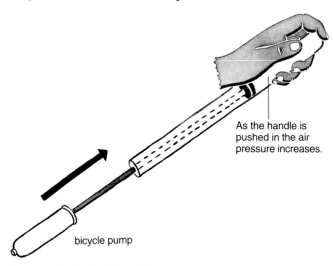

As the handle is pushed in the air pressure increases.

bicycle pump

Demonstrating the 'springiness' of air

The pressure increases because the molecules have less room to move around in, so they have more collisions with the walls of the container in each second.

Boyle's law

Over 300 years ago a famous scientist, Robert Boyle (1627–91), described experiments on the 'spring effects of air'. The diagram shows some modern apparatus used to investigate how the volume of a gas varies with the pressure on it.

The pump is used to increase the pressure of the oil which presses on the air trapped in the glass tube. The pressure of the oil and hence the pressure of the gas is measured using a Bourdon pressure gauge. The volume of the gas is read from the scale. After the volume has been recorded for several pressures the results can be plotted on a graph.

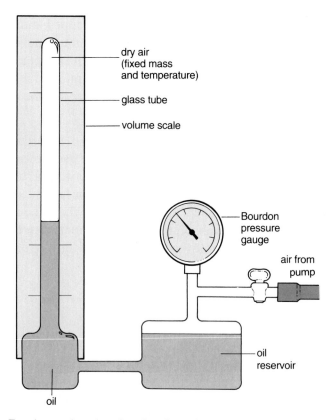

dry air
(fixed mass
and temperature)

glass tube

volume scale

Bourdon
pressure
gauge

air from
pump

oil
reservoir

oil

Experiment to investigate how the volume of a fixed mass of gas at constant temperature varies with pressure

The graph shows that when the pressure doubles the volume halves. We say that **the pressure is inversely proportional to the volume** provided that the temperature stays the same.

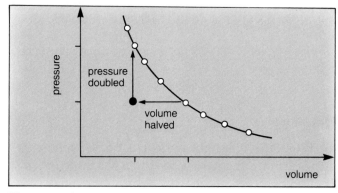

pressure

pressure
doubled

volume
halved

volume

*The pressure of a gas is **inversely proportional** to its volume – provided that the temperature remains constant.*

In other words, pressure multiplied by volume will always give the same value provided that the mass of the gas is not allowed to change and that its temperature remains constant. This is known as Boyle's law. In symbols we can write this as:

$$PV = \text{constant} \text{ (provided that } T \text{ remains constant)}$$

1 a) Name one common ore of each of the following metals:
i) aluminium ii) iron iii) copper.
b) Aluminium ore is much more plentiful in the Earth's crust than iron ore. Explain why pure aluminium is more expensive than iron.
c) Explain why we should recycle aluminium.

2 The diagram below shows a blast furnace.

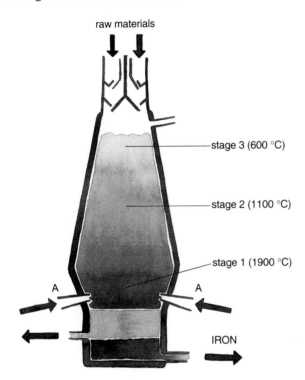

raw materials

stage 3 (600 °C)

stage 2 (1100 °C)

stage 1 (1900 °C)

A   A

IRON

a) What raw materials are added through the top of the furnace?
b) What is pumped into the furnace at A?
c) Describe what is happening at each of the stages labelled. Where possible give a chemical equation.

3 Draw a labelled diagram to show how you could nickel plate a piece of metal. Why is it essential that the piece of metal is completely clean?

4 Explain each of the following statements:
a) Sodium floats on water, most other metals don't.
b) Metals can be made harder and stronger by alloying.
c) Aluminium metal is relatively reactive yet the aluminium handlebars of a bicycle do not corrode.

5 Explain what you would see if the following experiments were carried out:
a) zinc placed in silver nitrate solution
b) iron placed in dilute sulphuric acid
c) clean magnesium left exposed to air for one month.

6 List three different alloys. For each one give an example of its use and explain why the alloy is particularly suitable.

7 a) A student says that only water and iron are needed to make rust. How would you demonstrate that air (or oxygen) is also needed?
b) Describe two different ways to prevent steel from rusting.

8 List the advantages and disadvantages of the materials chosen to make the following objects:
a) glass milk bottles
b) wooden window frames
c) 'foam' furniture
d) plastic cutlery
e) polyethene water pipes.

9 The diagram represents the kinetic theory model of a metal.

a) Is this metal a solid or a liquid? How do you know?
b) Use the model to explain how a metal conducts thermal energy (heat).
c) Use the model to explain why metals become superconductors at low temperatures.

10 The kinetic theory assumes that the molecules in a material are constantly in motion.
a) What evidence do we have to support this assumption?
b) How does the kinetic theory explain the fact that liquids cool down as they evaporate?

What is magnetism?

What is electromagnetism?

How can we use magnetism in technology?

What causes static electricity?

How can we use electrostatics?

What effect have electronic devices had on our lives?

How can information be stored digitally?

These all use magnetism to work.

Magnetism is a mysterious force which appears between magnets, and between magnets and materials like iron and steel. For example, a magnet will attract steel needles placed close to it.

A piece of steel or other alloy which has been magnetized so that it keeps its magnetic properties is called a **permanent magnet**. An electric current also exerts a magnetic force. We can use this fact to make magnets which can be turned on and off. These are **electromagnets**.

Magnetic forces act over relatively small distances, usually just a few centimetres, but we can use them to great effect. All the devices shown on this page use

magnetism. The can opener uses a permanent magnet to hold the lid, the motor of the electric drill uses electromagnets, and the headphones use both!

Activities

1 Make a list of all the devices in your home that use magnetism. Look for magnetic door catches, appliances with motors, loudspeakers, etc.

2 Design an experiment to test the statement **magnetic forces only act over small distances**. Draw the apparatus you would use and describe how you would carry out the investigation.

Magnetic effects: attraction and repulsion

A permanent magnet is very useful for picking up steel dressmakers' pins or steel nails, but it has no effect on copper wire or brass screws. In fact, there are only three elements which are strongly attracted to magnets: iron, nickel, and cobalt. Magnets also attract alloys which contain iron, nickel, or cobalt, for example steel.

Our planet also affects magnets. As a result, a bar magnet which is hung from a thread as shown in the diagram eventually settles down to point roughly north to south. The end of the magnet which points to the north is called the north-seeking pole. The other end is the south-seeking pole. We usually call these the north and south poles of the magnet, or just 'N' and 'S'.

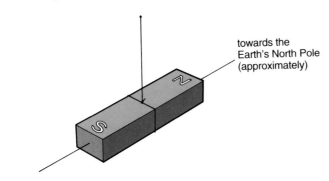

A magnet acting as a compass.

experiment	result
N pole brought near to S pole	attracts
S pole brought near to N pole	attracts
N pole brought near to N pole	repels
S pole brought near to S pole	repels
Like poles repel, unlike poles attract	

Questions

1 You have a bar magnet but the N and S poles are not marked. Describe briefly how you could find which end was south seeking.

2 A bar magnet is suspended from a piece of thin thread. What would happen if the following were brought near:
- **a)** an unmagnetized iron rod
- **b)** a copper rod
- **c)** the S pole of another magnet?

3 Some books say that 'repulsion is the only test for a magnet'. Why is attraction on its own is not enough.

Magnetic fields

When you bring a magnet close to a steel pin, the pin starts to move before the magnet touches it. The pin may even jump across a small gap to stick to the magnet. This is because there is a space around the magnet where magnetic materials 'feel' a force. We say that there is a **magnetic field** around the magnet.

Magnetic fields can be studied using iron filings and small compasses called plotting compasses. When iron filings are sprinkled on to a piece of card covering a bar magnet, each filing becomes magnetized and lines up with the magnetic field. This gives a pattern which tells us about the shape of the field. In fact, the field is all around the magnet in three dimensions. We can show this by dipping a magnet into iron filings.

The direction of magnetic field lines can be found using a plotting compass. The compass needle is a small magnet which can turn on a pivot. In a magnetic field its N pole is pulled one way and its S pole is pulled the other. The needle comes to rest in line with the magnetic field.

A typical field pattern for a bar magnet is shown in the diagram. Only a few lines are drawn to show the shape clearly. The spacing of the lines shows the strength of the field. Where the lines are close together, for example near the poles, the field is strong. A large force would act on a magnetic pole placed there.

The arrows on the field lines show the direction of the force which would act on a N pole. This is always from the N of the magnet to the S.

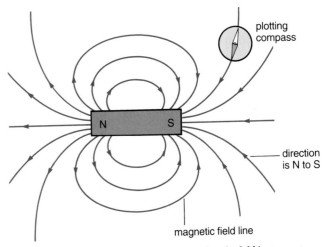

Magnetic field pattern for a bar magnet. Notice that the field is strongest near the poles.

A theory for magnetism

Experiments show us the basic properties of magnets and magnetic materials but they don't help to explain what is happening. We need a theory to explain the effects of magnetism and to help us use it in technology.

Evidence for the theory

A magnetized steel rod has a N pole at one end and a S pole at the other. It can be snapped in two. When each piece is tested it is found to be a complete magnet; each piece has its own N and S poles. If we keep breaking them into smaller and smaller pieces we get smaller and smaller complete magnets. We never get a N pole on its own, or a free S pole!

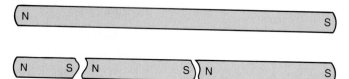

*When a magnet is broken **all** the pieces are complete magnets.*

We can think of magnetic materials as containing 'magnets' within their molecules. (These tiny 'molecular magnets' are actually due to the movement of electrons around atoms.)

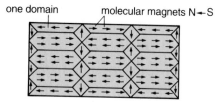

Unmagnetized iron

Inside a material like iron the molecular magnets can line up in groups called **domains**. The diagram shows how the domains are arranged in a piece of unmagnetized iron. Notice that the molecular magnets inside each domain are lined up, but that different domains line up in other directions. They seem to form loops which cancel each other out. This leaves the iron **unmagnetized**.

Now when the iron is placed near to a magnet, its molecular magnets start to line up. The domains in one particular direction start to grow. In the diagram of a magnetized piece of iron you can see that all the large domains point in the same direction. This leaves free poles at the ends. In the middle the N and S poles of the molecular magnets cancel out.

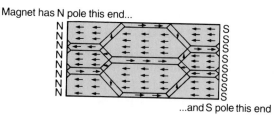

Magnetized iron

Using the theory

A piece of iron can be magnetized by stroking it repeatedly with a magnet.

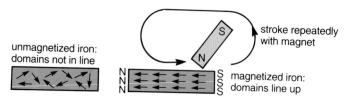

The N pole of the stroking magnet attracts the S poles of the 'molecular magnets' as it moves across the iron.

A permanent magnet can be demagnetized by heating it up and then quickly cooling it in cold water. The diagrams show what happens to the domains when this is done.

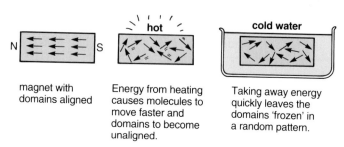

Demagnetizing by heating and rapid cooling

Questions

1 A carpenter finds that her screwdriver has become magnetized. She demagnetizes it by hitting it several times with a hammer.
   a) Using the domain theory, explain why this method works.
   b) Explain why science teachers get annoyed when students drop magnets on the floor.

2 If a piece of steel is heated and then allowed to cool slowly it becomes a magnet. Explain this using the idea of molecular magnets.

Magnetic induction

When a piece of iron or steel is placed near to a magnet the magnetic domains line up and it becomes magnetized. We say that the magnet has **induced** magnetism in the metal. You can see from the diagrams that the induced pole closest to the magnet's N pole is a S pole. This explains why magnets attract iron and steel.

When the iron is pulled away from the magnet it loses its induced magnetism. It was a **temporary** magnet. However when steel is used it keeps some of the induced magnetism and becomes a **permanent** magnet.

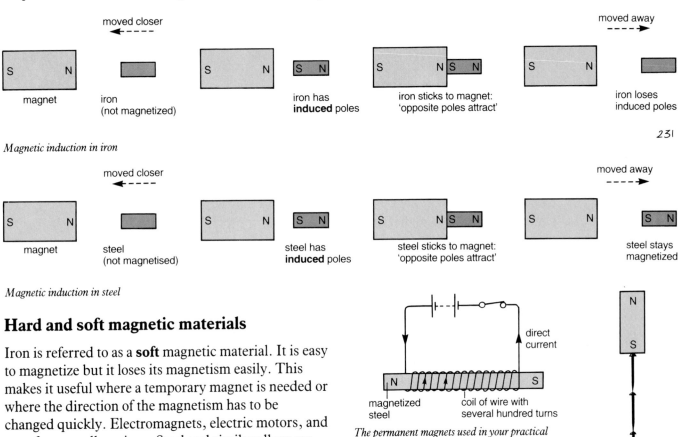

Magnetic induction in iron

Magnetic induction in steel

Hard and soft magnetic materials

Iron is referred to as a **soft** magnetic material. It is easy to magnetize but it loses its magnetism easily. This makes it useful where a temporary magnet is needed or where the direction of the magnetism has to be changed quickly. Electromagnets, electric motors, and transformers all use iron. Steel and similar alloys are **hard** magnetic materials. They are more difficult to magnetize than iron but do not lose their magnetism easily. They make good permanent magnets. They are also used in recording tapes and computer diskettes for storing information. (See page 110.)

Making a permanent magnet

You saw on the opposite page how a piece of steel can be magnetized by stroking it with a magnet. The magnet is moved over the steel many times, always in the same direction. Gradually the steel develops strong, induced poles. A better way of making a permanent magnet is to place the steel inside a coil of wire. When an electric current flows in the coil, strong magnetic poles are induced in the steel. (See page 104.)

The permanent magnets used in your practical work were probably made by this method.

Activities

1 The diagram shows a magnet attracting some steel pins. See how many steel pins or paperclips a strong magnet will support.

a) Explain how this happens using the idea of induced poles.

b) Use a plotting compass to test whether your pins or paperclips have been left magnetized by the experiment.

c) Explain how you could use the situation shown in the diagram to compare the strengths of two magnets.

d) Can you think of any other way of comparing the strengths of two magnets?

Electric currents and magnetism

In 1820 a Danish scientist called Oersted showed that if a compass was placed below a wire carrying an electric current, the compass needle moved. He had shown that a wire carrying an electric current has a magnetic field around it. We call this effect **electromagnetism**. The discovery of the connection between electric currents and magnetism was very important. Much of our modern technology depends on it.

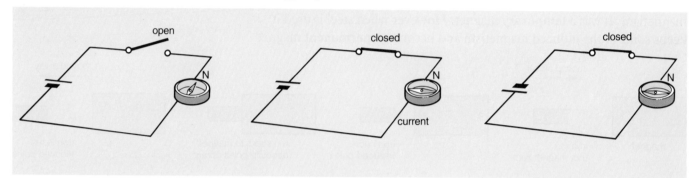

No current: compass lines up with Earth's field   *With current: compass needle deflected*   *With current reversed: compass needle deflected in opposite direction*

Experiments with iron filings and plotting compasses give the following results:

- The magnetic field lines are circles around the wire.
- The direction of the field (i.e. how a free N pole would move) is clockwise if we look in the direction of conventional current flow (+ to −).
- If the current is reversed then the magnetic field also reverses.
- If the size of the current is increased then the magnetic field gets stronger.
- The field is strongest close to the wire and gets much weaker as you move further away.

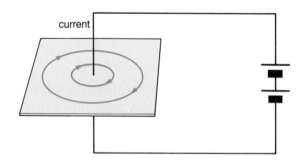

The current in the wire gives a circular magnetic field.

Magnetic fields and coils

When a current flows in a long coil with many loops of wire the magnetic field looks just like that of a bar magnet (see page 101). A coil like this is called a **solenoid**.

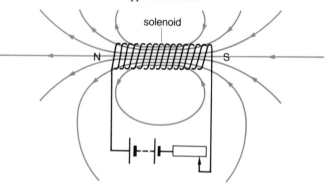

The field pattern of a solenoid is like that of a bar magnet.

The direction of the field in a solenoid can be found by using the fingers of your right hand to show the direction of the current in the loops of wire. Your right thumb then shows the N pole of the solenoid.

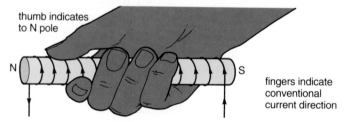

*This **right-hand grip rule** can be used to predict where the N pole of a solenoid will be.*

In a solenoid the field can be made stronger by:

- increasing the current
- making more loops of wire (in the same length)
- putting a core of iron or steel inside the coil (this makes the field much stronger).

Using electromagnets

Electromagnets are used for lifting scrap iron and steel. The magnet has a coil of copper wire wound around an iron core. The iron becomes strongly magnetized when a current flows in the coil. The core then loses its magnetism when the current is turned off. Iron is a soft magnetic material.

Electromagnets can also be used to separate ferrous metals like iron and steel from non-ferrous metals like copper and aluminium. They are also used in many other devices such as relays, loudspeakers, and motors.

Electromagnet lifting 'ferrous' scrap

Questions

1 The diagram shows the magnetic field pattern around a current in a wire. Copy the diagram, then draw (to the same scale) diagrams to show what happens when **a**) the current is increased **b**) the current is reversed.

wire carrying current into page

2 Look up the chemical symbol for iron. Suggest why scrap dealers call old car bodies 'ferrous scrap'.

3 Food cans are often made of steel plated with tin. Drinks cans are usually made of aluminium. Explain how a metal recycling plant could use an electromagnet. Explain why metal recycling is important.

4 Explain using the domain theory (see page 102) why the iron core inside a solenoid becomes magnetized.

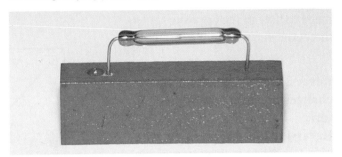

A reed relay can be operated by a small bar magnet (shown) or an electromagnet.

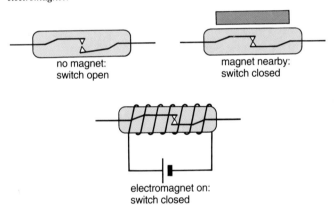

no magnet: switch open

magnet nearby: switch closed

electromagnet on: switch closed

Relays

A **relay** is an electrically controlled switch. It uses a small current to turn on a separate circuit, which may carry a large current. The diagram shows a relay to turn on the starter motor of a car. On starting, a very large current flows through the motor circuit. If it flowed through the wires to the ignition switch it would melt them!

In electronic circuits, small reed relays are used. These have a very thin, flexible piece of metal inside a glass tube. The metal acts as a switch. When a magnet is nearby, the switch becomes magnetized and the contacts touch. The relay can be activated by a small bar magnet or a small coil. Some reed relays have their contacts together under normal conditions. The switch then **opens** in a magnetic field.

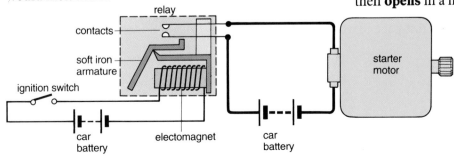

*When the ignition switch is closed a **small** current flows in the electromagnet. The iron armature is attracted to the electromagnet, closing the relay contacts. A **large** current flows in the starter circuit as the motor turns the engine.*

Magnetism, currents, and forces

The diagram shows an experiment to demonstrate the effect of a magnetic field on a current-carrying wire. A short piece of wire, W, rests on wires which make up the rest of the circuit. When the switch is closed a current flows in the direction shown. The wire W moves off to the right showing that there is a force in that direction. Notice that the wire is **not** attracted by the poles of the magnet.

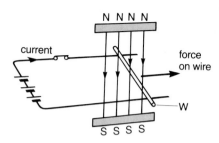

The motor effect

The experiment can be repeated with the magnetic field reversed. This time the wire moves in the opposite direction, i.e. to the left.

If the magnetic field is left as it is in the diagram but the current is made to flow in the opposite direction, the wire moves off to the left.

Reversing the magnetic field changes the direction of the force.
Reversing the current in the wire also reverses the direction of the force.

We can draw a diagram to show the relative directions of the current, magnetic field, and the force which makes the wire move. Notice that the force is at right angles to both the current and the magnetic field.

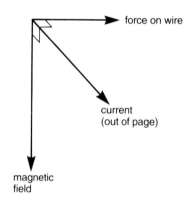

In the motor effect, the force is at right angles to the magnetic field and current.

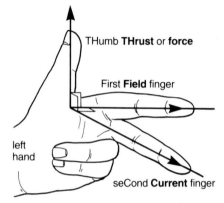

*Fleming's **left-hand motor rule** uses the first two fingers and the thumb of the left hand to show how the directions of the force, field, and current are linked.*

Questions

1 Copy the diagram on this page which shows the directions of the current, magnetic field, and force on the wire. Mark the arrows C, M, and F.

  a) Draw a similar diagram to show what happens to the direction of the force when the current is reversed

  b) Draw a third diagram to show what would happen if the current and the magnetic field were reversed.

2 The rule for finding the direction of the force is sometimes called **Fleming's left-hand motor rule**. Show that it only works with the left hand and that the right hand gives the wrong answer.

3 The diagram shows a loop of wire in a circuit. The wire passes between the poles of a magnet. Use the diagrams on this page to work out what will happen to the wire in the magnetic field.

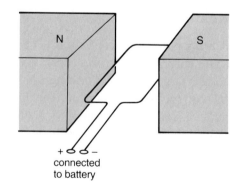

Electric motors

When an electric current flows in a wire in a magnetic field, a force is produced. The force can make the wire move. This is sometimes called the **motor effect**. Scientists and engineers have used this effect to build the electrical motors which are so important in our modern lifestyles. These range from the small motors which move the tape in cassette players to the powerful motors which move the trains on the electrified parts of our railway system.

In the diagram, a single loop of wire carries a current in the direction shown. The piece of wire on the left feels a force upwards, but the piece on the right feels a force downwards. These opposite forces make the loop of wire start to turn. This twisting effect is used in electric motors.

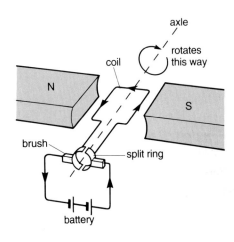

The two forces on this coil are making it twist.

Simple d.c. motors

In a real motor, we want the coil to keep spinning in the same direction. We do this by controlling the current direction. The diagram shows how this is done in a simple motor designed to work from a battery or other direct current (d.c.) supply The motor has a rectangular coil of wire between N and S poles of a magnet. The coil can spin on an axle. The coil is connected to two halves of a copper ring which has been cut through. The split ring is called the **commutator**. The battery is connected to the coil through two carbon blocks which rub against the commutator. (The carbon blocks are called **brushes** because early electric motors used brushes of metal wire to make the contacts.)

The commutator spins with the coil and makes sure that the current always flows in the right direction to keep the motor spinning.

Simple d.c. motor

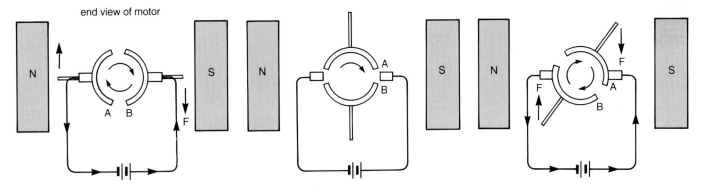

When the coil is flat, the forces on its sides are opposite, so the coil turns.

In this position there is no turning effect but the inertia of the coil keeps it turning.

As the coil passes the top, each brush connects with the other half of the split ring. This keeps the current flowing in the right direction.

Activities

1   List all the appliances in your home which use electric motors. For each appliance state whether the motor uses d.c. or a.c. current. (Think carefully about portable cassette players which can use batteries or mains!)

2   List all the devices in a car which use an electric motor. (Your answer will depend on the type of car you choose, but all cars have at least two.)

3   If you can, take the top off a motorized toy. Look for the motor and then identify the coil, the magnets, the commutator, and the brushes.

The motor effect again!

Another common application of the motor effect is in the **loudspeaker**. Cassette players, radios, and stereo systems usually use moving-coil loudspeakers.

The photograph shows a moving-coil loudspeaker and the diagram *underneath it* shows its parts. It has a permanent magnet shaped like a cylinder. This gives a strong magnetic field in the circular gap between the poles. A coil of wire rests in the gap. One end of the coil is fixed to a paper or plastic cone. Thin wires lead from the coil to connectors at the back of the loudspeaker cabinet. These are connected to a current supply. This can be an amplifier circuit inside a radio, television, cassette player, or even an electronic musical instrument. The output from the current supply will be an alternating current which has a frequency in the audible range (10 Hz to 20 kHz).

When an alternating current flows in the coil, the coil moves backwards and forwards making the cone vibrate at the same frequency as the current. The cone makes the air in front of it vibrate and move away as a wave. We hear this as sound.

If the volume is turned up, the size of the current is increased. This gives a bigger force on the coil and so the cone moves further. This in turn pushes the air molecules in front further. The result is a louder sound. If the current from the amplifier has a high frequency, the coil, and therefore the cone, moves backwards and forwards many times per second. This gives a high pitched sound.

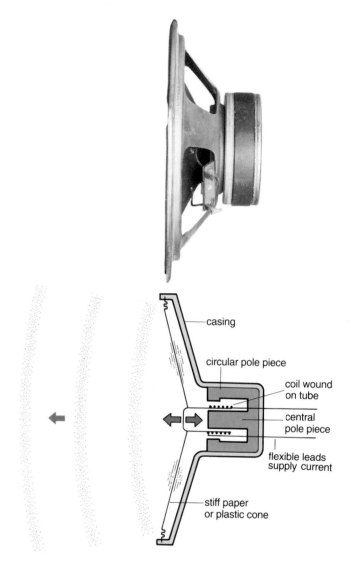

The photograph and diagram show a moving-coil loudspeaker. If you can, look at a real loudspeaker. Look for the magnet, the contacts for the coil, and the cone.

Questions

1 Give two ways in which a loudspeaker is like a motor. Give two differences between a loudspeaker and a motor.

2 Good loudspeakers have their paper cones attached to a heavy metal frame. Suggest why this is.

3 A student fixes a pair of loudspeakers into special wooden cabinets. After he has finished he finds that his screwdriver is magnetized. Suggest why.

4 The student uses speakers marked 'Maximum power 30 W'. He connects them to a stereo system marked 'Power output 50 W per channel'. Suggest what might happen if he turns the volume up to its maximum level. Explain your answer.

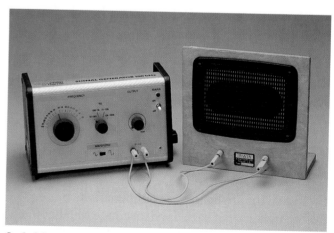

In the laboratory a signal generator can produce alternating currents at variable frequency. It can drive a loudspeaker to give sounds at different pitches.

Electromagnetic induction

We have seen that motion can be produced when a current flows in a magnetic field. It is possible to show that a current is produced when a wire is moved through a magnetic field. This is the opposite of the motor effect. It is called the **dynamo effect**. (See also Chapter 9.)

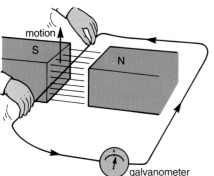

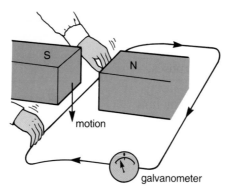

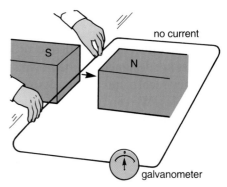

*As the wire is moved **through** the field, a current flows in the circuit.*

If the wire is moved in the opposite direction, the current reverses.

If the wire is moved parallel to the field lines so that it does not cut them, no current flows.

The size of the current can be increased by:

- moving the wire faster
- using a stronger magnetic field
- increasing the length of wire in the field by looping it around the magnetic poles.

A current can also be generated (**induced**) by moving a magnet towards or away from a coil of wire. The current is only induced when the magnet is moving. This is when the number of field lines linking with the coil is changing.

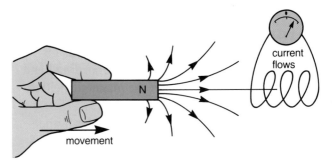

As the magnet is moved, the number of field lines linking with the coil changes. This induces a current in the coil.

The size of the current can be increased by:

- moving the magnet faster
- using a stronger magnet
- using more turns of wire in the coil.

Using electromagnetic induction

The moving-coil microphone. We have seen that a loudspeaker uses the motor effect to turn electrical signals into sound. The moving-coil microphone uses the dynamo effect to turn sound waves into an electrical signal.

The diagram shows the parts of a moving coil microphone. The sound waves make the thin diaphragm vibrate. This makes the coil move backwards and forwards in the magnetic field causing a small alternating current. This can be amplified to drive a loudspeaker, or the signal can be recorded on tape.

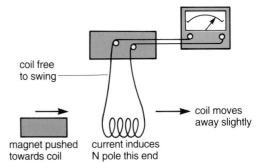

Lenz's law: the induced current flows in a direction to oppose the change producing it (in this case the motion of the magnet).

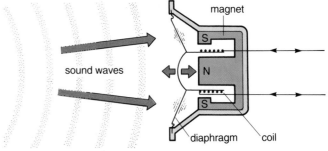

The moving-coil microphone

Storing information using magnetism

Magnetism has become very important in the modern world for storing information. It is used to record sound on audio tape, pictures on video tape, and data on computer diskettes. Credit cards and cash dispenser cards have a magnetic strip which stores details of the cardholder's bank account.

Computer disk drives, video recorders, and cassette players are designed for their own special purposes, but they record and play back using the same principles. We can understand these by studying how sound is recorded on magnetic tape.

Recording sound

Audio cassettes use plastic tape coated with a fine powder of magnetic material. This is mainly iron oxide, Fe_2O_3, sometimes mixed with other metal oxides to give better results.

To record on a blank cassette, the sound is turned into an electrical signal by a microphone. This signal is then sent to an electromagnet called a **recording head**. The signal varies the strength of the magnetic field in the narrow gap between the poles of the electromagnet. This magnetizes the particles in the coating of the tape as it is pulled past. The pattern of the magnetism then matches the signal from the microphone. Once the tape has passed the recording head the particles stay magnetized unless the tape is demagnetized or recorded over.

Playback

When a recorded audio cassette is played, a motor pulls the tape past a **playback head** which is just like the recording head. In fact, most cassette players use the same head for both jobs. This time the varying magnetic field of the particles in the tape induces a small current in the wires around the head. The signal is amplified and then fed into a loudspeaker where it is turned into sound which matches the original.

These can all be used to store information magnetically.

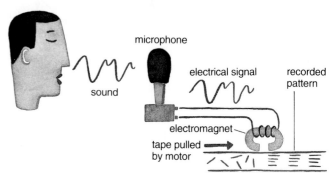

Recording on audio tape

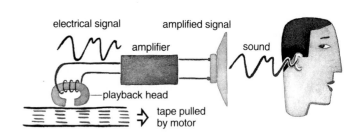

Playback of a recording on audio tape

Activities

1 Conduct a survey at home or at school to investigate how common magnetic recording is. Find the answers to the following questions:

a) How many audio cassettes are there at home/school?

b) How many cassette players are there?

c) Is there a video recorder?

d) How many video cassettes are there? What is their total playing time?

e) Is there a computer?

f) Does the computer use tape or diskettes?

g) How many tapes or diskettes are there at home/school?

h) On average, how many credit cards or other cards with magnetic recording strips does an adult carry?

2 A typical computer diskette can store around a megabyte of information. (One megabyte means 1 048 576 bytes – a byte can store one character. A character is a letter, a number, a punctuation mark, or even a space!) Calculate roughly how many pages of typing could be stored on a diskette.

Electrostatics

Lightning is nature's most spectacular demonstration of **static electricity**. The same effect can be seen on a smaller scale when a nylon jumper is taken off; crackling can be heard and, in a dark room, small sparks can be seen. There are lots of tricks you can do to demonstrate static electricity, and it also has some very important applications.

The effects of static electricity are referred to as **electrostatics**.

Lightning is the result of a build-up of static electricity in the atmosphere.

Activities

1   Rub a plastic ruler with a dry cloth and then hold it just above some small pieces of paper. The paper will be attracted to the ruler.

2   Rub an inflated rubber balloon on a woollen jumper and then hold it against a wall. The balloon may stick to the wall.

3   Turn on a tap so that a thin, steady stream of water runs into the sink. Rub a plastic pen vigorously on a piece of material and then hold it close to the stream of water. The water will be attracted towards the pen.

These activities show that insulating materials like plastic, rubber, and glass become charged with electricity when they are rubbed. They can then attract other objects.

Other experiments show that there are two types of electrical charge: positive (+) and negative (−). When rubbed, some materials like polyethene become negatively charged. Others, like Perspex, become positively charged.

Electrostatic forces

The forces between two charged plastic rods can be studied by hanging one from an insulating thread and bringing the other close to it.

The results of the experiment can be written as:

● **Like charges repel, unlike charges attract.**

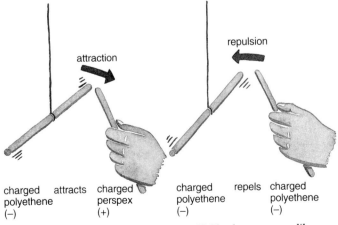

charged attracts charged | charged repels charged
polyethene perspex | polyethene polyethene
(−) (+) | (−) (−)

There is a force between two charged objects. Unlike charges attract; like charges repel.

A theory for static electricity

All materials are made up of **atoms** (see page 42). The diagram shows a model of an atom. In the nucleus there are particles called **protons**. These carry a positive charge. Around the nucleus are particles called **electrons**. These carry a negative charge. (There are only two types of charge.) Normally atoms are **neutral**. They have equal numbers of negative electrons and positive protons.

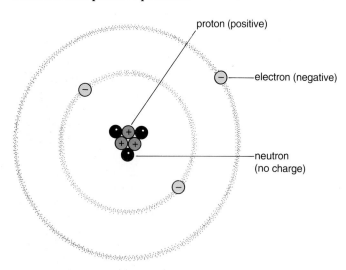

In this model of the atom there are two types of charged particle: electrons (−) and protons (+). Neutral objects contain equal numbers of positive and negative charges.

Rubbing a material with a cloth can pull away electrons. This leaves the material positively charged.

Sometimes the material pulls electrons from the cloth. This gives it a negative charge. Notice that it is always the electrons which move. This is because they are much lighter than protons.

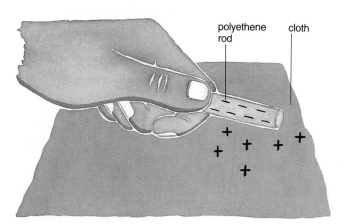

As the polyethene rod is rubbed, some electrons are pulled from the cloth. The rod becomes negatively charged . . . and the cloth becomes positively charged.

Using the theory

Example 1. A charged plastic rod can pick up a neutral piece of paper. This is because the charges on the rod separate some of the charges in the paper. Notice that this does not make any new charge. It just makes some electrons move closer, leaving unbalanced charges behind.

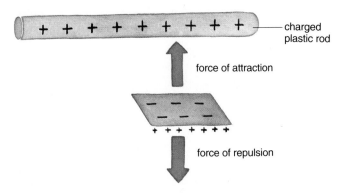

Example 2. In a warm, dry room with a nylon carpet, you may get an electric shock when touching a metal filing cabinet or a door handle. Friction between your shoes and the carpet charges you, as shown in the diagram. When you touch the door handle the charge can flow through the door to Earth. (*Note:* the Earth is so large it can take excess electrons or supply them without becoming charged.)

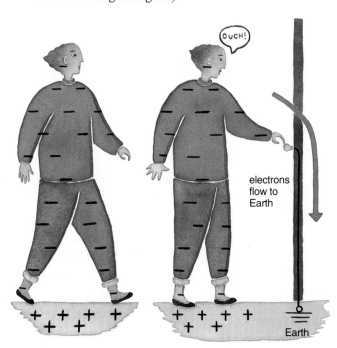

Person (and carpet) charged by friction

Person feels shock as charge flows to Earth as a current

112

Applications of electrostatics

Electrostatics has many important applications. Some of them are given here.

Electrostatic precipitation

Steel-making, producing electricity at coal-fired power stations, cement-making, and other industrial processes make smoke. The smoke which leaves factory chimneys contains small particles of ash and other solids suspended in the hot gases. When this ash is breathed in it can cause health problems. It can also pollute the environment by blackening buildings. One way of removing the dust is to use an **electrostatic precipitator**.

As the smoke and gases go up the chimney they pass wires at very high negative voltages of about 50 000 V. This causes electrons to be formed which start to move towards the earthed sides of the chimney. On the way, these charge up dust particles. The charged dust particles collect on the sides of the chimney. Every so often the chimney is given a sharp blow by a mechanical hammer so that the dust drops down into a large box for collection and disposal. In a power station up to 50 tonnes of dust can be collected in one hour!

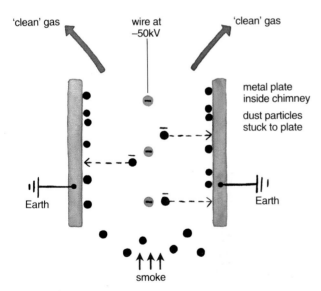

The wires at −50 kV charge up the dust particles in the smoke. These then move across to the earthed metal plates. Clean gases leave the chimney.

Photocopying

Photocopiers contain a drum coated with a material called selenium. This can be charged up, but it loses its charge in bright light. In the copier, a bright light reflects from the paper and an image is formed on the drum. The black parts of the image keep their charge but the white parts become neutral. Fine carbon dust (called **toner**) is blown on to the drum, but only sticks to the charged parts. A piece of paper is then pressed on to the drum, picking up the carbon dust pattern. The paper then passes through a heater where the toner is baked on.

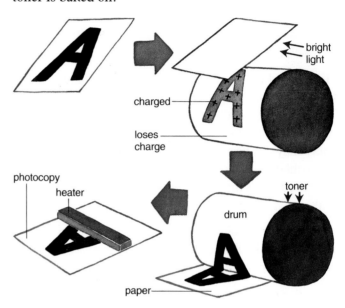

Stages in making a photocopy

Paint spraying

Paint spraying gives a high-quality, even finish to metal surfaces. Cars are sprayed with several layers of paint during their manufacture. However, paint spraying is messy and much of the paint is wasted. The quality and efficiency of spray painting can be improved by charging the paint droplets in the spray and charging the metal objects with the opposite charge. This attracts the paint droplets on to the charged surface.

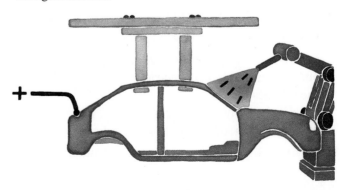

Using electrostatics to make paint spraying more efficient

Dangers of static electricity

Nearly all of us have experienced small electric shocks due to static electricity when taking off nylon clothes or getting out of a car on a dry summer's day. The voltage generated by the static electricity in these cases may be very high, up to several thousand volts, but the current is very small and unlikely to cause any real harm. The danger is that the spark caused as the charge flows could ignite explosive materials. There have been occasions when oil tankers have exploded when their tanks were being cleaned. Scientists believe that static electricity was to blame.

High-speed water jets are used to clean the tanks. The fine spray which is produced is electrically charged. This does not usually cause problems, but if larger drops of water or sediment pass through the charged spray they can become charged. If these pass close to an earthed piece of metal a high energy spark can be produced. This may ignite inflammable gases in the tank.

To prevent explosions the air and fuel vapour in the tanks should be flushed out with the exhaust gases from the ship's engines. These are not explosive.

A similar potential problem arises when aviation fuel is pumped at high speed into an aircraft. There could be a build-up of static electricity which could cause a spark. To prevent this, a metal strap is used to connect the fuel hose and the aircraft to Earth before large voltages can build up.

Questions

1 A scientist makes a new plastic called 'polyplas'. How would you find out whether 'polyplas' becomes positively or negatively charged when rubbed with material?

2 Explain, using diagrams, how a Perspex rod becomes positively charged when rubbed with a cloth. (Remember it is the electrons which move.)

3 a) Explain why, on a hot day, a person getting out of a car may get an electric shock when he or she touches the door.
b) Explain why this does not usually happen on a wet day. (Remember, water is a good conductor.)

4 Explain why a balloon rubbed on a woollen jumper will stick to a wall. (*Hint:* why does a charged rod attract a piece of paper?)

5 A student wants to stick two pieces of paper

Did a spark cause this damage?

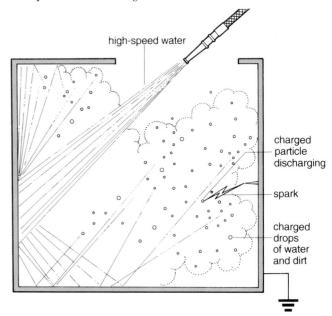

A spark can cause an explosion if the tank contains fuel vapour.

together using adhesive tape (an insulator). She pulls the tape from the roll but as she puts it close to the pieces of paper they move up towards the sticky tape. Suggest why this is.

6 Static electricity can damage some delicate electronic chips. Suggest why workers who make the chips at the factory wear shoes with conducting soles and are connected to their metal work benches by a metal strap or chain when working on these chips.

7 Photocopiers are very common, but not many people understand them. Write notes explaining to a friend how they work.

Electronics and information technology

In recent years a large number of electronic devices have been developed which have changed our homes and our work dramatically. Some of these are shown below.

Calculator. *Uses electronic circuits to solve mathematical problems quickly and accurately.*

Digital watch. *Uses an electronic timing circuit. These timers can be used in other devices.*

Central heating control unit. *Programmable electronic circuits allow easy control and are more reliable than mechanical switches.*

Computer. *Used for solving mathematical problems, business purposes, and . . . games!*

Electronic organ. *Uses electronic circuits to produce musical notes and rhythms.*

Satellite communications. *Used for international communications, military purposes, and satellite television.*

The electronics industry has worked to make electronic circuits smaller and cheaper. Mass production of **integrated circuits**, sometimes called **microchips**, has made things like digital watches and calculators much cheaper. They are also much more reliable and have more functions. Modern computers which sit on an office desk have more power than the early computers which filled a complete room.

One use of electronic systems which is becoming increasingly important is called **information technology**. Information such as words, numbers, and pictures is turned into electrical signals. This **data** can be stored in a computer's memory, rearranged using computer programs, printed on paper, or even sent down telephone lines to another computer. Information technology is changing the way that offices, shops, and even schools are working.

Activities

1 Carry out a survey of your friends and relatives to find out how much electronics affects their lives. Find out what percentage of the people interviewed have at least one of the following of their own or in their family:

calculator, digital watch, computer, satellite television, compact disc (CD) player, television with an information system such as Prestel or Teletext.

The diagram opposite shows the kind of trace produced when someone talks into a microphone connected to an oscilloscope. The voltage signal matches the **frequency** (pitch) and **amplitude** (loudness) of the person's voice. This is called an **analogue signal**.

Electronic circuits like those used in computers usually use information in the form of **digital signals**. These have just two voltage levels; on and off, or high and low. Because there are only two levels this is sometimes called a **binary signal**. By using 1 for on and 0 for off we can store numbers and other information.

Electronic circuits like the **central processing unit** (CPU) of a computer can store, add, subtract, and move these pieces of information.

Digital information can be put into a computer using a keyboard. Some systems use a scanner to take information from a printed **bar code**. The white and black lines give the high and low voltages of the digital signal. The information then goes directly into the computer. In shops the computer sends the price to the till and also counts the items sold for stock control.

Wordprocessing

Perhaps the most popular application of information technology is **wordprocessing**. This is a bit like typing, but a computer is used to store all the letters and punctuation marks as electronic bytes. A set of programs called a **software package** then displays these on the screen just like a typewritten page. But, because the characters are electronic signals, they can be erased, changed, or even moved around the screen. This makes wordprocessing much more useful than typing because documents can be corrected before printing.

Questions

1 Draw the electronic signal for the byte 01101101.

2 What is **a)** a bit **b)** a byte **c)** a kilobyte **d)** a megabyte?

3 Explain how barcode readers are used at supermarket checkouts. What are their advantages for **a)** the shop owner **b)** the customer?

4 Explain how a wordprocessor could help you with your school work.

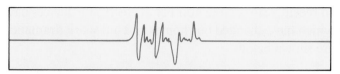

An analogue sound signal

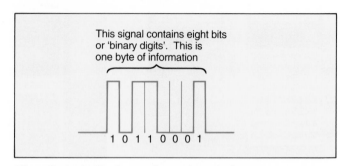

This signal contains eight bits or 'binary digits'. This is one byte of information

1 0 1 1 0 0 0 1

Electronic circuits like the central processing unit of a computer can store, add, subtract, and move these pieces of information.

ISBN 0-19-918292-2

9 780199 182923

A barcode contains information about the product. It can be read by a shop's computer system.

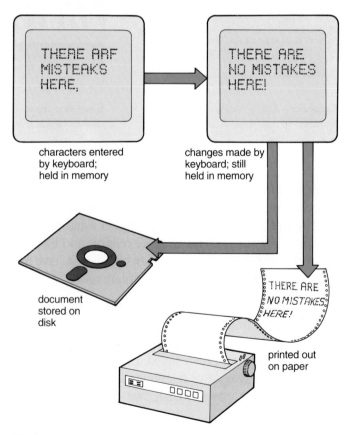

THERE ARF MISTEAKS HERE,

characters entered by keyboard; held in memory

THERE ARE NO MISTAKES HERE!

changes made by keyboard; still held in memory

document stored on disk

THERE ARE NO MISTAKES HERE!

printed out on paper

Wordprocessing allows the production of printed documents without errors.

Monitoring experiments

Computers can take in information quickly, store it in their memories, process it, and then give it back in a useful form. They are therefore very useful for controlling and monitoring experiments. This is particularly important when the changes being measured happen very quickly, when they happen very slowly, or when they are dangerous to observe. For example, a computer can record the current through a light bulb in the first few milliseconds after it has been switched on. It could also measure the growth of a plant over a few days or the radioactivity inside a nuclear reactor.

The experiment must be arranged to give an electrical signal so a **transducer** is used. This converts physical signals into electrical signals. A **thermistor** can be used where temperature is being measured or a **light-dependent resistor** where light intensity is changing.

The analogue signal is changed to a digital signal and then fed into the computer. The computer has a program which tells it what to do with the information. (Programs like this are called **software**.) The software then gives a display on the screen or prints it out on paper.

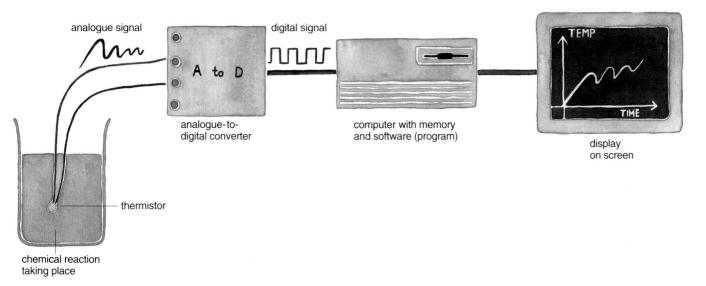

Monitoring an exothermic chemical reaction

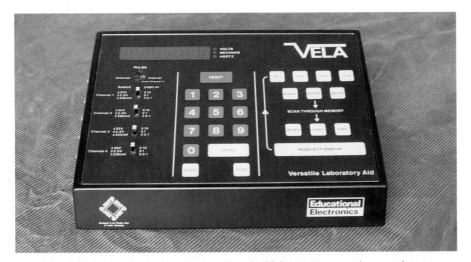

VELA is an electronic data storage device used in school laboratories to monitor experiments. Different programs (software) can make VELA act as a voltmeter, an ammeter, a thermometer, a data-logging device, and many other things.

Questions

1 State two advantages of using a computer to record measurements during an experiment.

2 A student uses a computer to measure how long a bell rings for after it has been hit once.

   a) Draw a block diagram to show how the apparatus should be set up.

   b) What transducer should be used to turn the sound of the bell into an electrical signal?

3 Suggest why different software is needed for different experiments.

Communications

Analogue signals can be used for sending information, but they are easily distorted so the message can be corrupted. You may have had difficulty understanding a telephone conversation on a bad line, or your television picture may not be clear during bad weather. Digital signals are also distorted, but because they can only have the value 1 or 0, they are easily 'cleaned up' when they are received at the other end. This makes digital signals very useful for sending information quickly and accurately. The diagram below shows how a letter can be sent to another country using a **fax** (facsimile) machine.

analogue signal
before transmission

analogue signal
after transmission

digital signal
before transmission

digital signal
after transmission

digital signal
after 'cleaning up'

Digital signals can be transmitted with little loss of quality. This means that the information received is accurate.

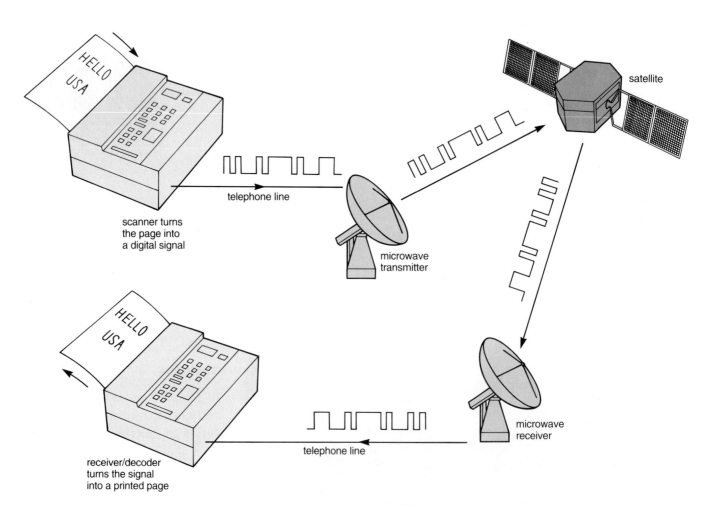

scanner turns
the page into
a digital signal

telephone line

microwave
transmitter

satellite

microwave
receiver

receiver/decoder
turns the signal
into a printed page

telephone line

Fax machines can 'send' printed material including diagrams and photographs by coding the image as a digital signal.

Information technology is very useful in many ways, but it can be abused. The data held on computer about people such as their address, their medical history, and their financial position should not be given to others who might misuse it. To protect people, organizations like the police, banks, and hospitals should have computer security systems. There is also a law called the Data Protection Act which allows people to find out what information is held about them on computer.

1 A student has a magnetic compass. He also has three metal bars painted to look the same. He knows that one is copper, one is unmagnetized iron, and the other is a permanent magnet. Describe how he could find out which bar was the magnet.

2 The diagram shows a piece of iron held by attraction to a magnet.

a) Copy the diagram. Mark on the iron bar where the induced N and S poles are.

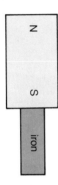

b) One theory of magnetism uses the idea that iron contains 'molecular magnets' or magnetic domains which can line up in magnetic fields. Use diagrams to explain how an unmagnetized iron bar is attracted to a magnet. (Use the symbol → to show the direction of a domain.)

3 Explain why a d.c. motor has   **a)** a commutator   **b)** carbon brushes and   **c)** an iron armature.

4 A credit card has a magnetic strip on the back.
a) Using your knowledge of tape recording, suggest how data could be stored on the strip.
b) At a shop the assistant slides the card through a machine which reads the information. Suggest how the machine might work.
c) A science teacher teaching magnetism carried magnets in her pocket, which also contained a bank cash card. The next day the cash dispenser at the bank would not accept the card. Suggest why.

5 **a)** What is the difference between an analogue signal and a digital signal?
b) Why are digital signals more use than analogue signals for sending information over long distances?

6 A compact disc (CD) stores music as a digital signal. A record stores the same music as an analogue signal. Explain why a CD player usually sounds better than a record player.

7 Write a short essay starting: 'All students should be provided with a computer and wordprocessing software because . . .'.

8 **a)** What information is likely to be held on computer about you?
b) What information is likely to be held on computer about your parents?
c) Why is a data protection act necessary?

What are oscillations and waves?

How can we use them?

What is meant by frequency and wavelength?

What is the electromagnetic spectrum?

How does visible light behave?

How can we use electromagnetic waves?

Sound waves travel from musical instruments to our ears. Knowledge of the science of waves helps architects design concert halls with good acoustics. In some circumstances sound can be a nuisance and even cause damage.

This telescope receives radio waves sent out by very distant stars. Understanding them helps us to understand more about the history of the universe.
We use radio waves for communication. Radio and television programmes are transmitted by waves and received in our homes.

Water waves arriving at a beach. Surfers may find large waves exciting but the constant pounding of waves erodes our coast. In other places the waves deposit sand and stones, building up the land.

This oven uses microwaves to heat food rapidly.
Microwaves can also be used for communications. By using satellites in orbit around the Earth messages can be sent over large areas using microwaves.

Vibrations and the **waves** they cause play an important part in our everyday lives. We hear sound waves wherever we go. Some, like music, are pleasant, but others are irritating and dangerous. We also see light waves scattered from the objects around us. Our senses cannot detect radio waves but we can use them to send information, for example in the form of television programmes. We can feel the warmth produced by infra-red radiation and we can use microwaves to cook food.

The science of waves is well understood. The simple ideas in this chapter can be used to explain nearly all aspects of wave behaviour, from the very smallest waves due to vibrating atoms to the large water waves we see on our beaches.

Activities

1 Count and list the devices in your home which produce light waves.

2 Count and list the devices in your home which are designed to produce sound waves.

3 Count and list all the devices in your home which are designed to receive radio waves (including televisions).

4 Describe how your life would be different if radios and televisions did not exist.

Oscillations

A pendulum clock keeps good time because the pendulum moves backwards and forwards regularly. We call this type of movement an **oscillation**. Many mechanical systems oscillate if they are disturbed. For example, a child's swing will swing backwards and forwards if it is pushed once. Similarly a mass on a spring will bounce up and down if it is pulled down and then released. Because oscillations are regular they can be used for timing.

The time taken for one complete oscillation is called the **period**. Often we need to know how many oscillations are completed in one second. This is the **frequency** of the oscillation. For example, if a pendulum has a period of $^1/_2$s it will make two complete swings in 1 s. Its frequency is 2 cycles per second.

We can see that:

frequency = 1/period

Usually the frequency is written in units called **hertz** (Hz). 1 Hz = 1 cycle per second.

It is not only large things that oscillate. Even the atoms in a crystal vibrate. For example, a modern quartz watch keeps very good time because it contains a quartz crystal which vibrates regularly several thousand times every second.

Investigating oscillators

A simple pendulum can be made by hanging a bob on a length of string as shown in the diagram. When the bob is pulled to one side, it gains gravitational potential energy. When the bob is released this turns to kinetic energy as the bob starts to move. As it passes the centre (rest) position the bob starts to slow down and the energy changes back to potential energy . . .

During each oscillation the pendulum loses some energy due to friction, so the size or **amplitude** of the swing gets less until eventually it stops. However, the period of the pendulum does not change.

One oscillation is often too fast to time so we can use a stopwatch to time, say, 20 oscillations and then calculate the average time for one.

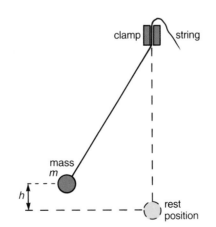

clamp   string

mass
m

h

rest
position

The mass is higher than its rest position. It has gravitational potential energy, mgh.

Activities

1 Set up a pendulum as shown and then investigate how its period depends on the length of the pendulum. Record your results in a table. (Don't forget to time complete oscillations.)

Measure the period for five different lengths. You will find that the period increases as the pendulum is made longer. Does doubling the length double the period? Can you find a pattern?

2 Using the same apparatus investigate whether changing the mass of the pendulum bob changes the time for one oscillation. (You will need to find a way of increasing the mass of the bob without changing the length of the pendulum.)

Questions

1 What is meant by
a) oscillation **b)** period
c) frequency?

2 A child on a swing goes backwards and forwards 100 times in five minutes. Calculate **a)** the period of the oscillation and **b)** the frequency in hertz.

3 The moon moves around the Earth once every 28 days (roughly). Work out the period of this 'oscillation' in seconds.

4 A pendulum clock is losing time.
    a) Is the period too long or too short?
    b) Should the pendulum be made shorter or longer?

More oscillators

There are many mechanical systems other than pendulums which oscillate. For example, the stretched string on a guitar oscillates when plucked (see page 130). Springs are also good oscillators.

The diagram shows a mass on a spring resting at the equilibrium position. When the mass is pulled down, energy is stored in the stretched spring. When released the mass starts to move upwards, accelerated by the force of the spring. It shoots past the rest position and starts to compress the spring. The compressed spring gives a force downwards. This force slows the mass down until it just stops. Then the mass accelerates downwards past the rest position, and stretches the spring again. The motion keeps repeating itself. Like the pendulum, a mass oscillating on a spring keeps good time. During each oscillation the mass loses some of its energy to the air due to air resistance. The spring also heats up a bit as it is continually stretched and compressed.

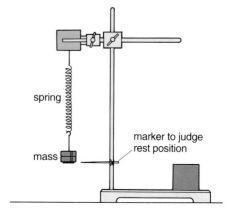

Apparatus for investigating oscillations in a spring

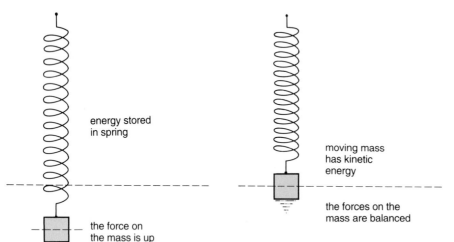

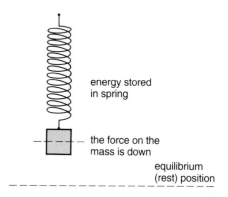

Activities

1 Set up a mass on a spring oscillator as shown. Investigate how the period of oscillation changes as the mass is changed. Measure the period for at least five different masses. Can you find a relationship?

2 Set up a loaded beam oscillator as shown in the diagram. When the weighted end of the beam is pulled down and then released, the beam and the mass at the end oscillate. In fact it is the elasticity of the beam which provides the force in this oscillator. As you push the end of the beam down the top edge is stretched a bit and the surface underneath is compressed slightly.

Investigate how the period of oscillation changes as the length of the beam is altered. Measure the period for at least four different lengths. Can you find a relationship?

Investigate how the period varies with the mass taped to the end of the beam. Can you find a relationship?

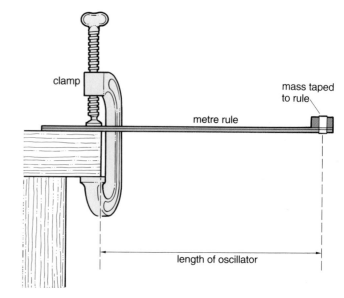

A loaded beam oscillator

Resonance

All things oscillate (if only for a short time) when they are pushed and released or even hit sharply. For example, a child on a swing swings backwards and forwards several times with just one push. We call the frequency of these 'free' oscillations the **natural frequency**. If we put more energy into the swing at just the right time, i.e. as the swing reaches the end of an oscillation, the amplitude gets greater and the child goes higher and higher. This is called **resonance**.

Resonance can cause a great deal of damage. This can be demonstrated by a trick which some opera singers can do. When a drinking glass is tapped with a spoon it makes a ringing sound as it oscillates. When the singer sings at exactly the same note, the sound wave makes the glass start to vibrate at its natural frequency. If the singer keeps singing at this frequency the oscillations in the glass get bigger and bigger due to resonance. Eventually the glass shatters.

Tall structures like chimneys also oscillate. Sometimes when the wind blows, vortices form as the air swirls around (see page 209). As the vortices break away the chimney vibrates. If resonance occurs the chimney sways further and further, perhaps eventually falling down. Some tall chimneys have spirals of metal around them to prevent the vortices that would cause oscillations.

Bridges can also oscillate as the wind blows past them. In a famous incident in 1940, a long suspension bridge over the Tacoma Narrows, USA, began to resonate as the wind blew past it. The oscillations got bigger and bigger until the bridge destroyed itself. Engineers now design bridges so that they are streamlined. This stops vortices forming.

Cars oscillate when they travel over ripples in the road surface. If the car is travelling at a steady speed the frequency of the bumps may match the natural frequency of the car. The car will then resonate. This may be unpleasant for the passengers, and could also cause damage to the car. To prevent this cars have shock absorbers. These use up some of the oscillation's energy and make it die away quickly. We say that the oscillations are **damped**. You can test this by pressing down on the front wing of a car and then letting go. The wing should bounce up and down but then die away very quickly within one or two oscillations. If it keeps bouncing up and down the shock absorber may need replacing.

To keep the swing going with a large amplitude it must be pushed at the right time.

*Factory chimneys often have **straikes** to prevent oscillation.*

Shock absorber on a motorcycle

Questions

1 Describe how you can make a swing go higher and higher by leaning backwards and forwards at the right times. Explain why this is a form of resonance.

2 A scientist connects a loudspeaker to a signal generator and then puts the speaker in front of a glass bowl. At a frequency of 1950 Hz the bowl cracks. Explain why.

3 Explain why a motorcycle needs a shock absorber attached to its front wheel.

4 A man notices that the television aerial on the roof of his house sways backwards and forwards when the wind blows steadily. He also notices that on some days the oscillations get so big that the aerial is in danger of snapping off.
   a) Explain why the aerial oscillates.
   b) Explain why on some days the oscillations are very big. Use the terms **natural frequency** and **resonance** in your answer.

Waves

Oscillations can be used to make waves. For example, if one end of a rope is tied to a fixed object and the other end is moved from side to side a wave can be seen moving along the rope. Notice that the person shaking the rope is putting in energy, and that the energy is moving with the wave. **Waves transfer energy from one place to another.**

This type of wave is called a **transverse wave**. It is transverse because the oscillation is from side to side at right angles to the direction in which the wave travels.

Other transverse waves can be seen in a laboratory ripple tank. As the electric motor makes the bar vibrate up and down a straight (plane) wave moves across the tank. If a small dipper is used instead then circular waves spread out across the tank. Notice that the waves move across the tank but the water level moves up and down as the wave passes. Looking at the water wave from the side we would see a shape like the wave on the rope.

This is a typical wave shape.

Frequency, wavelength, and speed

The **frequency** of a wave is the number of waves produced in one second. Frequency is measured in hertz (Hz).

The speed of a wave tells us how far each wavefront moves in one second. The speed is then calculated by:

$$\text{speed} = \frac{\text{distance travelled by wave}}{\text{time taken}}$$

The **wavelength** (λ) tells us the distance between two peaks (or two troughs).

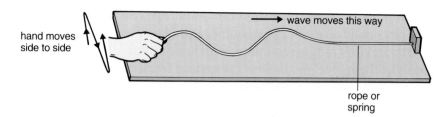

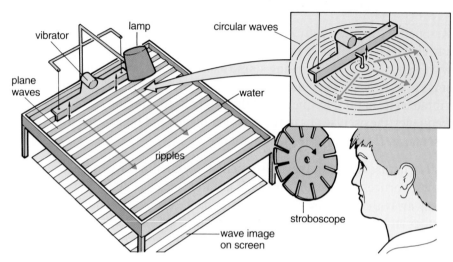

Straight (plane) and circular water waves can be investigated using a ripple tank. The speed of the stroboscope can be adjusted so that the water waves appear stationary.

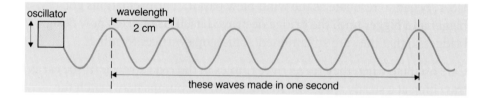

Connecting frequency, wavelength, and (wave) speed

If we look at all the waves made by an oscillator in one second we can find how frequency, wavelength, and speed are connected.

wave speed = frequency $\times$ wavelength

or in symbols,

$$v = f \times \lambda$$

Worked example

1   The end of a rope is moved up and down six times per second. Each wave in the rope is 0.2 m long. What is the speed of the wave in the rope?

$f = 6\,\text{Hz}, \lambda = 0.2\,\text{m}$
$\text{speed} = f \times \lambda = 6\,\text{Hz} \times 0.2\,\text{m}$
$\text{speed} = 1.2\,\text{m/s}$

Properties of waves: an introduction

Reflection

When moving waves meet a barrier they are **reflected**. The diagram shows what happens when plane water waves meet a flat barrier. The angle which the incident waves make with the barrier is the same as the angle made by the reflected waves. Notice that this is the same as the law of reflection for light rays meeting a mirror.

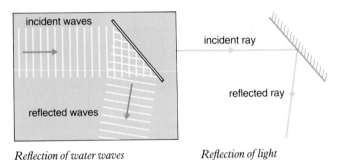

Reflection of water waves at a flat surface

Reflection of light at a flat mirror

Refraction

When water waves move into shallower water they slow down. This makes them close up giving them a shorter wavelength.

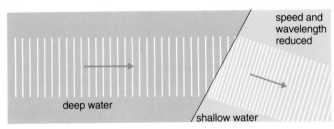

Refraction of water waves at a plane surface

This slowing down and change of wavelength is called **refraction**. When the water waves enter a shallow region at an angle then the refraction causes bending because one part of the wave slows down before the rest. On page 136 you will see how light is refracted when it enters glass from air.

Diffraction

When waves pass through a narrow gap they spread out. This effect is very noticeable when the gap is just a few wavelengths wide; a plane wave passing through a small gap spreads out as a circular wave.

Light waves are diffracted when they pass through gaps but this is only noticeable when the gaps are very small. The effect cannot be seen unaided.

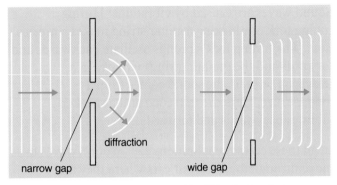

Water waves spread out as they pass through a narrow gap.

The diffraction here is almost unnoticeable because the gap is much wider than the wavelength of the waves.

Interference

Perhaps the most interesting property of waves is that they can add together or cancel each other out. This is called **interference**.

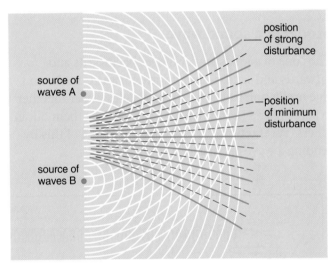

Two overlapping circular water waves give a complicated interference pattern. In some directions strong disturbances are seen. Between them the water is almost flat.

The diagram shows what happens when two circular water waves cross over. In some directions they add to give a strong wave but in other directions they cancel out leaving the water almost flat.

Constructive interference: *the two waves add together to give a bigger wave.*

Destructive interference: *the two waves cancel each other out.*

Sound as a wave

Sound waves are caused by vibrations. Hitting a tuning fork or plucking a guitar string makes a musical note. The tuning fork's prongs oscillate backwards and forwards and the guitar's strings vibrate. In a television or radio the sound comes from a loudspeaker. Here the thin cone of the speaker vibrates backwards and forwards.

In all these cases the vibrations cause sound waves to move through the air to our ears where they are detected.

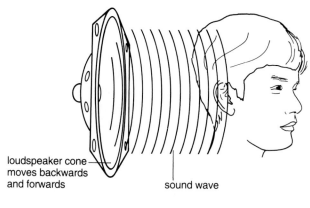

loudspeaker cone
moves backwards
and forwards

sound wave

Sound can only move where there is a material. It cannot exist in a vacuum where there are no molecules to vibrate. The diagram shows apparatus to prove this. With air in the jar the sound from the loudspeaker can be heard quite clearly. As the air is pumped out the sound gets quieter. Eventually no sound can be heard. When the air is allowed to leak back in, the sound gets louder, proving that the loudspeaker was vibrating all the time.

Model of a sound wave

The cone of a loudspeaker moves backwards and forwards and sends a sound wave forwards in the air. The oscillation forces the air molecules closer together in some places (**compression**) and spreads them out in others (**rarefaction**). We can make a model of this by sending a wave down a long 'slinky' spring.

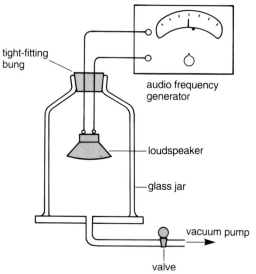

tight-fitting
bung

audio frequency
generator

loudspeaker

glass jar

vacuum pump

valve

When the air is removed, no sound can be heard. Sound cannot travel in a vacuum.

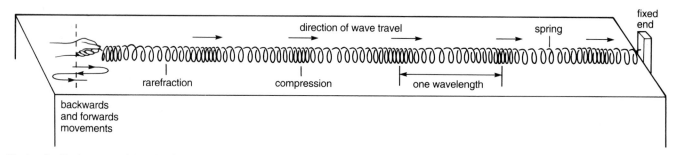

The longitudinal wave on this spring has regions of compression and rarefaction. This is like a sound wave moving in a material.

The wave on the spring and sound waves are **longitudinal** waves. The oscillations causing them are in the same direction as the wave's motion.

Activities

1 Design and carry out simple experiments to prove that sound can travel through gases, solids, and liquids.

Speed of sound

Sound waves take time to travel. A simple experiment can give an approximate value for the speed of sound in air. Two people stand 400 m apart in an open space. One has a starting pistol and the other has a stopwatch. When the gun is fired, the observer starts the watch immediately the smoke from the gun is seen. The watch is then stopped immediately the sound is heard. They do this three times and then change places and repeat the experiment in case the wind has been affecting the results. After three more timings an average time is calculated. The speed is given by:

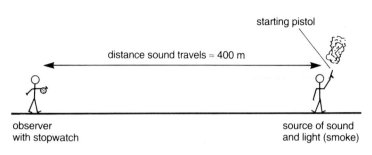

A simple experiment to measure the speed of sound

$$\text{speed of sound} = \frac{\text{distance between pistol and observer}}{\text{average time between smoke and sound}}$$

The speed of sound in air varies with temperature but is about 330 m/s at 0 °C. Sound travels at different speeds in different materials. In general it travels faster through liquids than gases and faster still through solids.

Questions

1 Science fiction films often show battles between spaceships. What would someone in space hear if an enemy spaceship exploded? Explain your answer.

2 A spectator at an athletics meeting is sitting about 200 m from the starter. She notices that the runners start off before she hears the starting pistol. Explain why.

3 At a swimming gala the time judges are at one end of the 33 m pool and the starter is at the other. They start their watches when they see the smoke from the starting pistol. Calculate what difference it would make if they waited to hear the sound before starting their watches.

4 In a thunderstorm the thunder is made at the same time as the lightning. Explain why an observer 1600 m away hears the thunder about 5 s after she sees the lightning. What time difference would there be if the storm was 2500 m away?

Finding distance using echoes

Ultrasound

The sound that we hear is a pressure wave in the air. Some pressure waves have a frequency too high for the human ear to detect. These are called **ultrasound**. They can be used at sea for finding depths or detecting shoals of fish. Because they can penetrate human tissue they can also be used to investigate inside the human body. The photograph shows an ultrasound source being used to study an embryo in the womb. The echoes from different substances and tissues are interpreted by the electronic equipment and shown on the monitor as a picture. This is a safe way of checking that the baby is developing normally.

Ultrasonic echoes allow the developing baby to be monitored safely.

Interference in sound

Sound waves interfere just like water waves. This can be shown by attaching two loudspeakers to the same audio signal generator as shown in the diagram. As you walk about in front of the speakers you find that the sound gets louder and quieter in a regular pattern. At the positions of maximum loudness the waves are arriving in step (**constructive interference**). Where the sound is very quiet the waves are arriving half a cycle out of step (**destructive interference**).

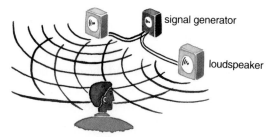

The two loudspeakers are driven by the same signal generator. Between them are areas of louder and quieter sound caused by interference.

Sonic booms

When a supersonic aeroplane like Concorde flies at the speed of sound a loud boom is heard on the ground below. This can be annoying to people living below and can cause damage to buildings. The boom is caused by constructive interference of sound waves.

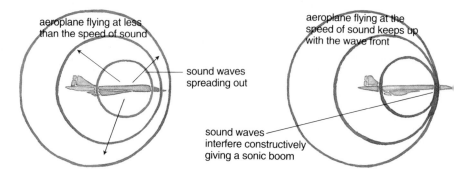

When an aeroplane breaks the sound barrier, i.e. flies faster than the speed of sound, a sonic boom is heard.

Sound pollution

The world has become so noisy that many people think of unnecessary sound as a form of pollution. You have probably had headaches caused by too much noise, but the effects can be much more serious. A very loud sound like an explosion can cause the thin membrane of the eardrum to split causing pain and deafness. People who work in noisy factories for long periods may also suffer loss of hearing if the small bones in the ear are damaged by the constant vibration.

To reduce noise pollution there are laws to limit sound levels of machines, vehicles, and even music at rock concerts. Where noise cannot be avoided ear defenders should be worn.

Sound can damage the ears. Our environment can be polluted by noise.

Questions

1 List 10 unnecessary sounds which you think contribute to sound pollution in local streets.

2 What laws do you think could be introduced to reduce noise pollution?

3 **a)** Explain why people on the ground hear a sonic boom when Concorde breaks the sound barrier (flies faster than the speed of sound).
b) Explain why a sonic boom can break the windows of houses.
c) Concorde is not allowed to 'go supersonic' until it is over the sea. Why is this a disadvantage for the passengers and an advantage for people living under its flight path?

4 Give two reasons why ultrasonic waves are useful in medicine.

Music and sound waves

Musical instruments make sound waves at frequencies which we find pleasing. These **notes** are then put together as music.

Stringed instruments produce notes by vibrating strings or wires. Percussion instruments are struck to make them vibrate.
Wind instruments produce notes when the air inside them vibrates.

Frequency and pitch

A signal generator connected to a loudspeaker gives a musical note. By adjusting the frequency of the generator the frequency of the note can be changed. When the frequency is low the notes heard have a low pitch. When the frequency is increased the notes have a higher **pitch**.

A young person with normal hearing can hear notes from very low frequencies of about 10 Hz up to about 20 000 Hz. Older people may have a reduced hearing range. Some other animals can hear higher notes.

frequency	notes
35 000 Hz	upper limit of hearing for dogs
20 000 Hz	upper limit of human hearing
10 000 Hz	shrill whistle
1 000 Hz	soprano singer
256 Hz	middle note on piano (middle C)
30 Hz	lowest note on piano

Waveforms

Musical notes can be displayed by connecting a microphone to a cathode ray oscilloscope (see page 186). A pure musical note from a tuning fork or from a signal generator has a typical smooth wave shape. If the note is played more loudly the amplitude of the wave gets bigger but the number of waves per second (the frequency) stays the same.

Other instruments can give the same basic frequency as the tuning fork but have other frequencies or **overtones** added in. This makes the same note sound different on different instruments. The number and size of the overtones give the notes from different instruments a different **quality** or **timbre**.

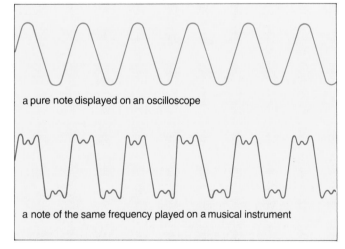

*The overtones give the note from an instrument its complicated waveform and also its **quality** or **timbre**.*

Questions

1 List three instruments which make musical notes in each of the following ways: **a)** vibrating a string **b)** vibrating air in a tube   **c)** vibrating a piece of metal or wood.

2 A tuning fork is supposed to give a pure frequency of 256 Hz. How could you check this scientifically?

3 A violin for use in the school orchestra costs about £80. A Stradivarius violin (made by Stradivari, 1644–1737) plays the same notes but costs about £500 000. Suggest two reasons why a professional violinist would prefer to play a Stradivarius.

Vibrating strings

When a stretched string or wire is plucked it vibrates. Most of the vibrations die away very quickly but some continue for much longer. These are vibrations or waves which fit exactly on the string. At the lowest or **fundamental frequency** there are **nodes** at the fixed ends where the string cannot move. In the middle there is an **antinode** where the movement is greatest. You can see from the diagram that half a wavelength fits on the string. There are higher frequency waves which will also fit on the string. These are the overtones or harmonics which give the note its timbre. Some of these are shown in the diagram.

The apparatus shown opposite is called a **sonometer**. It can be used to investigate how the note produced by a stretched string or wire can be changed. By adding more weights the tension (force) in the string can be increased. The movable bridge can be used to lengthen or shorten the vibrating section. Thicker and thinner wires can also be used. The results of changing these things are shown below.

change	result
use shorter wire	note is higher
use longer wire	note is lower
increase tension (force) in wire	note is higher
reduce tension in wire	note is lower
use thicker wire	note is lower

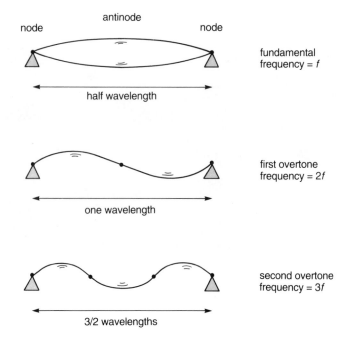

Vibrations on a string

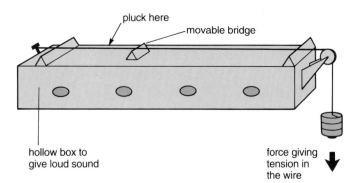

Investigating vibrations in a stretched wire

Activities

1 If you blow across the open top of a bottle you will hear a musical note. The note can be changed by pouring some water into the bottle and then blowing. (A note can also be produced by tapping the bottle with a spoon.) Investigate how the note changes as more water is added to the bottle. How do your findings compare with the result for a stretched wire?

Note that the bass (low pitch) strings on the guitar are thicker than the high pitch ones. The keys at the top allow the tension in the strings to be adjusted to tune the guitar. The guitarist can shorten the vibrating strings by pressing down with his/her fingers.

Vibrations in tubes

Air vibrating inside a closed tube or an open tube can give a musical note. This fact is used in the woodwind and brass instruments of an orchestra.

In a simple recorder, the air blown into the mouthpiece hits a sharp wedge. This breaks up the air flow and makes some of the air vibrate inside the tube. Just like the waves on a stretched string, only some of these waves will fit the length of the tube properly. These waves emerge as the notes we hear. To change the notes the player covers or uncovers the holes in the recorder. This is like changing the length of the tube.

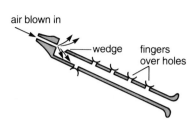

A recorder is a wind instrument. The notes are produced by vibrating air inside the tubular body of the recorder.

Modes of vibration

Blowing across the top of a bottle sets up a vibration in a closed tube. Air molecules close to the open top can vibrate a lot but those near the closed end cannot. We have an antinode at the open end and a node at the closed end. The illustrations opposite show this in diagram form. However, remember that the air molecules are really vibrating backwards and forwards (longitudinally), not from side to side.

The fundamental frequency fits just one quarter of a wavelength into the tube. The overtones have higher frequencies as shown.

If the tube is open at the end, as in a flute or recorder, there is an antinode at both ends and a node in the middle. This time the fundamental frequency fits half a wavelength in.

A closed tube gives a note one octave lower than an open tube of the same length (i.e. half the frequency).

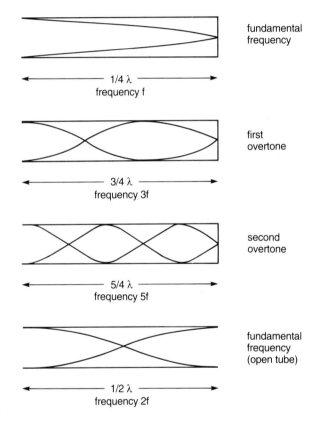

fundamental frequency

1/4 λ
frequency f

first overtone

3/4 λ
frequency 3f

second overtone

5/4 λ
frequency 5f

fundamental frequency (open tube)

1/2 λ
frequency 2f

Modes of vibration in closed and open tubes

Calculating the frequency

A flute is an open tube about 0.66 m long. The speed of sound in air is about 330 m/s. What is the lowest note a flute can play?

Answer

The fundamental note fits half a wavelength into the flute.
So one wavelength = $2 \times 0.66\,\text{m} = 1.32\,\text{m}$.
For any wave:

velocity = frequency × wavelength

$$f = \frac{v}{\lambda} = \frac{330\,\text{m/s}}{1.32\,\text{m}} = \textbf{250 Hz}$$

In fact flutes are tuned to middle C (256 Hz).

Activities

1 Find out how air is made to vibrate in **a)** a clarinet **b)** a flute **c)** a trumpet.

2 Find out how the length of the vibrating air column is changed in **a)** a trombone **b)** a flute **c)** a trumpet.

3 Blow across the hole in the end of a bicycle pump with the handle fully out. Listen how the note changes as the handle is pushed in. Explain the result in scientific terms.

Electromagnetic waves

Waves on strings, water waves, and sound waves can only move through a material. However, there is a whole family of waves which can move in a vacuum as well as in materials. These are called the **electromagnetic waves**. They can be thought of as a magnetic wave and an electric wave moving together. They are produced when molecules, atoms, or even electrons vibrate when they are given extra energy.

There are several different types of electromagnetic wave. The type of wave depends on its frequency and wavelength, but all electromagnetic waves travel at the same speed. In a vacuum they all move at about 300 000 km/s! This is sometimes called the **speed of light** because the light we see is an electromagnetic wave.

The speed of light is so great than an electromagnetic wave can travel around the world seven times in one second! The diagram shows the complete range or **spectrum** of electromagnetic waves.

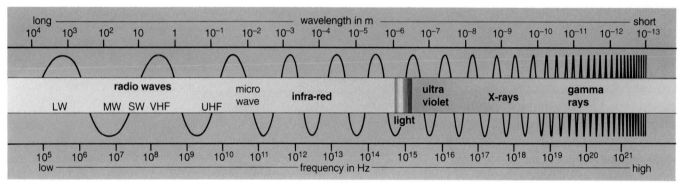

The electromagnetic spectrum

Radio waves

Radio waves have long wavelengths from about 1 m to several thousand metres. They are used to carry information over very long distances. An electrical signal coded with sound information is passed into an aerial. The aerial then sends out radio waves. This is shown in the diagrams opposite.

Radio waves reflect off layers of charged particles in the atmosphere. This means that signals can be sent around the curved surface of the Earth.

Ultrahigh frequency (UHF) radio waves are used to transmit television pictures. They cannot be reflected by the ionized layers in the atmosphere so you need a direct route between your aerial and the television company's transmitter. Alternatively the television signal can be 'bounced' off a satellite in orbit around the Earth. (See page 134.)

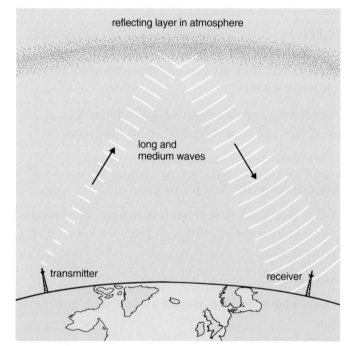

Reflection of radio waves

Questions

1 The moon is roughly 400 000 km away from the Earth. When men first walked on the Moon they sent messages home by radio. How long did it take the radio waves to reach Earth?

2 The Sun is about 150 000 000 km from the Earth. How long does it take light from the Sun to reach us?

3 Alpha Centauri is a star which is about 4 light years from Earth. A light year is the distance travelled by light in one year. How far away is Alpha Centauri in kilometres?

Sending information using radio waves

Audio signals are sounds we can hear. They have a frequency of up to about 20 000 Hz. Radio waves typically have frequencies of a few million hertz. The diagrams here show how a radio frequency signal can be shaped to carry an audio signal. The technique used here is called **amplitude modulation**.

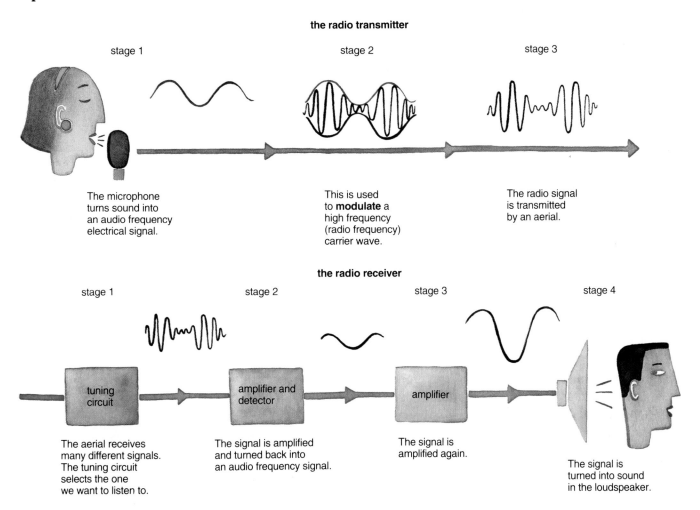

the radio transmitter

stage 1

stage 2

stage 3

The microphone turns sound into an audio frequency electrical signal.

This is used to **modulate** a high frequency (radio frequency) carrier wave.

The radio signal is transmitted by an aerial.

the radio receiver

stage 1

stage 2

stage 3

stage 4

tuning circuit

amplifier and detector

amplifier

The aerial receives many different signals. The tuning circuit selects the one we want to listen to.

The signal is amplified and turned back into an audio frequency signal.

The signal is amplified again.

The signal is turned into sound in the loudspeaker.

Sending information by radio waves

Questions

1 In some valleys people can receive radio signals perfectly well but their television pictures are fuzzy and poor. Suggest why.

2 Why does a radio set need an amplifier?

3 BBC Radio 4 broadcasts on 1500 m. This is the wavelength of its radio signal. Calculate its frequency.

4 A radio station uses a frequency of 500 kHz to broadcast. What is the wavelength of the radio waves used?

(Speed of light = 300 000 km/s.)
(Remember that for all waves $v = f \times \lambda$.)

Activities

1 Carry out a survey of houses near your home.
a) What percentage of houses have outdoor aerials?
b) Sketch the shape of a television aerial.
c) Do all the aerials in your road point in the same direction? If so, in which direction do they point? Suggest why.
d) How many houses have satellite dishes? In which direction do the satellite dishes point?

Microwaves and infra-red waves

Microwaves

Microwaves have wavelengths of a few centimetres. They are produced when electrons are made to oscillate in a specially shaped cavity. Like radio waves they can be used for communication. They can be directed towards satellites using specially shaped transmitting aerials. The satellite is placed in an orbit where it stays above the same place on Earth all the time. The satellite can then send the signal to receivers on Earth. One satellite can send signals across a huge area, so even though satellites are expensive to build and launch they are cheaper than building lots of transmitters on the ground.

Microwaves are also used in the home for cooking. In a microwave oven a transmitter sends a beam of microwaves into the food. The water molecules in the food absorb the energy from the microwaves and so the food heats up. This type of cooking is much faster than an ordinary cooker because the energy heats the food directly. In a gas or electric oven a lot of energy is wasted heating the oven itself and the air inside it.

Microwaves can cause damage to human tissue. In particular long exposure to microwaves can damage the eyes by causing cataracts. The cornea becomes cloudy and blindness may result. Modern microwave ovens have a metal grid inside the glass of the door. The metal absorbs and reflects the microwaves so that they can't escape.

Infra-red waves

Infra-red waves have wavelengths just a bit longer than the visible light that our eyes can detect. They are given out by all hot objects. They can be detected by special films or by electrical components such as phototransistors, which conduct electricity when infra-red waves fall on them. The hotter an object gets the more infra-red radiation it gives out. An infra-red picture of an engine can help an engineer to improve its efficiency or to find faults.

Infra-red waves have a heating effect when they are absorbed by materials. This is used for the medical treatment of aching or damaged muscles. A special infra-red lamp is used which gently heats the muscles. Sometimes massage is used at the same time. This helps to ease the pain.

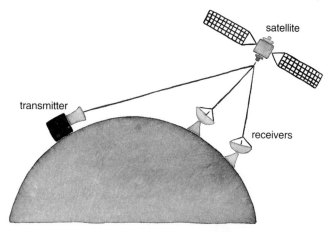
Communications satellites are used to send messages around the Earth.

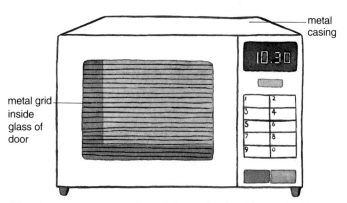
The microwaves cannot pass through the metal casing. The metal grid stops microwaves escaping through the door. A safety switch turns the microwaves off when the door is opened.

This photograph was taken at night. Special film was used which is sensitive to the infra-red radiation given out by the warm animal.

Questions

1 Explain why food cannot be cooked in metal containers in a microwave oven.

2 Microwave ovens have switches which turn them off as soon as the door is opened. Explain why.

3 Some security lights have infra-red detectors. The lights turn on automatically when anyone approaches the house. Suggest how they might work.

4 A friend says that microwave ovens cook food from the inside out. Suggest how this could be tested scientifically.

Visible light

Visible light is a small part of the electromagnetic spectrum which can be detected by our eyes. We can see objects because they scatter (reflect) this light into our eyes.

The visible spectrum can be seen by passing white light through a glass prism. The different wavelengths are refracted through slightly different angles. This is called dispersion (see page 136). Different wavelengths are seen as different colours. When Sir Isaac Newton did this experiment he thought that he could detect seven different colours in the spectrum: red, orange, yellow, green, blue, indigo, and violet.

Visible light can be detected by the eye, photographic film, phototransistors, and light-dependent resistors.

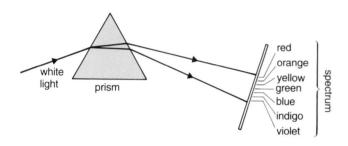

The dispersion of white light into a spectrum

Reflection of light waves

Light travelling in air is reflected when it meets a different material like shiny metal or glass. If a ray of light strikes a flat surface at an angle then it is reflected at the same angle, as shown in the diagram.

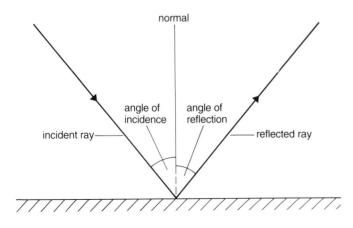

The angle of reflection is equal to the angle of incidence.

When light rays from an object strike a plane mirror all the rays are reflected in this way. The result is that we see an image when we look back into the mirror. The image appears to be the same distance behind the mirror as the object is in front. This is a **virtual image** because no rays of light actually pass through it. The image in the mirror is **laterally inverted**. (It appears swapped from left to right.)

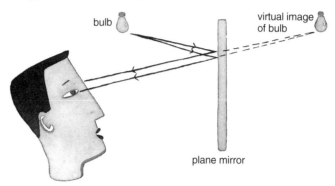

*The rays of light from the object (bulb) are reflected. The observer sees the image **behind** the mirror.*

Why are the words 'emergency ambulance' laterally inverted?

Questions

1 Draw a diagram to show what is meant by the angle of incidence and the angle of reflection.

2 Which capital letters of the alphabet look the same in a mirror?

3 A very small light bulb is placed 5 cm away from a plane mirror. Draw a full size diagram showing the bulb and the mirror. Add two rays of light from the bulb to the mirror and then carefully draw in the reflected rays. Show where the image of the bulb is.

4 **An image in a mirror is virtual and laterally inverted.** What does this statement mean?

Refraction of light

Electromagnetic waves, including light, travel at about 300 000 km/s in air but they slow down when they enter any other material such as water or glass. If a ray of light meets the new material at an angle it bends. This is **refraction**.

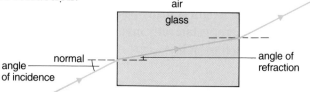

Refraction of light

The diagram shows that light entering a glass block bends towards the normal. As it leaves the glass it speeds up again and so bends away from the normal. The ray emerging form this rectangular block is parallel to the ray going in. Rays of different colours are bent through slightly different angles. In a prism this disperses the colours, spreading them out into a spectrum (see page 135).

Snell's law of refraction

When light enters a new material, the angles of incidence and refraction are connected by **Snell's law**, named after the scientist who found the relationship.

● **The sine of the angle of incidence divided by the sine of the angle of refraction remains constant. This constant is the refractive index of the material.**

The sine of an angle can be found by drawing a right-angled triangle as shown in the diagram. In fact we can find the values in trigonometry tables or from a calculator.

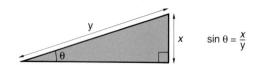

$$\sin \theta = \frac{x}{y}$$

Table of refractive indices

material	refractive index
air	1.00
water	1.33
Perspex	1.49
window glass	1.51
flint ('lens') glass	1.61

Refractive index and the speed of light

We already know that refraction is caused when light changes speed. The greater the change of speed the greater the change of direction. The **refractive index** of a material tells us the ratio of the speed of light in a vacuum to the speed in the material.

$$\text{refractive index} = \frac{\textbf{speed of light in vacuum}}{\textbf{speed of light in material}}$$

Worked example

The refractive index of glass is 1.5. Calculate the speed of light in this glass.

$$\text{refractive index} = \frac{\text{speed in vacuum}}{\text{speed in glass}}$$

$$1.5 = \frac{300\,000\,\text{km/s}}{\text{speed in glass}}$$

$$\text{speed in glass} = \frac{300\,000\,\text{km/s}}{1.5} = \textbf{200\,000\,km/s}$$

Apparent depth

One of the effects of refraction is that our brains can be tricked into thinking that pools of water are shallower or glass blocks are thinner than they really are. The **apparent depth** is given by the real depth divided by the refractive index. The refractive index of water is about $^4/_3$ so a 2 m pool only looks 1.5 m deep.

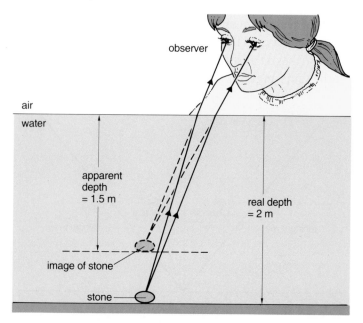

Refraction makes the water look shallower.

Refraction and the critical angle

In the diagrams below you can see what happens when the angle of incidence inside a glass block increases from 35° to 50°. At 35° most of the light gets out of the glass with just a small part being reflected. At about 42° the refracted ray just gets out of the block but much more of the light is being reflected. This is the **critical angle**. At angles greater than 42° all the light is reflected. This is called **total internal reflection**.

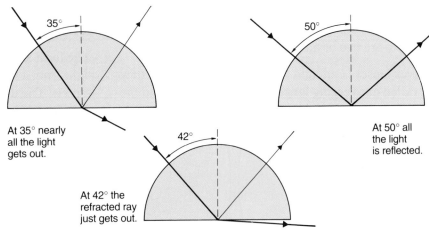

At 35° nearly all the light gets out.

At 42° the refracted ray just gets out.

At 50° all the light is reflected.

Using total internal reflection

Many optical instruments use total internal reflection inside prisms. The image is just like that formed by mirrors but there is no need for a reflective coating which can corrode.

Optical fibres

An **optical fibre** is a thin fibre of glass which light can pass down. The diagram shows that the light always hits the side of the fibre at an angle greater than the critical angle. All the light is reflected and so little energy is lost. The light emerges from the other end of the fibre almost as bright as it went in. The fibres are very thin so they can be bundled together and used as a **light pipe**.

Light pipes can be used for inspection inside machinery or even inside the human body. The outside fibres carry light down to illuminate the object. Light reflected from the object then travels up the middle fibres to a special camera or eyepiece.

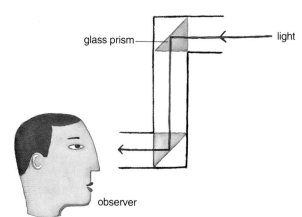

This periscope uses total internal reflection inside triangular prisms.

Optical fibres can also carry coded signals as pulses of light from a laser. These can then be changed into electrical signals at the receiving end. For example many of our telephone calls are now transmitted down light pipes which can carry several thousand conversations at once! Glass fibres are more efficient at transmitting messages than copper wires and so fewer booster stations are needed. This keeps costs low.

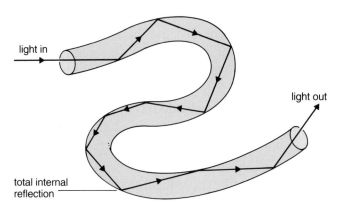

An optical fibre greatly magnified

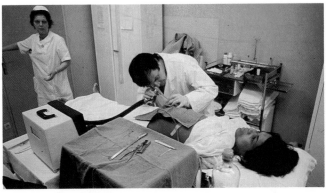

Fibre optics allow surgeons to watch as they manipulate instruments inside the body.

Lenses are pieces of glass shaped to have a focusing effect. They come in a huge variety of shapes and sizes but there are two basic shapes: **convex** and **concave**.

Convex lenses bend light towards a central axis so they are called **converging lenses**. Concave lenses bend the light away from the axis so are called **diverging lenses**.

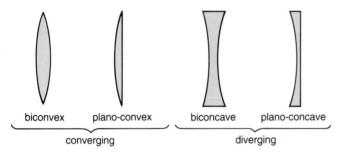

Lens shapes

The diagram shows how parallel light rays passing through a converging lens are brought together at a **focal point**. Parallel rays passing through a diverging lens are bent as if they came from a single focal point. The distance between the centre of a lens and its focal point is called the **focal length**. Powerful lenses have short focal lengths; weak lenses have long focal lengths.

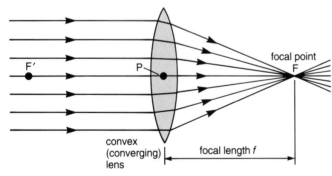

Action of a convex lens

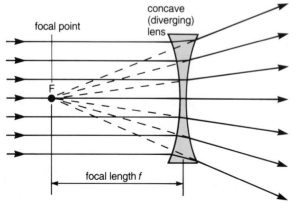

Action of a concave lens

Finding the approximate focal length of a lens

The focal length of a lens can be found by focusing light from a very distant object such as the Sun on to a screen. The distance between the centre of the lens and the screen (the focal length) is then measured.

In the laboratory it is easier to focus light from the windows on the other side of the room on to a wall or screen. The windows will be about three or four metres away so we can think of them as being fairly distant objects. When the image is sharply focused the distance between the centre of the lens and the screen can be measured. This gives a good approximation to the focal length of the lens.

When you do this experiment notice that the image is small, and upside down.

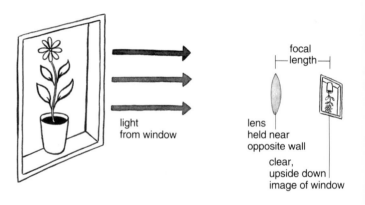

Finding the approximate focal length of a lens

Questions

1   Describe in words the shape of   **a)** a concave lens   **b)** a plano-convex lens.

2   After a practical lesson, a teacher finds that the students have not put the lenses back in the right packets. The lenses are all biconvex but some have focal lengths of 10 cm, others 20 cm, and the rest 25 cm.

   a)   How can she quickly sort the powerful 10 cm lenses from the weaker 20 cm and 25 cm lenses?
   b)   She can't see any obvious difference between the remaining lenses. How can she sort them out?

3   Explain why the experiment to measure focal length described on this page works for converging lenses but not diverging lenses.

Images formed by converging lenses

The position and size of the image formed by a convex lens depends on how far the object is from the lens. If the object is further away than the focal length of the lens then the image is **real**. This is because the lens can bring the light rays to a focus. If the object is so close that it is inside the focal length of the lens then the image is **virtual**. It cannot be seen on a screen. You see it by looking back into the lens.

We can draw ray diagrams to find what the image will be like. Usually two or three rays are drawn using these rules:

- **Any ray through the optical centre of the lens passes straight through without being bent.**
- **Any ray parallel to the axis of the lens passes through the focal point after it leaves the lens.**
- **Any ray through the focal point of the lens leaves parallel to the axis of the lens.**

Convex lens forming a small, real image of the Sun

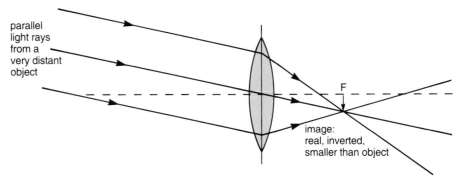

Ray diagram with the object a long way from the lens

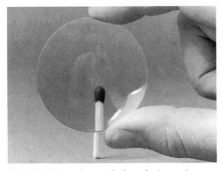

With the object close to the lens the image is magnified.

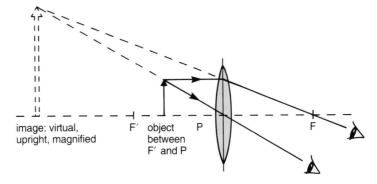

Ray diagram with the object less than one focal length from the lens

Images in concave lenses

The image formed by a concave lens is always virtual, upright, and smaller than the object.

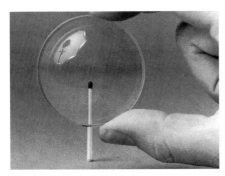

The image formed by a concave lens is smaller than the object and upright.

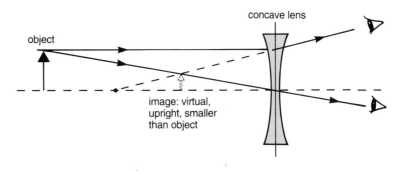

Ray diagram for an object viewed through a concave lens

Using lenses

One of the oldest and certainly the most common use of lenses is to improve the vision of people with poor eyesight. The lenses may be made of glass or plastic. They can be large lenses in spectacles or very small contact lenses worn in the eye.

Short-sighted people can see things clearly which are close but they cannot focus on things which are far away. For example they may see the print in a book but be unable to read a distant road sign. This is because the lens in the eye is too powerful or because the eyeball is too short.

Long-sighted people can see distant things clearly but cannot focus on things close to them. This may be because the lens in the eye is too weak. Old people tend to be long-sighted.

Opticians can provide lenses to focus the light from an object on the retina of the eye so that the person can see clearly. Short-sighted people need concave lenses and long-sighted people need convex lenses.

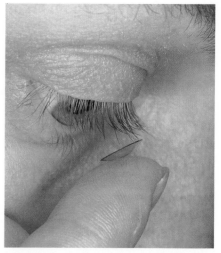

A contact lens is a thin, plastic lens which is placed on the cornea of the eye.

The camera

A **camera** has a convex lens at the front to focus light on to the film loaded into the camera. The image formed is real, smaller than the object, and upside down.

Behind the lens there is a shutter which is usually closed. This keeps all the light from the film. When the camera button is pressed the shutter opens for a short period of time (usually less than 0.01 second). This exposes the film. This image is recorded by chemicals in the film. The film is then developed and printed on special paper.

*A modern **single lens reflex** camera*

Cheap cameras have a lens fixed so that it is one focal length from the film. In photographs taken with these cameras things far away appear sharply in focus but things close to the camera are out of focus and blurred. The camera shown has a lens which can be moved backwards and forwards. This allows things which are far away *and* those close by to be brought into focus.

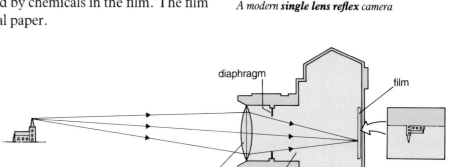

Ray diagram for a camera taking a photograph of a distant object

Activities

1 Cheap cameras have fixed lenses and so only distant things are in focus.
Design an experiment to find out how close the camera can be to the object before the photograph is blurred. If you have or can borrow a cheap camera carry out the experiment but remember that film and developing are expensive. (*Hint:* you could get away with taking just one photograph.)

2 If you have or can borrow a camera of the single lens reflex (SLR) type, design and carry out an experiment to find the effect of changing **a**) the shutter speed **b**) the size of the aperture. (*Note:* a camera with automatic controls only is not suitable for this activity.)

The telescope

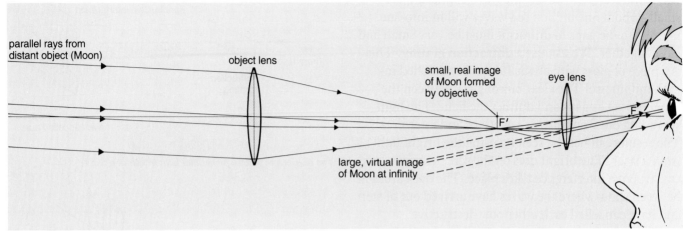

Ray diagram for a simple telescope

The simplest form of **telescope** has two lenses mounted in a long tube. The first lens, called the **objective**, is a convex lens. This brings light from the distant object into focus. A small, real image is formed. The second lens, called the **eyepiece**, is also convex but it is much more powerful than the objective.

The eyepiece can be moved so that the small image formed by the objective is at, or just inside, its focal length. It then acts as a magnifying glass and so a much larger image is seen. In this astronomical telescope the image is upside down. This doesn't matter much when you are looking at stars!

Binoculars

Binoculars are just like two telescopes joined together; one for each eye. To make them shorter, and therefore easier to use, two prisms are used to reflect the light and to turn the image up the right way.

Prisms inside binoculars make the image upright.

The projector

A **projector** makes a bright, real, and magnified image of a slide or film on a screen. The main parts of a projector are shown in the diagram.

The concave mirror reflects light from the bulb back towards the slide. The condenser lenses bend the light so that it all passes through the slide. These two parts make the image as bright as possible.

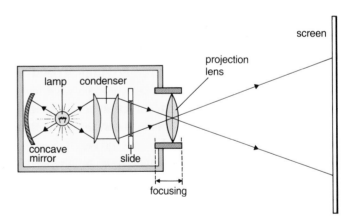

A slide projector

The projection lens is a converging lens and this brings the light to a focus on the screen. It can be moved backwards and forwards to keep the image in focus.

Notice that the light from the top of the slide is focused on the bottom of the screen. The image is upside down. It is also laterally inverted. This means that the slide must be put into the projector upside down and back to front.

141

Light as a wave

Visible light is a wave so it can be diffracted, and light waves interfere. However, the wavelengths are very small – about one million red waves will fit into one metre – so the gaps to diffract it must be very small and close together. We can use a **diffraction grating**. This is a piece of glass with about 1000 slits scratched in each millimetre! The clear bits of glass between the scratches act as gaps and diffract the light. The light spreading out from the gaps overlaps and interferes. The results can best be seen by using the bright light from a laser. The bright dots on the screen show where constructive interference takes place. The dark areas in between show where the waves have arrived out of step and have cancelled each other out (destructive interference).

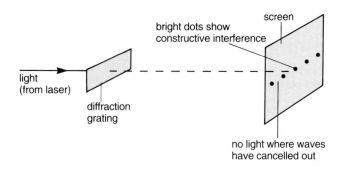

The interference pattern proves that light travels as a wave.

If white light is used the diffraction grating splits it into different colours. This is because each colour has its own wavelength and so constructive interference takes place at different angles. This can easily be seen by holding a compact disc at an angle near a window. The colours seen are due to interference of the light reflected from the reflective tracks of the compact disc.

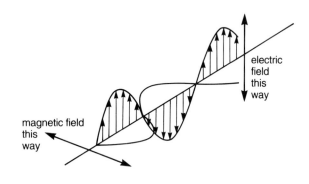

Light is an electromagnetic wave.

Polarization

All electromagnetic waves can be thought of as an electric wave travelling with a magnetic wave. Usually a light beam from the Sun or from a light bulb has lots of these waves travelling together with all the electric waves at different angles. This is called **unpolarized light**. It is possible to filter the beam so that only the electric waves in one particular direction get through. This is called **polarization**. It can be carried out with a special plastic called **Polaroid**. If two pieces of Polaroid are crossed in the beam no light can get through.

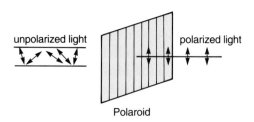

The piece of Polaroid only allows light through with its electric field in one direction.

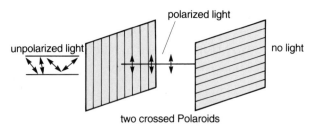

Here the second Polaroid does not allow the polarized light through.

Activities

1 On a bright day use one piece of Polaroid or one pair of Polaroid sunglasses to look at the light reflected from a very shiny surface such as the roof of a car. Gradually turn the polaroid around through 360°. What do you notice about the brightness of the reflected light seen through the Polaroid? Now do the same while looking at the blue sky (**not** the Sun). If you are very observant you may be able to prove that light is partially polarized by the atmosphere.

2 Hold two pieces of Polaroid (or two pairs of sunglasses) in front of one eye. Holding one still, slowly rotate the other one through 360°. What do you see?

3 Investigate what happens when you put a third piece of Polaroid between two crossed pieces of Polaroid and rotate it.

142

Ultraviolet light

Just beyond the violet end of the visible spectrum we find waves which have a slightly shorter wavelength. This is called **ultraviolet light** (UV). Ultraviolet light is given out by very hot objects and when certain atoms such as mercury are given energy. We also receive ultraviolet light from the Sun. It can be detected by photographic film or by chemicals which fluoresce (glow) when exposed to ultraviolet light.

Effects of ultraviolet light

Fluorescent chemicals absorb the energy from ultraviolet light and convert it into visible light. This makes them glow. Some washing powders contain fluorescent chemicals to make white clothes look brighter. A fluorescent light tube contains mercury vapour and the inside is coated with fluorescent powders. When the light is turned on the electricity makes the mercury vapour emit ultraviolet light. This then makes the powders give off white light.

Ultraviolet light can also affect living tissue. The most obvious effect is the tanning of fair skin caused by sunlight. A substance called **melanin** absorbs ultraviolet light and makes the skin turn brown. Having a suntan can make people feel healthier but too much exposure to ultraviolet light can damage the skin and cause skin cancers.

Ultraviolet light also affects natural fats in the skin and turns them into calciferol (vitamin D). Without vitamin D young children's bones do not form properly causing a disease called **rickets**. In sunny countries the sun helps to prevent this but in countries like the UK children's diets must contain enough foods with vitamin D like milk and eggs.

The ultraviolet light from the tubes of a sun lamp can tan fair skin. It can also cause damage to the eyes so goggles or sunglasses must be worn.

The ozone layer

Too much ultraviolet light would be harmful to living things on Earth. Fortunately we are protected by a layer of **ozone** gas in our atmosphere. Ozone is a special form of oxygen with three oxygen atoms joined together in each molecule. (Normal oxygen has two atoms in a molecule.) Ozone molecules absorb ultraviolet light. Without the ozone layer more people would get skin cancers. The Earth's temperature would also rise as more of the Sun's energy would get through and be trapped by other gases in the atmosphere which cause the **greenhouse effect**. Unfortunately some of the chemicals we use on Earth get into the atmosphere and break up the ozone molecules. The most common of these are called **chlorofluorocarbons** (**CFCs**). They are used in some aerosol sprays and in refrigerators and air conditioning units. Scientists have now proved that CFCs have started to make a hole in the ozone layer above the South Pole. To stop this getting worse we must reduce our use of CFCs and find harmless substitutes.

Aerosols which contain CFCs can damage the ozone layer. These products use harmless alternatives.

Activities

1 Gather information about the ozone layer. You may be able to get information from newspapers, scientific magazines, and environmental groups. Try to find the answers to these questions:

a) What would be the likely effects of destroying the ozone layer?

b) What products contain CFCs?

Coloured light

Our eyes can only detect electromagnetic waves with a small range of frequencies. However, we have already seen that white light can be split up into a range of colours called the visible spectrum (see page 135). In fact our eyes contain just three types of colour sensors. One type responds to red light, another to green light, and the third to blue light. Red, blue, and green are called the **primary colours**. If our eyes receive red, blue, and green light together we 'see' white light. This can be shown by shining three coloured spotlights on to a screen so that they overlap. Where the three primary colours combine we see white light. Where only two primary colours add we see **secondary colours**. The following table shows the rules of colour addition for light.

primary colours	colour 'seen' by eye
red + green + blue	white
red + green	yellow
red + blue	magenta
green + blue	cyan (peacock blue)

By varying the amounts of each primary colour present you can see any colour of the spectrum. This is used in the colour television.

In a black and white (monochrome) television there is an electron gun rather like the one in a cathode ray oscilloscope (see page 186). The beam of electrons is moved quickly across the screen and more slowly downwards. This gives parallel lines all over the screen. The picture is produced by varying the brightness of the spot as it moves. About 25 new pictures are produced every second so our eye sees a smoothly moving picture.

Television screens are coated with **phosphors**. These are chemicals which give out light when hit by the beam of electrons. In a colour television the screen is coated with thousands of small phosphor strips in groups of three – one which gives red light, one which gives green, and one which gives blue. The television has three separate electron guns, one for each colour. The colour seen on the screen depends on which phosphors are being struck by electrons. For example, when the red and green strips glow we see yellow.

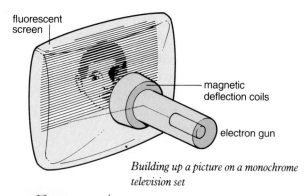

Building up a picture on a monochrome television set

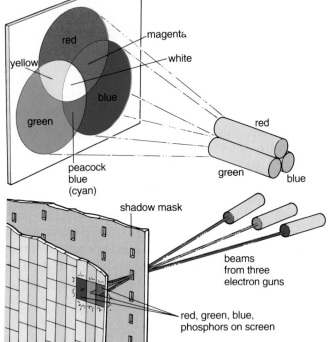

A colour television uses three electron guns

Questions

1 Name the colours of the visible spectrum. Which one has the longest wavelength?

2 Name the three primary colours for light. What colours do we get by adding the following coloured lights together:
    a) red + green **b)** blue + green **c)** cyan + red **d)** yellow + blue?

3 Explain why a colour television is more expensive than a monochrome (black and white) one.

4 Why are only three phosphors needed on a colour television screen?

5 What colours do you see on a television screen when the following phosphors glow:
    a) red + blue **b)** blue + green **c)** red + blue + green?

Looking at coloured objects

White light from the Sun or from a light bulb contains all the colours of the spectrum. Why do many objects look coloured? The answer is that the materials they are made of absorb some of the colours of the spectrum and reflect the rest. As a result we only see the colours of the reflected light. The diagram shows what happens when we look at a red rose in white light. We call chemicals which reflect only certain colours pigments. Paints, inks, and coloured crayons contain pigments. So do the petals and leaves of plants and the skins of animals. Some mixtures of pigments will absorb all the colours of the spectrum. These appear black.

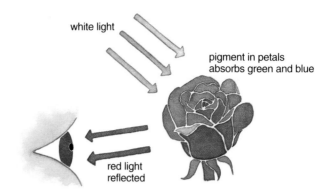
Red objects reflect red light.

Mixing pigments

There are three **primary pigment colours**: red, blue, and yellow. With them a wide range of other colours can be made. This is because the pigments do not reflect just one colour but a small part of the spectrum. For example, blue paint absorbs red, orange, and yellow light but reflects blue, green, and violet light. The diagram shows how green light is reflected from a mixture of blue and yellow pigments.

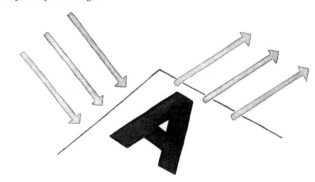
Black pigments do not reflect light.

Filters

A filter is a coloured piece of glass or plastic which lets through some colours but filters out all the others. For example, a red filter lets red light through but absorbs green and blue light. Looking through coloured filters or shining coloured light on objects may make them look different colours.

A green apple looks green because it reflects green light. If we now look at it in red light it looks black. This is because there is no green light to reflect!

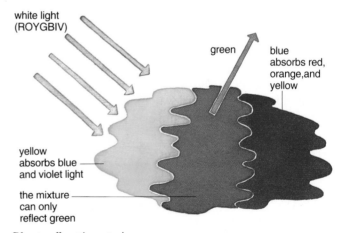
Blue + yellow pigments give green.

Questions

1 a) Why does a daffodil's flower look yellow and its leaves look green?
    b) What colour would a daffodil plant look through a red filter?

2 A set of snooker balls includes red, blue, green, yellow, black, and white balls. Explain why it would be difficult to play snooker under a blue light.

3 a) Write down the rules for mixing red, blue, and green light.
    b) Write down the rules for mixing red, blue, and yellow pigments (paint).

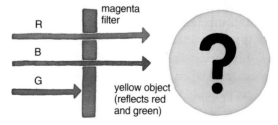
This yellow ball would look red under magenta light.

4 An actor wears a peacock blue (cyan) jacket. What colour does it look to the audience when he is lit by a spotlight covered by a) a green filter b) a red filter c) a magenta filter?

X-rays are electromagnetic waves. They have much shorter wavelengths than visible light. They are produced when fast-moving electrons hit metallic surfaces. They were discovered in 1895 when a German scientist, Wilhelm Röntgen, found that photographic plates placed near a cathode ray tube became fogged even when they were wrapped in paper. He called the radiation causing this X-rays (X for unknown). He found that these rays were able to pass through solid materials including human flesh and affect photographic film placed underneath. This effect is now used in hospitals to investigate damaged bones and joints, and even damage to the lungs. X-rays are produced in a modern X-ray tube using very high voltages – from 10000V to a few million volts. These voltages accelerate electrons, providing them with considerable energy. When the electrons hit a tungsten target (anode) some of their energy is converted to x-rays. (It heats up and has to be cooled.)

Using X-rays

Because of their great penetrating power X-rays are used to investigate inside solid objects. For example, at airports luggage is passed through an X-ray machine. The X-rays pass through soft items such as clothes and plastics but are stopped by metals. The X-rays getting through are detected and a picture is built up on a screen. The security guard watching the screen looks for the metal parts of guns and electrical wiring which could be part of a bomb. The same techniques can be used to check metal structures which have been welded together. A good weld stops X-rays but any small crack lets them through.

Care in using X-rays

X-rays are high energy waves. When they pass through substances they cause ionization, i.e. they can tear the electrons from atoms. If X-rays enter a human cell this ionization can kill it. We therefore have to be very careful when using X-rays. The following rules protect patients and doctors:

- X-ray photographs are taken with the lowest energy X-rays and the shortest exposure times possible to get a good image.
- Unless it is very important, X-ray photographs are not taken of pregnant women.
- People working with X-ray machines

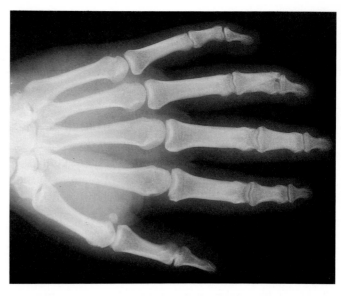

X-ray photographs help to diagnose disease and damage to bones.

(radiographers) wear protective clothing lined with lead.

- Where possible the person taking the X-ray stands behind a protective screen. (Your dentist may even step outside the room to X-ray your teeth!)

Questions

1 Compare the speed, wavelength, frequency, and energy of X-rays with those of red light.

2 Why does a modern X-ray tube have **a)** lead shielding **b)** cooling for the anode?

3 **a)** Why are suitcases checked using X-rays before they are put on to aeroplanes? **b)** Why shouldn't you pack film for your camera inside a suitcase before you fly?

4 The benefits of using X-rays for medical purposes far outweigh the risks.
- **a)** How are X-rays used for medical purposes?
- **b)** What are the risks?
- **c)** Do you agree with the statement above? Explain your answer.

Activities

1 When you next visit the dentist ask if you can see some X-rays of teeth. Ask the dentist to point out healthy enamel, healthy dentine, decay, and a metal filling.

(Some dentists now use an X-ray machine with a revolving camera. This can take an X-ray of all your teeth in one exposure.)

Questions

1 A pendulum is an oscillator.
   a) What is an oscillation?
   b) What is meant by   i) the period   ii) the frequency of an oscillation?
   c) Describe how you would measure the period of a simple pendulum 30 cm long.
   d) What would happen to   i) the period   ii) the frequency if the pendulum was made shorter?

2 The diagram shows the side view of a water wave.

   a) Copy the diagram and mark on the wavelength and the amplitude of the wave.
   b) The wave shown is moving at 2.5 m/s and has a wavelength of 15 m. What is the frequency of the wave?

3 All waves can transfer energy.
   a) Explain how energy can be transferred from a loudspeaker to your ear.
   b) Explain how energy from the Sun is transferred to the Earth.
   c) There is obviously lots of chemical activity on the Sun. Why can't we hear any noise from the Sun?

4 **a)** What is an echo?
   b) Some fishermen use echoes to locate shoals of fish beneath their boats. Suggest how this works.
   c) A mountaineer shouts for help. Half a second later (0.5 s) she hears the echo. How far away is the rock face which is reflecting her voice?
   (Take the speed of sound to be 330 m/s.)

5 A microphone is connected to a cathode ray oscilloscope. A tuning fork giving a pure musical note of frequency 256 Hz (middle C) is held in front of the microphone. The trace produced on the screen is shown below.

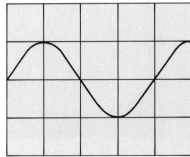

Draw to the same scale the traces you would expect to see if
   a) the tuning fork was held closer to the microphone so that the note was louder
   b) a tuning fork of lower pitch was held in front of the microphone
   c) the microphone was placed near to a piano and the note middle C played. Explain why this diagram is not the same as the one given in the question.

6 The main regions of the electromagnetic spectrum are given below.

   **radio waves   microwaves   infra-red
   visible light   ultraviolet light   X-rays
   gamma rays**

   a) State two things that all these waves have in common.
   b) Compare the wavelengths and frequencies of radio waves and X-rays.
   c) What do the letters UV stand for?
   d) How are X-rays produced?
   e) Give one use for X-rays.
   f) Explain briefly how messages can be sent by radio waves.

7 The diagram below shows an object 4 cm high at a distance of 9 cm from a convex lens of focal length 6 cm. The diagram is not to scale.

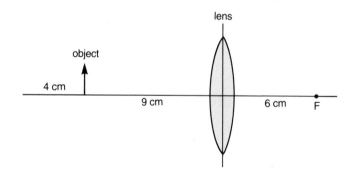

Draw the diagram to a scale of 1 cm representing 2 cm (i.e. half real size). Make sure that the object is on the left-hand edge of your page.

Draw two rays from the top of the image through the lens to find the position of the image.

Is the image real or virtual?

How large is the image?

How can we tell what is happening in a reaction?

How fast is the reaction?

How far does the reaction go?

How can we make use of all this information?

We are surrounded by chemical reactions: metals rust, plants grow and then die and decay, food cooks. Some chemical reactions are very fast, for example explosions, or very slow, for example buildings being eroded by acid rain. **In every chemical reaction a new substance is formed.** The new substance has very different properties from the starting substances.

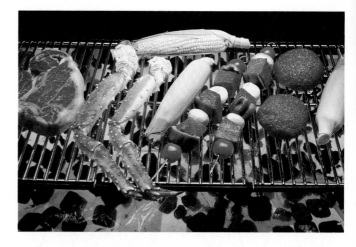

Some chemical reactions are very fast, others are slow.

Changes which are not chemical

No new chemical substances are made during a **physical change**. Physical changes are usually easy to reverse. Melting ice to form water is a physical change, and the water can be easily frozen back into ice.

When the ice has all melted, the water can easily be turned back into ice.

Chemical changes in the laboratory

1 Combination or synthesis

When two or more substances combine to form one new chemical substance, a **combination** or **synthesis** reaction takes place. For example, when hydrogen and oxygen explode together, they form a new substance called water. When elements combine like this, they form a single compound.

hydrogen + oxygen → water
$$2H_2 + O_2 \rightarrow 2H_2O$$

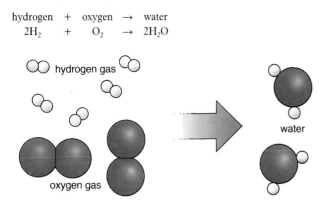

When a mixture of hydrogen and oxygen is exposed to bright sunlight, it reacts, forming water.

2 Decomposition

Sometimes a single chemical is broken down into two or more different substances – it is **decomposed**. In the production of cement, limestone (calcium carbonate) is decomposed by heating it strongly. It is decomposed into quicklime (calcium oxide) and carbon dioxide.

calcium carbonate → calcium oxide + carbon dioxide
$$CaCO_3 \rightarrow CaO + CO_2$$

Green copper(II) carbonate is decomposed into black copper(II) oxide and carbon dioxide gas when heated.

3 Oxidation and reduction

The rusting of metals is an example of **oxidation** (see page 72). When metals combine with the oxygen in the air, they are oxidized. Foods are oxidized in our bodies by a process called **respiration**. We breath in oxygen which reacts with food containing hydrogen and carbon. When the food is oxidized, energy is released, and carbon dioxide and water are produced.

A chemical is **reduced** when oxygen is taken away from it. Chemicals which reduce other chemicals are called **reducing agents**.

4 Precipitation

When two solutions are mixed together and form an insoluble product, the product is called a **precipitate**. A precipitate is formed when washing soda (sodium carbonate) is added to water to soften it. The hardness in water is due to dissolved calcium compounds. Sodium carbonate and these dissolved calcium compounds form insoluble calcium carbonate as a solid precipitate. Soft water remains.

Mixtures and compounds

A **compound** is made when two or more chemical substances are combined to form a completely new substance with different properties. Energy may be taken in during a chemical reaction, or it may be given out. For example when coal burns, heat is given out. When a new substance is formed chemical bonds are broken and made. The energy needed to make the bonds of the product can be greater or less than the energy needed to break the bonds of the reacting chemicals. If the energy needed to make the bonds is less than the energy needed to break the bonds, then heat is given out during the reaction.

Mixtures consist of two or more chemical substances mixed together which can easily be separated, for example salt and sand may be mixed. No new substance is formed, and no energy is needed to break or make bonds.

Questions

1 Write down five different chemical changes. What chemical is being changed and what new chemical substance is being formed?

2 How can you tell that a chemical change has happened?

3 What is meant by the term **reduction**?

4 What is the difference between a mixture and a compound?

149

Word equations

When a piece of solid magnesium is placed in some dilute hydrochloric acid, a chemical reaction happens. During this reaction a gas is given off. This gas is called hydrogen. The solution remaining contains magnesium chloride.

Magnesium reacting with dilute hydrochloric acid

The paragraph above describes what is happening during a chemical reaction. There is a much easier way of writing all this information down. It can be written as a **word equation**.

magnesium + hydrochloric acid → magnesium chloride + hydrogen

The **reactants** are on the left of the arrow. These are the chemicals that are added together at the beginning of the reaction. The **products** are on the right of the arrow. The products are the chemicals that are made during the reaction. The arrow tells us that a reaction happens.

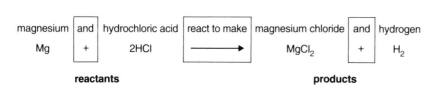

An equation is a chemical sentence. It is a shorthand way of writing down a chemical reaction.

reactants → products

If the reaction has to be heated to make it happen, then the word 'heat' can be written above the arrow, for example, in the decomposition of limestone into quicklime and carbon dioxide:

limestone $\xrightarrow{\text{heat}}$ quicklime + carbon dioxide

Questions

1   Write down the word equations for the following chemical reactions.
   a)   When sodium is put in a bowl of cold water, it immediately reacts giving off a gas. This gas is tested by putting a lighted splint near it. The gas 'pops', telling us that it is hydrogen. The solution that is left is tested with universal indicator and turns the indicator purple. An alkali has been made. The alkali is called sodium hydroxide.
   b)   Green copper carbonate is heated in a test tube. The gas given off turns limewater cloudy. It is carbon dioxide. A black solid is left in the test tube. This is copper oxide.

2   Describe the chemical reaction from the following word equations.

   a)   sodium carbonate + hydrochloric acid → sodium chloride + water + carbon dioxide

   b)   calcium carbonate $\xrightarrow{\text{heat}}$ calcium oxide + carbon dioxide

Formulae

The **formula** of a compound tells us what elements it contains and in what proportions. The formula of a compound can be used to:

- write the name of a compound in shorthand
- compare the relative masses of different molecules
- find the masses of elements that are combined in a compound
- find the mass of the **mole** (see page 162) of a compound.

It helps to know the symbols and relative atomic masses of some elements and ions when using formulae.

element	symbol	relative atomic mass
aluminium	Al	27
bromine	Br	80
calcium	Ca	40
carbon	C	12
chlorine	Cl	35.5
copper	Cu	64
hydrogen	H	1
iodine	I	127
iron	Fe	56
lithium	Li	7
nitrogen	N	14
oxygen	O	16
potassium	K	39
sodium	Na	23
sulphur	S	32

name of ion	symbol	relative molecular mass
carbonate	CO_3^{2-}	60
hydrogencarbonate	HCO_3^-	61
hydroxide	OH^-	17
nitrate	NO_3^-	62
phosphate	PO_4^{3-}	95
sulphate	SO_4^{2-}	96

State symbols

Sometimes equations give extra information. **State symbols** tell you whether a chemical is a solid, a liquid, a gas, or dissolved in water. These symbols are placed after the formula.

state	symbol
solid	(s)
liquid	(l)
gas	(g)
in aqueous solution (dissolved in water)	(aq)

Example

copper (II) carbonate + sulphuric acid → copper (II) sulphate + water + carbon dioxide

$$CuCO_3(s) + H_2SO_4(aq) \rightarrow CuSO_4(aq) + H_2O(l) + CO_2(g)$$

Questions

1 Some symbols for the elements are easy to learn, for example, sulphur is S, carbon is C. However, some are more difficult. Try to find out why these symbols are used for the following elements:

iron, Fe   copper, Cu   sodium, Na   gold, Au

2 Find the formulae of the following chemicals: sodium chloride, copper(II) sulphate, calcium carbonate, calcium hydroxide.

Equations

Word equations can only give a limited amount of information. **Chemical equations** are much more useful. A balanced chemical equation not only describes what chemicals are reacting to make other chemicals, but it also shows how many units of each chemical are involved. (The chemical unit is the mole.)

zinc oxide + hydrochloric acid → zinc chloride + water
$$ZnO + 2HCl → ZnCl_2 + H_2O$$

This equation tells us that one unit of zinc oxide reacts with two units of hydrochloric acid to make one unit of zinc chloride and one unit of water.

Rules for writing chemical equations

1 Write down the word equation.
2 Write down the correct formula for each of the chemicals.
3 Add up the atoms of each element on the left-hand side of the arrow.
4 Add up the atoms of each element on the right-hand side of the arrow.
5 If there are the same number of atoms of each element on the left-hand side of the arrow as there are on the right-hand side of the arrow, then the equation is **balanced**. If not, then balance the equation by putting numbers in front of the formulae.

Example

Write a chemical equation for the reaction of magnesium with hydrochloric acid to form magnesium chloride and hydrogen.

Step 1 Write a word equation:

magnesium + hydrochloric acid → magnesium chloride + hydrogen

Step 2 Write in the correct formulae:

$$Mg + HCl → MgCl_2 + H_2$$

Step 3 Add up the atoms of each element on each side of the arrow:

one magnesium, one hydrogen, one chlorine →
one magnesium, two chlorines, two hydrogens

Step 4 Balance the equation.

The magnesium atoms are balanced. There is one either side of the arrow. The hydrogen atoms and the chlorine atoms are not. We need more of both on the left-hand side. If we put a 2 in front of the hydrochloric acid, the equation balances.

Balanced equation:

$$Mg + 2HCl → MgCl_2 + H_2$$

Small amounts of copper(II) sulphate can be added to the water in countries affected by a parasitic worm which causes blindness in humans. Only a small amount is used. (magnification × 500)

Questions

1 Which of the following equations is balanced?

a) $Zn + HCl → ZnCl_2 + H_2$

b) $Na_2CO_3 + H_2SO_4 → Na_2SO_4 + H_2O + CO_2$

c) $K + Cl_2 → KCl$

d) $CaCO_3 → CaO + CO_2$

e) $Al + O_2 → Al_2O_3$

2 Write down those equations in question 1 that are not balanced, and try to balance them.

Rate of chemical change

Some chemical reactions are very fast. They only take fractions of a second to happen. Explosions are very fast reactions. Other chemical reactions, such as the ripening of fruit, can take days or even months. The **rate** at which chemical reactions take place can be measured very accurately. In industry it is very important to be able to make a substance in the most economical time possible. There are many different ways in which the rate of reaction can be controlled.

Explosives can be used destructively.

What is the rate?

We measure how fast we are travelling in a car by looking at the speedometer. If it tells us that we are going at a speed of 70 km/h, then in one hour we will travel 70 km.

In chemical reactions we use **rate of reaction** to tell us how fast a chemical reaction is happening.

$$\text{rate of chemical reaction} = \frac{\text{change in amount of a substance}}{\text{time}}$$

The change in amount of substance measured can be the amount of product formed or the amount of reactant used up, the change in volume, pressure, conductivity, or colour, with time. For example, if a reaction involves the formation of a substance that has a colour, and all the other chemicals involved are colourless, then the rate of the reaction can be followed by measuring how long it takes for the colour to appear.

Tomatoes take a few weeks to ripen – the reaction is controlled by chemicals in the fruit.

Measuring the rate of a chemical reaction

The rate of reaction of calcium carbonate with dilute hydrochloric acid can be measured using the apparatus shown below.

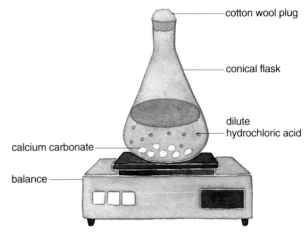

The decrease in mass during the experiment is noted at one-minute intervals.

calcium carbonate	+	hydrochloric acid	$\rightarrow$	calcium chloride	+	carbon dioxide	+	water
$CaCO_3$	+	$2HCl$	$\rightarrow$	$CaCl_2$	+	CO_2	+	H_2O

During the reaction carbon dioxide gas is given off, causing a reduction in mass. The cotton wool is placed in the mouth of the conical flask to prevent any liquid escaping, but at the same time allowing the carbon dioxide gas to escape. The results of such an experiment are plotted on the graph.

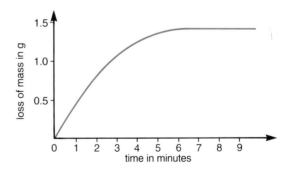

Questions

1 Look at the graph (above) showing the loss in mass during the reaction of calcium carbonate with hydrochloric acid.
  a) What mass of carbon dioxide has been lost from the flask after   i) 4 minutes   ii) 7 minutes?
  b) What is happening to the rate of reaction as time goes on?
  c) Why does the graph become horizontal after 8 minutes?

For a chemical reaction to happen, particles must come into contact with each other. To speed up a chemical reaction you need to increase the chance of particles colliding with each other. This can be done in four different ways:

- increasing the surface area
- altering the concentration (or pressure for gaseous reactions)
- altering the temperature
- using a catalyst.

Surface area

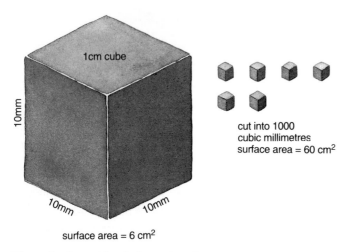

surface area = 6 cm²

cut into 1000 cubic millimetres
surface area = 60 cm²

The smaller the particles, the larger the surface area.

When a solid reacts with a liquid, the reaction can only happen on the surface of the solid. This is the only place where the particles have a chance to collide. If the surface area of the solid is increased, then the chance for collision is increased. More collisions means more reactions between particles. This results in a quicker reaction.

The reaction between calcium carbonate and dilute hydrochloric acid can be used to investigate the effect of surface area on reaction rate.

Example

20 g of large calcium carbonate chips were reacted with 50 cm³ of dilute hydrochloric acid using the apparatus in the diagram on page 153. The loss in mass was noted every minute. (Experiment 1)

The experiment was repeated using 20 g of calcium carbonate in small pieces. The results from both experiments were put in a table. (Experiment 2)

time in minutes	experiment 1 loss in mass in g	experiment 2 loss in mass in g
1	1.20	2.20
2	2.00	3.10
3	2.60	3.50
4	3.00	3.70
5	3.30	3.80
6	3.50	3.80
7	3.65	3.80
8	3.75	3.80
9	3.80	3.80
10	3.80	3.80

Questions

1 Plot a graph of loss in mass against time for the reaction with the large chips.

2 On the same graph plot the results of the experiment with the small chips.

3 Which experiment has the fastest rate at the start of the reaction?

4 Why do both graphs become horizontal eventually?

5 What does the graph tell you about the effect of surface area on the rate of reaction?

6 Why was cotton wool placed in the tops of the flasks?

7 When there was no more gas given off, some unreacted calcium carbonate was left in the flask in both experiments. Why?

Activities

These investigations can be carried out at home.

1 Measure out a mass of sea salt and add it to a cup of water at room temperature. Make a note of how fast it appears to dissolve without stirring the solution.

Repeat the same experiment using the same mass of table salt and then crushed sea salt. Which dissolves fastest? Why?

2 Carry out a similar investigation using stock cubes or sugar cubes.

Changing the rate (2): concentration

If the **concentration** of a solution is increased, then the number of particles in a given volume of the solution is increased. The more particles there are, the greater the chance of particles colliding. The rate of reaction will increase.

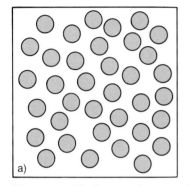 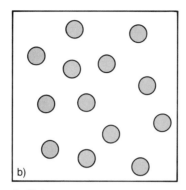

The more particles there are, the greater the chance of collision.

In the early morning there are few people on this beach . . .

When magnesium reacts with dilute hydrochloric acid, hydrogen gas is given off. The rate of the reaction can be measured by collecting the gas using the apparatus shown in the diagram.

$$\text{magnesium} + \text{hydrochloric acid} \rightarrow \text{magnesium chloride} + \text{hydrogen}$$
$$\text{Mg} + \text{2HCl} \rightarrow \text{MgCl}_2 + \text{H}_2$$

To start the reaction the flask is tilted and the tube falls over. The magnesium then starts to react with the acid. The gas is collected in a gas syringe. The volume of gas given off is noted every half minute. The results of two experiments carried out with two different concentrations of acid are plotted on the graph.

. . . collisions are much more likely later in the day.

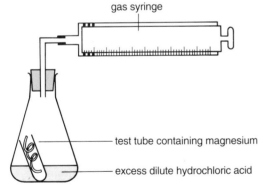

Apparatus used for measuring the volume of gas given off during a reaction

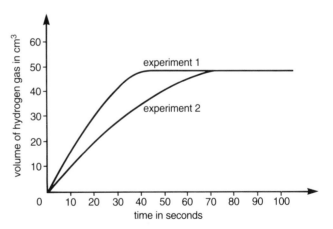

Questions

1 Which experiment used the more concentrated acid? (see fig right).

2 At about what time would the reaction be over if the concentration of acid was twice that of the acid used in experiment 1?

3 Why is it important to use the same mass of magnesium in each experiment?

Gas reactions

It is possible to increase the concentration of a gas by increasing the **pressure**. Some industrial processes are carried out at high pressures to help speed the reaction up. In the Haber process nitrogen and hydrogen gases react to make ammonia gas (see page 160) and high pressures are used during the reaction.

Changing the rate (3): temperature

Bread turns mouldy fairly quickly if it is left in a warm place. However, if it is in a freezer or even in a fridge it keeps fresh for much longer. Many foods are frozen to store them for long periods of time. Generally, chemical reactions go faster if the temperature is increased.

When the temperature of a reaction is increased the particles are given more energy When they have more energy they move about much faster. If the particles move faster and collide with more energy, then they are more likely to react with each other.

An experiment to investigate the effect of temperature on a reaction

When 50 cm³ of weak sodium thiosulphate solution reacts with 5 cm³ of dilute hydrochloric acid a cloudy precipitate of sulphur appears. As the reaction proceeds, more sulphur is precipitated. The cloudiness becomes thicker.

$$Na_2S_2O_3(aq) \ + \ 2HCl(aq) \ \rightarrow \ 2NaCl(aq) \ + \ H_2O(l) \ + \ S(s) \ + \ SO_2(g)$$

The rate of this reaction can be studied by putting a cross on a piece of paper and carrying out the reaction in a flask placed on this paper. The reaction is viewed from above and the time taken for the precipitate to make the cross 'disappear'. The results of experiments at different temperatures are given in the table below.

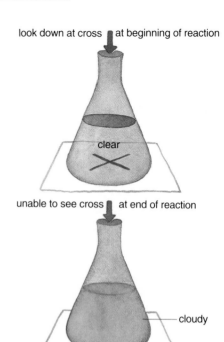

look down at cross at beginning of reaction

clear

unable to see cross at end of reaction

cloudy

The flask is placed on a piece of paper with a cross drawn on it. The time taken for the cross to disappear is taken as the time for the reaction to reach an end.

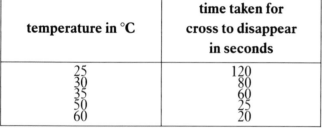

temperature in °C	time taken for cross to disappear in seconds
25	120
30	80
35	60
50	25
60	20

Why do you think food lasts much longer in a fridge, especially during hot weather?

Questions

These questions refer to the experiment using sodium thiosulphate.

1 If the temperature of the reaction is increased by 10 °C how does this affect the rate of the reaction?

2 Plot the results on a graph (temperature on the horizontal axis) and estimate the time it would take for the cross to disappear at 40 °C.

3 Copy and complete the following sentence:

'The rate of a chemical reaction _____ when the _____ is raised.'

4 Describe how you could investigate the effect of concentration on reaction rate using this chemical reaction.

Activities

You can carry out this experiment at home, using Alka-Seltzer tablets and water.

1 Investigate the effect of surface area on the dissolving of an Alka-Seltzer tablet. Remember to keep the volume and temperature constant for each experiment. Try the experiment with one whole tablet first. Cut another tablet into four pieces for the second experiment, and crush up a tablet for the final experiment.

Design an experiment to investigate the effect of temperature on the rate of a chemical reaction using Alka-Seltzer tablets as before.

Another way to alter the rate of a chemical reaction is to use a **catalyst**. This is a chemical that changes the rate of a reaction without being used up itself. Catalysts are used very extensively in the industrial production of ammonia and sulphuric acid (see pages 160 and 161). Our bodies contain catalysts. These are called **enzymes** or biological catalysts. Liver contains an enzyme, catalase, which decomposes hydrogen peroxide in the body.

How catalysts work

When molecules collide they will only react if they have enough energy. Catalysts can help reactions happen at a much lower energy than usual. The reaction speeds up without increasing the temperature or concentration. Using catalysts saves industry a great deal of money. However, catalysts usually need to be of a very high quality and are themselves expensive to produce.

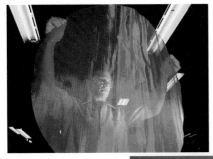

Production of nitric acid by oxidation of ammonia

Catalytic converters are fitted as standard on cars in the USA. Unfortunately, they do not remove carbon dioxide from the exhaust gases. Carbon dioxide contributes to the greenhouse effect.

Activities

1 Plan an experiment to investigate whether the amount of manganese(IV) oxide added to hydrogen peroxide affects the rate of reaction.

2 Some washing powders contain biological catalysts (enzymes) that help remove biological stains. Design and carry out an experiment to compare the stain-removing powers of biological and non-biological washing powders.

3 Find out how enzymes are used in the production of beer.

Uses of catalysts

Transition metals and their compounds are used extensively as catalysts. Nickel is used to speed up the change of vegetable oils into solid margarine. Vanadium(V) oxide is used in the manufacture of sulphuric acid. Iron is used in the Haber process for the manufacture of ammonia.

Biological catalysts are used increasingly in industry. Enzymes are used in the manufacture of beer, yoghurt, fruit juices, cheese, and in the pharmaceutical industry.

The harmful polluting gases that are emitted from a car exhaust can be converted into less harmful gases by a **catalytic converter** fitted to the car's exhaust system. These have been fitted to every new car in the USA since 1981. They help reduce harmful nitrogen oxides to nitrogen.

condition	effect on equilibrium
temperature	increase in temperature helps an endothermic reaction
concentration	increase in concentration of reactant increases amount of product
pressure	increase in pressure helps to move equilibrium towards the least number of gas molecules
catalyst	does not change the position of equilibrium, but the rate of reaching equilibrium is increased

Summary of the effects of changing conditions on equilibrium

Questions

1 What is a catalyst?

2 Give two examples of catalysts and their uses.

3 What is an enzyme?

4 List the four ways in which the rate of a chemical reaction can be changed.

Frying an egg is a one-way reaction. Once the egg has been fried it is impossible to change it back into a raw egg. The burning of fuel is another one-way reaction. Many chemical reactions are of this type. Reactions which are one way are called **irreversible reactions**.

Cooking eggs is not a reversible reaction.

Reversible reactions

There are some changes which can be reversed. A simple example is the physical change when ice is heated to form water. The water can be changed back into ice. The change can be written as an equation.

$$H_2O(s) \underset{\text{freeze}}{\overset{\text{heat}}{\rightleftarrows}} H_2O(l)$$

Another reversible change is the heating of blue (hydrated) copper sulphate. It decomposes to give white (anhydrous) copper sulphate and water vapour.

$$CuSO_4.5H_2O(s) \overset{\text{heat}}{\rightleftarrows} CuSO_4(s) + 5H_2O(g)$$

If water is added to the white copper sulphate the reaction is reversed and blue copper sulphate is reformed.

$$CuSO_4(s) + 5H_2O(l) \rightarrow CuSO_4.5H_2O(s)$$

The whole process can be written down in one equation.

$$\underset{\text{blue}}{CuSO_4.5H_2O(s)} \overset{\text{heat}}{\rightleftarrows} \underset{\text{white}}{CuSO_4(s)} + 5H_2O(l)$$

This is called a **reversible reaction**. The symbol for this is $\rightleftarrows$.

Reactions in equilibrium

When water is kept at exactly 0 °C it consists of a mixture of water and ice. There is a **balance** of ice and water. Provided the temperature does not change the amount of each will stay the same. In some chemical reactions the reactants and products are present together and the reaction seems to stop. These are called **equilibrium reactions**.

Icebergs are in equilibrium with the water around them. If the temperature is increased, then more ice melts into water. If the temperature is decreased, then the process is reversed. Holes in the ozone layer can cause icebergs to melt.

Someone walking up an escalator which is moving downwards may appear to stay in the same place. However, both the escalator and the person are moving at the same speed. They are in **equilibrium**.

The person and the escalator are both moving, but their relative positions do not change. This is a dynamic equilibrium.

An equilibrium reaction is a reversible reaction in which neither the forward reaction nor the backward reaction is complete. The symbol for equilibrium is $\rightleftarrows$. Therefore at 0 °C the 'reaction' between water and ice can be written as an equation.

$$H_2O(s) \rightleftarrows H_2O(l)$$

Equilibrium reactions

When ammonia gas and hydrogen chloride gas come into contact with each other, a white cloud of ammonium chloride vapour is formed. If solid ammonium chloride is heated it decomposes to give ammonia gas and hydrogen chloride gas. Under certain conditions this reversible reaction becomes an equilibrium reaction.

$$NH_4Cl(s) \rightleftharpoons NH_3(g) + HCl(g)$$

If solid ammonium chloride is heated in a sealed flask an equilibrium reaction is set up. When the gases are formed they cannot escape and so are able to reform ammonium chloride. Both reactions are happening at the same time. This is called **dynamic equilibrium**.

Many different industries make use of equilibrium reactions. The manufacture of ammonia and sulphuric acid both involve equilibrium reactions. There is an important equilibrium reaction going on in our bodies all the time. Chemicals in our blood, called **buffers**, help keep the pH of blood at 7.4. It is important to keep the blood at equilibrium since a change in pH of just 0.5 units can be lethal.

ammonium chloride

When ammonia and hydrogen chloride gases come into contact, white fumes of ammonium chloride are seen.

Changing the position of equilibrium

Concentration: When extra reactant is added to an equilibrium reaction, more product is formed. Adding more product will produce more reactant.

Temperature: If the energy needed to form chemical bonds is greater than the energy made by breaking bonds, then the reaction takes in heat. This type of reaction is called an **endothermic** reaction. Increasing the temperature helps this type of reaction. For example:

$$N_2O_4(g) \overset{heat}{\rightleftharpoons} 2NO_2(g)$$

In this reaction, the formation of NO_2 is an endothermic reaction. So by increasing the temperature, more N_2O_4 is changed into NO_2.

Pressure: Gases always try to make fewer molecules when the pressure is increased. In the reaction given above, one molecule of N_2O_4 is converted into two molecules of NO_2. If the pressure of this reaction was increased then more N_2O_4 would be produced.

Catalysts: These do not affect the position of the equilibrium, but they do allow equilibrium to be reached much more quickly.

Questions

1   What is meant by **reversible reaction** and **dynamic equilibrium?**

2   The heating of purple hydrated cobalt chloride, $CoCl_2.6H_2O$, is a reversible reaction. Blue anhydrous cobalt chloride is formed. Write an equation to represent this reaction.

3   Give two examples of a dynamic equilibrium.

4   How do temperature and concentration affect equilibrium?

Rate of reaction in industry

In many industrial processes it is important to produce a chemical as cheaply and quickly as possible. Concentration of chemicals, temperature of reaction, pressure, and the use of catalysts are all factors in the efficient production of a chemical.

Two important industrial processes are the **Haber process** for the manufacture of ammonia, and the **Contact process** for the manufacture of sulphuric acid.

Ammonia

85 million tonnes of ammonia are manufactured in the world each year. About 80% of the ammonia produced is used to make fertilizers such as ammonium sulphate, ammonium nitrate, and urea. The remainder is used to make nitric acid, nylon, and other chemicals.

The Haber process

In the early nineteenth century a German chemist called **Fritz Haber** solved the problem of how to make ammonia on a large commercial scale. Nitrogen gas is obtained from the fractional distillation of air, and hydrogen is produced from water (or methane). The main reaction in the Haber process is:

$$N_2 + 3H_2 \rightleftharpoons 2NH_3$$

An iron catalyst is used. The reaction is carried out at a pressure of 150–300 atmospheres. A temperature of about 400°C is used. Under these conditions about 25–50% of nitrogen and hydrogen are converted to ammonia, depending on the actual conditions used.

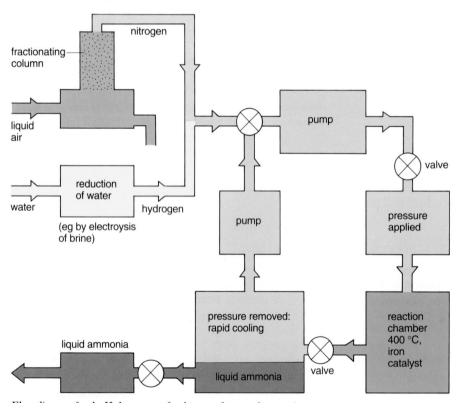

Flow diagram for the Haber process for the manufacture of ammonia

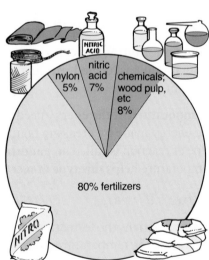

Uses of ammonia

Activities

1 Find out what chemicals are contained in fertilizers.

2 Find out what an NPK fertilizer is.

3 Fertilizers can be easily washed into rivers and streams. What effect does this have on our drinking water and on the life forms in the rivers and streams?

Questions

1 Draw a block diagram to show the Haber process.

2 How is the manufacture of ammonia speeded up?

3 More ammonia could be made by increasing the pressure to 400 atmospheres. Why do you think this pressure is not used in the Haber process?

Rate of reaction: the Contact process

The starting material for the production of sulphuric acid is sulphur. There are two main sources of sulphur. Some of it is mined from underground deposits in the USA. It is also obtained from fossil fuels before they are burnt. This reduces the pollution when these fuels are burned.

The first stage in the Contact process is the manufacture of sulphur dioxide.

$$S + O_2 \rightarrow SO_2$$

The sulphur dioxide is then filtered and cooled before being reacted with more oxygen to make sulphur trioxide.

$$2SO_2 + O_2 \rightleftharpoons 2SO_3$$

This is an equilibrium reaction. A catalyst of vanadium(V) oxide converts the sulphur dioxide to sulphur trioxide. The catalyst is used in the form of pellets to increase its surface area, hence the name the Contact process. A temperature of 450°C is used. The sulphur trioxide is then absorbed in 98% sulphuric acid. Water cannot be used to absorb sulphur trioxide as a sulphuric acid mist would be formed. This cannot be condensed and would cause pollution. Water is added to the acid mixture to produce concentrated sulphuric acid.

Uses of sulphuric acid

130 million tonnes of sulphuric acid are produced in the world each year. About 32% is used in the manufacture of fertilizers. Other uses include the manufacture of paints, soaps, detergents, fibres, and plastics.

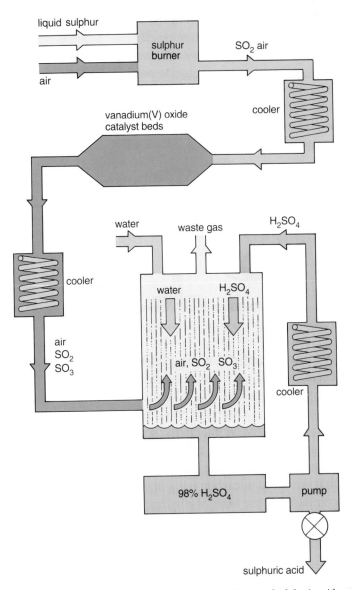

Flow diagram for the Contact process for the manufacture of sulphuric acid

Questions

1 All the reactions in the Contact process give off heat. How can this help to keep the costs of manufacture to a minimum?

2 Write equations for the three main reactions in the Contact process.

3 Most of the sulphur used in this process is imported from the USA by ship. It is very costly to transport the sulphur across land. What is the best site for a sulphuric acid plant and why?

4 List the uses of sulphuric acid.

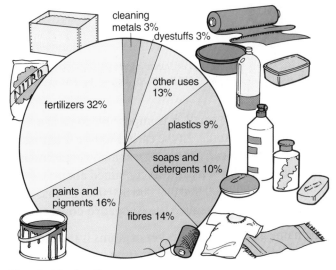

Uses of sulphuric acid

The mole

To avoid using too much or too little of a chemical in a reaction, we need to know exactly how much is needed. For example, we may want to know exactly how much limestone to use to produce 1 kg of quicklime. In industry this is very important to keep the cost of manufacturing chemicals to a minimum. It is also useful to know how much of a chemical you are going to make.

Twelve atoms of hydrogen have the same mass as one atom of carbon.

When you carry out an experiment to make a chemical, it is not enough to just weigh out equal masses of reagents. This is because atoms of different elements have a different mass. Each element has a different relative atomic mass (see page 42). For example, carbon has a relative atomic mass of 12 and hydrogen has a relative atomic mass of 1. This means that one atom of carbon has a mass of twelve units compared to the mass of a hydrogen atom. In chemical reactions it is important to know how many atoms react together.

The Italian scientist Amadeo Avogadro (1776–1856)

Since atoms are so small, it is impossible to measure out numbers of atoms. In the early 1800s, a scientist called **Avogadro** carried out a great many experiments and found that 1 g of hydrogen contained about 6×10^{23} (600 000 000 000 000 000 000 000) atoms. This very large number is called the **Avogadro constant**.

The name given to this number of atoms is the **mole**. So, one **mole** of hydrogen atoms (that is 6×10^{23} atoms) has a mass of 1 g.

A mole of atoms of any element has the same mass (in grams) as the relative atomic mass of that element.

Carbon has a relative atomic mass of 12
12 g of carbon contain one mole of atoms
One mole of carbon contains 6×10^{23} atoms

Magnesium has a relative atomic mass of 24
24 g of magnesium contain one mole of atoms
One mole of magnesium contains 6×10^{23} atoms

If half a mole of carbon atoms was needed in an experiment, you would need a mass of carbon equal to half of its relative atomic mass in grams.

0.5 mole of carbon has a mass of 6 g
0.5 mole of carbon contains 3×10^{23} atoms

If an experiment required three moles of carbon atoms, you would need to measure out three times its relative atomic mass.

3 moles of carbon has a mass of $3 \times 12 = 36$ g
3 moles of carbon contain $3 \times 6 \times 10^{23}$ atoms
(18×10^{23} atoms)

If you need to know how many moles there are in a certain mass of an element or compound:

$$\textbf{number of moles} = \frac{\textbf{mass}}{\textbf{relative molecular mass}}$$

Questions

1 Copy and complete the following table:

element	symbol	relative atomic mass	mass in g	
			1 mole	0.5 mole
magnesium	Mg			
carbon	C			
sulphur		32		
calcium	Ca		40	
nitrogen	N			
	O	16		

2 **a)** What is the relative atomic mass of sodium, Na?
  b) How many atoms are there in 23 g of sodium?
  c) How many atoms are there in 4 moles of sodium?

Working out formulae

The formula of a compound tells us what atoms it has and in what ratio. For example, suppose the formula of water was not known. It is possible to find out the formula by splitting water into its elements by electrolysis. The volume of hydrogen produced is twice that of oxygen. So for every two moles of hydrogen there is one mole of oxygen. Therefore their atoms must be in the ratio 2:1. Hence the formula for water is H_2O.

By knowing the masses of elements (or volumes if the elements are gases) that combine together to form a compound, and their relative atomic masses, it is possible to work out the formula of the compound.

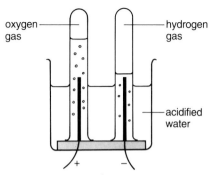

When water decomposes, twice as much hydrogen is formed as oxygen. In order to help the electrolysis proceed, a small amount of dilute acid is added to the water.

Activities

1 Finding the formula of magnesium oxide

When magnesium is burned in air, it forms magnesium oxide. It burns with a bright white light. The magnesium oxide formed is a fine white powder. The word equation for the reaction is:

    magnesium + oxygen → magnesium oxide

Weigh accurately about a 10 cm length of clean magnesium ribbon in a crucible with a lid. Heat it strongly in the crucible. The lid of the crucible should be lifted a couple of centimetres every minute. When you can see that the magnesium has finished reacting, leave the apparatus to cool and then reweigh it.

When magnesium burns, it gives off a very bright white light. **Take care not to look directly at this light or it will hurt your eyes.**

The results might be as follows:

mass of crucible	+	lid	+	magnesium	= 17.69 g
mass of crucible	+	lid			= 17.45 g
mass of magnesium used					= 0.24 g
mass of crucible	+	lid	+	magnesium oxide	= 17.85 g
mass of crucible	+	lid	+	magnesium	= 17.69 g
mass of oxygen used					= 0.16 g

a A piece of magnesium + crucible + lid are weighed.

	magnesium	oxygen
mass combining	0.24 g	0.16 g
relative atomic mass	24	16
number of moles combining	$\dfrac{0.24}{24} = 0.01$	$\dfrac{0.16}{16} = 0.01$
ratio	1	: 1
formula	MgO	

b The crucible is heated gently at first, then more strongly. The lid is carefully lifted at intervals.

Why was it necessary to lift the lid of the crucible at intervals during heating?

What safety precautions should be taken when carrying out this experiment?

In an experiment carried out by a pupil, the mass of oxygen used was less than expected. Think of a reason why this could be.

c After all the magnesium has reacted, the crucible is allowed to cool before weighing again.

Using the mole to calculate mass

The mass of one mole of a compound is calculated by adding up all the relative atomic masses of the elements in the compound. The mass of one mole of a molecule or compound is called its **relative molecular mass**.

Example 1

Find the mass of one mole of the compound sodium chloride (the relative molecular mass of sodium chloride).

> The formula of sodium chloride is NaCl
> In one mole of sodium chloride there is one mole of sodium and one mole of chlorine
> The relative atomic masses are Na = 23, Cl = 35.5
> The relative molecular mass of sodium chloride is $23 + 35.5 = 58.5$
> One mole of sodium chloride has a mass of 58.5 g.
> It contains 6×10^{23} sodium chloride **molecules**.

One mole of calcium carbonate, copper(II) sulphate, magnesium oxide, and sodium chloride

Using formulae to find the masses of elements combining

If the formula of a compound is known, then you can calculate the masses of the elements needed to make that compound.

Example 2

What mass of copper is contained in one mole of copper(II) oxide, CuO?

> In one mole of copper(II) oxide, there is one mole of copper atoms
> In one mole of copper(II) oxide, there are 64 g of copper

Using percentages

You can calculate the percentage (by mass) of each element present in a compound if you know its formula.

Example 3

Calculate the percentage of each element present in one mole of ammonium chloride, NH_4Cl. (Relative atomic masses; N = 14, H = 1, Cl = 35.5.)

Answer

The relative molecular mass (that is the total mass) of ammonium chloride, NH_4Cl, is:

$$
\begin{aligned}
1 \times N &= 1 \times 14 &&= 14 \\
4 \times H &= 4 \times 1 &&= 4 \\
1 \times Cl &= 1 \times 35.5 &&= \underline{35.5} \\
& && 53.5
\end{aligned}
$$

Percentage of nitrogen $= \dfrac{14}{53.5} \times 100 = 26.18\%$

Percentage of hydrogen $= \dfrac{4}{53.5} \times 100 = 7.48\%$

Percentage of chlorine $= \dfrac{35.5}{53.5} \times 100 = 66.36\%$

Activities

1   Using the table of relative atomic masses on page 151, calculate the relative molecular masses of the following compounds:

  a)   water, H_2O
  b)   methane, CH_4
  c)   potassium nitrate, KNO_3
  d)   sulphuric acid, H_2SO_4
  e)   chlorine (molecule), Cl_2

Questions

1   Calculate how much oxygen there is in each of the following:

  a)   one mole of zinc oxide, ZnO
  b)   2 moles of lithium oxide, Li_2O
  c)   0.01 mole of calcium carbonate, $CaCO_3$

2   What information can you obtain from this statement: **The formula for potassium iodide is KI**?

3   Ammonium nitrate, NH_4NO_3, is used as a fertilizer. How much nitrogen is there in 400 g of this compound?

Molar solutions

Many chemical reactions involve solutions of compounds dissolved in water. It is important to know the concentration of these solutions so that the correct volume can be used. Concentration is measured in g/dm^3. ($1\,dm^3 = 1$ litre $= 1000\,cm^3$.) However, it is more useful to know the concentration in moles/dm^3.

Moles/dm^3 is shortened to M. A solution with a concentration of 1 mole/dm^3 is called a **molar solution**. (A 1 M solution contains 1 mole of a material dissolved in one litre of solution – a 2 M solution would have 2 moles dissolved in one litre, etc.) A 1 M solution is weaker or more dilute than a 2 M solution.

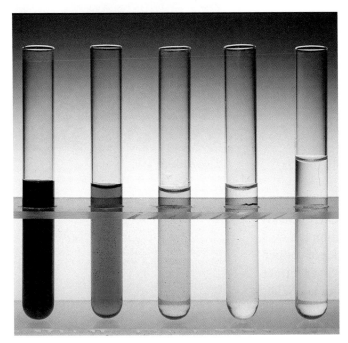

In coloured solutions it is easy to see different concentrations.

How to calculate the concentration of a solution

Example 1

A solution of sodium hydroxide, NaOH, is said to be 1 M. How many grams of sodium hydroxide are in $1\,dm^3$ of solution?

The formula for sodium hydroxide is NaOH
The relative molecular mass of sodium hydroxide is $23 + 16 + 1 = 40$
The solution is 1 M, therefore there must be 1 mole in $1\,dm^3$
40 g of sodium hydroxide are in $1\,dm^3$ of a 1 M solution

Example 2

How many grams of sodium chloride, NaCl, are needed to make $1\,dm^3$ of a 0.5 M solution?

To make $1\,dm^3$ of a 0.5 M solution, 0.5 moles of sodium chloride are needed
The relative molecular mass of sodium chloride is $23 + 35.5 = 58.5$
$$0.5 \text{ mole of sodium chloride} = \frac{58.5}{2} = 29.25\,g$$
29.25 g of sodium chloride are needed to make $1\,dm$ of 0.5 M solution

Example 3

How many grams of potassium iodide, KI, are needed to make $100\,cm^3$ of solution of concentration 1 M?

The relative molecular mass of potassium iodide is $39 + 127 = 166$
To make $1\,dm^3$ ($1000\,cm^3$) of a 1 M solution, 1 mole of potassium iodide is needed.
To make $100\,cm^3$ of a 1 M solution, 0.1 mole is needed
Therefore $\frac{166}{10} = 16.6\,g$ of potassium iodide are needed to make $100\,cm^3$ of a 1 M solution

Questions

1 Calculate how many grams are required to make the following solutions. Use the table of relative atomic masses on page 151 to help you.
a) $1000\,cm^3$ of 1 M sulphuric acid, H_2SO_4
b) $1000\,cm^3$ of 2 M nitric acid, HNO_3
c) $100\,cm^3$ of 1 M hydrochloric acid, HCl
d) $100\,cm^3$ of 2 M potassium hydroxide, KOH
e) $25\,cm^3$ of 1 M ammonium hydroxide, NH_4OH
f) $20\,cm^3$ of 2 M copper(II) sulphate, $CuSO_4.5H_2O$

2 Calculate the molar value of the following solutions:
a) 149 g of potassium chloride, KCl, in $1000\,cm^3$ of solution
b) 20 g of sodium hydroxide, NaOH, in $500\,cm^3$ of solution
c) 1.6 g of hydrogen bromide, HBr, in $10\,cm^3$ of solution
d) 55.5 g of calcium chloride, $CaCl_2$, in $4\,dm^3$ of solution.

Calculations in industry

In industry it is often important to know how much of a chemical can be made or is needed in a reaction. How much product can be made depends on how much reactant is available. To keep manufacturing costs as low as possible, the minimum amounts of reagents are used. All this information can be calculated from the equation for the reaction.

Example 1

What mass of lime (calcium oxide), CaO, could be obtained from 250 tonnes of limestone (calcium carbonate), $CaCO_3$?
(1 tonne $= 1\,000\,000\,g = 10^6\,g$.) Relative atomic masses: Ca $= 40$, C $= 12$, O $= 16$.

Calcium carbonate decomposes on heating according to the equation

$$CaCO_3 \overset{heat}{\rightarrow} CaO + CO_2$$

For every one mole of limestone that is decomposed, one mole of lime is produced
The relative molecular mass of calcium carbonate is
$(40 + 12 + 16 + 16 + 16) = 100$

$$250 \text{ tonnes} = 250 \times 10^6\,g = \frac{250 \times 10^6}{100} \text{ moles}$$

Therefore, 2.5×10^6 moles of lime are produced
The mass of lime produced $= 2.5 \times (40 + 16) \times 10^6\,g = 140$ tonnes

Lime has many uses.

Example 2

A chemical company has run out of silver, and needs some fairly quickly. The company has an enormous volume of silver nitrate solution left over from an electroplating process (see page 66). It also has 640 kg of copper metal available for use. It is possible to displace silver from silver nitrate solution by reacting it with copper which is a more reactive metal. What is the maximum mass of silver that could be displaced from the silver nitrate solution by 640 kg of copper? (Relative atomic masses: Cu $= 64$, Ag $= 108$.)

The balanced chemical equation for the reaction is:
$$Cu(s) + 2AgNO_3(aq) \rightarrow Cu(NO_3)_2(aq) + 2Ag(s)$$
For every mole of copper used, two moles of silver are displaced
$$640 \text{ kg of copper} = \frac{640\,000}{64} = 10\,000 \text{ moles of copper}$$
Therefore, $20\,000$ moles of silver could be produced
$$20\,000 \times 108 = 2\,160\,000\,g$$
$\qquad\qquad\qquad = 2160$ kg of silver could be produced if there was an unlimited supply of silver nitrate solution

When copper is placed in silver nitrate solution, silver can be seen after only a few minutes.

Questions

1 What is the maximum mass of copper(II) oxide, CuO, obtained by heating 1 kg of copper(II) carbonate, $CuCO_3$?

2 What volume of 2 M hydrochloric acid, HCl, is needed to completely react with 80 g of magnesium oxide, MgO? The equation for the reaction is:

$$MgO + 2HCl \rightarrow MgCl_2 + H_2O$$

Questions

1 List the following changes as chemical or non-chemical:
   a) burning a firework
   b) making ice
   c) adding sugar to a cup of coffee
   d) adding magnesium to dilute sulphuric acid
   e) melting iron.

2 Classify the following reactions as synthesis, decomposition, oxidation, or reduction:

a) calcium carbonate → calcium oxide + carbon dioxide

   b) iron + oxygen   →   iron oxide
   c) aluminium + chlorine→ aluminium chloride
   d) lead oxide + hydrogen→ lead + water

3 In an experiment to investigate the rate of a chemical reaction, $1.0\,g$ of manganese(IV) oxide was added to $100\,cm^3$ of hydrogen peroxide. The hydrogen peroxide decomposed into water and oxygen. The reaction was carried out at room temperature and pressure. The volume of oxygen gas given off was noted every minute.
   a) Draw a fully labelled diagram of apparatus that could be used to carry out this experiment.
   b) Using the results in the table, plot a graph of volume of oxygen (vertical axis) against time.
   c) In a similar experiment $1\,g$ of manganese(IV) oxide was added to $25\,cm^3$ of water and $75\,cm^3$ of hydrogen peroxide. What effect do you think this will have on the rate of reaction?
   d) Manganese(IV) oxide is a catalyst that speeds up the rate of decomposition of hydrogen peroxide. If you were given $1\,g$ of copper(II) oxide how could you compare its effectiveness as a catalyst with that of manganese(IV) oxide?

time in minutes	volume in cm^3
0	0
1	40
2	66
3	88
4	104
5	116
6	118
7	120
8	120

4 Iodine monochloride, ICl, reacts easily with chlorine gas, Cl_2. The solid iodine trichloride, ICl_3, is formed. However, the iodine trichloride, ICl_3, is not very stable and decomposes at room temperature back into chlorine and iodine monochloride:

$$ICl(l) + Cl_2(g) \rightleftharpoons ICl_3(s)$$

   a) What does the symbol $\rightleftharpoons$ mean?
   b) What effect would adding more chlorine have on the reaction?
   c) How could you increase the amount of ICl_3 formed?
   d) What do the symbols (l), (g), and (s) mean?

5 Hydrogen gas was passed over $8.0\,g$ of heated iron oxide in the laboratory. The reaction was stopped after 30 minutes. The mass of iron obtained was weighed and found to be $5.6\,g$.
   a) What is reduction?
   b) What is the reducing agent in this reaction?
   c) Draw a fully labelled diagram of apparatus that could be used to carry out this experiment.
   d) Using the information given, work out the formula of the iron oxide. (Relative atomic masses: Fe = 56, O = 16.)
   e) Write a word equation for the reaction.
   f) Write a full balanced chemical equation for the reaction.
   g) Another student carried out the same reaction using the same amount of iron oxide. However, the reaction was stopped after 20 minutes. The mass of iron at the end of this time was found to be greater than expected. Give a reason why this might be.

6 What percentage mass of water is there in one mole of hydrated sodium carbonate, $Na_2CO_3.10H_2O$? (Relative atomic masses: Na = 23, C = 12, O = 16, H = 1.)

What are acids?

Where can we find acids?

What are the effects of acids?

How can we neutralize acids?

How useful are acids?

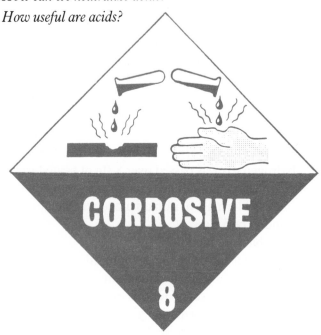

This warning label is found on all bottles of acid.

Milk that has turned sour contains an acid called lactic acid. Lemon juice and vinegar both contain acid and taste 'sharp' or 'sour'. There are a great many **acids** around us in everyday life. Some 'natural' acids are given in the table below.

name of acid	where it is found
hydrochloric	in the stomach
ethanoic	vinegar
methanoic	ants and stinging nettles
citric	lemon juice
lactic	sour milk
oxalic	rhubarb
ascorbic	fruits and vegetables
tartaric	grapes
tannic	tea

Acids that are used in the laboratory are much more corrosive than acids found naturally. If laboratory acids are spilt on clothing or skin they can cause a great deal of damage and must be washed off immediately with plenty of water.

All acids must be handled with care. They can cause damage to skin and clothing. Eyes should be protected, when using acids.

Acids in the body

The hydrochloric acid found in the stomach helps to break down food. Carbohydrates and proteins are broken down into smaller, more digestible compounds such as glucose and amino acids. Too much hydrochloric acid in the stomach can cause indigestion (see page 173).

The chemical balance of the blood is essential for a healthy life. Too much acid in the blood would be fatal. Special chemicals in the blood prevent the balance being affected by too much acid (see page 159).

What natural acids do these foods contain?

Look carefully at labels like these. What acids are contained in these foods and drinks?

Care must be taken with leaking batteries. They contain sulphuric acid. How could the spilt acid be cleared up safely?

Acids in food and drink

Many fruits contain acids. This gives them their slightly 'sour' or 'sharp' taste. Many foods like sauces and pickles contain ethanoic acid (vinegar). Vinegar preserves fruits and vegetables. If wine is exposed to the air for too long, the alcohol in it turns into vinegar.

Fizzy drinks are made by adding carbon dioxide gas to the drink under pressure. When carbon dioxide dissolves in water, a very weak acid, carbonic acid, is formed.

Other uses of acids

The acids you see in the laboratory have a great many uses. Sulphuric acid is used in car batteries and as a raw material for making many other chemicals (see page 161). About 2.5 million tonnes of sulphuric acid are manufactured in the UK each year. Nitric acid is another commonly used acid. At least three-quarters of the 770 000 tonnes of nitric acid manufactured in the UK each year is used to make fertilizers. Nitric acid is also used to make explosives.

Effects of acid rain

Acid rain

All rainwater contains a small amount of acid. Rain dissolves carbon dioxide from the air, making carbonic acid. However, other gases produced by industries such as coal-fired power stations cause rain to be much more acidic. These gases are sulphur dioxide and nitrogen dioxide. When they dissolve in water, they form sulphurous and nitrous acids. Burning fossil fuels such as coal and oil give off these gases creating acid rain. The damage done by acid rain is extensive. In many areas of Scandinavia, fish in the lakes are dying. Whole forests in Germany and Scandinavia are severely affected. Buildings are crumbling and metal constructions are rusting much faster because of acid rain.

Activities

1 Find out as much as you can about acid rain. Ask environmental pressure groups and local power stations. Present your findings as a report.

2 Carry out a survey in your own home, and list all the acids and their uses you can find.

Indicators and acid strength

Measuring the strengths of acids

Some acids are weak enough for us to eat, for example, vinegar. However, other acids such as sulphuric acid can be very strong. The strength of an acid is measured by its **pH**. Every acid contains hydrogen ions, H^+. The stronger the acid, the more hydrogen ions there are. pH is a symbol meaning **strength of acid** and comes from the German word 'potenz'. **The lower the pH number, the stronger the acid.** An acid with a pH of 1 is much stronger than an acid with a pH of 4. A substance which has a pH of 7 is **neutral**. Pure water has a pH of 7. A chemical with a pH greater than 7 is called an **alkali**. The higher the pH, the more alkaline the chemical is. An alkali with a pH of 14 is much stronger than an alkali with a pH of 9.

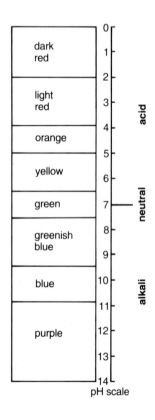

Universal indicator is a different colour in solutions of different pH.

The **strength** of an acid must not be confused with its **concentration**. Concentration depends on the amount of water present. Strength refers to the number of hydrogen ions. It is possible to have a dilute solution of a strong acid. For example, dilute nitric acid is a dilute solution of a strong acid. It has a pH of about 2, but is not very concentrated.

Indicators

An **indicator** is a dye that changes colour when it is put into an acid or an alkali. There are a number of different indicators. Many are made from plant extracts. **Litmus** is an indicator made from lichen. In neutral water it has a mauve colour. This turns red when acid is added to it. When it is put into an alkali, it turns blue. Indicators can be used in solution or as paper soaked in the solution and then dried.

indicator	colour in acid	colour in alkali
litmus	red	blue
phenolphthalein	colourless	pink
methyl orange	orange	yellow
bromothymol blue	yellow	blue

Some indicators and their colours

Universal indicator is a mixture of several indicators. It gives a different colour at each pH number.

Activities

1   Using either red cabbage or raw beetroot, you can make your own indicator.

–   Cut up the cabbage or beetroot into very small pieces.

–   Boil it in a little water for five minutes.

–   Leave to cool.

–   Strain and collect the juice.

–   Use the juice to test an acid such as lemon juice.

–   Test some baking powder (an alkali) with your indicator. What colour was the indicator in water, acid, and alkali?

–   Repeat the activity using other plant material or coloured flower petals.

Properties and reactions of acids

Properties of acids

- Acids are soluble in water.
- Acids turn blue litmus red.
- Acids contain hydrogen and produce H^+ ions in solution.
- Acids conduct electricity (they are **electrolytes**).
- Acids have a sour taste.
- Acids have a pH of less than 7.

name of acid	formula
hydrochloric	HCl
nitric	HNO_3
sulphuric	H_2SO_4
phosphoric	H_3PO_4
ethanoic (acetic)	CH_3CO_2H

Metals and acids

Many metals including magnesium and calcium react with dilute acids. However, there are some metals which do not react even with concentrated acids. Gold is an example. When metals react, they displace hydrogen from the acid. During the reaction a salt is also formed. For example, zinc reacts with dilute hydrochloric acid making zinc chloride and giving off hydrogen gas.

metal	+	acid	→	salt	+	hydrogen
zinc	+	hydrochloric acid	→	zinc chloride	+	hydrogen
Zn	+	2HCl	→	$ZnCl_2$	+	H_2

If a lighted splint is placed near the mouth of the test tube, the hydrogen explodes with a 'squeaky pop'.

Carbonates and acids

All **metal carbonates** eg calcium carbonate react with dilute acids giving off carbon dioxide gas. During the reaction 'fizzing' or **effervescence** is usually seen and heard.

calcium carbonate	+	hydrochloric acid	→	calcium chloride	+	water	+	carbon dioxide
$CaCO_3$	+	2HCl	→	$CaCl_2$	+	H_2O	+	CO_2

Carbon dioxide does not burn. Fire extinguishers are available that use the reaction of an acid with a carbonate to produce carbon dioxide foam.

The chemical test for carbon dioxide is to bubble it through **limewater** (calcium hydroxide solution).

Activities

1 Devise experiments to test the following:

   a) brown eggshells contain more carbonate than white eggshells

   b) stomach powders contain carbonate

   c) lemon juice is a stronger acid than vinegar.

Carbonates and baking cakes

Some cake recipes use flour and baking powder. Baking powder is a mixture of bicarbonate of soda (sodium hydrogencarbonate) and a weak acid called cream of tartar. It is used to make cakes rise during cooking. If less raising power is needed in a recipe, then bicarbonate of soda is used on its own. When bicarbonate of soda is heated or reacted with an acid, carbon dioxide gas is given off. The carbon dioxide produced by either method produces minute bubbles, making the cake mixture rise.

The reaction between a carbonate and an acid is useful in baking cakes.

171

Neutralization

If a metal such as magnesium reacts with a dilute acid the hydrogen in the acid is replaced by the metal. When the reaction is complete the acid is said to have been **neutralized**. Metal carbonates also neutralize acids. When an acid is neutralized a salt and water are formed. During the reaction, the pH of the acid changes. The reaction is complete and the acid neutralized when the pH of the solution reaches 7. The salt formed during the reaction depends upon which acid and which metal is used. Different acids make different salts, as shown in the table below.

name of acid	chemical formula	name of salt
hydrochloric	HCl	chloride
nitric	HNO_3	nitrate
sulphuric	H_2SO_4	sulphate
phosphoric	H_3PO_4	phosphate
ethanoic (acetic)	CH_3CO_2H	ethanoate (acetate)

A chemical that neutralizes an acid is called a **base**. Metal oxides and hydroxides both react with acids to make a salt and water.

acid + metal oxide → salt + water
acid + metal hydroxide → salt + water

For example, when copper(II) oxide reacts with dilute sulphuric acid the familiar blue salt of copper(II) sulphate is formed.

sulphuric acid + copper(II) oxide → copper(II) sulphate + water
H_2SO_4 + CuO → $CuSO_4$ + H_2O

The copper(II) sulphate crystals can be recovered by heating the solution gently to evaporate the excess water.

The salt formed in the reaction of sodium hydroxide with dilute hydrochloric acid is often called **table salt**. Its correct chemical name is sodium chloride, NaCl.

hydrochloric acid + sodium hydroxide → sodium chloride + water
HCl + NaOH → NaCl + H_2O

Ammonium hydroxide also neutralizes acids – this is an exception as it is a salt which does not contain a metal.

Understanding neutralization

An **ion** is a charged particle. All acids contain hydrogen ions, H^+. For example, hydrochloric acid, HCl, contains hydrogen ions and chloride ions, Cl^-. There are the same number of hydrogen ions as chloride ions. To neutralize an acid, the hydrogen ions have to be replaced by metal ions. Sodium hydroxide contains sodium ions, Na^+, and hydroxide ions, OH^-. When the sodium ions replace the hydrogen ions, the salt sodium chloride is made, NaCl. The hydrogen ions combine with the hydroxide ions to make water, H_2O.

$$H^+ + OH^- \rightarrow H_2O$$

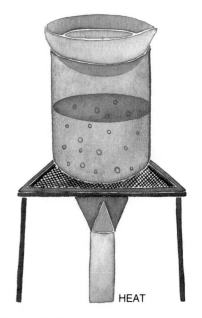

The more slowly the water is evaporated away, the better the crystals of copper(II) sulphate. This is one way of carrying out the evaporation slowly.

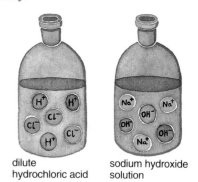

dilute hydrochloric acid   sodium hydroxide solution

neutralization

When dilute hydrochloric acid and sodium hydroxide solution are mixed, sodium chloride and water are produced.

Useful neutralization reactions

Curing indigestion

Dilute hydrochloric acid is found in the stomach. When you suffer from indigestion, there is usually more acid in the stomach than is needed. Indigestion tablets neutralize this excess acid. They contain metal carbonates or hydroxides.

Cleaning your teeth

During the day your teeth become coated in sugars and acids from the food you eat. Some toothpastes are slightly alkaline. They help to neutralize the effects of acids formed as a byproduct when microbes feed on sugar.

Taking the sting out

Bee stings contain acid. People often put calamine lotion on bee stings. Calamine lotion contains zinc carbonate, $ZnCO_3$. Wasp stings are alkaline. Vinegar is used to neutralize a wasp sting. Ant and nettle stings contain methanoic acid.

'Antacids' contain chemicals which neutralize excess acid in the stomach. Find out which chemicals in these indigestion preparations neutralize acid.

Rubbing dock leaves on nettle stings is said to relieve the stinging sensation. What type of chemical do you think is in a dock leaf?

Wasp stings are alkaline.

Activities

1 Find three different types of indigestion tablets. Devise an experiment to test the effectiveness of each tablet. Use vinegar or lemon juice as your acid. Compare the results of your experiment with the effectiveness of using sodium hydrogencarbonate (bicarbonate of soda) as a cure for indigestion.

Bases and alkalis

A **base** is a metal oxide or hydroxide. Copper oxide, magnesium oxide, and iron oxide are all bases. A base that is soluble in water is called an **alkali**, for example, sodium hydroxide. Ammonium hydroxide is also an alkali, but it does not contain a metal. Not very many bases are soluble in water. Bases and alkalis both neutralize acids. When they do so, a salt and water are formed.

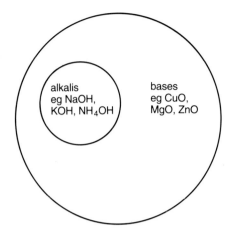

acid + base → salt + water

acid + alkali → salt + water

Venn diagram showing how some bases are also alkalis

Properties and uses of alkalis

- Alkalis are soluble in water.
- Alkalis turn red litmus blue.
- Alkalis have a pH of more than 7.
- Alkalis conduct electricity when in solution (they are electrolytes).
- Alkalis are soapy to the touch.

Sodium hydroxide is used extensively in industry. It is sometimes called caustic soda. It is used to make soap and soap powders. Animal fats or vegetable oils are boiled with sodium hydroxide to form, for example, sodium stearate (soap). Because alkalis react with fats, sodium hydroxide is a useful ingredient in oven cleaners. Sodium hydroxide is also used to remove the resins from wood pulp in the manufacture of paper.

Alkalis are used in all these products.

Some household bleaches contain ammonium hydroxide since it is very soluble in water. Calcium hydroxide (slaked lime) is less soluble than sodium or ammonium hydroxides. When calcium hydroxide is dissolved in water it forms limewater.

name of alkali	chemical formula
sodium hydroxide	NaOH
potassium hydroxide	KOH
ammonium hydroxide	NH_4OH
calcium hydroxide (limewater)	$Ca(OH)_2$

Questions

1 Write down the names of three alkalis.

2 Write down the names of three bases which are not alkalis.

3 List some uses of alkalis.

4 What would the pH of a strong alkali be? What colour would universal indicator be in a strong alkali?

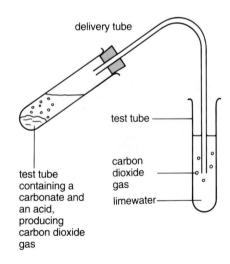

Limewater can be used in the laboratory to test for carbon dioxide gas. When the gas is bubbled through limewater, it turns milky.

174

Using alkalis in the laboratory

Sodium and ammonium hydroxides can be used in the laboratory to test for metal ions in a compound. Nearly all metal hydroxides are insoluble in water. When sodium hydroxide solution is added to a solution of a compound containing metal ions, a **precipitate** (solid) may be formed. This precipitate is an insoluble metal hydroxide.

When sodium hydroxide is added to magnesium sulphate solution, a white precipitate of magnesium hydroxide is seen.

metal in compound	result of adding a few drops of NaOH	result of adding excess NaOH
potassium	no precipitate	no precipitate
magnesium	white precipitate	white precipitate
calcium	white precipitate	white precipitate
zinc	white precipitate	precipitate dissolves
lead	white precipitate	precipitate dissolves
copper	blue precipitate	blue precipitate
iron(II)	green precipitate	green precipitate
iron(III)	red-brown precipitate	red-brown precipitate

Precipitates formed by metal ions and sodium hydroxide solution

Alkalis can be used in the laboratory to neutralize an acid by carrying out an experiment called a **titration** (see page 177). The reaction between potassium hydroxide and hydrochloric acid can be written down in an equation.

hydrochloric acid + potassium hydroxide → potassium chloride + water
$$HCl + KOH \rightarrow KCl + H_2O$$

Ammonium hydroxide, NH_4OH, does not contain any metal ions. However, it contains ammonium ions, NH_4^+. These ions can replace the hydrogen ions in an acid in the same way as metal ions. Salts which contain ammonium ions are used as fertilizers. Ammonium sulphate and ammonium nitrate are both fertilizers. Ammonium nitrate is made by neutralizing nitric acid with ammonium hydroxide.

Questions

1 Name three types of chemicals that can neutralize an acid.

2 What is the difference between a base and an alkali?

3 What are the main properties of alkalis?

4 List some uses of sodium hydroxide.

5 What is always made during the neutralization of an acid?

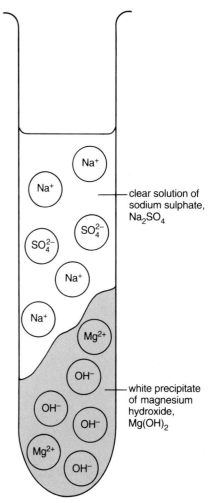

The precipitate is formed by magnesium hydroxide which is insoluble. Magnesium ions, Mg^{2+}, combine with hydroxide ions. OH^-, to form the precipitate.

The pH of soil

Soil contains minerals which when dissolved can make the soil acid or alkaline. Different plants prefer different conditions. This is very important to a farmer or gardener who can choose crops and control soil conditions to give the best results.

plants suitable for acid soils (pH < 7)	plants suitable for alkaline soils (pH > 7)
azaleas camellias ericas (heathers) lupins magnolias pieris rhododendrons	dianthus (pinks) gypsophila saxifrage lilac

If a soil is too acid or alkaline, it will not produce good crops. You can measure the pH of soil using indicators. Most of the soil in Britain is slightly acidic with a pH of about 6. Soil with a pH of about 6 or 6.5 is best for growing crops, though different plants require different conditions. Wheat needs a soil pH of 6.0–7.5. When the pH of the soil becomes less than 5 little grows well, though swedes need an acidic soil of pH 4.7–5.6 for the best growth!

The use of fertilizers makes soil more acidic. If a soil becomes too acidic for good plant growth then the correct pH value can be restored by using chemicals such as lime (calcium oxide is a base). Lime has the additional benefit of improving drainage conditions. Chalk (calcium carbonate), $CaCO_3$, is often used in place of lime since it does not dissolve as readily and therefore is not washed away so easily.

Questions

1 Why is chalk sometimes added to soil instead of lime?

2 Find out what you can add to an alkaline soil to reduce its pH.

3 What can be added to an acidic soil to improve its pH?

4 Some gardeners put the washings from their milk bottles on their garden plants. How do you think this might be useful?

The flowers on hydrangeas are blue in acid soils and pink in alkaline soils.

Lime is used to increase the pH of the soil in certain areas.

Different parts of the country have soils with different pH values. Soil in a limestone area will be alkaline. The soil on the Yorkshire Moors and in North Wales is very acidic. Wild rhododendrons which like acidic soils are growing profusely in Wales and causing problems. As time goes on, the soil will become more acidic with the fall of acid rain (see page 169).

Finding the pH of a soil sample

1 Dry the soil samples.

2 Quarter-fill a test tube with the sample to be tested.

3 Put about 5 cm³ of dilute universal indicator solution into the test tube and shake for 30 seconds.

4 Leave to settle and then note the colour and pH of the sample.

Activities

1 Collect some soil samples from around different plants. **Remember to wear gloves when digging in the garden.** Make a note of where each sample came from, what the plant is called, and how healthy the plant looks. In the school laboratory, find out the pH of each soil sample. Write up your results in a table with the following headings.

name of plant   health of plant   pH of soil   notes

Write a report on your findings. Compare your results with other members of your class. Can you draw any general conclusions about the type of soil in your locality?

Titration

When an acid and an alkali react together, a salt and water are formed. It is possible to find out exactly how much alkali is needed to neutralize an acid by carrying out a **titration**. This is an experiment using equipment that can measure the volume of a solution accurately. The reaction between hydrochloric acid and sodium hydroxide can be carried out as a titration.

hydrochloric acid + sodium hydroxide → sodium chloride + water
HCl + NaOH → NaCl + H_2O

A safety pipette filler is used to fill a pipette with a measured amount of alkali. The alkali is placed in a conical flask and a few drops of indicator are added. The acid is placed in a burette. Acid is then added to the alkali carefully, a small amount at a time. When the alkali has just neutralized the acid, the indicator changes colour. This is called the **neutral point** or **end-point**. The conical flask now contains a salt and water. If the salt is required, the titration is repeated without the indicator using exactly the same amounts of acid and alkali. The salt can be obtained by evaporating the water away. The table gives the results of a titration between hydrochloric acid and $25\,cm^3$ of $0.1\,M$ sodium hydroxide using universal indicator.

volume of 1.0 M HCl added in cm³	colour of indicator
0	purple
5	purple
10	blue
15	blue
20	blue
21	blue
22	blue
23	blue
24	green
25	yellow
26	pink
27	pink
28	pink
29	pink
30	pink
(Volume of 1.0 M NaOH used = 25 cm³)	

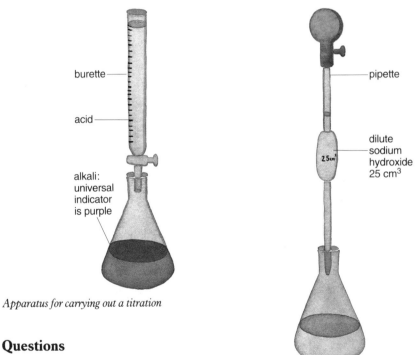

Apparatus for carrying out a titration

Questions

1   What is a titration?

2   What is meant by **neutral point** or **end-point**?

3   Draw a labelled diagram of the apparatus used in a titration.

4   What colour is universal indicator in a neutral solution?

5   Look at the table of results for the titration between hydrochloric acid and sodium hydroxide. How many cubic centimetres of acid are neutralized by $25\,cm^3$ of sodium hydroxide?

6   If the indicator litmus was used, what colour would it be at the end-point of the titration?

Titrations are carried out in analyical laboratories to find the concentrations of solutions.

Making substances pure

Sometimes we need a substance to be **pure**. Most naturally occurring substances are **mixtures** of different elements or compounds. Air is a mixture of different gases, both elements and compounds, for example nitrogen, oxygen, and carbon dioxide. Pure substances only contain one element or compound. If a substance is impure, it has different melting and boiling points than the pure substance. You can separate the impurities from a chemical substance using several different methods.

Differences between a mixture and a compound

mixture	compound
can be separated into its different components easily	can only be separated into its different components using a chemical method
has the same properties as its constituents	its properties are different from those of its constituents
no new substance is formed on making a mixture	a completely new substance is formed on making a compound

Filtering

If you have a mixture of two substances, one soluble in water and the other insoluble in water, you can separate them by **filtering**. Rock salt is a mixture of insoluble rock and soluble sodium chloride. If it is crushed and added to water, the sodium chloride will dissolve and the rock will not. The rock can be filtered away and the water evaporated leaving pure salt.

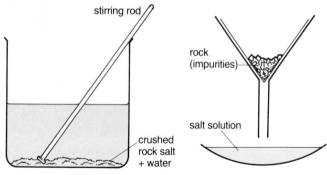

stirring rod

rock (impurities)

salt solution

crushed rock salt + water

Using filtration to take out the impurities in rock salt

Distillation

If you want to obtain pure water from salt solution, you do it by **distillation**. The evaporated water is collected as steam and then condensed. Distillation is more often used to separate a mixture of different liquids. This is called **fractional distillation** (see page 74).

Chromatography is used to identify the different substances in a mixture, and to see whether a substance is pure or not. Chromatography can be used to check whether a drug contains exactly what the manufacturer says it contains and also to identify amino acids in our bodies.

Questions

1 What method could you use to separate a mixture of sodium chloride (salt) and chalk dust?

2 How could you obtain pure water from sea water?

3 Here is the result of a chromatography experiment carried out with an unknown chemical X. It is thought that it contains another chemical. This chemical is either A, B, C, or D. Chromatography experiments have also been carried out on these chemicals. The results are shown below.
   a) What chemicals do you think X contains?
   b) How did you decide this?

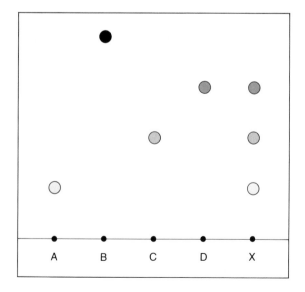

4 The boiling point of a liquid is 102 °C. Is this liquid pure water? Give a reason for your answer.

Solubility of salts

A salt is made when an acid is neutralized. The name of the salt made depends on the acid and the compound used to neutralize it. Nearly all salts are soluble in water. Sodium chloride, NaCl, is the most common salt. It is often just called salt. It is used to add taste to our food, and in its raw form on icy roads. However, 'salt' is a word that describes a group of chemicals all having the same properties.

- Salts have high melting points.

- Salts have high boiling points.

- Salts are often soluble in water.

- Salts can conduct electricity when dissolved in water or in the liquid state (they form electrolytes).

Some salts contain water in their crystals. These are **hydrated** salts. The water in their crystals is called **water of crystallization**. Examples of hydrated salts include Epsom salts, $MgSO_4 . 7H_2O$, and washing soda, $Na_2CO_3 . 10H_2O$. If the hydrated salt is heated and the water of crystallization evaporated away, the salt is then an **anhydrous** salt.

If you want to make a salt in the laboratory, it is important to know whether it is **soluble** in water or not. A salt is described as soluble if more than 1 g of the salt dissolves in 100 g of water.

- All sodium, potassium and ammonium salts are soluble.

- All nitrates are soluble.

- All chlorides are soluble except silver and lead chlorides.

- All sulphates are soluble except silver, lead, barium, and calcium sulphates.

- All carbonates, sulphides, and sulphites are insoluble except those of sodium, potassium, and ammonium.

Preparing an insoluble salt

Insoluble salts can be prepared by precipitation. For example, if you want to make some silver chloride salt, you add a solution containing silver ions to one containing chloride ions. When these two solutions are added together, a precipitate is formed. This can be filtered, washed, and left to dry. Suitable solutions for making silver chloride would be silver nitrate and sodium chloride. Both of these salts are soluble in water.

Questions

1 How much of a salt must dissolve in 100 g of water if the salt is soluble?

2 What is meant by **water of crystallization**?

3 Give three examples of hydrated salts.

4 Make a list of soluble salts.

5 Describe how you could prepare a pure, dry sample of the salt lead sulphate from lead nitrate solution and sodium sulphate solution.

Salting a road in winter.

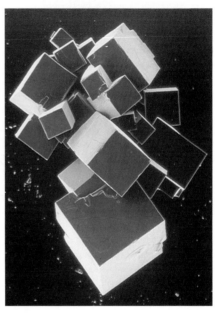

Sodium chloride has a cubic structure.

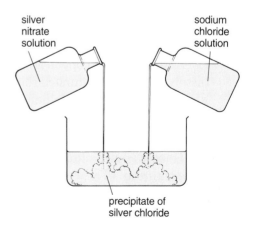

When a solution containing silver ions, Ag^+, is added to a solution containing chloride ions, Cl^-, a precipitate of silver chloride is produced.

Making salt crystals

Salt crystals have a definite shape. They all have straight edges, flat faces, and points or corners. Different salts have different shapes. Crystals of salts can be made and grown easily in the laboratory. They are made from a **saturated solution** of the salt. A saturated solution is a solution that will not dissolve any more of the solid.

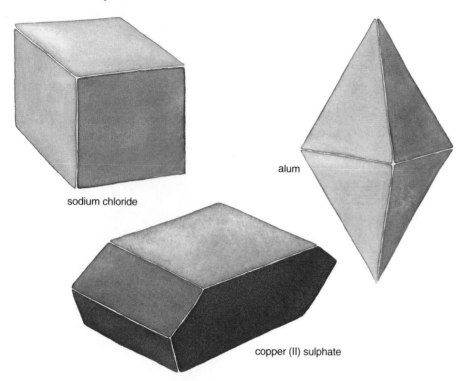

alum

sodium chloride

copper (II) sulphate

Salt crystals have a definite shape. They are not always easy to see. Try looking at them under a microscope.

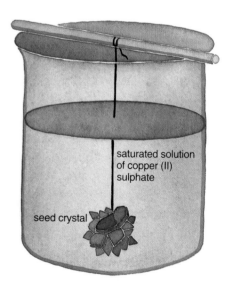

Can you see the shape of a copper(II) sulphate crystal?

Activities

1   Making a saturated solution of copper(II) sulphate

a)   Measure $50\,cm^3$ of pure water into a small beaker.

b)   Add two heaped spatulas of hydrated copper(II) sulphate powder.

c)   Stir until the powder has been dissolved.

d)   Keep adding the copper sulphate until no more will dissolve.

e)   Warm the solution.

f)   Add some more copper(II) sulphate and stir. When no more will dissolve you have a saturated solution.

g)   Leave the saturated solution to cool completely before starting to grow your crystal.

2   Growing a crystal

a)   Choose a small pure crystal of copper(II) sulphate and glue it to a piece of thread. (This is called a **seed crystal**.)

b)   Suspend the seed crystal in the saturated solution as shown in the diagram.

c)   Cover the beaker to avoid quick evaporation.

d)   After a few days you will notice that your crystal has started to grow.

saturated solution
of copper (II)
sulphate

seed crystal

Crystals of copper(II) sulphate can be grown to quite large sizes using this method.

Making soluble salts

There are four different ways of making a soluble salt.

acid	+	metal	→	salt	+	hydrogen
acid	+	metal oxide	→	salt	+	water
acid	+	alkali	→	salt	+	water
acid	+	carbonate	→	salt	+	water	+	carbon dioxide

The method used depends on the salt you want to make. The method using the reaction between an acid and an alkali is described on page 172.

Acid + metal

Not all metals react with dilute acids. This method cannot be used to make copper compounds, for example, since copper does not react with dilute acids. Lead reacts too slowly. Other metals, such as sodium and potassium, are too reactive to add to acid safely in the laboratory.

Zinc sulphate can be made using this method.

sulphuric acid + zinc → zinc sulphate + hydrogen
$$H_2SO_4 \quad + \quad Zn \quad \rightarrow \quad ZnSO_4 \quad + \quad H_2$$

Small amounts of zinc are added to the acid until no more reacts. When all the acid has been neutralized, there will be no more hydrogen gas given off. It is sometimes necessary to warm the flask gently to make sure that the reaction is complete. The excess zinc is filtered off. The remaining solution is crystallized to leave the salt.

Acid + metal oxide

This reaction is carried out in a similar way to the reaction with acid + metal. However, no hydrogen gas is given off during this reaction. To make sure that all the acid has been neutralized, the reaction can be tested with blue litmus paper. If the reaction is over, the litmus paper will remain blue. If it turns red, then either more metal oxide is needed or the reaction needs to be warmed slightly. The excess metal oxide is filtered off. The solution is evaporated to leave the salt.

Acid + metal carbonate

When a carbonate reacts with an acid, carbon dioxide gas is given off. All the acid will be neutralized if you add carbonate until no more gas is given off. The excess carbonate is filtered off. The solution is evaporated.

Questions

1 What are the four ways in which a soluble salt can be made in the laboratory?

2 Draw fully labelled diagrams to describe how to make copper(II) sulphate using copper(II) carbonate and sulphuric acid.

3 Which method could you use to prepare the following salts:
   a) magnesium chloride
   b) copper(II) chloride
   c) sodium sulphate
   d) calcium nitrate?

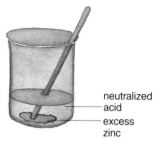

Making zinc sulphate from zinc and sulphuric acid

Geologists test rocks for carbonates by adding a few drops of acid.

Some common salts and their uses

Salt is found underground as rock salt. In the UK it is mined in Winsford, Cheshire. This rock salt is put on icy roads in the winter. The salt lowers the freezing point of water to below 0 °C. Salt water speeds up rusting (see page 72), so it is very important to wash cars carefully and frequently in the winter.

The correct amount of salt is very important in our diets. Too little salt can cause circulation problems. When we perspire, we lose a lot of salt through the pores of our skin. In very hot conditions people take salt tablets. However, too much salt is bad for you. It can cause high blood pressure and heart disease. Before the days of refrigeration, salt was used to preserve food. Pork was covered in salt and left in a cool building – it could be eaten months later.

The sea contains about 25 g of sodium chloride per litre of sea water. Sea water also contains many other salts, as shown in the table below.

salt found	amount in g per 100 g sea water
sodium chloride	2.6
magnesium chloride	0.3
magnesium sulphate	0.2
calcium sulphate	0.1
potassium chloride	0.1
magnesium bromide	0.01
magnesium iodide	0.0003

Salt is the main raw material for making chlorine and sodium hydroxide. A concentrated salt solution, called **brine**, is electrolysed.

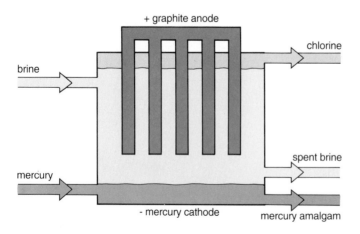

Flowing mercury cathode cell

Questions

1 What chemicals can be obtained from the electrolysis of sodium chloride?

2 What effects does sodium chloride have on our health?

3 List some uses of salt and compounds made from salt.

Salts as fertilizers

Ammonium nitrate is a useful fertilizer. It is a salt. It contains nitrogen which is an element essential for plant growth. A good fertilizer contains the elements needed to promote healthy growth in plants. It must also be cheap to produce and soluble in water.

Ammonium nitrate is used as a fertilizer.

In industry, ammonium nitrate is made by reacting ammonia with nitric acid. For this reason, the manufacture of ammonia and nitric acid are often carried out close to each other to reduce costs. Ammonia gas can be used directly as a fertilizer, but needs to be compressed to a liquid before it is injected into the Earth. This method is very popular in the USA.

Some other salts that are used as fertilizers include:

- calcium nitrate, $Ca(NO_3)_2$
- sodium nitrate, $NaNO_3$
- ammonium phosphate, $(NH_4)_3 PO_4$
- ammonium sulphate, $(NH_4)_2 SO_4$
- potassium sulphate, K_2SO_4.

Activities

1 Collect information about the chemical contents of fertilizers used by farmers and/or gardeners.

2 Try to find out the pH of a fertilizer by testing it with universal indicator.

3 Find out how fertilizers can cause pollution.

1   Copy and complete the following table:

name of chemical	pH	colour of universal indicator
	1	
pure water		
	14	
		blue

2   Answer the following questions in full sentences:
a)   What indicator turns red in lemon juice and blue in sodium carbonate solution?
b)   The 'fur' inside kettles is calcium hydrogencarbonate. What household chemical could be used to 'defur' a kettle?
c)   A gardener wishes to grow some turnips. They grow best in soil with a pH of 6. The soil in the garden is at a pH of 5.5. What could the gardener do to the soil to improve his chances of a good crop of turnips?

3   The labels have gone missing from four bottles. The bottles are known to contain the following colourless solutions:

● phenolphthalein
● hydrochloric acid
● sodium hydroxide
● sodium carbonate.

Using only test tubes and four pieces of magnesium, design an experiment to determine which bottle is which. Describe the results you would expect.

4   **a)**   List three differences between a mixture and a compound.
b)   Give two examples of a mixture and two examples of a compound.
c)   Describe how you could separate water from a solution of black ink in the laboratory.

5   What is the name of the salt that is made when the following chemicals react?
a)   phosphoric acid + potassium carbonate
b)   sulphuric acid + magnesium oxide
c)   hydrochloric acid + ammonium hydroxide
d)   nitric acid + zinc
e)   hydrochloric acid + silver nitrate.

6   Give brief details of how the following salts could be prepared in the laboratory:
a)   potassium chloride
b)   copper(II) nitrate
c)   lead chloride
d)   magnesium sulphate.

7   **a)**   Describe what you would see if a piece of zinc metal was placed in some dilute hydrochloric acid.
b)   How would you identify the gas that was given off during the reaction?
c)   Write an equation for the reaction.

8   What is the difference between a strong acid and a concentrated acid? What type of experiments could you carry out to illustrate your answer? Use ethanoic (acetic) acid (vinegar) and hydrochloric acid to help you answer this question.

What is alternating current?

How can alternating voltages be measured?

What is a transformer?

How is electrical power distributed?

How can we get d.c. from a.c.?

An electrical substation

Overhead cables carry electricity to where its needed

A coal-fired power station

All the photographs on this page are about the electricity used in offices, homes, schools, shops, and factories. As you travel around look out for power stations, overhead cables and pylons, and electricity board substations. You may also see electricity board workers repairing cables in the street. Our modern world would not be able to function without an efficient supply of electricity.

In this country our homes are supplied with **alternating current**. This chapter tells you how this is generated and how it is distributed around the country. It will help you understand this if you have studied electrical circuits and electricity and magnetism first.

Remember that electric shocks can kill. Never experiment with the mains supply and never get close to electricity board power lines or substations.

Activities

1 Describe briefly the area where you live. Is it in a town or in the country, mainly houses or industry, with a high or low population?

2 How is electricity delivered to your home? By overhead wires or underground cables?

3 Do you know where the nearest substation is to your home or school? Draw its warning sign.

Generating electricity

We saw in Chapter 5 that a magnet moving near a coil of wires induces a voltage. This can make a current flow in a circuit. **Electrical generators** like the bicycle dynamo in the photograph use this principle.

The energy which generates electricity in a bicycle dynamo comes from the rider. It is really his or her food which supplies the energy to turn the wheel which turns the magnet inside the coil of wire!

Bicycle dynamo

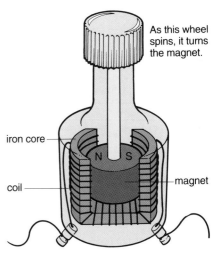

As this wheel spins, it turns the magnet.

iron core

coil

magnet

Inside the bicycle dynamo

When the magnet is lined up with the iron core there is a strong magnetic field in the coil of wire. As the magnet turns, the field gets weaker. It then gets stronger again but in the opposite direction. It is this changing magnetic field inside the coil which provides a voltage at the dynamo's terminals.

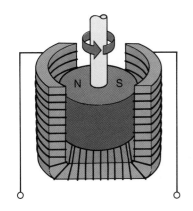

Large magnetic field inside the coil

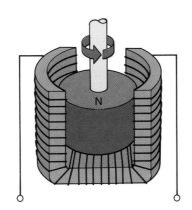

Small magnetic field inside the coil

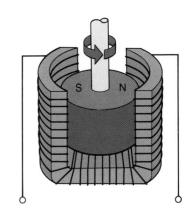

Large magnetic field inside the coil, but reversed

The size of the voltage produced by the dynamo depends on the speed of the spinning magnet. As it spins faster the voltage increases so the bicycle lights get brighter. When the bicycle stops the dynamo does not generate any electricity and the lights go out.

Questions

1 A student writes the following energy chain for a cyclist riding a bike with lights powered by a dynamo.

chemical energy → kinetic energy → electrical energy → heat + light

Explain where each energy change takes place.

2 Explain why lights powered by batteries are safer when cycling in traffic. Suggest one advantage that dynamo lights have over battery lights.

3 A girl rides a bicycle. The dynamo always rubs on the tyre, whether the lights are on or off. She finds that it is more difficult to pedal when she switches the lights on. Try to explain this fact.

When a bicycle dynamo is turning slowly the lights are not very bright and they flicker. This tells us that the output is not smooth.

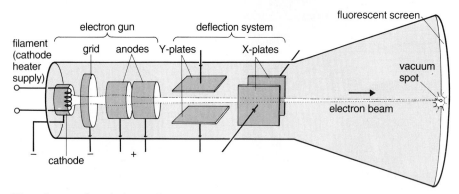

The main parts of a cathode ray tube

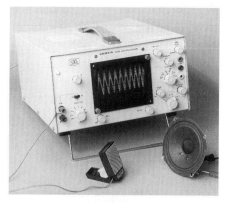

A CRO (cathode ray oscilloscope)

To investigate how the voltage changes with time we use a **cathode ray oscilloscope** (CRO). When the negative cathode is heated electrons are released from its surface. These are attracted to the positive anodes. The anodes accelerate the electrons and focus the beam. When the beam hits the fluorescent chemicals on the screen a bright spot of light is produced.

The X-plates are connected to an electronic time-base circuit. This gives a steadily changing voltage between the plates which makes the spot move across the screen at a steady speed. When it reaches the far side a sudden change in the voltage makes the beam fly back to its starting position. The speed of the moving dot can be adjusted. When it is moving quickly it looks like a continuous line.

The Y-plates are connected to two input terminals. This is where we apply the electrical signals to be investigated. When the top plate is positive the spot moves up the screen. When the bottom plate is positive the spot moves down.

The CRO has a gain control. This allows the size of the deflection to be set so that the voltage can be measured. For example, if the gain is set at 3 V/cm then a signal of 6 V will move the spot 2 cm up the screen.

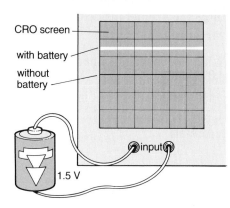

A dry cell connected to a CRO

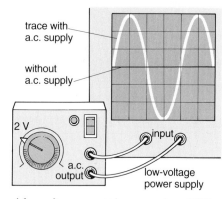

A low-voltage a.c. supply connected to a CRO

Investigating electrical supplies

When a dry cell (battery) is connected to a CRO the trace moves up the screen but remains a straight line. This tells us that the dry cell gives a steady, **direct current** (d.c.).

If the cell is reversed then the trace moves down from its starting position. This is because the voltage has been reversed.

When the input is a 3 V a.c. signal from a low-voltage power supply the trace looks like a wave. This shows how the voltage is changing with time.

When the output of a bicycle dynamo like the one shown on page 185 is connected to the CRO we get a complicated pattern. We can see, however, that the dynamo voltage changes direction. This shows that it is producing **alternating current** (a.c.)

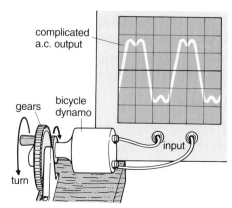

Output from a bicycle dynamo

Looking at alternating current

The electricity board supplies an alternating voltage to our homes. When we turn on, say, a light bulb, the alternating voltage makes an alternating current flow in the circuit.

We can use a CRO to investigate alternating voltages but **remember: never experiment with mains electricity – electric shocks can kill**. Instead we can look at the output of a low-voltage power supply.

The diagram shows what happens when a 3 V a.c. signal is applied to a CRO. The time base is set at 5 ms/cm. This means that the spot moves 1 cm across the screen in 5 milliseconds ($^{1}/_{200}$ s). The gain is set at 2 V/cm. This means that the spot moves 1 cm up the screen for every 2 V applied.

The smooth curve we get is called a **sine curve**. It has a special wave-like shape. Notice that it goes above and below the centre line showing that the voltage keeps changing direction: it is **alternating**. To find out how fast it is changing we measure its **frequency**.

Frequency

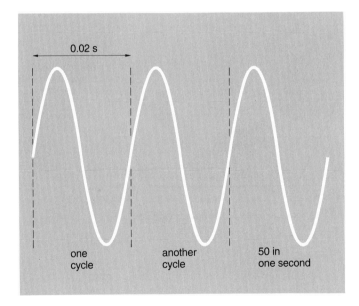

Anything which changes regularly with time has a frequency. This tells us how many times the cycle or pattern is completed in one second. The CRO trace above shows that the mains voltage completes one cycle in 0.02 s. Therefore it has a frequency of 50 cycles in each second. The scientific unit for frequency is the **hertz** (Hz). The frequency of the mains voltage in the UK is 50 Hz.

Voltage

The low voltage supply was set at 3 V a.c. but the CRO shows that it goes up to over +4 V and down to below −4 V! Because alternating voltages keep changing we need special ways of describing them.

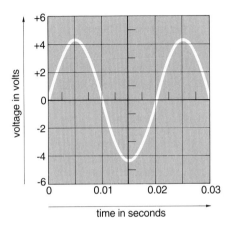

Peak voltage. This is the highest voltage produced. Our signal had a peak voltage of about 4.2 V.

Peak-to-peak voltage. The voltage actually swings from +4.2 V to −4.2 V so its peak-to-peak voltage is about 8.4 V.

R.M.S. voltage. The peak voltage is useful but we need a measure of the average voltage. In fact we really want to know what the equivalent steady d.c. voltage would be.

The steady voltage equivalent is called the **root-mean-square (r.m.s.)** value.

It is given by: $V_{r.m.s.} = \dfrac{V_{peak}}{\sqrt{2}}$ $(\sqrt{2} = 1.414)$

Questions

1 The label stuck to the back of an electrical appliance says '240 V, 50 Hz, 2000 W. Use 13 A fuse.'

    a) Does the appliance work on batteries or mains? Explain how you know.

    b) What does 50 Hz mean?

    c) The voltage given is the r.m.s. value. Calculate the peak voltage of the supply.

    d) What does a.c. mean?

    e) A light bulb is connected to the 50 Hz mains supply. Describe, in detail, what is happening to the current in the bulb's filament. Suggest why you can't see the bulb flickering.

Generators for power stations

At power stations fuel is used to heat water and turn it into steam. The steam then turns turbines connected to a.c. generators. These are called **alternators**. They work on the same principles as the bicycle dynamo. The voltage is produced by a magnet spinning inside fixed coils of wire. However, the power station alternator uses a spinning electromagnet. This is stronger than a permanent magnet. It can also be controlled easily; by changing the current in the electromagnet the output from the alternator can be accurately controlled without slowing the turbines. The current for the electromagnet comes from a small d.c. generator which is also driven by the turbines.

An alternator in a power station.

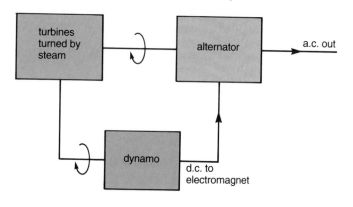

Block diagram showing a.c. generation at a power station

The bicycle dynamo only has one pair of coils. The alternator has three pairs. Each pair gives its own a.c. output with the peak voltages coming at slightly different times. We say that the alternator gives three **phases**. Only one phase is supplied to your home but factories may be supplied with all three.

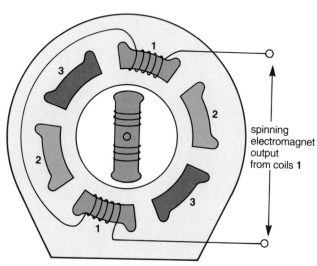
A three-phase alternator has three pairs of coils.

Questions

1   Write down two similarities and two differences between a bicycle dynamo and an alternator.

2   Explain why a power station alternator is attached to a d.c. generator.

3   A power station alternator can produce a current of 20 000 A at a voltage of 25 000 V.
   a)   Calculate the maximum power output of the alternator.
   b)   How many 100 W bulbs can be lit by the alternator?

4   A bicycle dynamo can just light two 3 V, 0.3 A bulbs fully. Calculate the maximum power output of the dynamo.

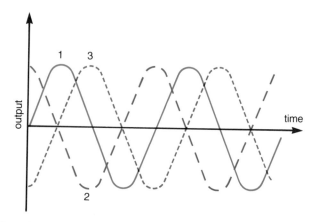
The three-phase generator gives three separate outputs.

Changing alternating voltages

We have seen that alternating voltages can be easily produced using rotating magnet dynamos and alternators. We also know that a.c. is just as effective as d.c. for lighting and heating. However, alternating voltages have one major advantage: they can be increased or decreased very easily using a **transformer**.

A simple transformer has an iron core with two coils wound around it. When a current flows in one coil, the core becomes strongly magnetized. When the magnetic field changes it causes an induced voltage in the second coil. This is **electromagnetic induction**.

The diagram shows a battery connected to one coil of a transformer. With the switch open there is no magnetic field. As the switch is closed the core becomes magnetized. The sudden change causes an induced voltage in the second coil. It is just as if a magnet had been pushed into the second coil.

If the switch is left closed the core stays magnetized and so the field remains steady and there is no voltage across the second coil. If the switch is opened the magnetic field suddenly collapses and so a voltage is induced across the second coil. This is like suddenly pulling a magnet out of the second coil. This time the induced voltage is in the opposite direction.

Remember: a voltage is only induced when the magnetic field is changing.

The second diagram shows the same transformer connected to an a.c. supply. The a.c. through the first coil is constantly changing its size and direction. This produces a magnetic field in the core which keeps changing size and direction. This gives an alternating voltage across the second coil. Notice that if the first coil is attached to a 50 Hz supply then the output from the second coil will also be at 50 Hz.

When the two coils have exactly the same number of turns the output voltage is exactly the same as the supply voltage. However, when they have different numbers of turns the voltage is changed. The voltage can be increased or decreased.

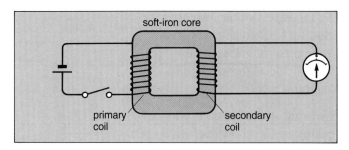

A voltage is only induced in the secondary coil when the switch is opened or closed.

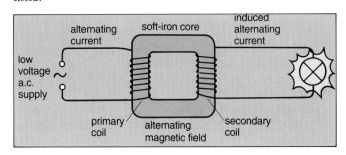

Transformers work on a.c.

A transformer

Questions

1 How can a magnet and a coil of wire be used to make electricity?

2 What is the iron core for in a transformer? Suggest why the coils are wound on a complete loop of iron.

3 How do transformers 'transform'?

4 Why can't a transformer be used to change the voltage from a battery?

To increase a voltage we use a **step-up transformer**. This has more turns on the secondary or output side as shown in the diagram.

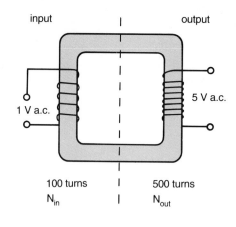

A step-up transformer

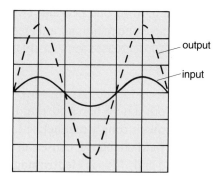

Voltages in a step-up transformer

By using an oscilloscope with two beams we can show that the output has the same frequency as the input but that the voltage is greater.

We can also show that the output voltage depends on the input voltage and the number of turns in the coils.

$$\frac{\text{voltage across secondary}}{\text{voltage across primary}} = \frac{\text{number of turns in secondary coil}}{\text{number of turns in primary coil}}$$

In symbols:

$$\frac{V_{out}}{V_{in}} = \frac{N_{out}}{N_{in}}$$

Step-up transformers are used to increase the voltage produced by power station alternators. This allows electricity to be distributed across the country with less loss of energy. (See page 192.)

A **step-down transformer** has fewer turns on the output side. This gives an output voltage which is lower than the input voltage.

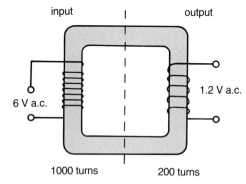

A step-down transformer

We can use the same formula:

$$\frac{V_{out}}{V_{in}} = \frac{N_{out}}{N_{in}}$$

Step-down transformers are used in many household appliances. This allows them to operate safely from the mains voltage. The photograph shows the inside of a portable cassette player. It can work from the six 1.5 V batteries seen at the bottom or it can be plugged into the 240 V mains – a small transformer then steps this down to 9 V.

This portable cassette player has a step-down transformer inside it.

Questions

1 The diagram shows the symbol for a transformer. What three parts of a real transformer do you think the symbol represents?

2 A transformer has 100 turns on the input (primary) side and 250 turns on the output (secondary) side.
    a) Does the transformer step voltage up or down?
    b) What would be the output voltage if the input voltage was   i) 10 V a.c.   ii) 50 V a.c.
    iii) 6 V d.c.?

Transformers and energy

You can get more voltage out of a step-up transformer than you put in. Does this mean that you are getting more energy out? The answer is no – transformers do not break the law of conservation of energy. You do get more voltage, but the current is stepped down.

The **power** transferred in an electrical component is given by:

power = current × voltage

A perfect transformer gives exactly the same output power as the input power.

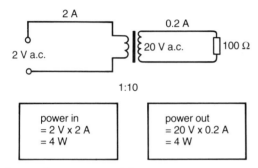

In a perfect transformer, no power is lost.

The diagram shows a step-up transformer connected to a 100 Ω resistor.
The power on the input side is 2 V × 2 A = 4 W.
The power on the output side is 20 V × 0.2 A = 4 W.
We have not gained or lost any energy.

In fact, real transformers are not this efficient. Some energy is used to push the current through the transformer coils. This is wasted as heat. The core of the transformer also gets warm as the changing magnetic field causes currents to flow in the iron. To reduce this the core is **laminated**. This means that it is made out of thin sheets of iron riveted together, rather than a solid piece of iron.

Some calculators and computers require separate step-down transformers.

Some calculators and computers use a step-down transformer so that they can work from the mains. The transformer gets warm as energy is wasted in the coils and core. Transformers like this often make a buzzing sound as the changing magnetic field makes the core vibrate.

Example

A step-down transformer converts 240 V a.c. to 12 V a.c.
The output current is 2 A and the input current is 0.11 A.

   a) What is the efficiency of the transformer?
   b) Comment on your answer.

   a) input power = voltage × current
                      = 240 V × 0.11 A
                      = 26.4 W
      output power = 12 V × 2.0 A
                      = 24.0 W

$$\text{efficiency} = \frac{\text{output power}}{\text{input power}} \times 100\%$$

$$= \frac{24.0}{26.4} \times 100\% = \textbf{90.9\%}$$

b) Transformers can be made to be very efficient. This one wastes 9% of the energy put in. This goes to heat up the transformer and its surroundings.

Questions

1 A transformer has 100 turns on the input side and 1000 turns on the output side.

   a) What does this transformer step up?
   b) What does it step down?

2 A transformer steps the mains voltage (240 V) down to 6 V. The current taken from the output is 0.5 A.

   a) What is the power output of the transformer?
   b) If the transformer is perfect (wastes no energy) what is its power input, and the current taken from the mains?

3 A transformer has an efficiency of 90%. Describe where the other 10% of the energy goes.

Transformers and the National Grid

When a power station is built the site has to be chosen carefully. It must be close to a coal field or there must be a way of getting fuel to it cheaply. It needs a large supply of water for cooling. It should also be far enough away from towns so that residents do not have to suffer noise and pollution. It is very important that nuclear power stations are not built near to where people live to minimize any risk of radiation effects. As a result most of our power stations are built in remote parts of the country far away from the towns where the electricity is needed. The electricity which is generated is distributed through a vast network of cables which crosses the country. This network is called the **National Grid**.

Overhead cables are used to transmit electrical energy over hundreds of kilometres. They are designed to be good conductors, but they do have some resistance. When a current flows in them they get warm and so some energy is wasted. The amount of wasted energy can be reduced if a low current is used, but this means that a high voltage must be used to transmit the same amount of power.

The advantage of using high voltages can be shown using model power lines. In the first case the lines are at 12 V. In the second case the voltage has been stepped up 20 times to 240 V. This means that the current can be 20 times smaller. (**Remember: power = current × voltage.**) Because there is less current there is less power loss in the cables. The voltage is stepped down at the far end and the bulb lights brightly.

Do overhead power lines spoil the environment?

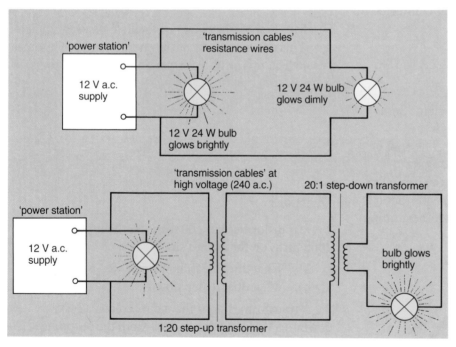

Model power lines

In the real National Grid the alternators at the power station give an output of 20 000 V. This is then stepped up to 275 000 V or even 400 000 V! The voltage is then stepped down for use in industry, offices, and our homes. The diagram on the opposite page shows typical voltage values in the National Grid.

A step-up transformer at a power station

The National Grid

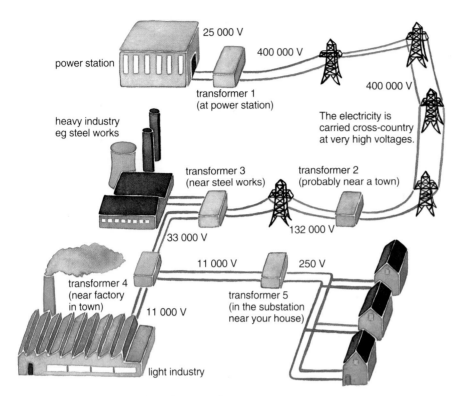

The National Grid – bringing electricity to your home

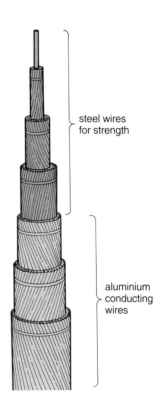

The structure of an overhead cable

Overhead or underground?

The cables used to transmit electrical energy can be hung from pylons or buried under the ground. Each method has advantages and disadvantages. Overhead cables are much cheaper to make and install. One kilometre of overhead cables costs about £500 000, but one kilometre of underground cables costs about £6 000 000!

Installing underground cables is much more difficult, and if they fail it takes much longer to repair them.

One disadvantage of overhead cables is that they are ugly and spoil the countryside. They are also much more dangerous than underground cables. Children flying kites near power lines have received severe shocks and youths climbing pylons have been killed.

Overhead cables

Overhead cables must have the lowest resistance possible but they must also be strong enough to support their weight. Light cables are best because then the pylons can be further apart. This saves money. In practice, aluminium wires are used to conduct electricity and steel wires are used for strength.

Questions

1 Explain why step-up transformers are used in the National Grid.

2 The electricity supply to your home has been stepped down to 240 V. Explain why.

3 Explain in scientific terms why it is dangerous to fly a kite near overhead power lines. Your answer should include the words voltage, Earth, current, and circuit.

4 Imagine you are an electricity board official responsible for putting up power lines near to a small village. Write a letter to the residents explaining why you are not using underground cables.

The light bulbs and heating elements in our homes work on a.c. but would work equally well on a 240 V d.c. supply. However, some electrical devices, particularly those with electronic components like transistors, must have a d.c. supply.

We can change a.c. to d.c. using components called **diodes**. Diodes only allow current to pass in one direction.

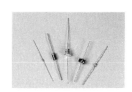

These are diodes. The cathode end is marked on each one.

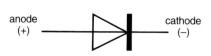

This is the diode symbol. The diode only conducts when the cathode end is connected to the negative side of the supply.

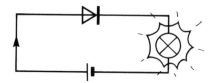

*In this circuit the bulb lights. The diode lets the current through. We say that the diode is **forward biased.***

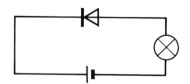

*In this circuit no current flows so the bulb does not light. We say that the diode is **reverse biased.***

Rectification

Diodes have many uses. For example, they can be used to change a.c. to d.c. This is called **rectification**. The simplest rectification circuit is shown in the diagram opposite. The diode stops a current flowing in the load resistor when the voltage is in the 'wrong' direction. When no current flows there is no voltage across the resistor. We can use a CRO to show that the output is always in the same direction.

This is called **half-wave rectification** because the negative half of the a.c. input is missing from the output.

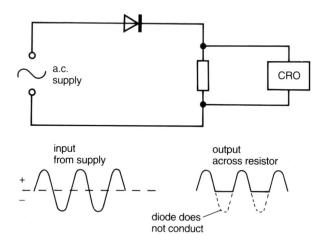

To get closer to a true d.c. supply we can use four diodes arranged in a special arrangement called a **bridge rectifier**. This does not block the current for half the cycle, but lets it follow a different path.

The output shows that we still have a changing signal but it is always in the same direction. This is **full-wave rectification**.

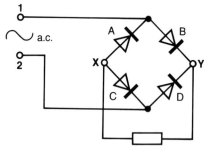

A bridge rectifier circuit

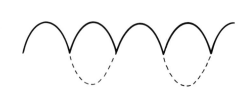

The output from a bridge rectifier. This is full-wave rectification.

Smoothing

To get a smoother output from the bridge rectifier a **capacitor** is used. Capacitors store electrical charge as the voltage across them rises. However, when the voltage starts to drop they discharge, keeping the output high. The diagram opposite shows how this gives a steadier output.

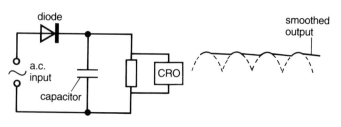

Using a capacitor to smooth a supply

Putting a power supply together

Batteries are very useful for portable electrical equipment, but they do not last very long and are expensive to replace. Many portable cassette players and radios work either from batteries or from the mains. Similarly many experiments in the laboratory could be carried out using batteries but a low-voltage d.c. power supply is more convenient, more reliable, and costs less to run. Such power supplies have to do three things:

- step the 240 V a.c. down to a low voltage
- rectify the a.c. so that it becomes d.c.
- smooth the output.

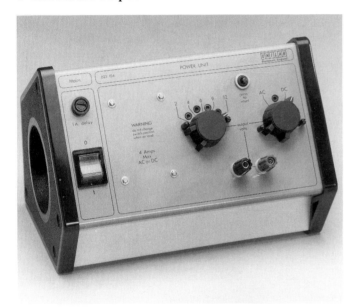

This power supply can be used instead of batteries.

The diagram shows a simple circuit for a power supply.

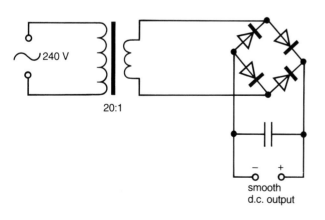

A low-voltage power supply

The 20:1 transformer steps the mains voltage down to 12 V. The four diodes are arranged as a bridge rectifier. This gives full-wave rectification.

The capacitor across the output terminals gives a smoothed output. You can test this using a CRO.

Questions

A portable cassette player uses six 1.5 V batteries. Each battery costs 25p. Using batteries, tapes can be played for about 8 hours. It can also work using a mains adaptor (transformer). The maximum power output of the cassette player is 10 W.

1 Calculate the cost of playing tapes for 1 hour using batteries.

2 Calculate the cost of playing tapes for 1 hour using the mains. (Mains electricity costs 6p for 1 kWh.)

3 Comment on your answers.

4 What d.c. voltage does the cassette player work on?

5 Design a mains adaptor for the cassette player to provide a smooth d.c. output of the correct voltage.

More power supplies

The bicycle dynamo at the start of this chapter gives a cheap source of electricity but only lights the bicycle lamps when the wheels are turning. A battery system is more expensive to run but safer. The best solution is to use a battery to take over when the dynamo stops.

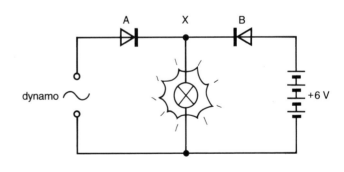

A dynamo system with battery back-up

When the dynamo is not working current from the battery flows through the bulb. Diode A stops the current passing through the dynamo. When the dynamo is working the voltage at point X becomes greater than +6 V. Diode B is now reversed biased so no current flows from the battery. The dynamo lights the bulb.

Alternators and transformers in cars

The electrical system of a car gets its energy from a 12 V lead–acid battery. The battery is charged by an alternator driven by the engine. The alternator produces a.c. This is converted by a bridge rectifier into d.c. The size of the current is electronically controlled so that the battery is always charged at the correct rate.

In a petrol engine, explosions are started inside cylinders by a **sparking plug**. A voltage of about 10 000 V is needed to make a spark jump across the gap. To get this very high voltage from a 12 V battery needs a special type of transformer called an **induction coil**.

The core of the coil is made up of iron wires. The primary side has a few turns of thick copper wire. The secondary side has thousands of turns of thin wire. When the primary coil is connected to the battery the iron core becomes magnetized. When the primary circuit is turned off the magnetic field suddenly collapses. This rapid change causes a very big induced voltage – big enough to cause a spark.

The coil has to be turned off at exactly the right time so that each cylinder gets its spark just as the piston reaches the top of the stroke. In modern cars this is done electronically. In older cars a mechanical switch called a **contact breaker** is used.

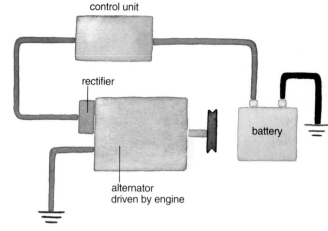

Generating electricity in a car

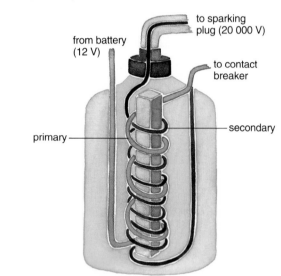

The induction coil is a step-up transformer.

Activities

1 Persuade a car owner to show you a car engine.

Look for the alternator. Find out how it is driven by the engine.

Look for the ignition coil. Look for the thin wires going to the primary side. Identify the wire from the secondary side. This comes from the centre of the cap of the coil. It will look thick because it is heavily insulated. Why?

If the car owner knows about the engine get him or her to point out the contact breaker or the electronic ignition system.

Identify the spark plugs. What do you notice about the leads going to them? Try to find out how big the gap is which the spark has to jump. (It will be in the car's handbook.)

Danger: this activity should only be carried out under supervision. Make sure that the ignition is turned off. High tension leads can give severe shocks.

A car engine

Questions

1 a) Draw a diagram showing the main parts of a bicycle dynamo.

b) Where does the energy come from to turn the magnet in a bicycle dynamo?

c) Describe two main differences between a bicycle dynamo and a power station alternator.

d) Where does the energy come from to turn the magnet in a power station alternator?

2 The diagram below shows an alternating voltage on a CRO screen. The Y-gain is set at 5 V/cm.

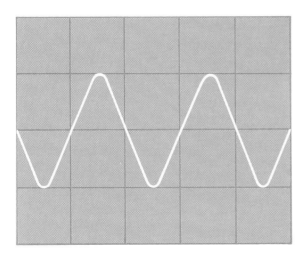

a) What is the peak voltage of the signal?

b) Is the r.m.s. voltage larger or smaller than the peak voltage?

c) Estimate the r.m.s. voltage.

d) Draw, to the same scale, what you would see if the time-base speed was doubled, i.e. speeded up.

3 The diagram below shows a transformer.

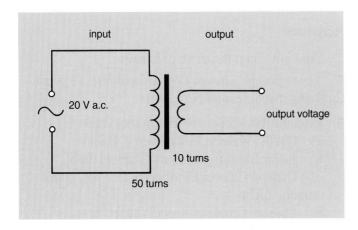

a) Is this a step-up or step-down transformer?

b) What will be the size of the output voltage?

c) What will be the frequency of the output signal?

4 The diagram below shows a step-up transformer.

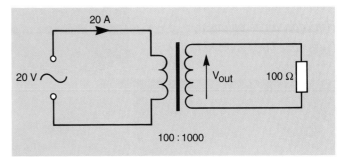

a) Calculate the output voltage V_{out}.

b) Calculate the current in the $100\,\Omega$ resistor. (Assume no energy is lost.)

c) Use your results to prove that transformers do not create energy.

5 a) What is the National Grid?

b) Give two reasons why our National Grid uses a.c.

c) Explain why National Grid cables are at many thousands of volts.

d) Underground power cables are much more expensive than overhead cables. Under what circumstances do you think that the electricity board should choose to use underground cables? Explain your answer.

6 The diagram shows a low-voltage d.c. power supply used in a school laboratory.

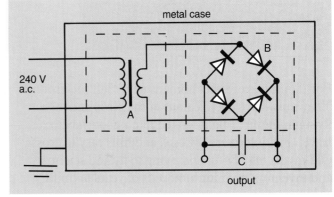

a) What are components A, B, and C? What does each one do?

b) Explain why the metal case is earthed.

7 You buy a portable cassette player which works on six batteries each costing 52p. The shop also sells a mains transformer for the cassette player at a cost of £10. Explain why it may be worth buying the transformer to use at home.

10 Falling and flying

Who do objects fall to Earth?
How do satellites stay in orbit?
How does an aeroplane fly?
How have birds evolved to fly?

For thousands of years humans never left the ground. They must have been jealous of the birds and insects flying in the air. Flight looked like a good way to travel, making rivers, forests, and hills easy to cross. Old myths tell of humans trying to fly and scientists and inventors tried for hundreds of years to build flying machines.

Most of the early designs were completely useless. In 1783 the first successful human flight took place in a hot air balloon designed by the Montgolfier brothers. Since then progress has been rapid and now flying is a common method of transport. Falling is a much more familiar experience and this chapter studies why things fall and how we can use this knowledge to our advantage.

Activities

1   Find out about the myth of Icarus.

2   Try to find pictures of Leonardo da Vinci's plans for flying machines and parachutes.

3   Find the dates for these important events:
   a)   Orville Wright: first powered flight
   b)   Louis Bleriot: first cross-Channel flight
   c)   Captain Charles Lindbergh: first solo trans-Atlantic flight
   d)   Captain Charles Elwood Yeager: first supersonic flight
   e)   Dick Rutan and Jeanna Yeager: first non-stop flight around the world without refuelling!

Mass, weight, and gravity

Over 300 years ago **Sir Isaac Newton** came up with the idea that all masses attract all other masses. He called this attraction **gravity**. The Earth has a mass of about six million million million million kilograms so its gravitational pull is large and easily measured. Newton's genius helped him to see that it is gravity which pulls an apple to the ground when it falls from a tree, and that it is the same gravity which keeps the planets in their orbits around the Sun.

Gravity and weight

When we lift a bag of sand from the ground we have to use a force. This is because the Earth's gravity is pulling downwards with a force. We call this force **weight** and we can measure it with a spring balance or newton meter. Because weight is a force it is measured in newtons. The **mass** which is being acted on by gravity is measured in kilograms. The weight of a 1 kg mass depends on the strength of gravity where the weight is measured.

This might seem confusing but it is easy to understand if you think about taking a 1 kg bag of sugar on a very long journey. In the UK the strength of the gravitational field is about 10 N/kg. This means that it gives a force of 10 N on every kilogram. The Moon is much less massive than the Earth – the strength of the Moon's gravitational field is about 1.6 N/kg.

An astronaut buys a 1 kg bag of sugar in London. Its mass is 1 kg. Its weight is 10 N. She takes the sugar to the Moon without opening it on the way, so its mass is still 1 kg. On the Moon it only weighs 1.6 N!

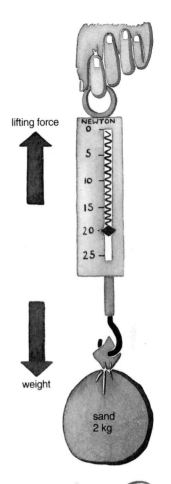

lifting force

weight

sand 2 kg

Working out weight

We know that things with a great mass are difficult to lift. This is because the gravitational force (weight) is large. Since the strength of gravity is the force on each kilogram we just multiply the mass and the field strength to get the weight.

weight = mass × gravity = *m* × *g*

Example

An exploration robot of mass 100 kg is built on Earth at a place where the strength of gravity is 9.8 N/kg. It is sent to Mars where the strength of gravity is 3.7 N/kg. What does the robot weigh on Earth and on Mars?

a) Mass on Earth = 100 kg
Strength of gravity on Earth = 9.8 kg/N
Weight on Earth = mass × gravity
$\qquad\qquad$ = 100 × 9.8 N = **980 N**

b) Mass on Mars = same as on Earth = 100 kg
Strength of gravity on Mars = 3.7 kg/N
Weight on Mars = mass × gravity
$\qquad\qquad$ = 100 × 3.7 N = **370 N**

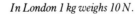

weight 10 N

In London 1 kg weighs 10 N.

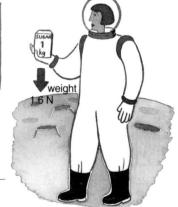

weight 1.6 N

On the Moon 1 kg weighs 1.6 N.

Activities

1 Using bathroom scales find your mass in kilograms. Use your result to calculate what your weight would be **a)** in Paris (*g* = 9.8 N/kg) **b)** at the North Pole (*g* = 9.85 N/kg) **c)** on the Moon (*g* = 1.6 N/kg) **d)** on Mars (*g* = 3.7 N/kg).

2 People who want to get slimmer may go to a club called 'Weight Watchers'. Explain why scientists might argue that it should be called '**Mass** Watchers'!

Balancing

Kitchen scales balance when the weights on each side are the same. If there is more weight in the left-hand pan then that side moves down. This is because the larger force has a bigger turning effect about the pivot.

The turning effect of a force is called its **moment**.

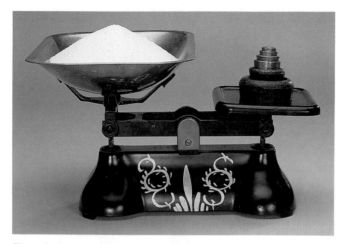

The scales balance when the forces on each side are equal.

The moment of a force depends on how big the force is. It also depends on the distance of the force from the pivot or fulcrum. The diagram below shows how a large force can be balanced by a smaller force. Notice that the smaller force is further away from the pivot. This increases its turning effect.

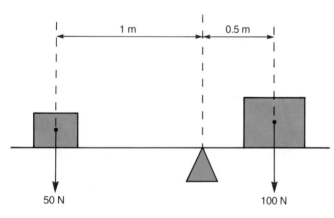

The moment of the force on the left-hand side is 50 N × 1 m = 50 Nm.
The moment of the force on the right-hand side is 100 N × 0.5 m = 50 Nm.
These balance.

Using moments

People have known how to use the moment of a force to do work for thousands of years. For example, the Egyptians used levers and other simple machines to move heavy blocks of stone to make the pyramids

about 50 000 years ago. The diagram below shows how a small force at the end of a long lever can overcome a large force close to the pivot.

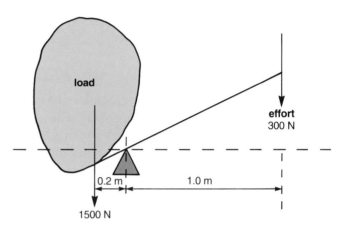

A long lever can enable a small effort to raise a large load.

The lever acts as a **force multiplier** but does not do more **work** than the effort puts in. The effort (300 N) moves through a large distance but the load (1500 N) is only raised by a small amount. In real life, the effort would need to be a bit bigger than 300 N to overcome friction at the pivot.

Useful levers

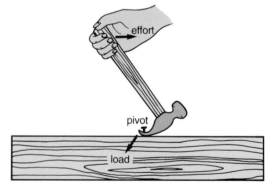

A small effort applied to the end of a hammer can overcome the force holding the nail in the wood.

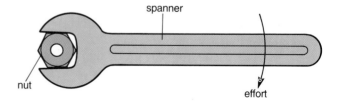

A long-handled spanner allows a small effort to overcome the large forces holding the nut on.

A metre rule will balance if it is supported at its mid-point. This is because the weights of all the particles on one side of the pivot are balanced by the weights of all the particles on the other side. To the person supporting the rule it is as though all the weight is acting at one point. This point is called the **centre of gravity** (or the **centre of mass**).

For uniform objects like metre rules and billiard balls the centre of gravity is where you would expect – right in the centre! For other shapes you may have to carry out a simple investigation to find it.

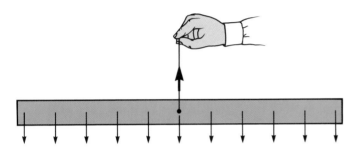

The weights of all the particles to the left of the centre of gravity balance those on the right.

Activities

1 Cut a shape out of a thick piece of card. Punch holes near to two corners.

Now hang the card from a nail or pin as shown in the diagram below.

Use a plumb line to mark a vertical line.

Repeat this with the card suspended from the other corner. Where the two lines cross is the centre of gravity.

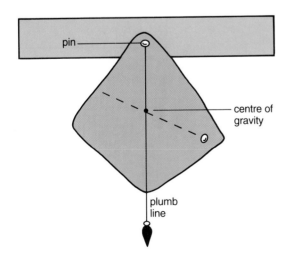

Stability

Some things fall over easily when pushed. They are **unstable**. Others are very difficult to topple. We say that these are **stable**.

The stability of an object depends on how far we can tip it before its weight moves outside its base. When this happens the moment of the weight tips it over.

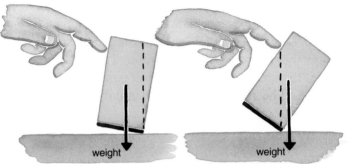

With a small push the weight will tip the box back to its original position.

With a larger push the weight is outside the base and so tips the box over.

Things with wide bases and low centres of gravity are most stable. Designers use this to make their products safer. For example, the Bunsen burners used in a laboratory have a wide, heavy base. This makes them very stable.

Racing cars have low centres of gravity and wide wheelbases.

Activities

1 Draw, in section, these pieces of laboratory equipment: beaker, test tube, conical flask, evaporating dish, measuring cylinder.

Try to get the proportions right.

Comment on the stability of each one.

Gravity and falling

If you hang a block of iron from a piece of string, the downward force (weight) is balanced by an upward force in the string (**tension**). Because the forces are balanced the iron block stays at rest. If you now cut the string the weight **accelerates** the block downwards. You can study and measure the acceleration due to gravity using ticker tape. The ticker timer is set up so that the falling mass can pull a tape through it. The mass is held close to the timer. The timer is turned on and then the mass is dropped. The tape can then be cut into five-tick lengths. When these are stuck side by side they form a speed–time graph. The results show that the speed of the falling object is getting steadily faster. **The acceleration due to gravity is constant**.

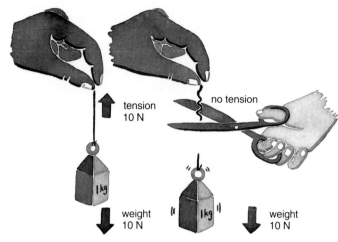

Balanced forces – no acceleration *Unbalanced force – mass accelerates*

g by free fall

It is not possible to get an accurate value for the acceleration from this experiment because the timer creates a lot of friction as it marks the tape. The best way to measure the acceleration due to gravity is to use **free-fall**. (see below right)

As the ball is dropped the electronic timer starts. As soon as it hits the switch at the bottom the timer stops. It records the time taken for the ball to fall through the distance S.

Calculation

The ball falls through the distance S in a time t.
Its average speed is given by S/t.
Since it starts from rest we know that its final speed is $2 \times S/t$.
Acceleration is (change in speed)/(time taken) so:

$$\textbf{acceleration } \boldsymbol{g} = \frac{2 \times S/t}{t}$$

Results

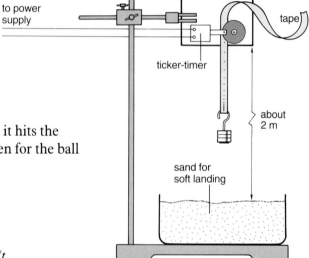

Investigating the acceleration due to gravity

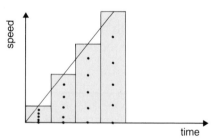

Results for a falling mass

S (measured with ruler)	t (measured with electronic clock)	t (average result)
1.8 m	0.62 s, 0.61 s, 0.57 s	0.60 s

$$g = \frac{2 \times (1.8/0.60)}{(0.60)} = 10.0 \text{ m/s}^2$$

The value of g in the UK is about 9.8 m/s². In calculations we often use the approximate value 10 m/s².

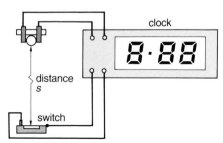

Apparatus to find g by free fall

Falling quickly and slowly

In the experiments to measure the acceleration of a falling object we didn't take the mass of the object into account. Was this a mistake? Do heavy things fall faster than light things? Common sense might suggest they do, but a simple experiment will show us that **all falling masses have the same acceleration due to gravity**.

The results show that all masses, large and small, accelerate at the same rate provided that there are no other forces, like air resistance, acting.

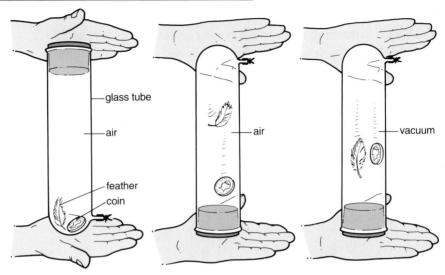

When the tube is turned upside-down the coin falls much faster than the feather. When the experiment is repeated in a vacuum (no air) the feather and the coin reach the bottom at the same time.

Explanation

If we drop an iron ball (mass = 2 kg) and a rubber ball (mass = 0.5 kg) of the same size, they hit the ground at the same time. The iron ball has a larger weight but it also has a bigger mass to accelerate. If we use the equation **acceleration = force/mass** for each ball we get the same value!

iron: $\dfrac{20\,\text{N}}{2\,\text{kg}} = 10\,\text{m/s}^2$ rubber: $\dfrac{5\,\text{N}}{0.5\,\text{kg}} = 10\,\text{m/s}^2$

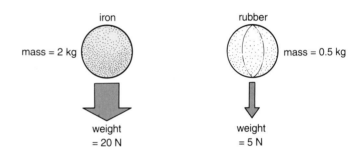

Using air resistance

Gravity makes all falling objects accelerate towards the centre of the Earth, but **air resistance** is a force opposing this motion. Air resistance depends on the size and shape of an object and its speed. As the object falls faster the resistance gets much larger. We can get a clear idea of this if we think of a skydiver jumping from a very great height.

Just leaving the aeroplane – moving slowly so little air resistance. Accelerating at about 10 m/s²

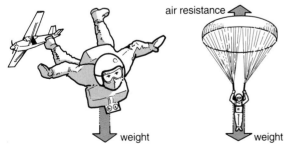

Eventually the parachute slows the skydiver down to a speed at which air resistance balances the weight. Continues to fall at this slow, steady speed until hitting the ground.

Questions

1 Skydivers like to fall for as long as possible before they open their parachutes. Suggest why they spread their bodies out flat as they jump out of the plane.

2 Beginners at parachuting are given large parachutes. Explain why this helps to reduce injuries.

3 Parachutists carry a spare parachute for emergencies. This is much smaller than the main parachute. Explain why you are much more likely to break a leg if you have to use your emergency parachute. (There are two reasons – think carefully.)

Activities

1 Investigate how the time taken to fall from a fixed height varies with the size of the parachute.

2 Investigate whether the time taken to fall from a fixed height depends on the weight the parachute carries.

3 Design an experiment to measure the terminal velocity of a parachute.

Gravity and energy

When we lift something we do **work** against gravity. This is because we have to apply a force to overcome the weight, and then move it upwards. Work is **force × distance** so in this case work done = weight × height lifted. In symbols: **work = mgh**

(m = mass, g = gravitational field strength, h = height)

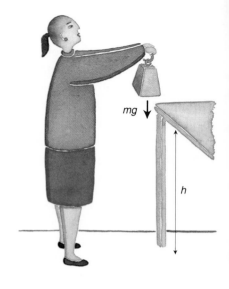

The work done against gravity is given by weight × height (mgh).

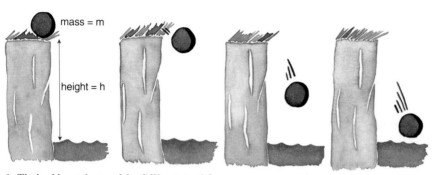

1 *The boulder at the top of the cliff has potential energy.*
2 *As it starts to fall its potential energy gets a little less. It now has some kinetic energy.*
3 *Half-way down it has potential energy $\frac{1}{2}mgh$. The rest is now kinetic energy.*
4 *Just before it hits the bottom all its potential energy has changed to kinetic energy, $\frac{1}{2}mv^2$.*

As we lift we transfer energy to the object. It now has energy stored in it because it is higher up than it was before. We call this energy **gravitational potential energy** (sometimes just **potential energy**, PE). When the object falls this potential energy is converted into **kinetic energy**, KE.

Worked example

On a building site a 50 kg bag of cement falls from a scaffold 15 m high. (Take $g = 10$ N/kg.)

a) What is the potential energy of the bag of cement before it falls?

PE = mgh = $50 \times 10 \times 15$ J = **7500 J**

b) What is the potential energy of the bag after it has fallen 10 m?

PE = mgh = $50 \times 10 \times (15-10)$ J = **2500 J**

c) What has happened to the rest of the energy?

It has been converted to kinetic (moving) energy. The falling bag has 5000 J of kinetic energy after it has fallen 10 m.

d) What is the speed of the bag just before it hits the ground?

All the PE has been changed to KE so the KE = **7500 J.**

KE = $\frac{1}{2}mv^2 = \frac{1}{2} \times 50 \times v^2$

$v^2 = \dfrac{2 \times 7500}{50} = 300$ (m/s)^2 therefore $v =$ **17.3 m/s**

Questions

1 A crane lifts a 1000 kg box from the ground to a height of 5 m. The lifting cable then snaps.

a) How much work does the crane do in lifting the box?

b) How much potential energy does the box gain as it is lifted?

c) Calculate the speed of the box just before it hits the ground.

d) Suggest what happens to the box's kinetic energy when it hits the ground.

2 An Olympic diver has a mass of 60 kg. He stands on a platform 10 m above the water and then dives.

a) How much potential energy did he gain in climbing to the platform?

b) What is his kinetic energy just before he hits the water?

(Take $g = 10$ N/kg.)

c) Give one reason why your answer to (b) is only approximate.

Bullets, missiles, and satellites

All objects accelerate when they fall straight downwards, but what happens if they are already moving along horizontally? The diagram shows a ball rolling along a table at a steady speed. When it reaches the edge of the table it keeps moving forwards at the same speed but also starts to accelerate downwards. The forwards and downwards motions together give a special curved shape called a **parabola**.

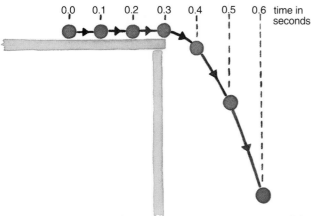

Horizontal motion + vertical acceleration gives movement in a parabola.

Activities

1 If the downwards acceleration is only due to gravity then the sideways speed should not affect time taken for the object to fall to the ground.

Take two coins, one in each hand, and stand on a chair. Hold your hands out in front of you at the same height. Drop them at exactly the same time. You should hear them hit the floor at the same time. Repeat the exercise but this time drop one coin straight down and throw the other one out sideways at the same time. This takes good co-ordination but after practice you should be able to do it. No matter how fast you throw the coin out sideways (provided it is thrown horizontally) the two coins will always hit the floor at the same time.

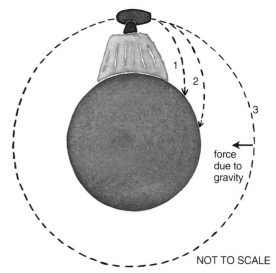

Satellites are kept in orbit by gravity.

The diagram above shows a gun at the top of a mountain. The curved surface of the Earth is greatly exaggerated.

Path 1 shows the parabola followed by a shell fired horizontally from the gun.

Path 2 shows what would happen if the shell left the gun at a greater speed. It would obviously travel further before it hit the Earth.

Path 3 shows a shell fired at an even greater speed. This one is travelling at so great a speed that it never reaches the ground. It keeps going around the Earth. It is a **satellite**!

Real satellites are launched by rockets. It is the pull of gravity towards the centre of the Earth which keeps them in orbit. (This force towards the centre is called the **centripetal force**.)

This satellite is constantly falling under gravity in a circular orbit around the Earth.

Flying (1)

A Boeing 747 Jumbo Jet can carry up to 500 passengers, their luggage, and some cargo. In fact a fully loaded Jumbo Jet may have a mass of over 300 tonnes! How can such a massive thing fly? All aeroplanes fly because of the shape of their wings.

Boeing 747 Jumbo Jet

Aerofoils

It we could cut through a wing we would get an **aerofoil** shape. The front edge is blunt and the rear edge is sharp. The top of the aerofoil is curved and the underneath is flatter.

An aerofoil

Activities

1 Make an aerofoil shape by folding and taping a piece of thin card as shown in the diagram. Tape a piece of thread underneath the aerofoil in the middle of the leading edge.

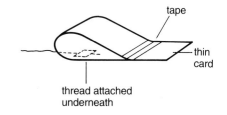

Using the thread pull the aerofoil along a smooth table or bench. Pull it quickly but keep the thread close to the table top. You should find that the aerofoil lifts into the air. Notice that you have provided a forwards force but the aerofoil has created an upwards force. We call this force **lift**.

Why does an aerofoil produce lift?

Our model aerofoil only gave lift when it was moving through the air. Similarly, aeroplanes have to be moving at high speed along a runway before they lift off. It is the movement of air over the shaped wing which produces lift. Two simple experiments show this.

Hold a piece of paper so that it bends in a curve. Blow hard across the paper. The paper lifts up towards the fast moving air.

Hold two pieces of paper so that they hang downwards with a gap between them. Blow down between the pieces of paper. They move inwards towards the fast moving air.

This is called the **Bernoulli effect**.

Blowing air over a curved surface causes lift.

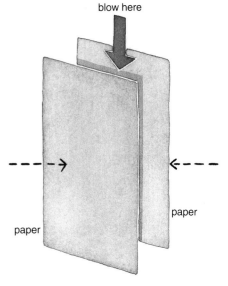

The pieces of paper move inwards because the pressure is lower in the middle.

The activities on the opposite page work because the fast-moving air produced a low pressure region.

The diagram below shows a piece of apparatus to demonstrate how air pressure varies with air speed. The air moves fastest at the narrowest part of the tube. Here the water rises up most showing that **the faster the air moves, the lower the pressure**.

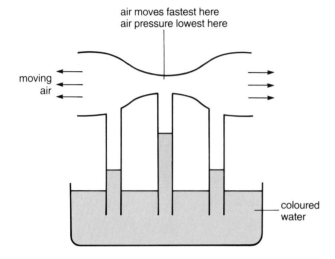

The Bernoulli effect

The Bernoulli effect and wings

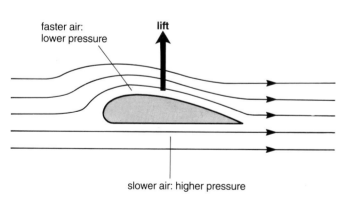

Wings use the Bernoulli effect to create lift.

Air moving over the top of an aerofoil moves faster than that going underneath. This makes the pressure over the wing lower. The result is an upwards force – lift.

Upside-down aerofoils

Using an aerofoil to give a downward force

Racing cars have aerofoils on the back. These aerofoils have the flat surface on top so they are like upside-down wings. The air passing underneath moves faster and so the lower air pressure is under the aerofoil. The unbalanced force is downwards. This holds the car down on to the track so that it can travel faster around bends.

Using air pressure in the carburettor

The Bernoulli effect is used in the carburettor of a petrol engine. The engine draws air through a tube in the carburettor. Because the air is moving quickly it is at a low pressure and so petrol is forced out of the float chamber and into the stream of fast-moving air. The mixture of air and petrol then gets drawn into the engine where it burns.

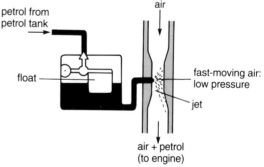

Fast-moving air in the tube of the carburettor gives a low-pressure region.

Questions

1   Imagine you are at an airport watching aeroplanes taking off. An adult says 'It's a miracle the way those things fly'. How would you prove that it is all to do with wing shape and air pressure?

2   What is the downward force which the lift has to overcome when an aeroplane flies?

3   Why would it be very dangerous if a mechanic fitted the aerofoil on a racing car upside down?

All aeroplanes need to make the air travel fast enough over their wings to create lift. They can use either propellers or jet engines to give the aeroplane a forward force. Well call this **thrust**.

The aeroplane shown has a propeller which has two blades shaped like aerofoils. These are set at an angle to one another. An engine turns the propeller at high speed. The blades force the air backwards. This action pulls the aeroplane forwards through the air.

An aeroplane with a single propeller

This aeroplane has turbojet engines. These move the aeroplane forwards by pushing air and hot exhaust gases out of the engine at very high speeds.

In general, jet engines are much more reliable than propellers. They do not vibrate so much and they produce a steady thrust. They can also be used at greater heights and higher speeds. However, propeller-driven aeroplanes are usually much quieter than jets and their engines are easier to maintain.

A Tristar jet uses jet engines.

Jet engines

The diagram shows the main parts of a jet engine. The rotating blades at the front suck air into the engine and force it into the combustion chamber. Kerosene fuel is pumped into the combustion chamber where it burns. The great amount of heat generated makes the gases expand and rush out of the back of the jet at very high speed. The reaction to this gives a forward thrust.

Notice that jet engines need air to mix with the kerosene so that it will burn. This means that aeroplanes with jet engines cannot fly out of the atmosphere. Spacecraft have rocket engines. These carry a liquid oxygen supply with them to burn the fuel. As in the jet engine, it is a reaction to the hot gases rushing out of the engine which produces the forward thrust.

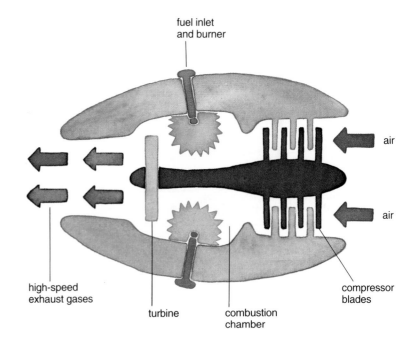

A jet engine gives an aeroplane thrust.

Forces on aeroplanes

The aerofoil-shaped wings give **lift**. For the aeroplane to take off the lift must overcome its **weight**.

Thrust moves the aeroplane forwards but air rubbing on its surface and the **turbulence** caused behind the aeroplane cause resistance to motion. This force is called **drag**.

In level flight at a steady speed, lift = weight and, thrust = drag.

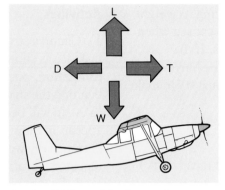

At take-off: lift > weight, thrust > drag.

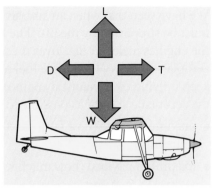

In level flight at steady speed: lift = weight, thrust = drag.

Streamlining and turbulence

When an aeroplane is travelling at a steady speed the thrust is being used to overcome the drag. If we can reduce the drag then we can use less thrust. This means that the engines will use less fuel and be more economical.

Much of the drag is caused when the air flowing over the wings and other parts of the aeroplane starts to swirl around like the water in a whirlpool. This is called **turbulence**. The amount of turbulence depends on the shape of the aeroplane.

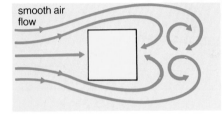

This shape causes lots of turbulence.

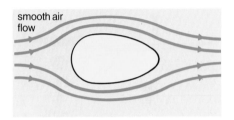

*This shape lets the air flow smoothly. It is **streamlined**.*

Activities

1 Take a candle and cut some of the wax from the top so that the wick is about 1 cm long. Stand the candle up on a heatproof surface. Make sure that it will not fall over. Light the wick. When it is burning well, blow the flame out but watch the smoke carefully.

Just above the wick you should see a smooth, thin stream of smoke. This is called **laminar flow**. Higher up you will see that the smoke stream breaks up and swirls around in a complicated pattern. This shows where the air is turbulent.

2 Find out what wind tunnels are used for and how smoke is used in them.

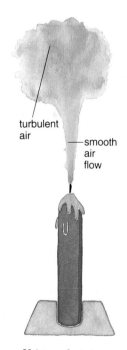

Using smoke to trace air flow

Stalling

To give maximum lift, the wings of an aeroplane are tilted slightly. They make a small angle of attack to the air flow.

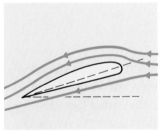

A small angle of attack gives maximum lift.

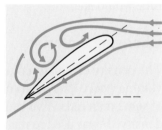

A large angle of attack causes turbulence – lift is lost.

If the pilot makes the angle of attack too large the air behind the wing becomes turbulent and lift is lost. This makes the aeroplane stall and begin to fall.

In aerobatic displays a stunt pilot may deliberately stall the aeroplane. It then suddenly drops towards the ground. It takes a great deal of skill to get the aeroplane back under control.

Questions

1 Airlines wash and polish their aeroplanes regularly. How does this help them to save fuel?

We have seen that when an aircraft is flying its weight must be supported by the lift. The lift is caused when the engines make air flow over the wings. If the aeroplane is heavy then more fuel must be burnt to keep it flying. Aeronautical engineers must try to make the aeroplane as light as possible to give:

- maximum range (how far it can fly without refuelling)
- maximum payload (how much weight it can carry)
- maximum fuel efficiency (how far it can fly on, say, 1000 litres of fuel)

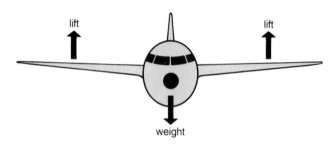

Aeroplanes must also be built to be strong. The diagram above shows that the lifting forces are on the wings and that the centre of gravity is in the middle of the aeroplane. This means that the wings must be firmly fixed to the body of the plane. They must also be flexible. (Passengers are sometimes surprised to see the wings moving up and down slightly. If they didn't, they would snap off!)

Choosing materials

The density of a material tells us the mass of a block of volume 1 cm³. The diagram below shows the densities of some materials. You can see that wood has a low density. It was used to make the framework for early aircraft and even some Second World War aeroplanes had a wooden structure. However, wood is not strong enough to make a large aeroplane.

Pure aluminium has a low density when compared with other metals but it is soft and cracks easily when bent.

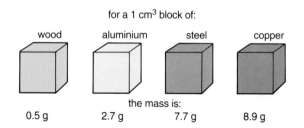

Activities

1   Clamp a strip of aluminium sheet about 2 mm thick in a vice as shown. **Wearing leather gloves for protection**, push the end backwards and forwards bending the strip a little more each time. Before long the strip will become very easy to bend and cracks will appear on the surface. Eventually, the metal will become very weak and snap off. This cracking, due to repeated vibrations, is called **metal fatigue**.

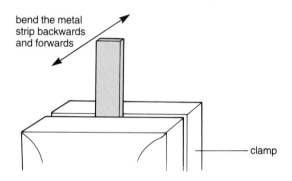

Making a better material

In 1910 a German metallurgist called Alfred Wilm made an alloy of aluminium which has a low density (7.8 g/cm³) but is much stronger and harder than pure aluminium. He called the alloy Duralumin. It contains approximately 94% aluminium, 4% copper, 1% manganese, and 1% magnesium.

When first made, Duralumin is soft and can be rolled into sheets or made into tubes. It is then heated and quickly cooled. This treatment leaves it hard, ready for use in building aircraft.

Questions

1   Explain why an airline would want its aeroplanes to be as light as possible before loading.

2   Suggest why airline passengers are limited to about 30 kg of luggage.

3   Early biplanes were made of a wooden frame covered with a thin fabric skin. Give two reasons why this was a good design. Suggest two disadvantages.

4   Steel is as strong as Duralumin and much cheaper.
   a)   Explain why Duralumin is used to build aircraft rather than steel.
   b)   An aircraft contains 4000 kg of Duralumin. How much more would it weigh if steel was used? (Not an easy question!)

Shaping for strength

Aircraft, boats, and buildings such as skyscrapers usually have a framework of beams to give them strength. Lighter material can then be used as a skin over the framework. The beams have to take two types of force: **compression** and **tension**.

Compression forces act when the beam is being squeezed; tension forces act when it is being stretched.

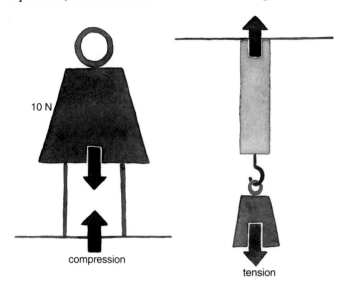

When a beam is bent, one side is compressed and the other side is stretched. The layer in the middle is not under stress so material can be removed from the middle leaving a strong beam which is lighter. Similarly, a metal bar can be replaced by a tube which is just as strong but lighter.

Shaped beams and tubes are used to make up the main skeleton of aircraft.

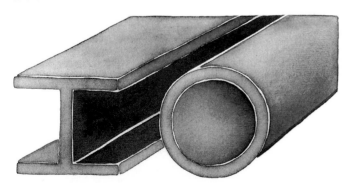

Girders and tubes are strong and light.

A single beam can be made stronger by adding extra beams to take some of the load. These are usually arranged in triangular shapes to make a **truss**. If you are passing a building site you may see the wooden trusses used for roofs.

Trussed bridges are stronger because the struts transfer some of the downward force of the load to the bridge supports. Triangles give strength.

The aircraft wing section shown below has much of the metal removed to make it light. The cross-pieces give it strength. The triangular holes have rounded corners. Sharp corners could help cracks to start.

Compare this diagram with that of the bone structure of a bird (see page 212).

Section through an aircraft wing

Activities

1 Use a strip of balsa wood as a simple bridge. Carefully load the middle of the bridge with weights until it breaks.

Use a similar strip of balsa wood and some balsa rods to make a trussed bridge as shown in the diagram. Load this bridge carefully until it breaks.

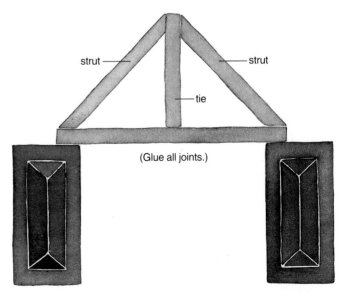

A truss bridge

Long before people learnt to fly many other animals had taken to the air. The most common flying animals are insects and birds. Bats are mammals which have evolved the ability to fly. All these have one thing in common – wings that flap! It is the flapping of the wings that creates lift.

Flight in insects

Flying insects like houseflies and bees have two pairs of wings made of very thin membranes. Because the insects are very light the wings do not have to provide much lift. They are flapped up and down by muscles inside the insect's body.

Flight in birds

Over millions of years birds have evolved many features which help them to fly. The most obvious are their **feathered wings**.

Birds are the only animals to have feathers. Each bird has several different kinds on its body. The most important are the flight feathers. These have a long central shaft or **quill**. The thin **barbules** which are attached to the quill have tiny **barbs** or hooks which fasten on to their neighbours. This helps to keep the feather together. If it comes apart the bird can repair it with its beak.

Wings have evolved from the forelimbs of prehistoric animals. The diagrams opposite shows the long bones at the front of the wing and the long flight feathers. These overlap to give a strong but flexible wing.

The bird's wing also has an aerofoil shape. This gives a streamlined shape and gives extra lift as the bird moves through the air. This is particularly important in birds which do a lot of gliding.

The **bones** of a bird must be strong but also very light. They have evolved to have a cellular structure with lots of air spaces.

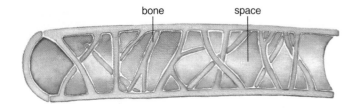

Birds' bones are cellular. This makes them strong and light.

Bats are mammals which have evolved wings for flight.

The vertical muscle contracts. This raises the wing.

The wing falls to the rest position when the muscles relax.

The horizontal muscle contracts. This forces the wing downwards.

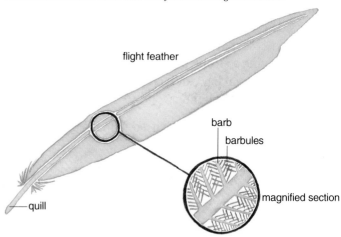

A flight feather

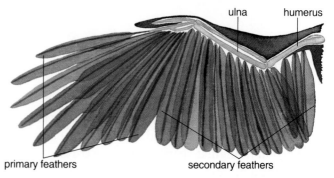

The bird's wing contains bones like those of a human arm. This is evidence that birds and humans evolved from a common ancestor.

Flying by flapping uses lots of energy and needs large **muscles** to provide large forces. In birds the skeleton has a strong breast bone with a large flat keel. The powerful flight muscles are attached to this. If you watch a roast chicken or turkey being carved you will see the large keel in the middle. The breast meat on either side is the flight muscle.

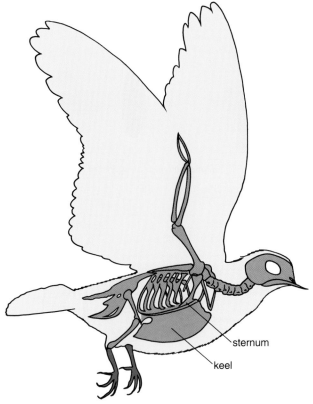

The large flight muscles are attached to the keel.

Using wings to get lift and thrust

Birds do not simply flap their wings up and down. They change the angle of the wing between the upstroke and the downstroke.

As the bird lifts its wing it keeps the leading edge above the trailing edge just like an aeroplane's wing. The air pressure builds up underneath helping to force the bird upwards. At the same time the feathers separate slightly so some air can get through.

On the downstroke the bird uses its powerful flight muscles to pull the wing downwards and forwards. The angle of the wing pushes the air backwards and this pushes the bird forwards.

Stalling

By lifting the front of its wing a bird can deliberately **stall**. This makes it lose lift and drop quickly. Birds of prey use this when hunting. They glide, using their wings as aerofoils, until they see a small animal below. They can then deliberately stall to start their dive to the ground. Other birds use a stalling technique when landing.

Activities

1 Look at a bird's flight feather under a microscope. Try to identify the barbules and barbs.

2 Observe birds flying in the wild. Look for birds gliding (e.g. seagulls), hovering (e.g. kestrels), flapping (e.g. pigeons), and stalling (e.g. ducks landing on water).

3 a) List three similarities between bird flight and aeroplane flight.

b) Some early designs for aircraft had flapping wings. Suggest why these were unsuccessful.

upstroke   downstroke

One stroke in a bird's flight

Flight in plants

Plants cannot fly, but some have evolved seeds which can travel large distances using air currents. In general seeds which are dispersed by the wind use **parachutes** or **wings**.

Dandelion seeds

After pollination many seeds develop in the dandelion's flower head. Each one is attached to a small parachute of fine hairs. On a dry day the wind can pull the seeds from the plant. The lightness of the seed and the parachute structure allows it to be blown a long distance before it falls to the ground.

The seed head of this dandelion contains many seeds ready for dispersal.

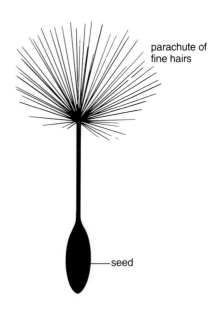

Dandelion seeds are dispersed by the wind.

Winged seeds

Some tall trees like the sycamore and maple have evolved seeds with wings. As the seed falls from the tree the wing spins in the air. This slows its fall. If the wind catches a falling seed it may carry it a long way. This means that if the seed grows the new tree will not be competing with the parent tree for food.

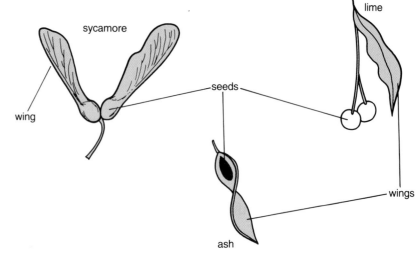

All these trees have seeds which are dispersed by the wind.

Activities

Model sycamore seeds can be made as shown in the diagram opposite.

1 Make two model seeds using exactly the same shaped and sized strips of card and paperclips, but do not fold the wings down on one model. Drop them both from a height and see what happens. The spinning effect of the wings should slow the fall considerably.

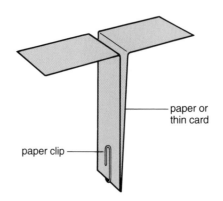

2 Using these models, design and carry out an experiment to find what effect wing size has on the time of fall.

3 If you can get some sycamore and/or maple seeds investigate their flight with and without their wings.

214

Questions

1 A friend says that heavy things fall faster than light things. To prove it he drops a piece of paper and a coin from the same height. The coin hits the floor first.

a) How would you explain the result of his experiment?

b) Describe an experiment to prove that in free fall all masses accelerate at the same rate.

2 An astronaut on the Moon fills a bag with moondust. When full it weighs 3.2 N. Back on Earth the bag weighs 19.6 N.

a) What is the mass of the bag of moondust on the Moon? (Take g on the Moon = 1.6 N/kg.)

b) What is the mass of the bag of moondust on Earth?

c) What is the gravitational field strength in newtons per kilogram on Earth?

3 The diagram below shows an aerofoil shape.

a) Copy the shape and label the leading (front) edge and the trailing (back) edge.

b) On your diagram draw lines to show smooth (non-turbulent) air flow over the aerofoil.

c) Show on your diagram where the air is moving fastest and where the pressure is greatest.

4 **a)** When an aeroplane is moving it has four forces on it – weight, drag, lift, and thrust. Draw a diagram to show the directions of these four forces.

b) Before take-off, as the aeroplane accelerates along the runway, the thrust is bigger than the drag and the weight is bigger than the lift. What can you say about these forces when   i) the aeroplane is in level flight at a stead speed   ii) it is coming in to land?

5 The table below gives information about an aeroplane.

aircraft type	BAC 111
mass (loaded)	43 400 kg
engine thrust	108 500 N
take-off speed	96 m/s
take-off distance	1920 m

a) Calculate the maximum acceleration of a loaded BAC 111. (Ignore friction. Remember $F = m \times a$.)

b) Show that the aeroplane takes about 40 s to take off at full thrust.

c) Explain why an empty plane can take off on a runway less than 1500 m long. In your answer use the words **mass**, **thrust**, **acceleration**, and **lift**.

6 After a meal of roast turkey a student investigates the skeleton. She finds a large, flat bone in the middle of the chest and when she cuts through the bones she finds lots of air spaces inside. How do these two facts show that birds are well adapted for flight?

7 The diagram shows the seed of an elm tree.

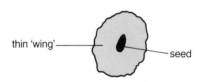

a) Suggest how the wing structure helps to spread the seeds.

b) Why is it important that the seeds are spread over large distances?

c) Only tall trees like elms and sycamores have evolved winged seeds. Suggest why this is.

d) Describe one way in which the seeds of low-growing plants can be dispersed by the wind.

How did the universe begin?

What is the solar system?

What causes days, months, and years?

Why do we have seasons?

Why are there tides?

How do people get into space?

our galaxy from the side   our galaxy from the top

Our solar system....

is about here!

The arrow shows the position of the Earth in the Milky Way. There are thousands and thousands of stars in the Milky Way. These stars give a milky appearance to the night sky, hence the name.

The universe contains everything that exists. We don't know how big the universe is, or even if there is a limit to its size. Planet Earth is just a tiny part of the universe. It is part of a galaxy called the **Milky Way**. Astronomers once thought that the Milky Way was the only galaxy. Today, however, we know that our galaxy is only one of many star systems scattered throughout the universe. Each galaxy contains millions of stars together with clouds of dust and gases.

The Horse Head nebula is a cloud of dust and gases hiding stars in the constellation of Orion in the Milky Way. It is about 5 light years across. (One light year is the distance travelled in one year by light travelling at 186,000 miles per second.) This is a dark nebula. Other nebulae consisting of glowing patches of gas are much brighter.

Galaxies are very far apart. The nearest large galaxy to the Milky Way is called **Andromeda**. Andromeda is two million light years away. This means that the light we see from Andromeda has taken two million years to reach us. We are seeing it as it was two million years ago – before there were humans on Earth.

When we look through a telescope into space we are looking at something not only very far away but also back in time. Some of the more distant galaxies that have been discovered are thousands of millions of light years away. Astronomers believe that there are many more galaxies further out into space that can't be seen.

Questions

1   What is a galaxy? What galaxy does the Earth belong to? How does it get its name?

2   What is a nebula? Suggest how the Horse Head nebula got its name.

3   Explain what is meant by a light year. How far is a light year in miles?

4   How big is the universe? How big is the planet Earth in comparison?

The expanding universe

Most objects in our galaxy are orbiting around some other object. Moons orbit planets, planets orbit the Sun, and the Sun, like other stars, orbits the centre of the Milky Way. The galaxy is so enormous that the Sun takes about 200 million years to move around it.

Galaxies, however, do not seem to be in orbit around anything. Astronomers have discovered that all the galaxies are in fact moving away from each other. They have calculated that the galaxies travel at speeds of thousands of kilometres per second. You can compare the expanding universe to a balloon being blown up. As you blow, the balloon expands, every bit of rubber moving away from every other bit. This has led scientists to suggest that the universe first formed after a 'big bang'.

The **big bang theory** suggests that the universe began 10 000 million years ago with an enormous explosion. Scientists believe that all matter now in the universe was contained in one primitive atom. They call this atom a **primordial atom**, but have no idea of its size. The primordial atom blew up and its contents flew off in all directions. As the primordial material spread out, it cooled, joined together and made the galaxies. The galaxies are still flying apart. Unfortunately this theory doesn't suggest where the primordial atom came from in the first place!

Will the expansion of the universe go on forever? Or will the process stop and go into reverse?

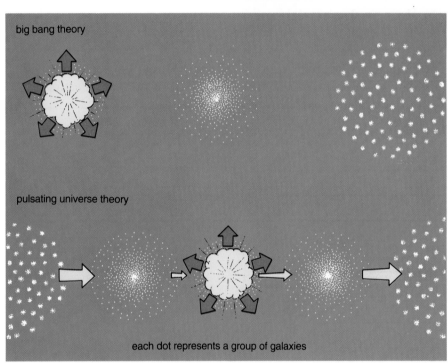

The making of the universe

The **pulsating universe theory** assumes the universe to be continually contracting and expanding. When the universe has expanded to a certain size it will begin to shrink. The galaxies will be pushed closer and closer together. Eventually they will explode causing the universe to expand again.

The **expanding universe theory** suggests that the universe will never collapse but keep on expanding. This theory implies that there has only ever been one 'big bang'.

Questions

1 What is an orbit? How long does the Sun take to orbit the Milky Way?

2 What evidence is there to suggest that galaxies are not in orbit?

3 Briefly describe the big bang theory.

4 Briefly compare the expanding universe theory with the pulsating universe theory for the origin of the universe.

Days, months, and years

The Earth is constantly spinning. It rotates around an axis through the North and South Poles. The time taken for one complete rotation of the Earth is 24 hours or one day. If you watch the Sun at different times in the day you will see that it appears to move from east to west. In fact this motion is due to the Earth spinning on its axis.

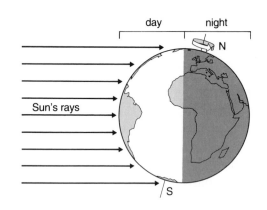

When the part of Earth on which you live is facing the Sun it is daytime. Night-time falls when your part of the Earth faces away from the Sun, towards where there is no light.

The Moon revolves around the Earth once every 27.3 days. This is a **lunar month**. When the side lit by the Sun faces the Earth we see a **full Moon**. Sometimes we see no Moon at all. This is when the Moon is on the side of Earth nearest to the Sun. This is called a **new Moon**. Between these two positions we see only a part of the Moon. These sections of reflecting surfaces are called the **phases of the Moon**.

Why do we see the Moon differently at certain times of the month?

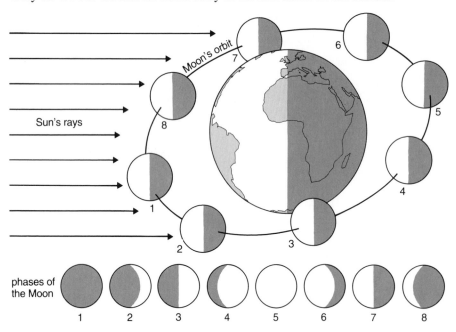

Whilst all this is going on, the Earth is revolving around the Sun. One complete orbit takes about 365.25 days or **one year**. Obviously we can't have a quarter of a day at the end of each calendar year. So the quarters are added together to produce an extra day every four years. Years that have the extra day are called **leap years**. The extra day is 29 February. A year has an extra day if its number divides exactly by four, e.g. 1992. If the year divides exactly by 100 it is not a leap year, e.g. 1900. On the other hand, if a year divides exactly by 400 it is a leap year, e.g. 2000. This correction means that three days are lost every 400 years. It is called the **Gregorian correction** and it keeps the Christian calendar in line with the movements of the Sun and the stars.

Questions

1 Which direction does the Earth spin in?

2 Why is it dark at night?

3 What is the difference between a full Moon and a new Moon?

4 What is **a**) a day **b**) a month **c**) a year?

5 Draw diagrams showing the eight phases of the Moon.

6 Why do we have leap years? Which of the following are leap years: 1596, 1600, 1700, 1760, 1800?

What year were you born? Was it a leap year?

The seasons

The Earth's axis is tilted at an angle of 23° to its orbit. During the year the Earth revolves around the Sun. This means that at certain times of the year the North and South Poles are tilted towards the Sun in turn. The part of the Earth which is tilted towards the Sun gets more light and is warmer. It has its **summer**. The part which is tilted away from the Sun gets less light and is colder. It has its **winter**.

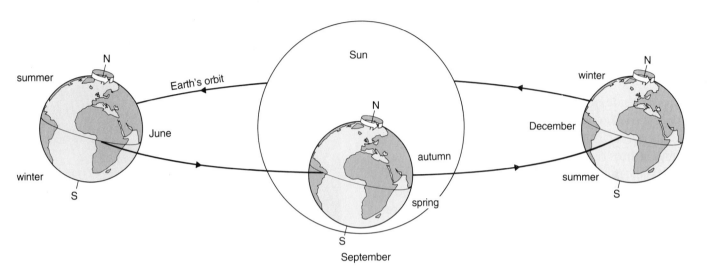

During spring and autumn in the UK, we get equal amounts of light because the Earth is tilted neither towards nor away from the Sun.

Activities

1 Hold a piece of plain white card vertically and shine a lighted torch or bicycle lamp onto it.

– Tilt the card slowly to an angle of about 45°.

How does **a)** the shape **b)** the brightness of the light change? Why is this?

– Now try the same exercise with a football. Set up your investigation like this:

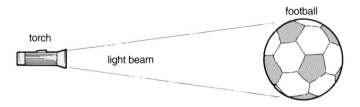

Is the brightness of the light the same over the whole surface of the football?
If not, how does it differ?

– Mark the position of the equator on your football with a pencil.

– Hold the football at an angle of about 25°. Shine the torch on the football from four different positions around it like this:

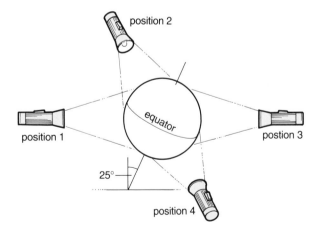

Describe the brightness of the upper and lower halves of the football with the torch in each of the four positions.

Why can Australians have Christmas dinner on the beach?

219

The Moon – the Earth's satellite

The Moon is the Earth's natural satellite. It orbits Earth in the same way as the Earth and the other planets orbit the Sun. It is our nearest neighbour in space and the only other part of our solar system to have been visited by humans.

The Moon lies 384 000 km from the Earth and has a diameter of about 3500 km. It is much less dense than Earth and has only one-sixth of Earth's gravity. It has no atmosphere and no signs of life. The Moon rotates very slowly. It rotates once in the same time as it takes to complete one orbit of Earth. This means that the Moon always keeps the same side facing the Earth. The dark side can only be seen from space. This slow spin speed also means that Moon days and Moon nights last for 14 Earth days. During a Moon day, temperatures rise to as much as 120 °C. At night, however, temperatures may fall to − 150 °C or lower. The surface of the Moon is dry, hard, and covered in loose dust. It is pitted with many large impact **craters**. These craters are caused by **meteorites** as they collide with the Moon. Some craters are over 100 km across.

Lunar eclipse

A **lunar eclipse** happens when the Earth comes between the Moon and the Sun. In most lunar eclipses we can see the shadow of the Earth slowly moving across the face of the Moon.

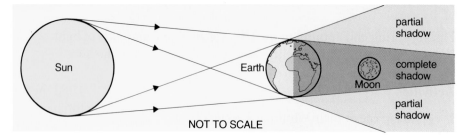

Activities:

1 How far is the Moon from the Earth?
For this activity you will need:

- a piece of straight stick about 1 metre long (a broom handle will do)
- a 1p piece
- some Plasticine
- a tape measure
- a clear night with a full Moon!

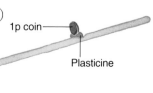

– Arrange the apparatus as shown in the diagram. Make sure that your eye, the stick, and the Moon are in line. (You may need to support the stick on a windowsill or get someone to hold it for you.)

– Move the coin up and down the stick until it just covers (eclipses) the Moon. Fix the coin in place with Plasticine and check its position. Adjust it if necessary.

– Measure the distance from the coin to the end of the stick nearest your eye and write it down.

– The Moon diameter is 3500 km. The distance of the Moon to the Earth =

$$\frac{\text{Moon dia(m)} \times \text{coin to eye dist(m)}}{\text{coin diameter (m)}}$$

If you have been to the seaside you will have noticed the sea level rise and fall during the day. This rise and fall is called a **tide**. High tide is when the tide is in and low tide is when the tide is out. There are two high tides in a day. Sometimes tides come very high up the shore and even flood surrounding land. At other times, however, high tides stop lower down the shore.

Scientists have shown that the tides are related to the position of the Moon. The water on Earth is not fixed in position. The Moon's gravity exerts a force which pulls the water into a bulge beneath it. There are in fact two bulges, one on either side of the Earth. This is because the Earth is also pulled by the Moon's gravity, leaving a bulge of water behind it.

As Earth spins, a piece of coastline enters a bulge causing a high tide. As it leaves a bulge behind the tide goes out. Remember that the Earth rotates once every 24 hours, hence the tide rises and falls twice daily. Each day high tide is about 50 minutes later than the day before. This is because the Moon slowly changes its position as it orbits the Earth.

Spring and neap tides

The Sun also exerts a gravitational pull on the Earth and therefore affects the tides. However, its effect is much less than that of the Moon because it is much further away.

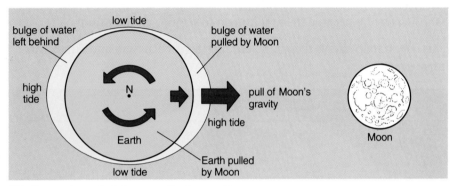

This diagram shows the bulges on an Earth covered in water.

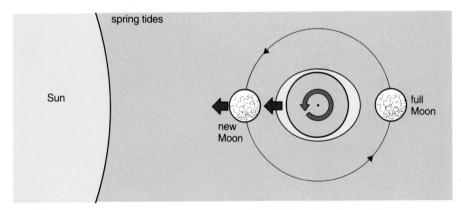

*When the Earth, Moon, and Sun are in line, the combined effects of the Sun and Moon cause an extra high tide called a **spring tide**.*

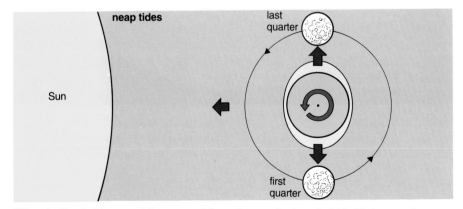

*When the Earth, Moon, and Sun are at right angles to each other, the high tide is not as far up the shore. This is a **neap tide**.*

Walking on the Moon

Before humans could land on the Moon it was important for scientists to find out what the surface of the Moon is like. Both the USSR and the USA sent a number of unmanned spacecraft to the Moon. The first ones crashed and were destroyed. However, in 1966, the Russian *Luna 9* landed successfully and sent television pictures of the Moon's surface back to Earth. *Luna 9* was followed shortly after by America's *Surveyor 1*. More *Luna* and *Surveyor* spacecraft followed, each one sending back more important information. This information was carefully studied before the USA launched the first of six manned expeditions to the Moon on 16 July 1969. *Apollo 11* carried three astronauts, Edwin 'Buzz' Aldrin, Neil Armstrong, and Michael Collins. The lunar module *Eagle* carrying Aldrin and Armstrong landed on 20 July in an area called the Sea of Tranquility. Neil Armstrong became the first human to set foot on the Moon.

This Moon map shows the main landing sites for Russian and American lunar expeditions.

When Neil Armstrong and Edwin Aldrin landed on the Moon they wore carefully designed spacesuits. The suits have to be very flexible to allow the astronauts to move around easily. They carry oxygen and are pressurized to stop dissolved gases in the blood forming bubbles. The suits also have cooling jackets. Water was fed through a series of thin tubes close to the skin to keep body temperature stable. There was even a built-in toilet!

- ● *Apollo* references
- ■ *Luna* references

Apollo 11 *20 July 1969.*
Astronauts Aldrin, Armstrong, and Collins. Moon rock and soil collected.

Apollo 12 *19 November 1969.*
Astronauts Bean, Conrad, and Gordon. More Moon rock and soil collected along with parts of Surveyor 3.

Luna 16 *20 September 1970.*
Robot Moon probe. Core samples from Moon crust collected and returned to Earth.

Luna 17 *17 November 1970.*
Remote controlled vehicle, Lunokhod 1, sent information back to Earth for a period of almost one year.

Apollo 14 *5 February 1971.*
Astronauts Mitchell, Shephard, and Roosa.

Apollo 15 *30 July 1971.*
Astronauts Irwin, Scott, and Worden.

Luna 20 *21 February 1972.*
Robot vehicle extracted more core samples.

Apollo 16 *16 April 1972.*
Astronauts Duke, Mattingly, and Young.

Apollo 17 *7 December 1972.*
Astronauts Cernan, Evans, and Schmitt.

And just in case you were wondering!
Apollo 13 *11 April 1970.*
Mission aborted after an oxygen tank ruptured. Astronauts Haise, Lovell, and Swigert returned to Earth safely.

Why do you think there have been no more Moon walks for over 10 years?

A star called the Sun

You probably think of stars as tiny specks of light twinkling in the sky billions of miles away from Earth. There is one star, however, that we see every day quite close to Earth. This star is the **Sun**. The Sun is the star of our solar system.

The Sun is an enormous body. It has a mass of about 330 000 times that of Earth and is about 1 384 000 km in diameter. The distance between Earth and the Sun is about 149 million kilometres. This is a relatively short distance compared to the vast expanse of space. It is because the Sun is so near that it appears so large. In fact the Sun is small in comparison to other stars. Our next nearest star, **Alpha Centauri**, is much bigger but looks tiny because it is further away.

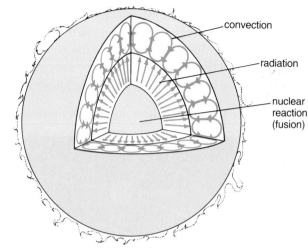
The Sun – a thermonuclear reactor

Scientists think the Sun was formed from gas and dust over 5000 million years ago. As gases collected together, the core became compressed, temperatures rose, and hydrogen atoms fused to form helium atoms. As helium atoms form, energy in the form of heat and light is released. This is a nuclear fusion reaction. Large numbers of helium atoms form every second and the heat is intense. Temperatures at the centre of the Sun are estimated at over 14 000 000 °C. The surface temperature is about 6000 °C.

The visible part of the Sun is called the **photosphere**. Surrounding this is a region of glowing gases called the **chromosphere**. Outside the chromosphere are the transparent gases of the **corona**. Flowing away from the corona is a solar wind of charged particles which bombards the Earth and distorts its magnetic field.

Sometimes glowing gases stream out in great arches from the chromosphere. These are called **prominences**. Prominences can leap thousands of miles before falling back to the surface.

Sunspots are dark patches on the surface of the Sun. They appear mainly in pairs or in small clusters in areas where the Sun's surface has cooled to about 4000 °C. Charged particles are shot out of sunspots far into space. Sometimes these reach the Earth's atmosphere and produce brilliant light displays called **aurorae**. The Northern Lights are an example of an aurora. Unfortunately the particles also cause interference to radio and television broadcasts. Scientists have found that sunspots become more frequent every 11 years or so. They cannot yet explain why this pattern occurs.

The Sun showing a huge prominence.

Solar eclipses

A solar eclipse is caused when the Moon, in its orbit around the Earth, comes between the Earth and the Sun. Light from the Sun is hidden and the Moon appears as a black disk surrounded by the chromosphere and corona.

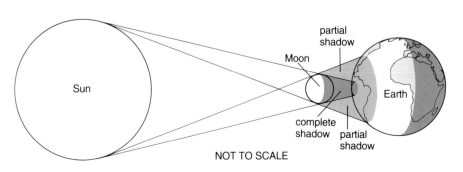

NOT TO SCALE

The planets of our solar system

The Earth is one of at least nine planets which travel around the Sun. The planets follow elliptical paths or orbits so their distance from the Sun is always changing. Moons orbit some of the planets. Like the Earth, the planets rotate on their axes although they rotate at different speeds. Only Earth appears to be capable of supporting life as we know it.

This diagram shows the planets in order of their distance from the Sun.

Planet facts: Earth
Distance from the Sun: 149M km
Diameter: 12 800 km
Time for one rotation: 213 h 56 min
Time to orbit the Sun: 365.25 days
Surface temperature: −90°C to +60°C
Atmosphere: water vapour, nitrogen, oxygen
Number of moons: 1

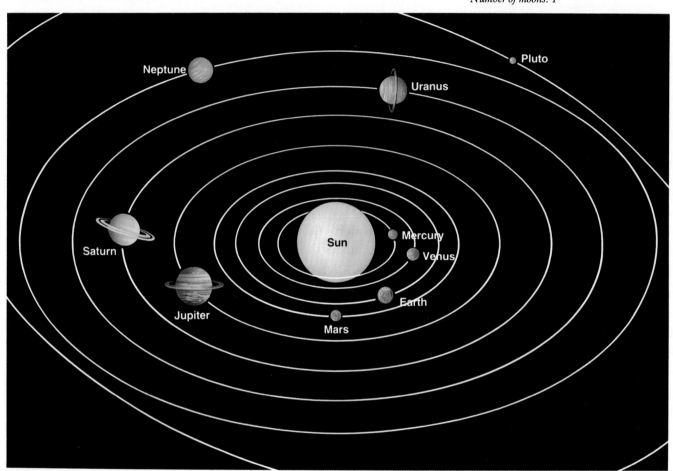

Planets of the solar system

Some astronomers have suggested that another planet may lie far beyond the orbit of Pluto. They have come to this idea after studying the paths of comets, including Halley's comet. As comets pass beyond Pluto and out of our solar system, they appear to be influenced by other gravitational fields.

All the planets and other bodies revolving around the Sun are held in orbit by the force of gravity. The Sun is by far the biggest body in our solar system. It therefore exerts a gravitational force that is strong enough to hold the largest and most distant planets.

Activities

1 Think of an easy way to remember the order of planets in our solar system. You could try making up a sentence with words beginning with the initial letter of each planet. On the other hand, you may think of some other way!

Mercury, Venus, and Mars

Mercury

Mercury is one of the smallest planets in the solar system and the one nearest the Sun. It is slightly less than half the size of Earth. Mercury turns on its axis very slowly. However, it is the fastest moving planet, travelling around the Sun at over 100 000 miles per hour. The surface of Mercury is covered in rocks and, because of its small size and low gravity, there is almost no atmosphere. The lack of an insulating atmosphere means that there is an extreme temperature range.

Venus

Venus is our closest planet and about the same size as the Earth. It travels within 41 million miles of the Earth. It is difficult to see the surface of Venus because it is always covered in thick white clouds. Venus rotates very slowly in the opposite direction to the Earth. The dense atmosphere on Venus is mainly carbon dioxide. Like the greenhouse gases on Earth, this carbon dioxide retains heat from the Sun. With its high surface temperature and an atmospheric pressure about 90 times that found on Earth it is hardly surprising that there is no life on Venus!

Mars

The atmosphere on **Mars** contains less oxygen and water vapour than that on Earth but it could be enough to support some simple form of life. People have thought there was life on Mars ever since 1877 when the Italian astronomer Schiaparelli thought he saw irrigation channels crossing the planet. Space exploration has, however, now put a stop to these ideas. Information sent back from *Viking 1* and *Viking 2* in 1976 indicates that the climate and the planet surface are unsuitable for any advanced life forms.

The variations in temperature cause large pressure differences leading to winds of up to 500 km/h. However, because there is little atmosphere on Mars, the winds lack energy. Atmospheric pressure is less than one-tenth that on Earth. Like Earth, Mars has two polar icecaps. It is thought that they consist of solid carbon dioxide (dry ice) mixed with some water ice. During the Martian summer, the ice appears to melt, causing the icecaps to shrink. As winter approaches, the icecaps extend over a larger surface of the planet.

There are four seasons on Mars just like on Earth. But because Mars takes twice as long as Earth to orbit the Sun, Martian seasons are twice as long as ours.

Questions

1   Explain why there is such a wide temperature range on Mercury and yet Venus, the next planet to it, has a temperature that doesn't change very much.

2   Explain why an astronaut would not survive if he or she got out of a spacecraft on Venus.

Planet facts: Mercury
Distance from the Sun: 57M km
Diameter: 4800 km
Time for one rotation: 58 days 16 h
Time to orbit the Sun: 88 days
Surface temperature: 200°C to +400°C
Atmosphere: very little
Number of moons: 0

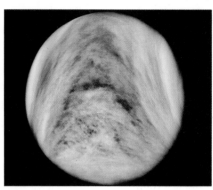

Venus

Planet facts: Venus
Distance from the Sun: 108M km
Diameter: 12 200 km
Time for one rotation: 244 days 7 h
Time to orbit the Sun: 224 days
Surface temperature: 480°C
Atmosphere: mainly carbon dioxide, sulphur, and sulphuric acid
Number of moons: 0

Mars

Planet facts: Mars
Distance from the Sun: 228M km
Diameter: 7000 km
Time for one rotation: 24 h 37 min
Time to orbit the Sun: 1.9 years
Surface temperature: −40°C to +25°C
Atmosphere: very little
Number of Moons: 2

Jupiter and Saturn

Jupiter

Jupiter is the giant of our solar system. Its radius is more than ten times that of the Earth and has nearly twice the mass of all the rest of the planets put together. It is because the planet is so massive that its gravity can attract so many moons. (It has at least sixteen).

Jupiter's atmosphere is made up mainly of hydrogen with some helium. The surface of the planet is liquid hydrogen. Below the surface, increasing pressure and temperature change this liquid hydrogen to a solid state. Some scientists think that Jupiter has a small rocky core only a few thousand miles in diameter.

Jupiter spins on its axis faster than any other planet. The equator travels much faster than the poles and bulges out giving Jupiter an oval shape. This fast rotation also produces wide bands of different colours on the planet's surface.

An interesting feature in the cloud belt around Jupiter is the **Red Spot**. This is a massive cloud of gases which swirl around like a tornado. Sometimes the spot shrinks until it almost disappears. At other times it grows. The red colour, which gives the spot its name, is due to the helium in the gas cloud.

Saturn

Saturn is the second largest of the planets and probably the most beautiful to look at. It is surrounded by hundreds of narrow rings. From time to time, Saturn's rings appear at different angles as the planet orbits the Sun. At one time astronomers thought that there were only three rings. However, *Voyager 1* and *Voyager 2* have revealed many more. Even the gaps have rings in them!

The appearance of Saturn and its chemical composition are very similar to those of Jupiter. Once again hydrogen and helium are the main gases but these are much less dense than on Jupiter. This means that the planet is unlikely to have any rock in it at all, only frozen and liquid gases.

Saturn spins on its axis almost as fast as Jupiter; more than twice as fast as Earth. This fast rotation produces very fast winds of up to 1400 km/h which constantly blow around the planet.

The biggest and brightest of Saturn's moons is called Titan. Titan is 8000 km in diameter, larger than the planet Mercury. It has an atmosphere of nitrogen gas and is very cold.

Planet facts: Jupiter
Distance from the Sun: 780M km
Diameter: 143 000 km
Time for one rotation: 9 h 50 min
Time to orbit the Sun: 11.9 years
Surface temperature: −150°C
Atmosphere: methane, ammonia, hydrogen, helium
Number of moons: 16

Jupiter

Planet facts: Saturn
Distance from the Sun: 1425M km
Diameter: 120 000 km
Time for one rotation: 10 h 14 min
Time to orbit the Sun: 29.5 years
Surface temperature: −180°C
Atmosphere: methane, ammonia, hydrogen, helium
Number of moons: 15

Saturn

Questions

1 Why has a spacecraft never landed on Jupiter?

2 What causes the coloured bands around Jupiter?

3 How is the Red Spot formed? Why is it red?

4 Why do you think Saturn has no rocky parts?

5 Why does Saturn have such strong winds?

6 Why are there no life forms on Titan?

7 Name one of Jupiter's moons. Explain why Jupiter and Saturn have more moons than any other planet in our solar system.

Uranus

Uranus is thought to be the first planet discovered by use of a telescope. It was found in 1781 by William Herschel, an English astronomer. Like Jupiter and Saturn, Uranus is a very large planet. Uranus is a blue-green colour. It also has rings. The ring system seems to consist of small pieces of ice-covered rock.

Uranus is very cold and clearly no life could exist there. Ariel, Titania, and Oberon are the largest of Uranus's moons.

Neptune

Neptune is about the same size as Uranus and is the last of the large planets. Three complete rings have been discovered. Because of its great distance from the Sun, Neptune doesn't have a proper day. The Sun's rays have so far to travel that daylight on Neptune is like dawn and dusk on Earth. Temperatures never rise above $-200\,°C$. *Voyager 2* discovered a great dark spot. This is a huge storm, big enough to swallow the Earth! Winds on Neptune reach speeds of over 1100 km/h. Neptune has seven moons. Triton is by far the biggest. On Triton there are signs of active volcanoes.

Pluto

Pluto was the last planet to be discovered. An American astronomer, Percival Lowell, first suspected its existence in 1905. But Pluto wasn't actually seen and identified until 1930. Clyde Tombaugh located a spot of light on the outer edge of our solar system. This light appeared to move as though in an orbit around the Sun. Tombaugh called this light Pluto.

Pluto is very small and has a very low density. It is thought to consist mainly of frozen methane. It is extremely cold as it is so far from the Sun. Pluto has an elliptical orbit which takes about 248 years to complete. Occasionally the planet passes inside Neptune's orbit.

In 1978 a moon was discovered close to Pluto. This moon is called Charon. Charon and Pluto are very close to each other, 19 000 km apart, a small distance when compared to others in our solar system! In fact it is difficult to tell Charon and Pluto apart, even with the most powerful telescope.

Some astronomers believe that Pluto is not really a planet. They think that it was once one of Neptune's moons. This moon broke out of Neptune's gravitational field and went into orbit around the Sun.

Questions

1 List the similarities between Uranus and Neptune.

2 Why is a day on Uranus so short?

3 Why is there no 'real daylight' on Neptune?

4 Explain why life as we know it could not exist on Uranus and Neptune.

Planet facts: Uranus
Distance from the Sun: 2900M km
Diameter: 49 000 km
Time for one rotation: 10 h 49 min
Time to orbit the Sun: 84 years
Surface temperature: −190°C
Atmosphere: methane
Number of moons: 5

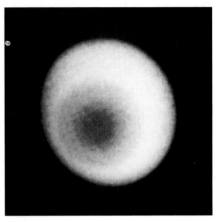

Uranus

Planet facts: Neptune
Distance from the Sun: 4500M km
Diameter: 50 000 km
Time for one rotation: 16 h 3 min
Time to orbit the Sun: 165 years
Surface temperature: below −220°C
Atmosphere: methane
Number of moons: 8

Neptune

Planet facts: Pluto
Distance from the Sun: 5900M km
Diameter: 4000 km
Time for one rotation: 6 days 9 h
Time to orbit the Sun: 248 years
Surface temperature: −250°C
Atmosphere: unknown
Number of moons: 1

Getting into space

Much of our knowledge about the solar system has come from investigations carried out by people or machines.

To get people and machines into space, powerful rockets had to be developed. These rockets have to be strong enough to break out of the Earth's gravitational field. Speeds of over 11 km/s must be reached by a rocket if it is to overcome gravity.

How do rocket engines work?

If you blow up a balloon then suddenly let it go, it flies off into the air. This is because the air rushing from the open end produces a reaction in the opposite direction. This is called **thrust** (see page 208). A space rocket engine uses thrust.

Most space rocket engines use kerosene and liquid hydrogen as fuel. Liquid oxygen is needed to enable the fuel to burn outside the Earth's atmosphere. Both the fuel and the oxygen are carried in huge, separate tanks. Oxygen and fuel are fed into a combustion chamber where they are burnt. Escaping exhaust gases rush through a nozzle at high speed producing thrust.

The *Saturn V* rocket was used to send the first people to the Moon. It had a mass of almost 3 000 000 kg and was 120 m tall. The fuel used in the first stage is kerosene. All the other stages use liquid hydrogen (and liquid oxygen to burn it).

The age of the shuttle

The Space Shuttle is a true space vehicle. It takes off like a rocket, moves about in space, and lands like an aeroplane.

Like rockets, the Space Shuttle can carry heavy loads into space. However, unlike other launch vehicles, the Space Shuttle orbiter can be used over and over again.

Saturn V

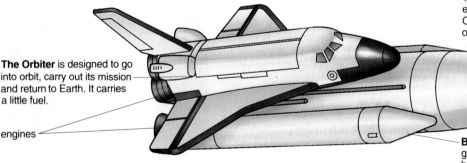

The Orbiter is designed to go into orbit, carry out its mission and return to Earth. It carries a little fuel.

engines

The space shuttle and how it works

The fuel tank carries fuel for the orbiter's engine. The tank has two compartments in it. One contains liquid hydrogen, the other liquid oxygen. the fuel is used up just as the orbiter enters orbit at a height of 200 km. Then the tank is ejected. It enters the atmosphere and burns up.

Booster rockets help the shuttle to get off the ground. When the shuttle has reached a height of 50 km, the fuel in these rockets is completely used up. The rockets are ejected. They parachute back to Earth to be used again.

Questions

1 Why do rockets need to be so powerful?

2 What is thrust?

3 How does the use of a Space Shuttle cut the cost of space exploration?

4 Why must space rockets carry liquid oxygen?

5 Why are clouds of steam produced when the Space Shuttle takes off?

6 Why is space a good place to carry out experiments?

What shape is the Earth?

In the Middle Ages most people believed that the Earth was flat. They thought that if ships sailed too far away from land they would fall over the edge.

Long before this, however, some people thought the Earth was a sphere. About 235 BC, the Greek astronomer Eratosthenes actually calculated the circumference of the Earth. Eratosthenes found out that at noon in Alexandria the Sun's rays fell at an angle of 7.5° to the vertical. At Aswan, 800 km due south of Alexandria, the noon Sun was directly overhead. Using the calculation shown alongside, Eratosthenes found the circumference of the Earth to be about 40 000 km. When we remember that he did this without any of the advantages of modern technology it is remarkable that Eratosthenes' estimation is only 5% away from the present-day value!

Evidence for a spherical Earth

If the Earth were flat, then the same stars would be seen from anywhere on its surface. But we know that this is not so. As travellers move around the world they see stars appear and disappear over the horizon.

If you stand on the seashore and watch a ship sail out to sea, you will notice that it not only appears smaller but also disappears over the horizon, rather like someone walking away from you over the top of a hill. This could only happen if the surface of the Earth were curved.

You can travel on a ship or an aeroplane on a journey all around the world and return to exactly the same place.

During a lunar eclipse the shadow of the Earth falls on the Moon. This shadow is always circular, no matter what position the Earth and Sun are in. The only solid that casts a circular shadow when lit from any angle is a sphere.

Today, space exploration has made it possible for us to see the true shape of the planet Earth. Photographs of our planet from outer space provide the ultimate proof that the Earth is spherical.

Questions

1   Why do you suppose sailors didn't travel very far from the coast in the Middle Ages?

2   Explain how Eratosthenes calculated the circumference of the Earth. How near to the present-day value was he?

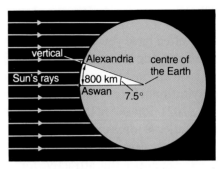

Measuring the circumference of the Earth

Calculation

If 7.5° corresponds to 800 km around the circumference of the Earth, then 360° corresponds to:

$$\frac{800 \times 360}{7.5} = 38\,400 \text{ km}$$

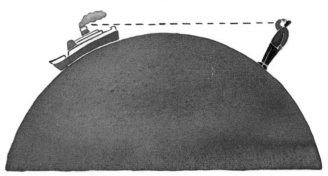

A ship disappears over the horizon.

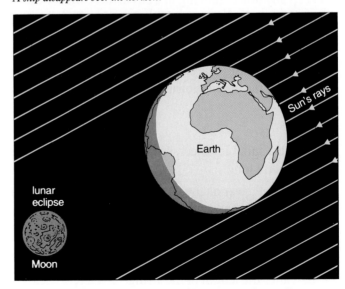

The Earth's circular shadow falls on the Moon during a lunar eclipse.

3   Your next-door neighbours tell you that they believe the Earth is flat. How would you try to convince them that they are wrong?

The force of gravity

How often have you dropped a piece of crockery when doing the washing up? Everyone knows that an object falls to the ground when it is dropped. This downward motion is the result of the force of **gravity**, or **gravitational force**, pulling the object towards the centre of the Earth (see page 202). It was Sir Isaac Newton who came to the conclusion that a gravitational force exists between all bodies. Not only are objects attracted towards the centre of the Earth, but they also attract each other. Usually we do not notice this attractive force because the objects are so small. However, the larger objects become, the greater the gravitational force between them. For example, scientists have measured a gravitational force of 180 newtons between two large tankers lying side by side at sea.

Newton came up with a law of gravitation. It says:

● **Any two particles of matter attract one another with a force which is proportional to the product of their masses (mass$_1$ × mass$_2$) and inversely proportional to the square of their distance apart (1/distance^2).**

This means, in simple terms, that the pull of gravity between two objects depends upon the mass of the objects and the distance between them.

Every object in the universe attracts other objects. It is gravitational force which keeps the Moon in orbit around the Earth and the planets of the solar system in their orbits around the Sun.

Gravity causes this apple to fall. It also keeps the planets in their orbits.

Centripetal force

To keep any object moving in a circle there must be a force acting on it directed towards the centre. This force is called a **centripetal force**. The planets of the solar system keep moving very quickly through space because there is nothing to slow them down. Centripetal force is needed to produce the continuous change of direction which occurs in an orbit. It is provided by the gravitational attraction between the planets and the Sun.

Activities

1   Attach a suitable object, such as rubber bung, to the end of a piece of string 1 metre long.

2   Stand well clear of any obstruction (including anyone else!) and swing the object round and round.
The pull on the string is providing the centripetal force.
What happens to this force if you:
  a)   increase the speed of rotation
  b)   alter the length of the string
  c)   change the mass of the object?

Questions

1   What force causes objects to fall to the ground?

2   What two things affect the gravitational attraction between objects?

3   Why do you suppose the planets orbiting the Sun   **a)** never slow down   **b)** are not drawn towards the Sun by the Sun's gravity?

4   Communication satellites are launched using rocket power. They orbit the Earth for a time before they lose speed and fall back towards the Earth.

Explain these events.

1 Use diagrams to explain the following:

a) Day and night are always of equal length at the Equator.

b) Day and night are of equal length twice a year in the U.K.

c) It never goes dark even at night for a few weeks in June at the North Pole.

d) Average temperatures are lower near to the North and South Poles than at the Equator.

2 The table gives information about four of the planets in our solar system.

planet	distance from Sun	diameter	time to orbit Sun	surface temperature	atmosphere
Jupiter	780 Mkm	143 000 km	11.9 years	-150°C	hydrogen/helium
Pluto	5900 Mkm	4000 km	248 years	-250°C	unknown
Mars	228 Mkm	7000 km	1.9 years	-80 to +40°C	carbon dioxide/nitrogen/oxygen
Mercury	57 Mkm	4800 km	88 days	-200 to +400°C	very little

Use this information to answer the following questions.

a) Which is i) the largest ii) the smallest planet?

b) Which of the planets has i) the shortest ii) the longest year?

c) Which planet is furthest from the Sun?

d) Which planet has the greatest temperature range?

e) Some scientists have suggested that there is life on Mars. Give one reason why i) they could be right ii) they could be wrong.

3 a) What is an eclipse?

b) Draw diagrams to show the difference between a lunar and solar eclipse.

c) Explain why the Sun appears as a black disk surrounded by a halo of light during a solar eclipse.

d) Why do you think full solar eclipses are so rare?

e) This diagram shows part of a lunar eclipse. The shadow of the Earth is almost covering the Moon.

i) Carefully trace the shape of the Moon on to a large piece of paper.

ii) See if you can work out the diameter of the Moon by completing the circle with a pencil and pair of compasses.

iii) Try to find out the diameter of the Earth in the same way.

iv) What is the ratio of the two diameters (Moon diameter: Earth diameter)?

v) Calculate the actual diameter of the Moon using the formula:

$$\text{actual diameter of Moon} = \frac{\text{Moon diameter}}{\text{Earth diameter}} \times 13\,000$$

How close are you to the real diameter of the Moon? (See page 220).

4 Little George started building a sand castle on the beach. He took his parents' advice and worked well away from the water's edge. George came back the next day to finish the sandcastle but it had gone. His mother told his father that he had seen someone do exactly the same one week earlier and their sandcastle had not disappeared overnight.

a) Explain these events as fully as you can.

b) What advice would you give to someone who wanted their sandcastle to remain on a beach for a few days?

What is biotechnology?

What are genes made of?

What is genetic engineering?

How can biotechnology help us?

What use is biotechnology to industry?

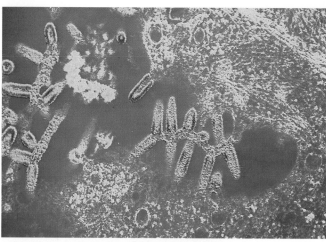

Microorganisms can be useful to biotechnologists (magnification × 20000).

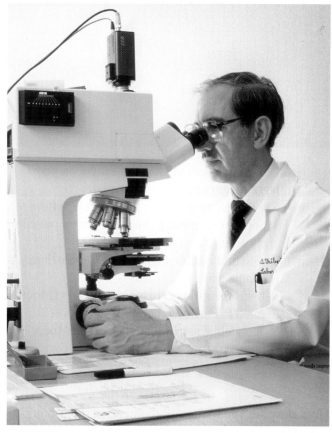

Biotechnology uses organisms that can only be seen with a microscope.

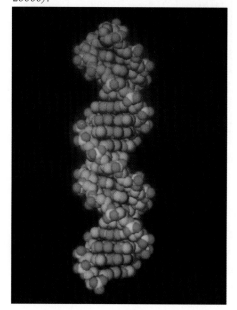

Model of the DNA molecule

Biotechnology has been around for thousands of years. People have been making bread and cheese, brewing wine and beer, and preserving food in vinegar for generations. Today we know a lot more about how these processes work.

Biotechnology is using cells to make useful things. It brings together the knowledge of the biologist and the skills of the technologist to provide food, medicines, and new materials for industry. It can also help to clear up much of the waste that pollutes our environment.

The biotechnologist may use whole cells or parts of cells such as DNA (see page 234) to control complex chemical reactions. Micro-organisms can be grown in vast quantities before being 'harvested' for food. They are also a source of important molecules such as antibodies.

By engineering genes (see page 234), rare and expensive chemicals such as **insulin** can be made cheaply and efficiently.

Work with micro-organisms has to be carried out in sterile conditions.

Biotechnology past and present

Biotechnology probably began thousands of years ago with **fermentation**. This process was used to make bread, wine and beer, and vinegar. You probably know that fermentation is brought about by yeast. Yeast is a single-celled organism called a **microbe**. Other examples of microbes are **bacteria** and **viruses**. Bacteria were used to make yoghurt from milk and mould fungi were used to make cheese.

Of course we still use this 'old' biotechnology. In fact most modern work is based on the old methods. Modern biotechnology is on a much larger scale but it still depends on microbes.

Bread, beer, and cheese are all products of biotechnology.

Why use microbes?

Microbes grow quickly when given the right temperature and food supply. It is therefore easier to grow microbes in large quantities than to develop ways of growing plant and animal cells on their own. Also, microbe cells are relatively simple. This makes it easier for scientists to genetically engineer new microbes for specific jobs.

The biotechnology calendar

10 000 BC	Neolithic men and women ate fermented grain.
6000 BC	Babylonians used yeasts to make beer.
4000 BC	Egyptians used yeast to make bread dough rise.
2000 BC	The Chinese developed the fermentation process.
AD 1400	Distillation of wines and spirits was widespread.
AD 1500	Aztecs harvested algae from lakes for food.
1686	Leeuwenhoek made the first microscope and discovered microbes.
c. 1870	Pasteur proved that microbes were responsible for fermentation and for the decomposition of food.
c. 1890	Alcohol was first used as fuel.
1897	Buchner discovered that enzymes in yeast are responsible for converting sugar into alcohol.
1912	Microbes were first used in sewage works.
1912	Weizmann used bacteria to produce acetone (propanone) and butanol by fermentation.
1928	Fleming discovered penicillin.
1943	Avery provided evidence that DNA carries genetic information.
1944	Chain and Florey developed large-scale production of penicillin.
1953	Watson and Crick discovered the structure of DNA.
c. 1960	The genetic code was cracked.
1972	The first gene cloning was carried out.
1973	Brazil introduced its National Fuel Alcohol Programme.
1975	Kohler and Milstein first produced monoclonal antibodies.
1976	Guidelines on genetic engineering were drawn up.
1977	The first human gene was cloned.
1982	Human insulin was made by genetic engineering.
1987	Field trials of the first genetically engineered microbes started.
1988	Genetic 'fingerprinting' techniques were developed.

Questions

1 Name two products that can be made by fermentation.
2 Some people say that biotechnology hasn't changed.
   a) Give one reason why they might be right.
   b) Give one reason why they might be wrong.
3 Give two reasons why biotechnologists use microbes.

DNA – it's all in the nucleus

All living things are made of **cells**. You may remember that the nucleus of a cell contains long, thread-like structures called **chromosomes**. Chromosomes carry bits of information called **genes**.

Genes instruct our bodies to make **proteins**. Proteins determine the shape of the body and how it behaves. Each gene controls the production of one particular protein.

Chromosomes and genes are made of **DNA** (*d*eoxyribo*n*ucleic *a*cid). DNA is a sort of plan that determines how the body is constructed. It is often called the 'blueprint for life' – every cell in an organism contains a copy of the blueprint. Notice how the DNA molecule is like a twisted ladder. This is called a **double helix**. The double helix is coiled up tightly on itself so that all DNA molecules can fit inside the cell nucleus.

The rungs of the ladder are made from pairs of **bases**. There are four kinds of bases. They have complicated names so we will use their initials.

Bases can only fit together in one way.

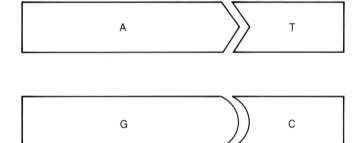

When cells divide the DNA first duplicates itself. A copy of the blueprint is passed from one generation to the next. This is the reason why we inherit characteristics from our parents. The diagram opposite shows how this duplication happens.

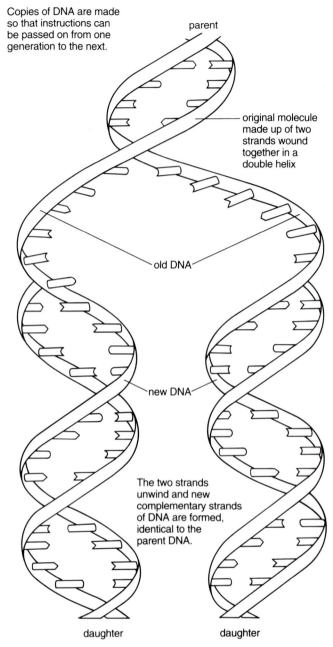

Copies of DNA are made so that instructions can be passed on from one generation to the next.

parent

original molecule made up of two strands wound together in a double helix

old DNA

new DNA

The two strands unwind and new complementary strands of DNA are formed, identical to the parent DNA.

daughter   daughter

DNA can make new strands identical to the old ones.

Questions

1 What are chromosomes?

2 What do genes make in our cells?

3 What does DNA stand for?

4 How would you describe the shape of the DNA molecule?

5 Why is DNA called the 'blueprint of life'?

6 Why do you suppose a large base is always paired with a small base in the DNA molecule? (*Hint:* think what would happen if two small bases were paired together.)

DNA – copying and reading the code

The order in which the bases appear on the DNA molecule forms a coded message. The code is read as blocks of three letters, such as ACA. Each block of letters signals a particular amino acid. The order of letters on the DNA determines the order of amino acids in a protein and therefore the kind of protein to be made.

Copying the code

Another molecule called **RNA** (ribo*nu*cleic *a*cid) is also present in cells. RNA is like a DNA molecule split down the middle – a 'half ladder'. Instead of having pairs of bases, RNA has single bases attached along its length.

Messenger RNA copies the code from the DNA molecule and carries it out of the nucleus into the cell cytoplasm.

Reading the code

Transfer RNA molecules bring specific amino acids up to the messenger RNA. The order in which the amino acids are brought together depends upon the order of letters in the three-letter blocks on the original DNA molecule.

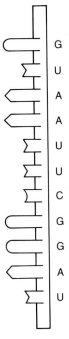

A 'half ladder' RNA molecule. RNA has no T base. T is replaced by U.

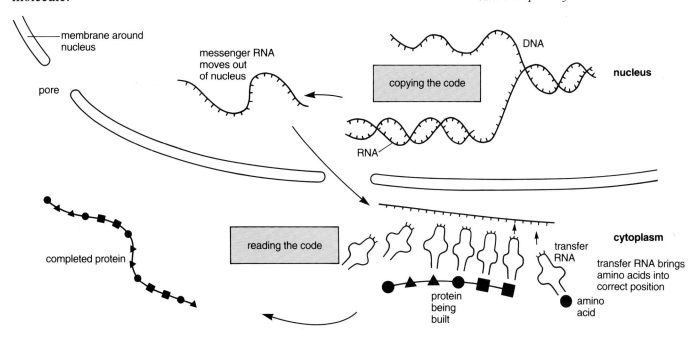

How DNA determines the sequence of amino acids in proteins

Activities

1   There are four kinds of bases in the 'rungs' of the DNA molecule.

What are they?

2   Each amino acid has its own code of three letters. For example, ACA codes for an amino acid called threonine. Another amino acid, glycine, has the code GGC.

There are 20 amino acids altogether, each with its own code.

Are there enough codes to go round?

Work them out and see.

Genetic engineering

Genetic engineering involves removing genes from one type of cell and transferring them to another completely different cell. The techniques involved require a lot of precision and genetic engineers must be highly skilled.

Animal and plant products used in industry, agriculture, and medicine are often in short supply or very expensive. The genes controlling the production of these materials in animals and plants can be inserted into microbe cells. These genes then instruct the microbial cells to produce something they would not naturally do. Since microbes reproduce and grow at a rapid rate they produce the required materials in much greater quantities than the original animal or plant cells.

How is it done?

Cells contain thousands of genes. So the first step is to locate and then collect the required gene. Finding a gene is not easy, as you can imagine. The gene is removed from the chromosome by using special enzymes – like 'chemical scissors'.

Getting the gene into a microbial cell involves the use of **plasmids**. Plasmids are found in bacterial cells. They are small circles of DNA which are smaller than the single circular bacterial chromosome. Plasmids can move from one cell to another and make copies of themselves. By fixing the required gene into its correct position on a plasmid it can be introduced into a microbial cell. Once there it will be duplicated every time the microbial cell divides. Each of the new cells is called a **clone** because they all have the same genetic make-up. In just a few days there will be millions of cloned cells, each one carrying a copy of the original donated gene. This is called **gene cloning**.

All that remains is to persuade the microbial cell to begin making the appropriate product and then devise an economical method of collecting it.

Questions

1 What is genetic engineering? Explain the process briefly.

2 Why have genetic engineering techniques been developed?

3 Why are microbes used in genetic engineering?

4 Why do you suppose enzymes are called 'chemical scissors'?

5 What are plasmids?
Give two reasons why plasmids are used in genetic engineering.

6 What is a clone?

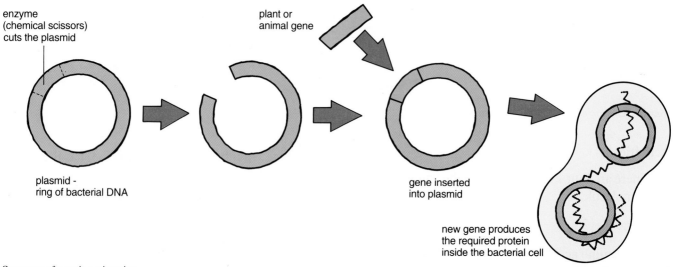

enzyme
(chemical scissors)
cuts the plasmid

plant or
animal gene

plasmid -
ring of bacterial DNA

gene inserted
into plasmid

new gene produces
the required protein
inside the bacterial cell

Summary of genetic engineering

Human insulin from genetic engineering

Insulin is a hormone that allows the body to take up sugars from our blood. Insulin is made in the pancreas. Unfortunately some people cannot make enough insulin so their blood sugar level rises. They suffer from the disease **diabetes mellitus**. People who suffer from diabetes are called **diabetics**. Some diabetics can regulate their blood sugar levels by controlling their diets and avoiding sugary foods. Others, however, must inject themselves regularly with insulin.

Until recently the only insulin available for diabetics came from the pancreas of pigs or cattle. This insulin is not exactly the same as human insulin and in some people it produces allergic responses. Also, the number of diabetics is increasing and it is unlikely that the supply of animal insulin will meet the demand.

Now, by using genetic engineering techniques, biotechnologists can use bacteria to produce human insulin. Using human insulin avoids any possible side-effects of animal insulin. It can also be produced in the quantity required to meet the needs of known diabetics.

Some diabetics have to inject themselves with insulin.

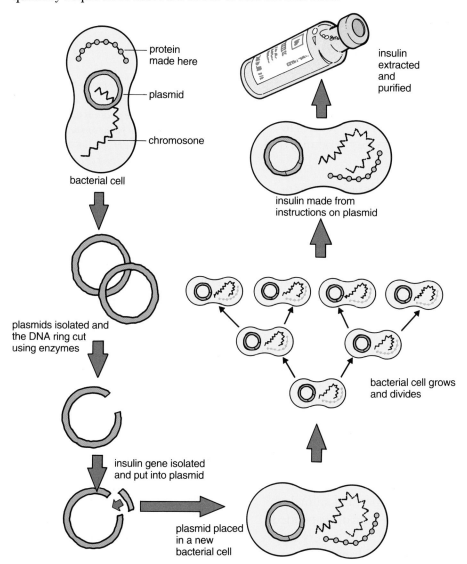

Making insulin by genetic engineering

Questions

1 **a)** What is insulin?
b) Where is it made in the body?
c) What does it do in the body?

2 **a)** What disease do diabetics suffer from?
b) What symptons do they show?
c) How can diabetics overcome their illness?

3 **a)** Name one 'old' source of insulin.
b) Why is genetically engineered insulin better?

4 Briefly describe how biotechnologists make human insulin.

Engineering plants and animals

Biotechnologists use genetic engineering to develop new kinds of plants and healthier and more productive farm animals. They can also save rare animals from extinction.

Nitrogen is a vital component of proteins. Plants get their nitrogen from the soil in the form of nitrates. Animals eat plants to obtain their proteins. Although the air is about 80% nitrogen this is of no use to plants until it has been converted to nitrates. This process is called **nitrogen fixation**. Some plants called **legumes** such as beans, peas, and clover have **root nodules** containing nitrogen-fixing bacteria. This fertilizes the soil naturally and removes the risks and expenses of adding artificial fertilizers.

Unfortunately, most of the world's major food plants such as rice and wheat do not have bacteria-filled nodules on their roots. Scientists are using genetic engineering techniques to modify the nitrogen-fixing bacteria so that they will live in the roots of these important plants.

Large areas of the world are not suitable for growing food crops. This may be because of poor rainfall, high temperatures, or insect pests. If genes can be found to improve the ability of food plants to survive in these conditions then we may see the end of food shortages in countries such as Ethiopia and the Sudan.

Healthier animals

Biotechnologists have genetically engineered a number of vaccines to protect animals against disease. Newcastle's disease virus in poultry and the pig disease 'scours' are just two of their successes.

Sickness in animals is often the result of infection by parasites. There are two kinds of parasites. Parasites such as worms that live in the gut are **endoparasites**. **Ectoparasites** like ticks live outside the body. Scientists discovered a mould fungus in the soil that killed parasitic worms. As more work was done it was found that it also killed ticks. This has lead to the development of new kinds of pest control products called **endectocides**.

More productive animals

The use of **BST** (*bovine somatotropin*) has greatly increased productivity in cattle. BST is a hormone that cattle produce naturally. By isolating and cloning the gene that codes for the production of BST, scientists have genetically engineered bacteria to produce the hormone. The same techniques can be used to improve production in other farm animals such as pigs and sheep.

Safe from extinction

Scientists are able to store the unfertilized eggs and sperm of animals for long periods of time. Even embryos can be kept in a state of suspended animation. The process involves carefully cooling the cells to very low temperatures. In this way the valuable genetic material from rare and endangered animals will never be lost.

Some types of plant can be grown from a tiny piece containing only a few cells. This is called **tissue culture**. *Tissue culture is useful because thousands of identical plants can be grown from just a few cells. The technique can be used in the production of vegetables such as carrots and potatoes, and especially to produce ornamental plants such as orchids where each individual plant is very valuable.*

Questions

1 Why is nitrogen important to plants?

2 Why don't crops such as peas and beans need to be fertilized?

3 Give two advantages of developing cereal plants with root nodules.

4 What are the advantages of tissue culture?

5 What is a common cause of sickness in animals?

6 **a)** What are endectocides?
    b) Where do they come from?

7 Briefly describe how biotechnology can help to save rare and endangered animal species from extinction.

Microbes – new sources of food

Although the thought of eating microbes may not be very pleasant, we do in fact eat quite a few. Cheese and yoghurt contain microbes, bread and beer are made using microbes, and yeast extract is almost pure microbes! Algae, fungi, and bacteria can all be used directly as sources of food.

Algae are simple plants that live in water. They contain a lot of protein, vitamins, and minerals. Hundreds of years ago the Aztecs collected and ate an alga called *Spirulina maxima*. It didn't have much taste but it was a valuable source of nutrients.

Today food scientists are once again showing interest in *Spirulina* as a food. In hot countries where cereal crops are difficult to cultivate, *Spirulina* is grown in long plastic ponds.

Fungi such as mushrooms have been eaten for centuries. Recently, however, attention has been directed to a mould fungus called *Fusarium*. *Fusarium* contains about 45% protein and 13% fat – about the same as the protein: fat ratio of meat. The big advantage that *Fusarium* has over meat is that it contains a lot of fibre and is cholesterol free.

Fusarium will grow on any material containing carbohydrate such as potatoes, starch, or wheat. These are relatively cheap. Afterwards the fungus can be collected and used to make artificial meat. You will find this fungal protein in a number of products at your local supermarket. Look out for it on the label – it is called **mycoprotein**.

A bacterium called *Methylophilus methylotrophus* grows well on methanol. Methanol can be made quite cheaply from natural gas. Mineral salts, ammonia, a plentiful supply of air, and a suitable temperature are essential for successful growth of the bacteria.

When removed from the ethanol the bacteria are dried. The dried bacterial cells contain protein. The commercial name for this protein is **Pruteen**. As in the production of mycoprotein, conditions for Pruteen manufacture must be sterile. In fact, very few other microbes will grow in methanol so there is little risk of contamination.

A **continuous culture** process is used in Pruteen production. This means that as bacteria are removed they are replaced with similar amounts of starting materials.

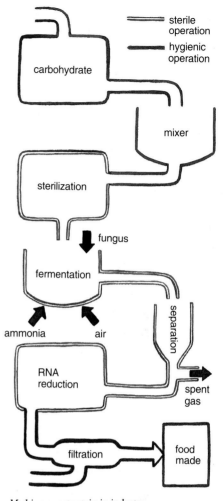

Making mycoprotein in industry

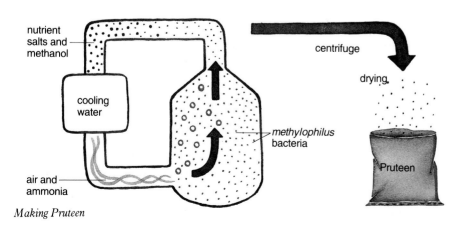

Making Pruteen

Questions

1 Name three foods that contain microbes.

2 What nutritional value is there in the alga *Spirulina*?

3 How are meat and the mould fungus *Fusarium* **a)** similar **b)** different?

4 What three things are needed for the successful growth of *Methylophilus* bacteria?

5 Why must the conditions for making mycoprotein and Pruteen be sterile?

6 What is a continuous culture process? What do you think is the advantage of such a process?

Biotechnology and fuel (1): alcohol

New sources of fuel are needed if we are to conserve traditional fossil fuels such as coal and oil and reduce the harmful effects that their use has on the environment.

One such alternative is **alcohol**. An alcohol called ethanol is produced when yeast feeds on sugar in the absence of oxygen. The properties of alcohol make it good for use as fuel.

Using Gasohol

The Brazilian alternative

Brazil has no fossil fuels of its own and cannot afford to buy them in the quantities it needs. However, it does have a lot of land on which sugar cane is grown – in fact it has more sugar that it needs. As a result the Brazilian government introduced its National Fuel Alcohol Programme. The idea was to produce ethanol from the surplus sugar and mix it with petrol to make 'Gasohol'. Gasohol sells well as an alternative to petrol, it is cheaper, and most vehicles can use it with only minor adjustments.

Increasing oil prices have lead to the development of engines that can run on pure ethanol. This fuel is cheaper still, about half the price of petrol.

Most of the production costs are spent on making the alcohol strong enough to use as a fuel. Yeast will usually die at alcohol concentrations between 11% and 15% so the fermenting liquid must be distilled to concentrate the alcohol. If yeasts could be developed that are more alcohol tolerant, alcohol could be much more widely used as a fuel, especially in poorer countries.

Gasohol has also been available for some years in America as an alternative to petrol. America used to import its alcohol from Brazil; today it makes its own from maize (corn-on-the-cob).

In some tropical countries a root crop called **cassava** is used in the production of alcohol. Despite having less sugar than sugar cane, cassava is a valuable energy source in countries that have few other resources.

What's in the future?

Biotechnologists are currently trying to genetically engineer a yeast that is able to break down starch into sugar before fermenting the sugar in the normal way. If they are successful any plant material could be used as a basis for the production of alcohol.

Research is also going on into the use of vegetable oils as fuels. You are probably familiar with vegetable oils such as palm oil, sunflower oil, and corn oil, especially if you are concerned about your health! It may not be too long before these oils are used in motor vehicles. Brazilian scientists have already produced a suitable 'cocktail' for use instead of diesel fuel. The cocktail is made up of 73% diesel oil, 20% palm oil, and 7% ethanol. It appears to work well, with the palm oil actually making the fuel last longer.

Questions

1 Why are new sources of fuel needed?

2 Give two reasons why Brazil introduced its National Fuel Alcohol Programme.

3 What is Gasohol?

4 How is alcohol made 'stronger' for use as a fuel?

5 Name three plants that can be used for making fuel alcohol.

6 What is the advantage of producing a yeast that can break down starch into sugar?

7 Briefly describe a successful use of a vegetable oil as a fuel.

8 Why do you think there hasn't been a worldwide swing towards using biofuel?

Biotechnology and fuel (2): flammable gases

Like alcohol, methane is a product of a natural process. It is produced whenever plant and animal remains decompose in the absence of oxygen. There are lots of places where this could happen, such as in the mud at the bottom of stagnant ponds. You may have seen bubbles of methane gas rising to the surface of the water. Don't try lighting it though, methane is a flammable gas!

Methane is produced on a much larger scale inside the Earth's crust. For millions of years bacteria have been breaking down organic material into methane gas. Today we can drill deep into the Earth to extract it. North Sea gas or 'natural gas' is methane.

Like ethanol, methane is produced by fermentation. It is made by bacteria feeding on organic waste rather than yeast on sugar.

Biotechnologists are already considering the uses of methane-producing bacteria. The bacteria could provide us with a renewable source of natural gas. There are plenty of raw materials around, including unwanted waste. Household and farmyard sewage, industrial waste, and rubbish provide ideal materials for use in fermenters. Some scientists have even suggested using fast-growing seaweeds. These could be grown in huge floating grids in the sea.

Digester

Some farms and sewage works use methane-powered generators to produce their own electricity. Cattle produce the raw materials on farms. In the sewage works it comes from us. The methane is produced in large closed tanks called **digesters**. It is important that the temperature inside the digester is kept at about 35°C because this is an ideal temperature for the bacteria.

How do digesters work?

Methane production is slow and is quite a complicated process. There are two stages:

1 Acid formation – animal and human waste contains acid-forming bacteria. These bacteria break down the waste into simple organic acids.

2 Methane formation – the organic acids are broken down by methane-forming bacteria. Methane gas is produced.
The sludge left at the bottom of the digester is removed and used as fertilizer.

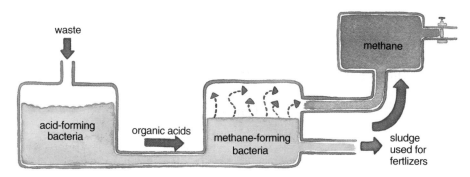

What happens in a digester

Questions

1 How is methane produced?

2 Name a place where methane is produced naturally.

3 Why do you think North Sea gas is called natural gas?

4 Give   a) one similarity
b) one difference between the production of ethanol and that of methane.

5 List four raw materials that could be used in methane production.

6 What are digesters?

7 What effect would the use of hydrogen as a fuel have on the environment?

8 Why is hydrogen not produced as a fuel at the moment?

241

Biotechnology and health (1)

Biotechnology and health have been closely linked for many years. It was in the middle of the nineteenth century that Louis Pasteur and Robert Koch first discovered that microbes were the cause of most common diseases. The production of useful medicines such as vaccines and antibiotics is the job of the biotechnologist.

A **vaccine** is a liquid containing dead or weakened microbes. Vaccines work by stimulating the natural defences of the body. Antibodies are produced by white blood cells every time microbe cells enter the body. These antibodies destroy the invading microbes and disease symptoms are removed.

Unfortunately there are still some diseases for which there are no vaccines. Those such as the common cold and mumps are not so serious because, given time, the body can cure itself. However, a much more serious example is AIDS. There is no known cure for AIDS.

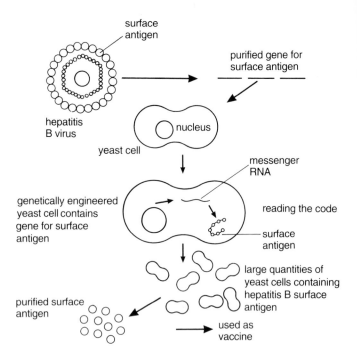

Producing a vaccine by genetic engineering. A problem facing scientists is finding a way to produce large amounts of vaccine quickly. Recently success has been achieved with the production of a vaccine against the serious liver disease hepatitis B. This is how it is done.

Antibiotics destroy bacteria. It was Alexander Fleming who, in 1928, discovered the first antibiotic. It was called **penicillin**. The name penicillin comes from the mould fungus *Penicillium notatum*. Fleming discovered penicillin almost by accident. By mistake, the mould infected some bacterial cultures he had been working on. Instead of throwing the cultures away Fleming looked at them and noticed there were no bacteria around the blue-green mould. The mould was giving off a substance that prevents bacterial growth. This substance was penicillin.

How do antibiotics work?

Penicillin is not the only antibiotic. There are a number of others including **cephalosporin** and **streptomycin**. It is important that new antibiotics are developed because bacteria can become **resistant** to them. When penicillin was first used many major bacterial infections could be cured. However, some types of bacteria that were once easily killed by penicillin are now able to survive. Mutations have occured in some bacteria making them resistant to penicillin. The resistant bacteria have survived – they have been favoured by **natural selection**.

Cephalosporin comes from the fungus *Cephalosporium*. Fortunately it is effective against penicillin-resistant bacteria. Penicillin and cephalosporin work in the same way – by stopping bacteria building a cell wall.

Streptomycin works in a different way. It stops bacteria making protein by interrupting the reading of the genetic code carried by messenger RNA.

Questions

1 What is a vaccine?

2 Name **a**) one disease that can **b**) one disease that cannot be prevented by a vaccine.

3 Briefly describe a vaccine that can be produced by genetic engineering. Why is this technique an important step in vaccine production?

4 a) Who discovered penicillin? **b**) What kind of organism produces it? **c**) What colour is this organism?

5 a) Name two other antibiotics. **b**) Briefly explain how they work.

6 How can we help overcome bacterial resistance to antibiotics?

Biotechnology and health (2)

What are monoclonal antibodies?

The surface of a microbe is made of protein called an **antigen**. The shape of this protein coat is unique to a particular kind of microbe. **Antibodies** are shaped so that they can join up with antigens and so make them harmless. White blood cells called **phagocytes** then come along and digest them.

Antibodies are produced by other white blood cells called **lymphocytes**. Lymphocytes are made in the lymph glands or the spleen. You can sometimes feel swollen lymph glands under your arms or just beneath your ears when you are ill. Since antibodies are made here, this is where most of the 'fighting' takes place, hence the swelling. You may remember that a **clone** is a large number of identical cells. When a clone is produced from only one type of cell it is called a **monoclone**.

Monoclonal antibodies are antibodies produced by clones of one type of lymphocyte.

How do they work?

Antibodies can recognize the protein coat of one type of cell. These cells are called **target cells**. During the production of monoclonal antibodies only one type of lymphocyte is grown. This produces only one kind of antibody that recognizes only one kind of target cell.

If a drug is attached to a monoclonal antibody, it will be taken directly to its target cell. The drug will be able to act exactly where it is needed. Monoclonal antibodies have been called **magic bullets**.

What are they used for?

Monoclonal antibodies can be used to detect diseases with speed and accuracy. Body fluids such as blood and urine can be tested easily. If microbes are present monoclonal antibodies seek them out and a chemical indicator changes colour. Genetic engineering combined with monoclonal antibody production has led to the development and manufacture of new bacterial and viral antibodies.

Questions

1 What do antibodies do to bacteria that invade the body?

2 **a)** What are antigens?   **b)** How do antibodies make them harmless?

3 Explain why your lymph glands may swell when you are ill.

4 **a)** What are monoclonal antibodies?   **b)** Why are monoclonal antibodies sometimes called 'magic bullets'?

*Making monoclonal antibodies. Antigens are injected into a mouse which produces antibodies to them. The antibody-producing cells are removed and fused with tumour cells which reproduce rapidly. The resulting **hybridoma** cells produce one type of antibody each. They are separated and the antibodies produced in bulk.*

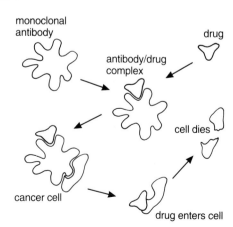

The drug is attached to a monoclonal antibody which recognizes cancer cells. When it finds them the drug destroys only the cancer cells.

Biotechnology and industry

Many of our industries depend upon oil, coal, and gas for their raw materials. As natural resources become scarce, industrial scientists are looking to biotechnology as a source of materials and products.

Getting more oil from oil wells

Only about one-third of the oil in the ground is brought to the surface. The rest remains clinging to rock particles deep below the ground. Biotechnology has provided a way to extract this remaining oil using xanthum gum. Xanthum gum is made by a type of bacteria called *Xanthomonas*.

water and xanthan gum
pumped into oil deposits

water and gum

xantham gum loosens
oil from rocks

oil removed
at oil well

to refinery

Some oil companies are developing another way of removing oil. This involves pumping bacteria down an oil well and feeding them with nutrients while they are deep underground. Despite the high temperature and pressure below ground, the bacteria soon grow and increase in numbers. The bacteria produce chemicals that wash oil from surrounding rock particles. They also produce a gas which builds up enough pressure to force the oil to the surface.

Getting materials from the ground

Some types of bacteria live in the spoil heaps around coal and mineral mines. These bacteria feed on the traces of minerals in the rock and oxidize them to produce energy. Sulphuric acid and iron(II) sulphate are produced as by-products. Surrounding rocks are attacked by these chemicals and many kinds of metals are leached out. Copper, iron, and uranium are leached out in this way. Biotechnology has used these bacteria to extract mineral ores from places where it has not been economical in the past.

Methylococcus lives in the hot water baths in the historic city of Bath!

New plastics

Alkene oxides are widely used in the plastics industry. Scientists have been able to add oxygen to alkenes with the help of a bacterium called *Methylococcus capsulatus*. The process is a lot cheaper than the traditional method and produces no pollution.

Questions

1 What is the name of the bacterium that produces xantham gum?

2 How does xanthum gum help remove oil from oil wells?

3 Why are scientists looking to biotechnology to provide materials and products for industry?

4 Name two metals that bacteria remove from rocks.

5 What contribution has the City of Bath made to biotechnology?

Questions

1 Josie's pet dog, Skip, became ill so she took him to the vet. Skip had a bacterial infection. The vet prescribed some antibiotics. She told Josie to give Skip two tablets every day after meals for the next ten days.

After four days Skip seemed much better so Josie stopped giving him the tablets. Unfortunately Skip became very ill again a few days later.

Josie started giving Skip the tablets again but this time they did not make Skip better.

Once again Skip was taken to the vet. The vet was very annoyed with Josie for not completing the course of antibiotics. She gave Josie some different antibiotics for Skip. This time Josie made sure she gave Skip all the tablets as instructed. Skip got better.

a) What are antibiotics?
b) What do they do?
c) Explain why Skip got better after the first four days of treatment.
d) Suggest why Skip became ill again and only recovered when different antibiotics were given.

2 The diagram shows a pressure cycle fermenter used by ICI to make Pruteen.

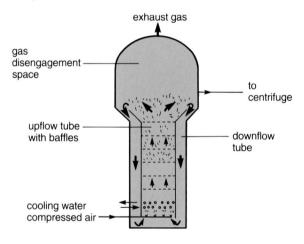

a) What does the compressed air do?
b) What is the job of the cooling water pipes?
c) Why do you suppose there is an exhaust valve?
d) Why do you think the fermenter is called a pressure cycle fermenter?
e) Why does the mixture rise in the centre tube?
f) ICI claims the pressure cycle fermenter is more sterile than fermenters fitted with stirrers.
Why is it important for the fermenter to be sterile?
g) Explain how a centrifuge is used to remove the product.

3 The diagram shows a summary of the processes involved in genetic engineering.

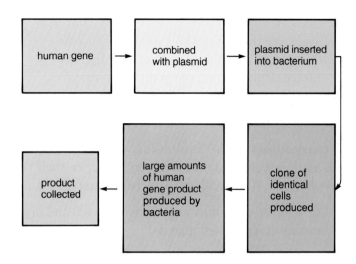

a) What is i) a gene ii) a plasmid iii) a clone?
b) List the four main stages in genetic engineering.
c) Give two reasons why microbes such as bacteria are used in genetic engineering.
d) Genetic engineering is used to produce human insulin. Why is insulin important in the body?
e) What happens to a person who cannot produce enough insulin of their own?
f) Why is it better to produce human insulin by genetic engineering than to use the insulin from large animals such as cattle?

4 Farmer Stone generates his own electricity using a methane-powered generator. He collects all the manure from his cows and puts it into a large tank. Inside the tank the manure is decomposed by bacteria and methane gas is produced.

a) What does **decomposed** mean?
b) Give two reasons why methane can be used as a fuel.
c) The tank into which Farmer Stone puts the cow manure is called a **digester**. Why is this?
d) Give one precaution that Farmer Stone should take when making methane gas.
e) What use could Farmer Stone make of the sludge left behind in the tank?
f) Suggest how Farmer Stone i) can save money ii) can help to protect the environment by making and using his own methane gas.

Ideas for investigations and extension work

Chapter 1

1 Design and carry out an investigation to find out how much food a caterpillar eats in one day.

2 Investigate the rate at which a fruit decomposes when placed in different parts of a garden. Do different fruits decompose in different ways?

3 Design and carry out an investigation to find out whether greenfly are attracted to all kinds of roses.

4 Carry out a study of the birds that visit your garden. List the species and their numbers. Describe their behaviour. What evidence is there of 'competition'?

5 Carry out an experiment to compare the wet and dry biomass of some plant material.

6 Design and carry out an experiment to compare the flight of sycamore and ash fruits in terms of speed and distance of descent.

7 Design and carry out an investigation to show that houseflies are scavengers.

8 Design a questionnaire and make a survey of how local gardeners control garden pests, e.g. greenfly; slugs.

Chapter 2

1 Design and carry out an investigation of the effect of environmental factors, such as light intensity on plant growth. List the environmental factors you have chosen to study. Explain how you have tried to isolate the effects of each factor.

2 Devise a simple but effective method of measuring the height of a large tree.

3 Investigate the germination of seedlings on fine soil and on rough soil and on other media such as sand or rock:
  a) what kind of surfaces become colonized quickest
  b) what kind of surfaces are never colonized.
  c) why some surfaces are never colonized.

4 Design and carry out an experiment to enable you to measure the growth of a yeast population.

5 'Mowing a lawn regularly has no effect on the population of plants that grows on it.' Test this hypothesis.

6 Carry out a survey to enable you to draw a population pyramid of the area in which you live.

Chapter 3

1 Sir Humphrey Davy discovered more elements than any other scientist. Find out about Davy's life and work.

2 Find out how the elements in the periodic table came by their names.

3 Research the history of the discovery of the atom and the various parts from which it is made up: the nucleus, the electron, the proton, and the neutron. List the dates of 'discovery' and the names of the scientists involved.

4 Carbon is in group IV of the periodic table, between the true metals and the non-metals. Design and carry out an experiment to show that carbon (graphite) will conduct electricity (like a metal). Design and carry out an experiment to show that carbon powder burns in air to produce a gas which dissolves in water to give an acid (like a non-metal).

5 Design and carry out an experiment to measure the solubility of the following compounds: sodium chloride, NaCl; potassium sulphate, K_2SO_4; calcium chloride, $CaCl_2$; magnesium carbonate, $MgCO_3$; copper(II) nitrate, $Cu(NO_3)_2$; sodium carbonate, Na_2CO_3; calcium nitrate, $Ca(NO_3)_2$.
Can you find any general patterns from your results?

6 Design and carry out a series of simple experiments to show that sodium chloride contains ionic bonds.

7 Find out about Henry Cavendish and the discovery of the noble gases. Why were they originally called the **inert gases**?

8 Design a series of demonstrations by which a teacher could show the following trends in the periodic table to a class. Name any chemicals which he or she should use.
   a) 'As we move across a period, the trend is from metals to non-metals.'
   b) 'As we move down a group, reactivity increases.'
   c) 'The salts of transition elements tend to be coloured.'

Chapter 4

1 Find out the prices of the following metals from the financial pages of a newspaper (they are sometimes called 'commodities'): lead, copper, aluminium, gold, silver, platinum.
Compare the prices of the various metals and suggest why they are so different from each other.

2 Choose *one* of the following materials and find out as much as you can about its abundance, its ores, its extraction, and its uses: aluminium; copper; iron.
Display your findings on a wall poster.

3 In recent years the following materials have been used to make window frames: wood; galvanized steel; aluminium. List the advantages and disadvantages of each material.
Conduct a survey of the homes in your area to find the proportions of wood, steel, and aluminium window frames. Display your results as a pie chart.

4 A manufacturer says that its new wood preservative protects wood better than paint or creosote. Design an experiment to test the manufacturer's claim.

5 Lead pollution is a problem in developed countries. Find out all you can about the causes and effects of lead pollution. List the ways in which the effects can be reduced.

6 Compare the properties of plastic with those of glass. List the advantages and disadvantages of using glass containers for liquids.
Conduct a survey at a local supermarket to find what proportion of liquids are packaged in plastic.

7 Design and carry out a survey of the number of drinks cans used by members of your class in one year. What proportion of the cans are aluminium? How much aluminium would be saved in one year if all the drinks cans were recycled? What would it be worth?

8 Grow and compare crystals of copper(II) sulphate, sodium chloride ('salt') and magnesium sulphate (Epsom salts). Crystals can be grown in the following way:
   • dissolve each solid in warm water until no more will dissolve
   • decant some of the saturated solution into a glass dish, cover the dish with perforated paper and then leave it to stand so that the solution slowly evaporates.
(You may need a hand lens to study the crystals.)
Care: Copper(II) sulphate is poisonous. Wash your hands afterwards!

9 Design and carry out an experiment to find whether copper, steel, or aluminium is the best conductor of thermal energy (heat).

10 Use a data book to make a table showing the melting points and boiling points, in kelvin and degrees Celsius, of the following elements: hydrogen; nitrogen; oxygen; sodium; chlorine; iron; tin; lead.

11 Look for evidence that engineers leave gaps in structures to allow for thermal expansion. Study bridges, road surfaces, and large buildings.

Chapter 5

1 Find out why the Earth's magnetic field is important to us.

2 Design and carry out a simple experiment to show that the magnetic field around a wire depends on the size of the current in the wire.

3 Design and carry out an experiment to find out how the current taken by a motor varies when it is used to lift different loads (weights).

4 Design and carry out an experiment to find the power of a small electric motor.

5 Design and carry out an experiment to show that when the armature of a motor is turned, the motor acts as a dynamo (see Chapter 9).

6 Find out about loudspeaker design. Some loudspeaker cabinets contain two or even three speakers. What is the difference between a 'tweeter' (for high frequencies) and a 'woofer' (for low frequencies)? What is a 'cross-over'?

7 Design and carry out an experiment to find whether expensive audio cassettes give better quality sound than cheap ones. You will have to make sure that the recording conditions are the same for each tape.

8 Find the maximum number of characters (letters, numbers) you can store on a single side of a piece of A4 paper. Compare this to the maximum number of characters you can store on a single floppy disk.

9 Study a computerized checkout in a large supermarket. What advantages does the computerized system offer customers? What advantages are there for the supermarket owners? Are there any disadvantages for the customer?

10 Try to find out how much information is held about you on computer: check at school, at the library, at the doctor's, etc.

Chapter 6

1 A mass on the end of an elastic band will oscillate up and down. Design and carry out an experiment to find out how the frequency of the oscillation varies with the mass.

2 A real pendulum loses some energy during each swing until it eventually comes to rest. Design an experiment to show that this **damping** is caused mainly by air resistance.

3 Find the frequencies and wavelengths for Radio 1, Radio 2, Radio 3, Radio 4 and Radio 5. What is the relationship between frequency and wavelength for radio waves?

4 If your school has a sound-meter, measure noise levels around the school and in the local environment. Is noise pollution a problem?

5 Design and carry out an experiment to find whether human hearing range (frequency range) is related to age.

6 Add various amounts of water to eight bottles so that they give a musical scale when tapped with a spoon. When you have 'tuned' them try to find whether there is a relationship between the pitch of the note and the depth of air in the bottle.

7 Conduct a survey to find out how many people suffer from sight defects. Your survey should include details of sex, age, occupation, type of sight defect, and method of correction. Can you draw any conclusions?

8 Prove by experiment that long-sighted people have converging lenses prescribed for their glasses.

9 Design an experiment to estimate the maximum magnification you can get when using a 15 cm focal length biconvex lens as a magnifying glass.

10 Carry out an experiment to find the approximate size of the individual phosphors on a colour television screen.

11 Find out what the letters in the word LASER stand for. Find out about the use of laser light. Find out about holograms.

12 Ask a dentist to estimate how many X-rays he or she takes in one week. Also find out what safety precautions are taken when X-raying patients.

Chapter 7

Safety warning: you should not carry out your own investigations in the laboratory without checking your plans with your teacher. You must always wear eye protection when heating any substance or when using corrosive liquids such as acids or alkalis.

1 Investigate the action of heat on blue copper(II) sulphate crystals. Write down all changes you observe. What safety precautions should you take? Investigate the action of water on the solid produced when copper(II) sulphate is heated. What evidence is there that you have investigated a reversible chemical reaction?

2 Granules of zinc will react with cold, dilute sulphuric acid to produce hydrogen gas. Design and carry out an experiment to show that a small quantity of copper(II) sulphate solution acts as a catalyst for this reaction.

3 Marble chips (calcium carbonate) will react with dilute hydrochloric acid to produce carbon dioxide gas. Design experiments to find out whether the rate of this reaction depends on **a)** the temperature of the acid **b)** the size of the marble chips.

4 When sodium hydroxide solution, NaOH, is added to a solution of copper(II) sulphate solution, $CuSO_4$, a blue precipitate is formed.

$$2NaOH(aq) + CuSO_4(aq) \rightarrow Cu(OH)_2(s) + Na_2SO_4(aq)$$

1 cm^3 portions of 3.0 M NaOH were added to 9 cm^3 of 1.0 M $CuSO_4$ in a boiling tube. The tube was shaken and then placed in a centrifuge for two minutes. The height of the precipitate was measured after the precipitate had been allowed to settle. Here is a table of results:

volume of 3.0 M NaOH added (in cm^3)	1 2 3 4 5 6 7 8
height of precipitate (in mm)	4 8 12 16 20 24 24 24

a) Plot a graph of the results.
b) Explain the shape of the graph.
c) How many moles are there in 6 cm^3 of 3.0 M sodium hydroxide solution, NaOH?

d) How many moles of copper(II) sulphate react with this number of moles of sodium hydroxide?

e) Does your answer confirm the equation given for the reaction?

5 Manganese(IV) oxide is a black powder. It can be used as a catalyst to speed up the decomposition of hydrogen peroxide into water and oxygen.

$$2H_2O_2 \rightarrow 2H_2O + O_2$$

If you were given a small quantity of four different black powders and 100 cm^3 of hydrogen peroxide, design an experiment that you could carry out to find out which powder was the most effective catalyst.

6 Draw a diagram of the apparatus you would use to reduce copper(II) oxide with dry hydrogen gas. Write down any safety precautions you would take.

Chapter 8

1 Design and carry out an experiment to show that acetic acid (ethanoic acid) can be neutralized using sodium bicarbonate (sodium hydrogencarbonate).

2 Simple indicators can be made from various materials such as beetroot, red cabbage, and flower petals. Test a selection of home-made indicators in various acid and alkaline conditions and record your results in a table. What happens if you combine indicators?

3 The fertilizer potassium nitrate can be made by neutralizing potassium hydroxide solution with nitric acid. Describe how a titration could be used to find the right volumes of solutions to use. Explain how dry potassium nitrate can be produced from the neutral solution.

4 Carry out an investigation of the acidity of the rain falling in your area. It may be necessary to carry out this investigation over a long period of time.

5 Carry out an investigation of the acidity or alkalinity of the soil in your area. Does it vary from place to place?

6 If you live in an area with an acid-soil, carry out an investigation to find out how much 'lime' must be added to each square metre to increase the pH to about 7.

7 Using a book on garden plants or by visiting a garden centre, make a list of plants which prefer alkaline or acidic soils.

8 Design and carry out an experiment to compare the effectiveness of two different fertilizers. Include controls to ensure that other factors are not responsible for different growth rates.

Chapter 9

Remember: never experiment with mains electricity!

1 Design and carry out an experiment to find how the output power of bicycle dynamo varies with speed.

2 Compare the cost of using battery-powered bicycle lights with the cost of using a dynamo set. You will need to consider initial outlay as well as running costs.

3 Design and carry out an experiment to see how the voltage output of a battery changes with time when it is connected in series with a bulb which it lights brightly. You may choose to use a voltmeter, a CRO, or a data logging device such as VELA.

4 Design an experiment to show that the output signal (voltage) of a transformer has the same frequency as the input signal.

5 Carry out a survey in your locality to identify important parts of the National Grid. Look for overhead power cables and pylons, underground cables being repaired or installed by the Electricity Board, substations, and transformers mounted on pylons or poles near, for example, farms. If possible record your findings on a map and take photographs of the different parts of the Grid.

Remember: never climb pylons or enter Electricity Board substations. Never ignore the warning signs!

6 Design and carry out an experiment to compare different brands of batteries. Your experiment must have controls to ensure that it is a fair test. Is it worth buying 'long life' batteries?

7 Carry out an experiment to find the cost of running a cassette player from batteries. Is it worth buying a transformer so that you could use mains electricity?

8 Study the construction of a car sparking plug. What materials are used and why? Where does the spark occur? How large is the gap across which the spark 'jumps'? How do mechanics measure this gap accurately? Suggest what might happen if the gap was **a)** too big or **b)** too small.

Chapter 10

1 Design an experiment to prove to a doubting adult that all masses fall at the same rate and that it is air resistance which makes feathers fall more slowly than stones.

2 Design and carry out an experiment to measure the greatest angle at which a disconnected bunsen burner can be tilted before it falls over.

3 If possible, visit an airport, an air show, or an air museum so that you can study aircraft design. Look at the wing shapes and wing spans, number and type of engines, streamlining, etc.

4 Carry out a comparison of a Boeing 747 'jumbo jet' and Concorde. You should include as much technical information as possible, including maximum speed, maximum payload, number of passengers, maximum range, etc. Also find the cost of a return ticket from London to New York travelling on Concorde and compare it with the cost of flying on a 747.

5 Organize a competition to find the best design for a paper aeroplane made out of one sheet of A4 paper.

6 Make a simple balsa wood glider from a kit. Can you improve on the design?

7 An engineer says that a tetrahedron (triangular pyramid) is a much stronger structure than a cube. Test this statement by building models and testing them to destruction.

8 The same engineer says that tubes are as strong as solid rods. Test this statement by building and testing models. What is your conclusion?

9 Collect samples of seeds dispersed by the wind. Include those that use parachute mechanisms and those that use wings. Identify the plants from which your seeds came. (Summer and early autumn are the best times for this activity.)

10 Design and carry out an experiment to find out how many seeds a dandelion plant produces in one season. Use your answer to explain why a seed dispersal system has evolved.

Chapter 11

1 Design and carry out an experiment to find out how much thrust is exerted when you a) jump into the air b) start sprinting.

2 Investigate the changing pattern of day length and average temperatures during each of the seasons.

3 How would you show the Earth is rotating?

4 Design and carry out an investigation to find out the diameter of the Sun.

5 Design an experiment to show that high tides do not always reach the same height.

6 Space suits are made of a shiny material and are pressurized. Design and carry out experiments to explain these facts.

7 'Life as we know it could not exist on any other planet of the solar system.' What evidence is there to support this hypothesis?

Chapter 12

1 Carry out food tests on mycoprotein and meat. How do they differ? In what ways are they the same?

2 What conditions are needed for the decay of plant material in a compost heap? Carry out an investigation into the speed at which different materials decompose in a compost heap.

3 Find out what happens at a sewage treatment works. What use is made of biotechnology in sewage treatment?

4 Design and carry out an experiment to find out whether soil fungi produce antibiotics.
Safety warning: discuss your plans with your teacher before starting your experiment.

5 Find out where good use is made of the gas produced from rubbish tips. What is the gas used for? What role does biotechnology play in the production of this gas?

6 Design an experiment to compare the 'thickness' of some different brands of natural yoghurt.

7 Design and carry out an investigation to find the best growing conditions for tissue cultures.

8 'Mineral oils are better lubricants than vegetable oils.' Design and carry out an investigation to test this hypothesis.

Index